TRIED & TRUE

THIRDS BOOK 10

CHARLIE COCHET

Tried & True

http://charliecochet.com

http://reesedante.com

Edits by Desi Chapman, Blue Ink Editing

https://blueinkediting.com

Proofing by Susi Selva

TRIED & TRUE

When THIRDS agent Dexter J. Daley met Team Leader Sloane Brodie, he couldn't have imagined how slamming into his new partner—literally—would shake both their worlds. Now four years later, they've faced dangers, fought battles both personal and professional… and fallen deeply in love. Now their big moment is finally in sight, and they're ready to stand up together and make it official. Unfortunately, as the countdown to their big day begins, an enemy declares war on the THIRDS….

With their family in danger, Dex and Sloane are put to the test on how far into darkness they'll walk to save those they love. As secrets are unearthed, a deadly betrayal is revealed, and Dex and Sloane must call on their Destructive Delta family for one last hurrah to put an end to the secret organization responsible for so much devastation.

Dex and Sloane will have plenty of bullets to dodge on the way to the altar, but with happiness within their grasp, they are determined to get there come hell or high water….

CHAPTER ONE

HE WAS ON HIS OWN.

Dex breathed in deeply through his nose, then let the breath out slowly through his mouth. He steadied his heart, his pulse, his breathing. His body answered to him, not the other way around. It was three against one, though there was only one he had to worry about. He had to stay on his guard with that one.

"You're going down."

Dex opened his eyes, his focus on the huge tiger Therian before him. His dear delusional friend had no idea what he was getting himself into. Seb would be the one going down, but first... Dex curled his lip up on one side as he moved his gaze to Hudson. The good doctor would be the first down but the last man standing. Dex would make sure of it. His most challenging target, however, slowly circled Dex. He could feel his mate's eyes burning over every inch of him.

Sloane came back into view, the predator inside him looking out at Dex through molten amber eyes, his pupils dilated. His Felid was awake, ready to hunt, and Dex was his prey, or so Sloane believed. Sloane flexed his fingers, the knuckles stretching the blue wraps around his hands. The black racerback tank accentuated his broad muscular shoulders, and Dex allowed his gaze to travel down the thick biceps to his deliciously corded forearms. The tank was snug against his expansive chest, down to his torso and tapered waist. The loose black yoga pants rested low on his hips, and his feet were bare.

"Holy shit, your eyes."

Dex ignored Seb and kept his gaze on Sloane and the smug smile now on his face. He knew the change in Dex's eye color was his doing. Didn't matter. It wouldn't change what was going to happen. His mate was going down.

"You boys going to stand around all day?" Dex balled his hands into fists at his sides, the orange wraps shifting against his skin.

As expected, Seb charged first. Dex ducked beneath his right hook, spun, and slammed his hands into Seb's back, sending him reeling forward. Dex lashed out, grabbed Hudson's arm, and kicked his leg out from under him. He used his weight to flip Hudson over his shoulder and throw him onto the mat. Seb lunged at him, but Dex was quicker. Much quicker. He dropped and rolled out of the way, then popped up behind Seb and kicked at the back of his bad knee.

Seb roared, and Dex smiled.

That's it, big guy. Get pissed, but don't get sloppy.

Seb snarled as he pushed through the pain and came after Dex, his Felid half shining through his green eyes. Dex ducked and dodged. He slapped Seb's fists away from him. Movement from the corner of his eye caught his attention, and Dex brought both fists down against Seb's arms, then came up with a fierce uppercut and a kick to the abdomen that sent Seb rolling across the mat. Then Dex spun and ducked under Hudson's right hook, landing a punch against Hudson's ribs that left him gasping for breath. Dex pulled Hudson's leg out from under him and brought both fists down against Hudson's back, slamming him down hard into the mat, knocking the wind out of him. Hudson inhaled sharply as he writhed in pain. A low growl rose through him, and when he tried to get up, Dex put his foot on Hudson's back and pushed down.

"You're not even trying," Dex growled.

"Dex," Seb warned.

Dex stepped back and motioned for Seb to advance. "I'm not going to baby him, Seb. You want him to be prepared? You want him to survive out there? Then he has to learn." Dex moved his gaze to Sloane, who was circling him, a barely there smile on his face.

I haven't forgotten about you, baby. Your turn will come.

Hudson was still on the mat, his forehead pressed against it.

"Get up, Hudson," Dex demanded. "Get your ass up off that mat right now."

Seb and Hudson might have been sworn in and were officially TIN, but they were behind in their training. Sparks arranged for them to start their TIN Operative Training Program as soon as Dex and Sloane returned from their honeymoon. Since their recruitment, Seb and Hudson had been doing the same TIN Associate Training Program Dex and Sloane had been doing for months. The two had a hell of a lot to catch up on, and Dex felt for them; he did. Especially Hudson. As a medical examiner, Hudson had never been put through the same training as a THIRDS Defense agent, so he had the most to learn. Making him the most vulnerable. Not to mention the most hesitant. Hudson was a wolf Therian, and although he could be as fierce as any Felid, he was soft-hearted and tended to be a nurturer. Hudson was a logical thinker, which was great, but his new role with TIN required instinct and action.

Dex wouldn't go easy on them because they were his friends. His family. In fact, it was precisely for that reason he *couldn't* go easy on them. Shit was about to get real, and he needed those he cared about to be prepared. If he had to be the one to push, to break them and help put them back together, then so be it.

Hudson glared at him and sat back on his heels.

Dex marched over, grabbed his arm, and hauled him to his feet. He thrust a finger in Hudson's face. "I said get your ass up."

Hudson's wolf Therian growled at him, his steel-blue eyes intense. *Good.* Hudson had a temper buried deep down behind all that sweetness and timidity, and Dex knew just how to expose it.

Dex took a step back, his attention moving between Seb and Hudson. The two exchanged glances, and Dex grinned. *Now we're talking.*

The pair came at him at the same time, and Hudson even managed to land a hit, punching Dex across his jaw. Finally, they were getting somewhere. Dex maneuvered around Seb, making sure none of Seb's punches landed. If they did, he wasn't too worried. Not that he wanted to get punched in the face by a tiger Therian, but where it once might have broken his jaw, now he could take the hit and bounce back.

"Why do you keep trying to punch me?" Dex asked Seb.

Seb spun with a snarl. "What the hell are you talking about?"

"I'm talking about the fact you're underestimating me, seeing me as a Human, as someone smaller and weaker than you that you can overpower. Your punching me is not going to knock me out."

"I never said you were weaker," Seb replied, his eyes narrowing.

"No, you're just treating me like I am." Dex motioned to Sloane. "Would you attack Sloane the same way?"

Seb frowned, puzzled. "Well, no, obviously."

"Why? Because he's bigger? Stronger? A jaguar Therian?" Dex shook his head. "Never underestimate your opponent." Seb took a step forward, and Dex put a hand up to stop him. "Stay there. Both of you. Observe." Dex turned to Sloane and took his position. "How about showing them how it's done?"

Sloane ducked his head, his amber eyes almost black as he met Dex's gaze. "My pleasure."

Dex readied himself. This was going to hurt oh so good. He'd done it before, several times. Dex grinned wickedly. Sloane wouldn't attack first. He never did. His Felid half wanted to stalk, to catch Dex unawares, which was why Dex wouldn't give him the opportunity. He took off in a run toward Sloane. Sloane was heavier, bulkier, and weighed a fuckton more than Dex, which worked to Dex's advantage.

Whatever Dex did, Sloane would do his damn best to keep his feet on the mat. The floor was not where he wanted to be. Which was why it was exactly where Dex had to get him. The bigger the Therian, the harder they fell. Sloane took his stance—left leg forward, right leg back, knees slightly bent as he anchored himself. He held up his fists, ready to strike. Dex picked up speed, grabbed Sloane's shoulder, flung himself up in a flying scissor kick, and wrapped his legs around Sloane's neck, using the force of his momentum to bring Sloane down, flipping him over onto the mat. Dex kept his legs wrapped around Sloane's neck. This was where Dex would have gouged out the dude's eyes, but he wasn't about to do that to his beloved, so instead, he tightened his hold and smacked Sloane in the face.

With a feral growl, Sloane rolled with Dex still on him so Dex had his back to the mat. He thrust his hands down against Dex's groin and jerked backward, but Dex only squeezed his legs around Sloane's neck. He grabbed Sloane's thumb and bent it back, forcing Sloane's arm—and more importantly his elbow—away from Dex's groin area. Had this been a real scenario, Dex would have won by now. Sloane twisted and threw his weight against Dex, thrusting his elbow back and hitting Dex in the balls.

"Fuck," Dex said through gritted teeth, loosening his grip enough for Sloane to force one leg off him and giving Sloane the room he needed to slip out. Dex rolled away just as Sloane came down elbow first, hitting the mat right where Dex had been. That would have hurt like a son of a bitch. Dex pushed through the pain to his boy bits and got to his feet in time to have Sloane slam into him from the side. Dex landed several feet away, his whole left side throbbing from being bodychecked by a two hundred forty pound—probably more like two hundred fifty pounds now—Therian.

All he could do was push through it and get on his feet quickly. When Sloane lunged at him, Dex dug deep. His eyesight sharpened, and he let out a fierce growl as he threw one arm around Sloane's waist and grabbed at the back of Sloane's right leg, jerking it forward so he could lift Sloane off his feet and slam him onto the mat where he brought his knee down against Sloane's stomach, knocking the wind out of him. He was mindful to use just enough force to hurt but not seriously injure his boyfriend. With an arm pressed to Sloane's neck, his knee ready to do some damage, and a fist over Sloane's face, Sloane tapped out.

Dex grinned down at him and kissed him before rolling off. Sloane laughed softly as he lay on the mat, his chest rising and falling in rapid breaths. He wiped the sweat from his brow with the back of his wrapped hand. He turned his head to look at Dex.

"Nicely done."

"Thanks." Dex got to his feet and held his hands out to Sloane, then helped him up. He turned to Seb and Hudson, who were gaping at him. "Obviously that would have ended a lot sooner had I gouged out his eyes, but I kind of like his eyes," Dex said, batting his lashes at Sloane. "They're pretty."

Sloane chuckled. He shook his head and wiped more sweat from his brow.

Rolling his shoulders, Dex turned back to Seb and Hudson, his expression stern. "Now, let's try that again."

"Holy..." Pant. "Crap." More panting.

Sloane dropped onto the mat. He was dripping with sweat, and every muscle in his body ached. He wiped his face with a clean towel, then chuckled at Seb, who dropped next to him and lay sprawled on his back.

"I think... my heart... is going to... explode," Seb said, breathless.

"I warned you, didn't I? But you didn't listen. Your exact words were 'how strong can he really be?'"

Seb turned his head to pout at Sloane, his brows drawn

together. “I was wrong, Sloane. So very wrong. I will never doubt your words again.” He sat up with a groan and grabbed one of the rolled-up towels beside him to wipe the sweat off his face. “I can’t believe Dex took me down.”

“The bigger they are, the harder they fall.”

Seb narrowed his eyes at Sloane. “I’m a tiger Therian. Your not-even-two-hundred-pound boyfriend is not supposed to be able to take me down.”

“Except he’s been training his ass off, is no longer Human, and I’m pretty sure he’s still getting stronger.” Every time Sloane sparred with Dex, he noticed an increase in Dex’s strength. It was in minimal increments, but enough for Sloane to see the difference. “It seems to come in little bursts when he gets worked up or pissed off, but when that happens, he’s stronger than I am. If this keeps going, he may even end up stronger than you, or who knows, maybe even Zach. Not even TIN knows what’s going on inside him. The tests are starting to come back inconclusive again.”

“How is that possible?”

Sloane shrugged. “No one knows. TIN’s brought in their top specialists, and every time they run a test for something, whatever they’re looking for, it’s gone, but they know it’s there because they can see it. They did a blood test, and it came back Human, but when they did a different test that wasn’t specifically looking at his blood, it pinged Therian. It’s like his DNA and everything that makes him a hybrid is trying to protect itself by avoiding detection.”

Seb seemed to think about it. “So if someone ran a test to see if he was Therian, they’d get something else?”

Sloane nodded. “Not sure if that’s a good thing or not. My worry is when he’ll need to get treatment. Unless whoever’s treating him knows what he is...”

“Fuck. It’ll be a mess.”

Which scared the living shit out of Sloane. They had Hudson and TIN to provide the best medical attention possible, but what if either wasn't an option? How the hell did a regular hospital treat a half Human, half Therian? Especially if every test they ran came back screwed-up? Hopefully they'd be able to get to the bottom of it soon. Sloane didn't like the idea of them not being able to get Dex medical treatment when he needed it.

Seb stared at him. "Shit, Sloane. What the hell is in that DNA of yours?"

"I don't know, but as long as it doesn't hurt him, I'm okay with it. Knowing he can hold his own against whatever he faces out there is good enough for me. Hopefully the rest will get sorted out."

A slew of British curses met Sloane's ear, and he cringed.

"Your man does not like to lose."

Seb's eyes went slightly wide. "Are you kidding me? Everyone's always surprised when he kicks their ass at pool, or football, or soccer, thinking that he's this awkward science nerd, but he is ruthless when it comes to competition, and yeah, he *hates* losing." Seb drew his knees up and let his elbows rest on them. "He doesn't get pissed at his opponent, though. He gets pissed at himself. As if his losing reflects how inadequate he is. A complex gifted to him by his asshole father."

Sloane turned his attention to Hudson, whose brows were drawn together in concentration as he circled Dex. Both had their shirts plastered to their skin with sweat, and Hudson had smartly worn contacts, even though he hated them. Sloane lost count of how many times Dex had dropped Hudson to the mat. Hudson charged, and Dex spun on his heels, ended up behind Hudson, threw his arms around his waist, picked him up, and slammed him down.

"He's being a little hard on Hudson, don't you think?" Seb asked, concern etched on his face.

Dex wasn't holding back, but he had his reasons. "Hudson means a lot to Dex, and he wants to make sure Hudson's prepared for whatever we face. If that means he pisses Hudson off, then he'll do it. Dex might be a joker in a lot of respects, but when it comes to the safety of those he cares about, he's hard-core."

"I can see that."

Even though Sloane felt for Hudson, especially every time he hit the mat, he couldn't help but admire Dex. His perfect posture, his expertly calculated moves, the way his muscles flexed beneath his clothes. The loose black workout pants accentuated Dex's perfectly rounded ass, and the sweaty shirt stuck to his skin outlined the delicious curve of his spine and the muscles of his finely sculpted torso. He'd wiped the floor with Sloane, and Sloane couldn't be prouder.

Seeming to have had enough of being floored, when he next hit the mat, Hudson wrapped his legs tight around Dex, and the two crashed down together, thrashing about as each one tried to get the upper hand. They rolled around, grunting, Hudson's legs wrapped around Dex's waist, Dex's head in a choke hold. Somehow, they ended up with their shirts halfway up their bodies, and Seb cleared his throat.

"I know this is probably inappropriate, but is it me, or is this kinda... porny?"

Sloane tilted his head for a better angle as Hudson arched his back to try to budge Dex, but Dex had managed to get out of the choke hold and had Hudson's wrists pinned above his head.

"Uh, yeah, definitely porny." Sloane stood at the same time as Seb. "Maybe we should take a break," Sloane called out. Dex looked his way, and Hudson twisted his body, flipping the tables on Dex and rolling them over so he was sitting on Dex's stomach.

"Ha!" Hudson threw his arms up in victory when Seb took hold of his wrist and pulled him up. Hudson smiled at his husband. "Hello, darling." He put a hand to Seb's cheek. "Your face is so red. Didn't you get any rest?"

Seb cleared his throat again. "Um, yeah, just, you know, why don't we hit the showers and meet up for something to eat later?"

Before Dex could reply, Sloane spoke up. "Great idea." He helped Dex to his feet, pretending he hadn't noticed Dex narrowing his eyes at him. They agreed to meet up later, and Sloane took hold of Dex's hand and quickly led him out of the training bay.

"Um, Sloane? What's going on?"

Sloane shook his head. "Nothing. Just going to hit the showers."

"The locker room is the other way."

Sloane had no intention of showering anywhere near anyone else.

"Sloane?"

Sloane led Dex back to his new private training bay, and more importantly, his office with the fully stocked, brand-new shower. As soon as they got into his office, he put the room in privacy mode, turned, and pounced.

Dex had no idea what had gotten into Sloane. Not that he was complaining. The moment Sloane put the room into privacy mode, he captured Dex's lips, his tongue demanding entrance. Dex happily obliged, parting his lips, meeting Sloane's tongue with his own as they tangled in a searing kiss. Sloane ran his hands over every inch of Dex, groping, caressing, squeezing, as he stripped Dex of his clothes while walking him backward toward the bathroom.

When they were naked, Sloane trailed kisses down Dex's jaw to his collarbone, down his chest to a nipple that he tongued then sucked into his mouth. Dex dug his fingers into Sloane's shoulders, his head back and his eyes closed as Sloane's tongue drove him crazy. He sucked and teased one nipple before moving on to the other one, his fingers digging into Dex's skin. He slipped a finger between Dex's ass cheeks, and Dex bucked his hips when Sloane's finger teased at his hole.

"Sloane... please."

Sloane pulled away long enough to turn on the shower and check the water's temperature. The entire bathroom was tiled, so they had plenty of room to maneuver. There was even a padded bench.

"Sloane? Talk to me."

Sloane pulled back, his pupils so wide his amber eyes were almost all black, his feral half lingering beneath the surface.

"When I saw you on the mat, all sweaty and writhing underneath Hudson, I couldn't keep my eyes off you. Don't get me wrong, I don't share, and no one is ever laying a finger on you in that way except me, but seeing you move like that, your face flushed, I had to get my hands on you."

Dex's brows shot up. "Are you saying my training session with Hudson turned you on?" No wonder Seb had been in such a hurry to get Hudson to himself. A sinful smile spread across Dex's face, and he ran a finger down

Sloane's arm. "You like to see me all sweaty and groaning, don't you?"

"Only when it's me causing you to make those noises." Sloane grabbed the soap and led him under the shower before proceeding to wash Dex. He stood behind Dex, their bodies all but pressed against each other as Sloane soaped him up, his hands running over every inch of Dex, over his arms, down his legs, and between his ass cheeks. He quickly washed himself before rinsing off and turning Dex to face him. Dex shivered at the hunger in Sloane's molten amber gaze. "I want you on that bench, on your hands and knees so I can fuck your ass with my tongue."

Dex almost came right then. He nodded fervently and quickly went over to the bench, where he got on his hands and knees. He lowered his head against the soft padding of the bench, his ass in the air as Sloane stood behind him, his fingers kneading Dex's cheeks. Dex moaned when he looked back in time to find Sloane getting down on his knees. He parted Dex's cheeks and licked at Dex's hole. Dex did his best not to wriggle too much or he might end up falling off the bench, and that was most certainly not sexy. He'd fallen off their bed plenty of times, but here there was no cushy carpet to break his fall. However, it was hard remaining still with Sloane working that sinful tongue over Dex's hole, spearing Dex, nipping at his skin, and driving Dex out of his mind.

When Sloane moved away, Dex whimpered. He glanced over his shoulder at Sloane, a shiver going through him as Sloane lined up his beautiful, hard cock with Dex's entrance. Fuck, that was hot. Dex let out a low groan, his body trembling with need. He couldn't get enough of Sloane, of his touch, his kisses, the way he set Dex's body on fire.

"That's it, baby. I want to hear how much you like having my dick inside you."

"Sloane, please."

"Please what?" Sloane growled.

"Fuck me. Make me come." Dex was all but vibrating with need. He wanted it hard and rough, wanted to feel Sloane inside him for hours. His muscles already ached from training, but he wanted to feel the burn left behind by Sloane's fucking him.

Sloane plunged inside Dex, and Dex cried out. He gripped the edge of the bench until his knuckles were white, holding on with all his strength as Sloane plowed into him over and over. Steam filled the room, along with the sounds of Dex's loud moans and panting. His wet hair was plastered to his face, and he thrust back as Sloane plunged in deep, making Sloane release a hoarse cry. Dex loved it when Sloane lost himself, when his feral half growled and roared.

Dex reached under him and took hold of his cock, jerking himself off. "Sloane..."

"No."

"Please."

"*No*."

Dex whimpered. He was so painfully hard. Behind him, Sloane's fingers dug into Dex's hips as skin slapped against skin. Sloane changed his angle, and Dex saw stars. He screamed Sloane's name, his muscles tightening around Sloane's cock as Sloane let out a roar and folded himself over Dex as he filled Dex with his come. Sloane's body was racked with shivers as he held on to Dex until he'd emptied himself in Dex's ass.

"Please, Sloane." Dex was begging, and he didn't care. He was so painfully hard and so very close.

"Sit," Sloane ordered, his voice low and rough.

Dex did as asked, turning to sit up on the bench and spreading his knees so Sloane could kneel between them. Sloane kissed Dex before swallowing down Dex's cock.

"Oh fuck!"

Dex slipped his fingers into Sloane's hair and grabbed fistfuls of it. When Sloane stopped moving, Dex planted one hand on the bench, and with the other braced himself so he could thrust up into Sloane's mouth. Sloane let out a guttural moan, and Dex could feel his orgasm looming.

"You like that? You like it when I fuck your mouth, don't you?"

Sloane nodded around Dex's cock, and Dex almost came right then. He grabbed hold of Sloane's hair again with one hand as he thrust into Sloane's mouth over and over.

"You look so fucking hot with your lips around my dick."

Sloane's tongue was sinful as it did dirty things to Dex's cock, the tip pressing into Dex's slit, then pushing against the underside of Dex's cock before once again moving to work Dex's slit. His cheeks hollowed as he sucked, his free hand fondling Dex's balls.

"Oh God, Sloane. I'm gonna come."

Sloane picked up his pace, the sweet friction building inside Dex as he watched his cock moving in and out between Sloane's full lips. A white light burst in front of his eyes, and Dex screamed Sloane's name, his muscles straining and his body shivering as he emptied himself inside Sloane's mouth. Sloane swallowed every drop, and when Dex was a boneless mess, Sloane stood and kissed Dex so he could taste himself.

"Holy fuck, babe," Dex murmured, his knees a little

unsteady as Sloane led him back under the shower to wash them again. "I think training just got a whole lot more interesting."

Sloane chuckled as they finished up and turned off the water. As Sloane dried Dex, he nuzzled his hair, his voice soft, yet full of promise. "As long as I'm the one taking you home and getting you all sweaty in bed."

Dex turned and slipped his arms around Sloane's waist. "You've got a deal."

CHAPTER TWO

"TWENTY MINUTES," Dex announced before thrusting a spatula in Sloane's direction and lip-synching to "Do Ya, Do Ya Want My Love" by Electric Light Orchestra, making Sloane laugh.

"I already got your love," Sloane said, giving Dex a quick kiss on the lips before placing the groceries he'd just brought home on the island counter to put away.

"Damn right you do." Dex went back to singing into his spatula and bopping around the kitchen in his Peter Venkman *Ghostbusters* apron Letty gifted him for his birthday. His wearing it usually resulted in *Ghostbusters* movie quotes or scene reenactments, with his favorite scene to perform being Venkman getting slimed. Dex's one-man show included him playing the part of Peter, Ray, *and* Slimer. It made Sloane laugh his ass off every time.

"Mmm, that smells good. What's for dinner?" Usually Sloane did the cooking and Dex washed up. Dex was a great cook, but he loved to eat the food more than he liked to make it. He was also very particular about how things should be cleaned and stored, so Sloane didn't even attempt to do the washing up afterward. Unless it was a lone mug or cereal bowl, he left the cleaning up to Dex. Also, with Sloane doing the cooking, it meant there was always some kind of vegetable on their plate rather than double the carbs.

"Lemon and herb chicken, baked garlic parmesan potato wedges, *and* parmesan baby broccoli."

Sloane gasped. "You cooked little trees?" Several months ago, Dex decided vegetables were too annoying to be called by their names and therefore renamed every vegetable to cross his plate. As if renaming them would somehow get him out of eating them. Broccoli was now referred to as "little trees." Carrots were "veggie vampire killers," sprouts "shrunken cabbages," and asparagus "pee stinkers." The list went on.

Dex rolled his eyes. "Yes, oh love of my loins." He narrowed his eyes at Sloane, his lips curling into an evil grin. "I baked alive your precious baby trees. Muahaha."

"And I bet they'll taste delicious."

"Did you get dessert?"

"Of course." Sloane held up a carton of Ben & Jerry's ice cream in each hand. "Cherry Garcia and Phish Food, as requested."

"You're the best," Dex said, then blew Sloane a kiss before he started washing up the dishes he'd used to prep dinner. Dirty dishes in the sink gave Dex hives. Once all the groceries had been put away, Sloane turned to Dex, momentarily captivated by his beautiful partner. Today's socks were ninjas leaping and summersaulting—a Christmas gift from Cael. The charcoal gray distressed T-shirt Dex had on with a Nintendo controller on it and the words "Classically

Trained" was fitting a little snugger these days, thanks to the muscle he'd put on, and although the black pajama bottoms he wore were loose, they couldn't hide that delicious ass. The man really was a feast for the eyes.

Unable to help himself, Sloane slipped his arms around Dex, his chest pressed against Dex's back and his fingers splayed on Dex's chest, keeping him close. A sweet love song floated up from the Bluetooth speakers in the living room, and Sloane hummed softly, stopping only long enough to kiss Dex's cheek. He began to sway, head pressed to Dex's.

"Less than two weeks," Sloane murmured. "In less than two weeks, we'll be having our first dance as husband and husband."

Dex dried his hands on a dish towel before placing them over Sloane's. He laced their fingers together and joined Sloane, swaying in time to the music. Sloane's heart skipped a beat at the thought of their upcoming wedding. Part of him was nervous as hell, but the other side of him couldn't wait to stand with Dex, hand in hand before the whole world, as they exchanged vows. Dex had been prepared to write his own, but Sloane asked if they could keep the traditional wedding vows. There had been no hesitation on Dex's part when he'd agreed.

Details like color scheme, type of cake, and venue were all things Sloane left to Dex, and he preferred it that way. It was too much for him. He never thought he'd be lucky enough to find someone who'd love him the way Dex did, much less get married, so he'd never given any thought to what kind of wedding he'd have. Dex, on the other hand, had very specific ideas. For Sloane, making sure Dex was happy was more important than Sloane randomly choosing a certain flavor of cake, which was what would have ended up happening had the choice been his.

When Sloane asked to keep a few traditions, Dex beamed at him. The fact Sloane was asking was enough for Dex to know it was important to him. After the vows, they discussed what other traditions Sloane wanted to keep. The big ones for him were keeping the ceremony traditional as far as vows, music, wedding party, and attire. Together they'd approved the venue, and Tony had insisted on taking care of the rehearsal dinner, since Dex was paying for the wedding. Tony hadn't been happy about it at first, and he'd been prepared to argue with Dex, thinking Dex was just trying to save him from a huge bill, but the truth was, Dex intended on following tradition and having his parents pay for his wedding.

After John and Gina Daley were killed, their life insurance policies had paid out a *huge* amount of money. When Dex had added Sloane's name to the house—a house Dex bought with some of his parents' insurance money, along with his car—he'd disclosed how much money he still had left. It had shocked the shit out of Sloane. Now, not only had Dex found the perfect use for a portion of that money, but he'd also found a way to include his parents in his wedding day. The three of them had sat in Tony's living room, not one dry eye among them. Tony had smiled through his tears and agreed it was a wonderful idea.

Sloane closed his eyes, loving the feel of Dex's warm body pressed to his, how perfectly he fit against Sloane, and the delicious scent that was all Dex. God, how he loved this man. He couldn't imagine his life without Dex. Without his gorgeous smile, infectious laugh, and his big heart full of so much love. Despite the emotional roller coaster of the last few years, after everything Dex had suffered, he hadn't lost any of what made him Dex. He still laughed at his own silly jokes, wore crazy socks, rocked out to eighties music, and enjoyed driving Ash crazy.

Dex turned his head so Sloane could kiss him. "I can't believe it'll be four years since we met. Do you remember?"

"Remember?" Sloane chuckled. "How could I forget? You left me speechless."

"Yeah, it wasn't one of my better moments," Dex said with a laugh, most likely recalling the instant their lives changed forever.

"I'll admit, when you smacked your head against mine, my first thought was that you were an idiot."

"I kinda felt like one at the time," Dex muttered.

"That wasn't what left me speechless, though."

"Oh?"

Sloane released Dex and gently turned him so they were face to face. Dex's beautiful smile stole Sloane's breath away. What could he possibly have done to be so lucky? "It was your eyes." Sloane stroked Dex's eyebrow with his thumb and cupped Dex's cheek. "Four years. It seems like only yesterday, but at the same time, it's like I've always known you." He brushed his lips over Dex's, coaxing his beautiful mate to let him in. Dex parted his lips, and Sloane slipped his tongue inside, savoring the taste of him. Dex stroked Sloane's right arm where his—as of five months ago—tattoo was. He smiled against Sloane's lips before pulling back to look down at it.

"I can't believe you had this done for me."

Sloane smiled, his fingers brushing along Dex's own half-sleeve tattoo on his left arm. Calvin designed Dex's first, which meant when Sloane approached him, asking him to design a matching one, Calvin was able to design it so when they stood with their arms together, the images fit. Sloane's ship faced Dex's lighthouse, both sharing the same starry night and swirling sea.

"When you said you were getting one and I saw the design, I knew right away I wanted one too. So you'd always be with me."

The oven timer beeped, and Dex kissed Sloane before cheerfully announcing dinner was ready. "Grab a plate, sexy pants." He removed the trays from the oven, and Sloane went to the fridge.

"What are you drinking?"

"Water's fine."

That answer would have surprised him several months ago, but Dex was doing a great job in cutting back on the sugary drinks, especially in the evenings. Sloane grabbed them a couple of bottled waters and placed them on the counter so he could serve himself. Once they'd both filled up their plates, they each grabbed their water, cutlery, and paper towels before heading into the living room. They sat on the couch, and Dex turned on the TV and flipped channels until he got to one of his favorite cop shows. It was the only one they watched, not for the realism, but because it was full of action, great banter, and Sloane agreed with Dex that the bromantic lead couple were pretty damn sexy.

As they ate and watched TV together, Sloane realized he was stupidly happy. After all the crazy they'd been through, they had six weeks off, three leading up to the wedding and three for their honeymoon. The thought made him smile like a dope.

"What's got you all smiley?" Dex asked before chomping down on one of his potato wedges. Potatoes had not been renamed, as they were "awesome and tasty" and therefore not considered true vegetables in Dex's book—unless Sloane was bugging him to eat more veggies, and then suddenly potatoes transformed into temporary vegetables. Sometimes living with Dex was like living with a Human jigsaw puzzle where all the pieces were the same color.

"Well?"

Sloane snapped out of it. "Oh. I was thinking about spending three weeks with you on the sandy beaches of Curaçao."

Dex hummed. "You in an itsy bitsy teeny weenie yellow polka dot bikini."

Sloane laughed. "Yeah, no."

"You're right. Mankini is more your style."

"Mankini is no one's style. Just no."

"You know, they make tux mankinis with little bow ties. I think we should totally trade our tuxes in for those. What do you say? Walk down the aisle with me, bare assed."

Sloane laughed around a mouthful of potato. "That's just wrong. Besides, then we'd have to get turquoise and tangerine ones for the wedding party. Ash would make sure we never made it to the altar." A thought occurred to him, and he had to swallow before he choked on his laughter.

"What?" Dex asked.

"I dare you to call up Lou and tell him we're switching our tuxes to tux mankinis."

Dex let out a bark of laughter. "Oh my God, yes!" He put his plate on the coffee table and swiped up his phone to call Lou. Within seconds, Lou picked up. "Hey, Lou. Yeah, everything's great. Listen, so I was thinking about our tuxes for the ceremony, and we thought maybe we'd go for something a little more... creative."

Sloane put a fist to his mouth so he wouldn't laugh. He could just see Lou's face. The poor guy.

"Yeah, we were thinking of, you know, being a little different, and figured why not just go for it? So we decided to go with tux mankinis."

Sloane waited.

"What's a mankini?" Dex's lips twitched, and Sloane could tell he was trying desperately not to burst. "Why don't you google it. I can wait." Dex winked at Sloane when a roar of expletives in both Spanish and English came blasting through the phone. They couldn't hold it any longer and busted into peals of laughter.

"But, Lou, it'd still be classy. They got little bow ties, and—I only understood the word *saints*. Lou, are you blaspheming right now? Think of your poor abuelita." Dex quickly moved the phone away from his ear. "Oh, he really didn't like that." With a chuckle, he held the phone out to Sloane. "He said your name."

Sloane shook his head. "No way. He still wants to smother me in my sleep over the color scheme incident." Dex waved the phone at him, and with a groan Sloane took it. "Hi, Lou."

"Sloane," Lou said through gritted teeth. "If your fiancé so much as hints at any ridiculous changes, I'll be forced to do the unthinkable."

"And what's that?"

"I will send my mother to your house."

Having dealt with few mothers in his lifetime, Sloane wasn't exactly sure how that was a threat. Dex arched an eyebrow at Sloane, and Sloane shrugged. "He said he's going to send his mother to our house."

Dex's eyes went so wide Sloane thought they were going to pop out of his head. Before Sloane could say a word, Dex dove for the phone and snatched it out of Sloane's hand.

"Lou, hey. Let's not be too hasty now. I was just kidding. Of course, I wouldn't do such a thing. I'll be on my best behavior. At least until the reception. I promise. Please, *please* don't send your mom to our house. Pinky swear. Cross my heart. Do you need me to put it in writing? Sign something? A contract? I'll do it. Whatever it is, I'll do it. Just don't tell your mom!"

Sloane went back to finishing his dinner, amused by Dex's panicked look. Was Dex really afraid of Lou's mom? How bad could she be? After promising profusely that he wouldn't cause Lou any more near heart attacks, Dex hung up.

"Okay. Crisis averted."

Sloane laughed and placed his plate on the coffee table. "You should have seen your face. You're really scared of Lou's mom?"

Dex turned to face Sloane. "You have no idea of the horror. Lou's dad is Dominican and a chef. Oh my God, his food is to die for. That's where Lou got his love of good food. Lou's mom is Cuban. She also makes awesome food, but I swear to you, Sloane, I have never, *ever* faced a more terrifying adversary."

"Adversary? You make her sound like some kind of Bond villain."

"Pfft, amateurs compared to this lady. She's this tiny little woman with a supersweet smile and a perfect little bob, and holy shit, she will bust your shit up without laying a finger on you. I don't know how she does it, but she has this death stare. Like Medusa. If you look directly at her, you're screwed, except she doesn't turn you to stone, she destroys you with her mom guilt. Like how can you break her heart? How can you crush her soul? Which is what you're doing by saying no or disagreeing with her. You say yes, and you fucking run. You run fast, Sloane."

Sloane was in tears from laughing. He could picture it so clearly. "Are you telling me there's someone out there who's immune to your Daley charm?"

"You have no fucking idea. I shit you not. You know how Darla does that Southern 'I'm smiling, and sweet-sounding words are coming out of my mouth, but I'm actually about to shank you with a spork' thing? Well this is worse. So much worse."

Sloane thought about it. "Like Julia?"

Dex shook his head. "I would walk through fire for Julia. No one wants to disappoint Julia. Lou's mom is more like, if you disappoint her, you're the biggest asshole to walk this earth and you're going to hell for causing this poor innocent little lady so much pain. She's pure evil, I tell you. Evil wrapped in floral chiffon."

Sloane fell over onto his side, holding his stomach, which started to cramp from laughing so hard. His face hurt. He was dying to call Lou up and have him send his mom over just so he could witness this great feat. He needed to get some tips from the woman.

"I know what you're thinking," Dex said with a sniff as he stood with his empty plate. "If you so much as even hint at what you're thinking, there will be no sexy times for you for the foreseeable future."

Sloane sat up with a scoff. "Please. Like you would last a day." He picked up his plate and followed Dex into the kitchen. Dex took it from him and started washing, grumbling under his breath, making Sloane laugh. He wrapped his arms around Dex from behind and nuzzled his temple. "And why would you want to?" He kissed behind Dex's ear, loving the shiver it sent through his sexy-as-sin partner. "Don't worry. I wouldn't subject you to such horrors."

Dex finished washing up, his lips doing that adorable pouty thing. When he'd dried his hands, Sloane took his hand and pulled him into a twirl before dipping him. Dex let out a laugh, and Sloane planted a quick sweet kiss on his delicious lips, then brought him back up. Dex shoved at him playfully, shaking his head before he turned to walk away.

"Come here, baby," Sloane said in a low sultry tone that immediately got Dex's attention. His sexy man turned to him, laughing when Sloane crooked his finger. He bit down on his bottom lip before giving Sloane his hand. Sloane pulled Dex against him, and they danced around the kitchen, through the dining room, and into the living room. Sloane's heart was ready to burst from how happy he was. This right here, this was what mattered. Whatever happened in their work lives, whatever job they were doing, whatever operation they'd find themselves in, this was what he would look back on, what he would draw strength from. *This* was worth surviving whatever trials came their way, and hopefully someday soon, they could retire and spend every evening in each other's arms, dancing, laughing, and loving each other unconditionally.

After dancing, they went back to watching TV before showering and changing into their pajamas. Cael called, and while Dex chatted with his brother, Sloane put some laundry away. Afterward, he was in the mood for some ice cream. They'd gotten so caught up in their being sappy that he'd forgotten about dessert.

Sloane headed into the kitchen and searched the freezer with a frown. Where the hell was it? "Babe, where's my ice cream?"

"Oh."

Sloane closed the freezer door and turned to find Dex standing in the middle of the kitchen, spoon near his mouth and what looked suspiciously like Sloane's Cherry Garcia in his hand. Or rather an empty carton of what was once Cherry Garcia. Considering the carton of Phish Food had also been absent in Sloane's search of the freezer, he was going to hazard a guess that a certain someone had devoured that as well.

"Um." Dex dropped his gaze to the carton, then looked back up at Sloane, big blue eyes wide and innocent. "I can explain."

Sloane leaned against the counter, his arms folded over his chest. "I can't wait to hear this." He arched an eyebrow at Dex and motioned for him to proceed.

"The thing is," Dex began, and Sloane could almost see all the little wheels and cogs working furiously in that sweet little Dex brain. "I, um..." A lightbulb went off somewhere, and Dex met Sloane's gaze, his expression serious. "Sloane, I didn't know how I was going to tell you this with everything going on, but..." He sniffed, and Sloane straightened.

"What's wrong?"

Dex's bottom lip wobbled, and he let out a shaky breath. "I'm pregnant."

Sloane's expression turned deadpan. "Really?"

Dex nodded. "It was a craving. I'm so sorry. I'm eating for two, you know." He put the spoon and the empty carton in the sink before placing a hand on his belly. He gasped. "Quick, give me your hand. I can feel him kicking."

Sloane rolled his eyes, and Dex let out a loud, disturbingly long burp. "False alarm. It was just gas."

"Classy." Sloane shook his head and walked around the counter as Dex washed his spoon. Dex then dived onto the couch when Sloane sat down. Sloane flipped through the channels, and Dex rolled onto his back, his head in Sloane's lap.

"Don't be mad."

Sloane wasn't mad, but that didn't mean he was going to let Dex off the hook that easily. Dex knew better than to eat *two* cartons of ice cream in one night.

"You ate your ice cream and mine."

Dex pouted. "I'm sorry. Being half Therian is hard. I'm hungry all the time."

Sloane scoffed. "Nice try. You were hungry all the time before."

"Yeah, but now it takes more food to fill me up."

"Which we buy," Sloane reminded him. "Admit it. You wanted ice cream, and since you'd eaten all of yours, you thought you'd eat mine and then pretend like I'd finished it." It wouldn't be the first time. Sloane knew Dex far too well by now. Sloane rarely ate dessert, which meant his lasted longer, or at least until Dex gave him the sad puppy eyes and Sloane gave in.

Dex threw a hand dramatically over his brow. "I can't help it, Sloane. I'm weak, and ice cream is so tasty."

"It also bloats you."

"This is true." Dex got up and shoved his butt in Sloane's face, making him laugh. Damn it. He didn't want to give in that quickly. "Does my ass look bigger?"

"Get your butt out of my face," Sloane said, trying hard to sound annoyed.

"But you like my butt in your face." Dex wiggled his ass, and Sloane slapped it. "Ooh, yeah, baby, just like that. I've been a naughty boy."

Sloane let out a bark of laughter. "Oh my God, all right. I give up. I'm not mad."

Dex dropped down onto the couch and resumed his spot with his head in Sloane's lap. His smile was ridiculous.

"I knew you loved me."

"Shut up."

Dex did the opposite. He was relentless. Until he had Sloane where he wanted him, he wouldn't give up. He snapped his fingers, and *Retro Radio* came floating through the speakers. Dex rolled off the couch, popped up like a jack-in-the-box, and broke off into song, replacing the lyrics "the boy" in "Let's Hear It for the Boy" with "my Sloane" all while pulling his best *Footloose* moves.

Oh dear God. Sloane pressed his lips together and shook his head. He was not giving in. He was strong. He could do this.

Dex arched an eyebrow at him. He snapped his fingers, and the Eurythmics "Sweet Dreams" started playing. Dex arched his brows and sang along as he did deep lunges across the living room, his eyes never leaving Sloane no matter which way he turned.

Not happening, Daley. No dice.

With narrowed eyes, Dex snapped his fingers, and "Two of Hearts" came on. Sloane inhaled deeply and braced himself as Dex did his best eighties Jazzercise. Seeing as how that didn't work, Dex moved on to the next song, and Sloane knew he was in trouble the moment he heard the first chord. He closed his eyes and shook his head. The couch cushions dipped, and Sloane was forced to open his eyes. He bit down on his bottom lip to keep from smiling as Dex lip-synched to Chicago's "You're the Inspiration," dramatic hand gestures and all. Dex straddled Sloane's lap and put everything he had into his performance, one hand going to his heart, the other out grabbing air. During the chorus, he grabbed Sloane's head and brought it against his chest.

"Okay, okay. I give," Sloane said with a laugh before he was smothered. Dex released him, and he sat back. "If I hold it in anymore, I'm going to pop a spleen."

"Yes!" Dex jumped to his feet, then fist-pumped the air. He lowered his voice, mimicking a certain burly gladiator. "Call me Victorius Maximus."

"All right, Victorius Maximus. Get over here."

Dex happily obliged, lying down on the couch with his head in Sloane's lap once more. Sloane grabbed one of the throw pillows. "Head up."

Dex lifted his head, and Sloane placed the pillow under him. They settled in together, and Sloane ran his fingers absently through Dex's soft hair as they watched TV together. Sloane couldn't remember the last time they got to just hang out and spend time together like a normal couple without some kind of crisis hitting. So this was how the other half lived? Waking up, running errands, doing chores, cooking, watching TV, spending time together. They'd griped about how their laundry detergent wasn't as good as it used to be and that they should try out a new brand. It was all so oddly satisfying.

Sloane dozed off at some point and woke up to find Dex gone. He checked his watch, surprised he hadn't actually been asleep very long. The house was oddly quiet, with the only sounds coming from the TV. Maybe Dex had just popped upstairs to the bathroom. After half an hour and still no Dex, Sloane got up. He headed upstairs to their bedroom. It was empty, but the bathroom door was closed. Was Dex not feeling well? Sloane had a habit of worrying when Dex was sick. With Dex's mutation, there was no telling whether a cold or stomach bug was just that or the start of something more.

Sloane stopped in front of the bathroom door and reached up to knock but paused when he heard sniffling. Putting his ear to the door, he could hear Dex clearly on the other side. Dex was crying, and it broke Sloane's heart. He felt the pain then. The heartache. Dex's heartache. Sloane was torn. He desperately wanted to draw Dex into his arms and comfort him, but he also wanted to give Dex his privacy. It was clear Dex wanted to be on his own, or he would have woken Sloane up.

Instead of disturbing him, Sloane went back downstairs and checked the house, making sure everything was locked. He switched off all the lights, then returned to the bedroom. After turning down the bed and switching on his bedside lamp, he climbed into bed under the covers. He'd just settled down on his side and closed his eyes, when he heard the bathroom door open. A heartbeat later, Dex joined him in bed, and Sloane's heart skipped a beat when Dex slipped his arm under Sloane's and around Sloane's chest, his body pressed against Sloane's back from head to toe. Sloane placed his hand over Dex's and laced their fingers together. He didn't have to wait long.

"I'm sorry if I worried you," Dex said, his voice quiet and rough. "I was thinking about the wedding when I kind of dozed off. I was half-asleep, but still awake, and I had this vision of us getting married, and my parents were there. I woke up, and..." Dex let out a shuddered sigh. "I realized it had been a dream. It hit me harder than I expected."

Sloane turned to face Dex and wiped a tear from his wet cheek. Dex pressed his lips together and shook his head. He didn't want to talk about it. That was okay. Sloane drew him close, and they lay together, limbs entangled. He rubbed circles on Dex's back and kissed his brow, offering the comfort Dex sought.

"I love you," Dex said, his voice so quiet Sloane wouldn't have heard him if he wasn't so close.

"I love you too, baby." Sloane stroked Dex's cheek—his mind, body, and soul feeling at peace. He inhaled the scent he'd know anywhere—his beautiful mate, his best friend, and his whole world.

CHAPTER THREE

"I CAN'T BELIEVE we have to train during our time off," Dex whined loudly.

Sloane refrained from saying a word as he walked alongside his disgruntled husband-to-be. Mostly because Sloane was aware Dex wasn't really annoyed they had to train during their vacation time. Dex was eager to get in as much training as possible. Even though they'd be spending the next six months after swearing-in getting their asses handed to them in TIN's Covert Operative Training Program, Dex wanted to be ready. Dex was whining because it bugged the ever-loving shit out of Sparks, and it had become Dex's life mission to drive her insane at every possible opportunity. To what end, Sloane had no idea. His job was to make sure she didn't end up pushing Dex in front of a moving bus.

"TIN doesn't take time off," Sparks informed them, oh so calmly.

"Never?" Dex eyed her. "You're telling me we don't get to take a vacation *ever*?"

Sparks rolled her eyes. "Every operative gets time off.

However, if you're needed while you're on said time off, you report in. Criminals don't take vacations."

"I'm pretty sure they do. Are you telling me Moros didn't have paid vacation time?"

Sparks arched a perfectly shaped eyebrow at him but didn't respond, just kept walking.

"Fine, whatever, but not in the face. I don't want to walk down the aisle sporting a black eye. It'll clash with my color scheme."

Sparks came to a halt and turned to face him, her hands on her hips. "Are you serious?"

Dex mimicked her pose. "Do *you* want to explain to my dad how I got a black eye during my time off before the wedding?"

"That would not be good," Sloane agreed. "Tony's already nervous about being the officiant."

Sparks narrowed her eyes at Dex before spinning on her high heels and marching off.

Dex waggled his eyebrows at Sloane, and Sloane leaned in to whisper in Dex's ear, "She's dying to put you in a sleeper hold. I can feel it."

Dex chuckled, and Sloane shook his head. Fine. If Dex wanted to continue baiting the scary cougar Therian, he only had himself to blame when he got bit. It wasn't like Dex was going to listen to reason. He was on a mission of optimum annoyance.

They followed Sparks down yet another drab gray corridor that looked like every other drab gray corridor they'd visited over the last few months. Not that he expected TIN to put up any artwork or framed portraits, but would it kill them to slap some paint on these walls? Something to differentiate one facility from another? Since they weren't officially sworn in yet, the location of each facility remained undisclosed, and although they had been informed that each site served a unique purpose, they all looked the same. The corridors varied in length, but it was always the same dull gray with the same steel doors, always closed. How many of these facilities were scattered around the city, most likely hiding in plain sight?

"So what'll it be today?" Dex asked, breaking the silence. "Ooh, please tell me I get to ride some kickass motorcycles. I've had my eye on the Dodge Tomahawk." Dex rubbed his hands together, and Sloane chuckled at his excitement. Something told Sloane whatever Sparks had in store for them did not involve a half-a-million-dollar motorcycle.

Sparks sighed. "Yes, because that would be so inconspicuous. Flashy equipment is used only when an operation calls for it."

"Okay, how about a Kawasaki Ninja?"

Sparks didn't so much as blink. "No. There are no motorcycles involved in today's training."

"Fine. You plan on telling us what today's training is?"

They finally reached the end of the corridor and a set of doors. Sparks turned to them, her eyes intense.

"For months you've been trained in various forms of combat in a controlled environment. Today the real training begins, and when you return from your honeymoon, we're going to be putting everything you've learned to the test, and then some."

Sloane had no idea what that meant, but his inner Felid was awake and alert. Something on the other side of the door smelled familiar. Sparks opened one of the doors and motioned for them to step through. Was this an exit? It looked like there was a street on the other side.

Dex stopped in his tracks, and Sloane did the same.

"What the fuck is this?" Sloane asked, looking up and down the street. He turned and looked up at the building they'd just been in. It belonged to an apartment building just down the street from their house.

"This is the street you live on."

Dex held up a hand. "Are you telling me you have a TIN facility on our block?"

"Your neighborhood and every home on these two blocks has been under surveillance for several months. After today, the facility will be relocated."

Sloane's brows shot up. "You planted surveillance equipment in every home?"

"In other words, TIN wiped their asses with the Fourth Amendment," Dex scoffed.

Sparks folded her arms over her chest. "Allow me to impart some truth to you boys and your very naïve view of privacy. We're creatures hardwired for connection, now made ever easier by the internet and social media. This privacy you seem to think we all have, it doesn't exist. You leave a digital trail every time you turn on your computer, use a bank card, or even start your pretty orange car. Every aspect of our lives is out there, ready to be harvested with a few clicks of a mouse or strokes at a keyboard. It's our job to make sure that doesn't happen. But what about when lives are at risk? What then? Do we sit back and wait for criminals and murderers to slip up? Do we allow law enforcement agencies to set up task forces and undercover operations that could stretch on for years with no results while citizens lose their lives?"

Dex opened his mouth to reply, but Sparks held up a hand.

"You do realize you've joined a covert intelligence

agency. Most of our ops are undisclosed to even the president."

"Okay, I get it. But we're not talking about infiltrating a terrorist cell here. We're talking about my neighbors."

"Beck Hogan was someone's neighbor. Isaac Pearce was someone's neighbor."

Sloane couldn't help but flinch at the mention of Isaac Pearce. He should probably feel remorse for Pearce's death, but he didn't. The son of a bitch had killed Gabe and had planned on killing Dex. Sloane hoped he was rotting away in hell like he deserved.

Sparks let out a sigh, and Sloane was surprised when her gaze turned sympathetic. "I know this is all difficult for you to come to grips with, and I don't expect you to flip a switch and suddenly see things the way we do. You need to ask yourself, how far are you willing to go to protect people? How far is too far? We're the ones who get our hands dirty so no one else has to. When you look around you, all you see is your quiet neighborhood filled with Humans and Therians going about their daily lives, but what you don't see are the operatives who risk their lives every day to make sure that's possible." Sparks pointed to the house three doors down from theirs. "You know Mr. Jonas, correct?"

Dex nodded. "Yeah, he's a sweet old guy. A Pre-First Gen who fought in Vietnam."

"His wife makes us cookies all the time," Sloane added.

"Did you know Mr. Jonas has been losing the battle against his illness?"

Dex cursed under his breath. "I knew he wasn't well, but he doesn't like to talk about it, and when I asked Mrs. Jonas once, she burst into tears, so I didn't ask again."

"Mr. Jonas shares the same illness as several other Pre-First Gens we were monitoring who were dying at an alarming rate. They were all on the same prescription drug. Our operatives traced the drug to a large American pharmaceutical corporation located abroad. We quickly learned the drug should never have made it past the trial stage. Four out of the ten clinical trial subjects died after eight months of taking it. While the CEOs made billions, Therians were dying."

"How come we never heard about it at the THIRDS?" Dex asked.

"Cause of death for each patient was determined to be complications brought about by the illness. Not only were the drugs not helping the patients, but they were slowly killing them. Our intel led us to Mr. Jonas, and our surveillance led us to the corporation responsible for killing hundreds. Had TIN not become involved, how many more Therians would have died before the truth was revealed? I'm certain you believe alternative, lawful means could have reached the same conclusion, but what if we made it personal? We managed to do in weeks what could have taken other law enforcement agencies years."

"But you don't know that," Dex argued.

"True. Would the timeline matter if I were to say the same medication was prescribed to Thomas Hobbs four months ago?"

Sloane swallowed hard. *Fuck.* "Was it?"

Sparks nodded. "Mr. Hobbs's physician was convinced this new drug would alleviate Mr. Hobbs's pain for a period longer than his previous medication. We made certain to collect every prescription out there, including the one sitting on the shelf at the pharmacy waiting for Sebastian Hobbs to pick up."

"Does Seb know?" Dex asked, his voice quiet.

"Yes. As you can imagine, this particular operation was

of great interest to Seb. How do you feel about our involvement now? It shouldn't matter, should it? But it does because you care. You care what happens to these people. The world isn't black and white. You need to be prepared for the worst and be willing to do something about it."

Sloane hated to admit it, but Sparks was right. They kept telling each other and everyone else that they were ready, but were they really? They'd spent most of their adult lives following their moral compasses and the laws their country was governed by. There was no telling where their operations would take them or what would be asked of them. In the end, they had to trust in their own judgment and hope they were making the right choices for the right reasons.

Rather than answering Sparks, Dex motioned to the street. "So, what are we doing here?"

"You've just received intel that a very dangerous enemy agent is inside one of the homes on your block. You need to find them, detain them, and bring them in for questioning before their extraction team arrives."

Dex peered at her. "Which is in how long?"

"One hour."

"An *hour*? Do you know how many apartments there are on this block?"

"Maybe you'll get lucky and they're sitting in the restaurant on the corner." Sparks turned back toward the door they'd come from. "If you blow your cover, the operation is aborted and you've failed."

"Got it. Equipment?"

Sparks's grin was wicked. "You're wearing it."

Dex looked down at himself. "But… I don't have anything on me."

"Then I suggest you be resourceful."

"In other words, we're on our own," Sloane muttered, not really surprised. It wasn't like he expected to go into every situation perfectly prepared. If his time at the THIRDS had taught him anything, it was to always expect the unexpected and shit was always guaranteed to go wrong.

"Are you saying you need me to hold your hand?" Sparks asked, amused.

"We got this." Dex turned to Sloane and motioned toward the street. "Come on." The door closed, and Dex stepped closer to Sloane. "This is so freaking weird."

"I know. Okay, where do we start?"

"Our house," Dex replied with a grin. "And more importantly, our closet."

Sloane returned Dex's grin. They were so all over this. "Let's go. We've got a lot of area to cover." Not to mention it was Sunday, so a good number of their neighbors were probably out enjoying the nice September weather before winter came to kick all their asses, and someone could arrive at any moment and catch them.

They jogged over to their front steps, and Dex quickly unlocked the door. It was so surreal.

"This is crazy," Dex said as he scanned their living room before running for the stairs leading up to the bedroom, Sloane on his heels. In their bedroom, Dex gave Sloane a wry grin as he pointed. "Oh look, TIN got to see the wet towel you always leave on the bed."

Crap. It wasn't bad enough Sloane always forgot the damn towel; apparently, now there were witnesses.

"Sorry," Sloane said as he walked over to the bed to pick up the towel.

"What are you doing?" Dex asked, amused.

"Shit. Right. Covert operation." He dropped the towel

back on the bed. "This whole thing is messing with my head." He joined Dex at the closet as Dex pulled out the locked weapons and ammunitions crate they had stored in there. It used to just be a small case with a couple of Glocks, but after all the craziness they'd been through, they'd agreed an upgrade was in order. The crate was programmed to open with a thumbprint from Dex or Sloane only. Inside were several different firearms, tranq guns, zip ties, ammunitions, and more. Dex checked his Glock's magazine and frowned.

"Fuck."

"What is it?" Sloane asked, picking up one of the tranq guns.

"I can't believe we're going to break into our neighbors' homes."

Sloane shook his head. "We can't shoot that."

Dex blinked at him. "Why?"

"Because someone will hear and call it in."

Dex peered at him. "So, we're supposed to break into our very possibly armed neighbors' homes, face an 'enemy agent,' not blow our cover, and all in less than an hour, without firing a shot?"

Sloane nodded.

"Fuck. This is why we need silencers," Dex muttered.

"Why would we need silencers?"

"Because of this right here."

"This right here has never happened before, so there was never any need for silencers."

Dex threw up a hand. "And look how well that's turned out."

"Oh my God, seriously? Babe, we have less than an hour or we fail our first fake operation."

"Shit. Okay, stock up on tranqs, then. You take this end

of the street, I'll start at the other end." Dex put in an earpiece and handed Sloane the other. "Stay in communication, and be safe." Dex kissed Sloane before hurrying off. Sloane called out behind him.

"You too." Sloane shoved some Therian-strength zip ties into his pockets. He left the house, noticing Dex was nowhere to be seen. With his gun tucked in the back of his waistband, covered by his shirt, Sloane closed the front door of their house and discreetly scanned the street of their quiet little West Village neighborhood. No one was outside, and no movement caught his eye. The end of the block was a completely different story. Their house was only four buildings down from the corner of a typical busy New York City street intersection. There were people walking, riding bikes, milling about, waiting for their burgers at Five Guys or heading into the pizza place across the street.

Right. Break in next door without getting caught. The basement windows were out of the question, since they all had bars, and seeing as how TIN had yet to issue them any nifty gadgets, Sloane had to think of another way in.

Just his luck, one of his neighbors, Sandra, headed in his direction. She waved as she went up the stairs. Well, it was time to do this. He quickly jogged over, flashing his brightest smile.

"Hey, Sandra. Do you know if Brian's in? He borrowed my power drill, and I need it to fix a loose shelf before Dex gets home. It's been driving him nuts."

Sandra smiled brightly at him. "I'm not sure, but why don't you go ahead," she said, standing to one side of the open front door.

"Thanks. You're a lifesaver." He slipped inside and turned to give her his most appreciative smile. "If I don't get this thing fixed, I'm going to end up in the doghouse. Or the cat house, I guess."

Sandra giggled before waving at him and heading upstairs. As soon as she was out of sight, Sloane waited until he heard her apartment door close before turning to Brian's apartment. He leaned in, listening for any signs Brian might be home. It was doubtful, since their young neighbor was most likely out with his girlfriend. Sloane rapped gently on the door. As a Felid, Brian had exceptional hearing. If he was home, he'd have heard Sloane.

How many times had he told Brian he needed to change his door? This one was total shit with a crappy lock. All it took was one forceful push of Sloane's shoulder, and the door was open. He quietly closed it behind him and stilled, listening for any movement. When he heard nothing, he moved around the tiny apartment. He couldn't imagine where an agent would find a place to hide in here unless they also happened to be a contortionist. Nonetheless, he checked every nook and cranny, while also listening to Dex on the other end of Sloane's earpiece.

"Holy fuck."

Sloane straightened, his heart pounding. "What is it? Did you find the agent?"

"No, but I found something even better. Dude, Mrs. Bauman's into BDSM."

"What?" Sloane let out a breath he hadn't even realized he'd been holding.

"Mrs. Bauman. She has an entire closet full of leather stuff, paddles, whips..."

"Why are you searching Mrs. Bauman's closet?"

"For our guy, or girl, agent."

"And a highly skilled enemy agent is going to be hiding in Mrs. Bauman's closet?" Maybe they were taking a page out of Dex's book. *Dexter J. Daley's 101 Places to Hide If You Want to Get Caught. Number 1. Bedroom Closet.* Sloane let out a snort at the memory of a naked Dex hiding from Ash in the bedroom closet back when they'd thought they were being sneaky about their relationship. Of course the closet was the first place Ash looked.

Dex let out a bark of laughter. "Oh my God!"

"What now?" Sloane was going to strangle him.

"Mrs. Bauman has a strap-on."

"I did not need to know that."

"Ooh yeah, get your freak on, Mrs. Bauman. Just goes to show, you're never too old to get jiggy with it. Man, I hope we're this adventurous when we get to her age. We're probably going to need a little something-something to help with the, uh, you know, gravity, but we can make it work. Shit. What if Mrs. Bauman *is* the agent?"

"Really?"

"Think about it, Sloane. She always happens to pop up when I'm either compromised or half-naked."

"I think that says more about you than it does our elderly neighbor."

"I bet her walking that tiny prehistoric dog—which I'm convinced is some kind of wingless pterodactyl—is her doing surveillance. She's probably got all kinds of explosives hidden in her housedress. Have you seen how ginormous the pockets are?"

"You're ridiculous."

"Am I, Sloane? Am I really?"

"Yes."

"Fine, but when she springs out at you like the wrinkly ninja she is and tries to strangle you with her hairnet, don't say I didn't warn you. I bet those rollers are actually grenades."

"Stop talking." Sloane heard a board creak up in the ceiling. "Um, Dex."

"A lot of people would probably be grossed out by Mrs. Bauman's sexual prowess, but she's a mature woman. A very, very, very, *very* mature woman. But who says she's not allowed to have some fun? People are so judgey."

"I'm not talking about Mrs. Bauman's sex life," Sloane hissed. "Would you stop for a second and listen?"

"Listening."

Sloane silently moved around the apartment, his eyes up at the ceiling. There was another creak. "Mrs. Lloyd spends the day with her mom on Sundays, right?"

"Yeah, while her wife is at dance practice. Why?"

Sloane lowered his voice to a whisper. "Because someone's upstairs in their apartment."

"On my way."

"Don't blow your cover," Sloane warned, and he hurried to the door. Cracking it open, he peered out into the hall. It was empty. After slipping out of Brian's apartment, he edged toward the stairs and took them two at a time until he was on the second floor. The old brownstone, like countless others around the city, had been converted into apartments, with three apartments occupying the structure. Sandra lived up on the third floor, and Mrs. Lloyd and her wife on the second.

Sloane reached back into the waistband of his jeans and removed his tranq gun. Sticking close to the wall, he approached the apartment. The door was closed, but that didn't mean it was locked. Reaching across the door, he silently wrapped a hand around the doorknob and very gingerly tested it. It was unlocked. Would an enemy operative leave a door unlocked? Unless they were so completely certain they wouldn't be found, or they were confident they wouldn't get caught.

Slowly, Sloane pushed the door in, remaining on the other side of it in case someone decided to shoot through the open door. When there was no gunfire, he leaned in closer to peek through the opening. He didn't see or hear anyone. Gun in hand, he slipped inside the room and quickly scanned it. The apartment was long and narrow, the living room tastefully decorated in creams and browns. It was also empty, which made sense seeing as how there was no place for anyone to hide. One wall had a fireplace and across from it a couch with a glass coffee table in the center. Next to the fireplace was a bookshelf, and from where he stood, Sloane could see partially into what looked like a bedroom.

"Sloane, I'm at the front door. It's open."

"It was unlocked," Sloane replied quietly. "I'm in the living room."

Dex was at his side seconds later. Sloane motioned to the bedroom and then nodded toward the kitchen. Dex nodded back, and with his tranq gun lifted, he headed for the kitchen while Sloane silently made his way toward the bedroom, making sure to stay close to the walls and away from the open doorway. When he reached the bedroom, he glanced down at his watch. Twenty-five minutes until extraction. Shit. They needed to find this agent soon. If the agent wasn't in here, they were screwed.

Sloane carefully checked the bedroom. He checked the obvious places—behind the door, in the closet, and under the bed. As he got to his knees to stand, he found himself staring at a pair of Chucks. His gaze traveled up, and he frowned.

"Austen?"

Austen winked at him before kicking him in the chest, knocking the wind out of Sloane. He fell onto his back, sucking in a lungful of air as he held a hand to his chest. Austen jumped off the bed, and Sloane scrambled to his feet.

"What the hell?" Sloane wheezed.

"Sorry, Sloane. This is going to hurt you more than it does me, but if it's to make you a stronger operative, to make sure you're prepared, then I gotta." Austen launched himself at Sloane, and Sloane dodged, slapping away Austen's fist when it came at his ribs.

"I don't want to hurt you," Sloane said, deflecting Austen's blows, but Austen was much quicker, his training far exceeding Sloane's.

"That's your first mistake," Austen growled, using Sloane's bent knee to hop up and wrap his legs around Sloane's neck, twisting and using his weight to throw Sloane off-balance.

"What's going on?" Dex ran into the room, tranq gun in hand. His eyes went wide, and Sloane hit the bed, front first, and bounced off. He managed to regain his balance and grabbed Austen's leg with one hand while wrestling him with the other. Dex aimed his gun at them.

"Damn it, I can't get a clear shot." Dex threw himself at Sloane, and the three of them went crashing to the floor, their guns skidding across the wooden floorboards. Austen released him, and Sloane scrambled for his gun while Dex got to his feet.

"What the hell are you doing?" Dex asked, fists up, as he faced Austen.

"Teaching you boys a valuable lesson."

"And what's that?" Dex asked.

Sloane spun, tranq gun in hand. He aimed it in Austen's direction but hesitated. Did Sparks really want him to tranq one of their own? Austen wasn't just a friend; he was family. Sloane had watched the kid grow up from a gangly street punk into a fearless operative. Austen met Sloane's gaze from across the room.

"You need to be prepared to do whatever is necessary to complete your op."

Sloane swallowed hard.

"Sloane, shoot him."

Sloane aimed but didn't pull the trigger.

"Sloane," Dex snapped.

Sloane flinched. He attempted to pull the trigger but was too late. Austen hopped on the bed and jumped on Dex, who stumbled but didn't fall.

"Fuck, he's like a spider monkey!" Dex threw himself back into the dresser, and Sloane ran to help, but when Dex moved away, Austen brought a drawer with him, swinging it at Sloane. Not having time to avoid the blow, Sloane turned to his side, the drawer breaking against his shoulder.

"Motherfuck!" Sloane made a grab for Austen, but Austen released Dex, dropped to the floor, and kicked at Dex's leg, sending Dex into Sloane. Before they could even get their balance, Austen grabbed another drawer, pulled, and swung it, hitting Dex in the back.

"Dex!"

The momentum propelled Dex forward, and he slammed into the wooden closet door, sending the whole thing crashing along with him.

"Come on, Sloane," Austen snarled. "Your partner and fiancé is down. Get fucking mad."

Sloane shook his head. "Austen, please."

Austen shook his head. "You're not getting this, are you?" He pulled out a gun and aimed it at Dex. Sloane didn't hesitate. His inner Felid woke up with a roar, and

Sloane lunged at Austen, smacking the hand holding the gun away from Dex before shoving his elbow into Austen's face. The blood from Austen's nose splattered over Sloane. Austen cursed up a storm, but Sloane didn't give him time to react before he swiped Austen's feet out from under him, bringing him hard onto his stomach. A knee to Austen's back, and Sloane pulled his arms up behind him. He grabbed a couple of Therian-strength zip ties from his pocket and slipped them around Austen's wrists. He took another one and slipped it around Austen's ankles. With a hand wrapped around Austen's neck, he brought Austen to his feet.

Blood trickled down Austen's nose and over his mouth. He spit out saliva with blood, his teeth red when he grinned at Sloane.

"I knew you had it in you," Austen said.

Dex groaned and pushed to his feet. "Fuck." He held on to his side.

"You okay?" Sloane asked, worried.

"Yeah, I just got the wind knocked out of me." Dex looked Austen over with a frown before moving his gaze to Sloane. "You okay?"

Sloane nodded, not trusting himself to say anything right now. At least he hadn't had to tranq Austen, but what if they hadn't been so lucky?

"Aren't you two sweet. Sloane, you may want to kiss your bride later. My extraction team is going to be here any minute. You still have to turn me in without blowing your cover, so let's get moving."

"First you try to kick our asses, now you're giving us advice?"

Austen laughed at Dex. "Dude, there was no *try*. I totally kicked your ass."

Dex rolled his eyes. "We should have brought a gag."

"Ooh, kinky." Austen waggled his eyebrows.

"That's enough." Sloane looked around the bedroom, then out into the living room. "Dex, the rug."

Dex followed his gaze and grinned.

"Oh my God," Austen groaned. "Please tell me you guys aren't about to do what I think you are."

Sloane hoisted Austen over his shoulder and carried him into the living room.

"Can't complain about the view, though."

"Stop staring at Sloane's ass," Dex demanded, shoving away furniture until the rug was clear. "Definitely big enough for short stuff."

"Screw you, Daley." Austen wriggled, and Sloane dropped him none too gently onto the accent rug.

"Ouch, man. Why you gotta be so rough?" He winked at Sloane. "I like it."

"Sweet Jesus." Dex shook his head. "Let's just get this over with. Hold him down."

Sloane laid Austen at the end of the rug, and then he and Dex rolled him up into it. Dex helped Sloane get the rug onto his shoulder, then started to move the furniture back into place.

"What are you doing?" Sloane asked.

"He's being a blond," Austen said from inside the rolled carpet, his voice slightly muffled.

Dex smacked the rug. "Shut up." They quickly headed for the front door, and Dex peeked out into the hall. "Coast is clear." He opened the door for Sloane, and Sloane hurried out, making sure Dex closed the door behind them. Checking the coast was clear outside, they casually walked down the steps and to the street. Austen wriggled, and Sloane hissed at him.

"Stop moving or I'm going to drop you right here in the middle of the sidewalk."

The wiggling stopped, and they approached the building where they'd come out from. Dex looked around. "So what do we do now?"

Sloane shrugged. "Ring the doorbell?"

Dex did, and the door opened. They carried the rug inside, and Sparks approached, looking amused.

"Not bad."

Dex stared at her. "Not bad? We captured the enemy agent."

"Did you?"

Wait. Why did the rug feel lighter all of a sudden? Sloane placed the rug on the floor with a frown. Something wasn't right. Quickly he unrolled it, then cursed under his breath. "He's gone."

Dex spun around. "What?" He dropped his gaze to the carpet. "How the fuck did we lose him?"

"You didn't frisk me," Austen said, strolling past them to stand beside Sparks, a tissue to his nose. He reached into his pocket and pulled out a small butterfly knife. "I took it out when you two weren't looking and hid it between my wrists. I cut my hands loose, wriggled my way out the back of the carpet, and cut my feet loose. Easy peasy."

"It was a good effort, but it could have been over much quicker had you shot Austen when you had the chance."

Dex folded his arms over his chest. "I know."

"All right, yes. I get it. I fucked up." Sloane turned to Dex. "But what if it had been your brother, or Hobbs, or someone else you cared about? Would you have pulled the trigger without hesitating?"

Dex let out a sigh. "You're right. I would have hesitated. I'm not upset because you couldn't take the shot,"

Dex said, turning to face Sloane, the disappointment in his eyes squeezing at Sloane's heart. "I'm upset because *I* didn't take the shot. If you couldn't do it, for whatever reason, I understand, but I should have been able to do it. Just like if I couldn't do what I needed to do, you would be there to back me up and make sure it happened. I failed you."

Sloane stared at Dex. He certainly hadn't been expecting that. "Dex..."

Dex shook his head and walked off, leaving Sloane standing there wondering what the hell had just happened.

"He's right," Sparks said gently. "You're a team. If one of you is compromised, it's up to the other to complete the op. I was watching. You weren't the only one who hesitated."

"What are you talking about?"

"Dex had a clear shot of Austen, and he hesitated. He could have tranqed Austen, but in his inability to cause you heartache, he didn't shoot. That's something you both will need to work on or you leave yourselves both vulnerable."

Sloane nodded. They were dismissed, and Sloane turned to head back outside and go home. Austen caught up with him and grabbed his wrist. Sloane turned, motioning to his nose.

"Sorry about that."

Austen shrugged, a big boyish smile on his face. "I've had worse. You guys did really great."

Sloane sighed. "Yeah? It doesn't feel like we did."

"Don't be so hard on yourselves. You don't even officially start training until you get back, so don't worry about it. You guys have one hell of an advantage. Not everyone was THIRDS before being recruited, you know." He winked at Sloane. "You guys are gonna be awesome. Have a little faith. Your boy has chutzpah. You just need to remind him."

Sloane chuckled. "Thanks. Take care, yeah? See you next weekend at the rehearsal dinner."

Austen gave him a salute as he walked backward. "Wouldn't miss it."

Feeling somewhat better, Sloane hurried off home and found his solemn-looking partner in the kitchen leaning against the counter, staring off into space.

"TIN dude was here. He removed the surveillance cameras," Dex mumbled, looking out at nothing in particular. Sloane hated seeing him so despondent. He stopped in front of Dex, his feet to either side of Dex's and his hands on Dex's hips.

"You're being too hard on yourself," Sloane said.

Dex frowned and averted his gaze. "What if that happens out in the field? What if we're in the middle of an op and I hesitate because I'm afraid of hurting you and you end up injured or worse? I hesitated, Sloane, and look how quickly it escalated. I didn't see an enemy operative; I saw Austen. I know how much he means to you, and I thought 'fuck, if I do this, I'm going to hurt Sloane,' and there I was telling *you* to shoot him, and fuck." He ran his hand over his face. "What if I suck at this? What if joining TIN was just me stroking my ego, thinking I could be this superspy, and I end up getting you killed?" Dex sucked in a sharp breath. "You want a family, and fuck, I really want a family with you too, and what if I fuck it all up because I convinced you to go traipsing around the world to play James Bond with me? Oh God."

"Stop," Sloane insisted gently, cupping Dex's face. "Take a deep breath."

Dex nodded, following Sloane's tender order.

"That's it. Just breathe. Now look at me."

Dex did, his beautiful eyes filled with doubt. "We're getting married next weekend, Sloane. Am I being a selfish prick?" His shoulders slumped, and he wrapped his hands around Sloane's wrists. "You're everything."

"And you're everything for me. Do you think I would have gone along with this if I didn't think we were capable? If I didn't think we were going to make a real difference out there? Baby, I have never seen *anyone* take to this as quick as you have. You've been working your ass off. Between picking out invites, working on assigned seating, getting fitted for tuxes, choosing a cake, and all the dozens upon dozens of wedding prep items, you've been pushing yourself beyond anyone's expectations. You've been training in combat techniques I've never even heard of, all of which you're excelling at. I'm just blown away by how amazing you are." He kissed Dex's cheek and ran his fingers down Dex's jaw. "Do you want to know what I think is happening here?"

"What?" Dex asked.

"I think you're nervous about the wedding, you're exhausted, and today's session messed with your head." Sloane brushed his lips over Dex's. "This was good for us. It showed us what we need to work on, and I have no doubt that we're going to rock this." He let their heads rest together. "You, Dexter J. Daley, are an inspiration, and I'll be right with you every step of the way when you go out there and show these guys how it's supposed to be done."

Dex pulled back, his smile stealing Sloane's breath away. "You always make me feel like I can do anything."

"Because you can." Sloane believed it with every fiber of his being. There was nothing Dex couldn't do. Sloane had never known a more fearless, strong-willed force of nature than the man in front of him, and Sloane was about to be officially tied to him for the rest of his life.

Dex shook his head with a soft laugh.

"What?" Sloane asked, nuzzling Dex's temple.

"For some reason, I thought of that night not long after I joined the THIRDS. The one where I took your picture. You chased me all over Unit Alpha and we ended up in the parking garage next to a black SUV." He nipped at Sloane's chin. "You were so pissed, and then we got each other off."

Sloane groaned. "God, I was such a fucking mess back then. I didn't know whether I wanted to punch you or fuck you."

Dex laughed. "Both. You definitely wanted to do both."

"Seems like such a long time ago." Had he changed that much? He'd been so angry all the time. "I was a real asshole to you, wasn't I?"

Dex shook his head. "You were in a lot of pain."

"That's no excuse." Sloane took Dex's hand in his and brought his fingers to his lips for a kiss. "But thank you. Thank you for all your patience, for your smile, for taking a chance on a guy who thought he was too broken to ever know what real happiness looked like."

"And now you know what it looks like?"

Sloane smiled. "Yeah. Looks like you."

"You know what Ash would say if he were here?"

Sloane lowered his voice and did his best Ash impression. "You two are disgusting. I'm getting cavities just from breathing the same air as you."

Dex threw his head back and laughed. "Oh my God, that was perfect."

Sloane took advantage of Dex's exposed neck and nipped at his skin. "You know what we should do tomorrow?"

Dex melted against Sloane with a moan. "Hump like bunnies?"

"After that. I think we should call the gang up and have a night out at Dekatria."

Dex let out a dreamy sigh. "Karaoke, booze, and shenanigans. You know me well."

Yes, he did.

CHAPTER FOUR

Sloane peered at the full coffeepot, then checked his watch. By this time, Dex was usually sitting at the counter next to Sloane, drinking his coffee as he roused himself from his zombie-like state. Like most mornings, Sloane woke up before Dex. Sometimes he stayed in bed watching TV or reading until Dex woke up, but this morning he wanted to get a few chores out of the way. Maybe yesterday's scenario hit Dex harder than Sloane thought. After finishing his coffee, he washed out his cup and headed back upstairs to check on Dex. What greeted him when he walked into the bedroom was a decadent, mouthwatering feast for his senses. Dex lay in the center of the bed, on his stomach, not a stitch of clothing in sight. His perfectly plump ass had Sloane biting down on his bottom lip. Fuck, he was stunning. He was also very awake.

Dex propped himself on his elbows and looked at Sloane from over his shoulder, his now amber eyes hooded and filled with molten desire. Sloane would never get tired of seeing the change in his sexy partner's eyes, especially since it was usually a result of Dex being so aroused by

Sloane that he couldn't help the change. Dex ran his tongue over his lush bottom lip, and Sloane was forced to adjust himself.

"Hey, handsome. Why don't you come join me? I'm feeling a little lonely here on this big bed."

Sloane all but dove onto the mattress. Dex turned and sat with his back to the headboard as he drew his knees up and spread his legs. He leisurely stroked his hardening cock. His hair was wild, and the tattoo on his arm made Sloane's dick twitch in the most erotic way. He'd never seen anything so fucking hot.

"Fuck," Sloane groaned.

"That's the plan," Dex purred, sliding his hand over his chest to tweak one nipple.

As much as Sloane wanted to watch, he wanted to touch a whole lot more. He purposefully kept himself from mauling his gorgeous man, and raked his gaze over Dex's body, appreciating the results of Dex's hard work. Dex had been pushing himself during every training and workout session for months, and it showed in his sculpted muscles, in the thickness of his biceps and thighs. He was still leaner than Sloane, with a slim waist Sloane loved to wrap his arms around, but Dex was at his physical peak, and no matter what he was wearing, whether it was a faded T-shirt and jeans or a suit, he turned heads.

Sloane grabbed the bottle of lube from his nightstand drawer and tossed it on the bed before kneeling and leaning in to kiss Dex, hungry and eager to see what Dex had in store for him. Dex got on his knees, returning Sloane's kiss with enough heat and fervor to have Sloane moaning. His hands roamed Sloane's body, Dex's fingers caressing, pressing, squeezing. Sloane brought their bodies flush against each other, their hard, leaking cocks rubbing together.

"How do you want it?" Sloane growled, nipping at Dex's jaw, loving the scruffy stubble.

Dex pulled back, turned, and gripped the top of the headboard, his knees spread, and his back arched. *Holy fuck.* Sloane snatched up the lube, flipped the cap open, then poured a generous amount into his palm. As he slathered his cock up, he traced Dex's spine with his fingers, loving the sensual curve that ended down at Dex's perfectly rounded ass. The muscles in Dex's back flexed, and his breath hitched when Sloane slipped a lubed finger between Dex's ass cheeks.

"Sloane," Dex breathed. "More."

Sloane teased Dex's hole, making Dex shiver. "You want me to fuck you with my finger, baby?"

"God yes. Please."

Sloane placed a kiss on Dex's shoulder and reached around to palm Dex's rock-hard erection, pressing a finger into him. Dex's gasp was music to Sloane's ears. Speaking of music... There was nothing Dex loved more than a good hard fuck to some classic rock. Releasing Dex for a second, Sloane snapped his fingers, and Foreigner's "Juke Box Hero" filled the room. Dex laughed.

"Oh yeah. Rock my world, baby." Dex leaned into Sloane, his hand cupping the back of Sloane's head as he craned his neck to crush his lips to Sloane's. It was sloppy, messy, wet, and so fucking incredible.

"I aim to please," Sloane said, breathless. "Now brace yourself because I'm about to put stars in *your* eyes."

Dex laughed and turned to face the headboard, his back arched as he wiggled his ass for Sloane. With a groan, Sloane continued to finger-fuck his sinful love. When Dex was writhing and all but ready to fall apart, Sloane lined himself up, then gently pushed in. He moved slowly, sinking himself inch by inch until he was balls-deep inside Dex's sweet round ass before pulling almost all the way out and then plunging back in, making Dex cry out in surprise. Sloane groaned at the sight of his painfully hard cock being swallowed by Dex's tight heat time and time again.

"Oh fuck. Sloane."

"You're so damn beautiful."

"I need..."

Sloane sank closer, then leaned in to murmur in Dex's ear, "Tell me what you need, baby." Dex pushed against him, and Sloane followed his lead, sitting on his heels. Dex held on to the headboard, pulled up, then impaled himself on Sloane's cock.

"Holy fuck!" Sloane dug his fingers into Dex's hips as Dex pulled almost all the way off, then slammed himself back down onto Sloane, the fast-paced guitar riff and pounding drums from AC/DC's "Thunderstruck" setting the pace for Dex fucking himself on Sloane. Sloane's heart hammered in his chest as he was swept up in the vigorous ride.

Needing more, Sloane gripped Dex's hips tight, spread his knees, and thrust up every time Dex came down on him.

"Oh fuck, *fuck*!" Dex panted, his gorgeous skin flushed, and muscles strained as he rode Sloane hard.

"Dex," Sloane growled, throwing an arm around Dex's chest as he pushed himself to his knees and plastered his chest to Dex's back. He covered Dex's hand with his, their fingers lacing together as Sloane pounded into Dex, the headboard slamming against the wall and the bed rocking beneath them, the music barely drowning out Dex's cries. Sloane shifted his angle, and Dex jerked against him.

"*Fuck me*! That's it. Right there, baby. Fuck me right there. Make me fucking scream."

Sloane hit Dex's prostate again, and Dex clamped his left hand over Sloane's arm, the tips of his claws only just piercing Sloane's skin, and Sloane lost it. He thrust himself deep and hard, frantically chasing his orgasm as it rolled and thundered right in front of him. With a fierce growl, he bit down on Dex's shoulder as he flew over the edge, his orgasm slamming into him. He let out a roar as he came hard inside Dex. He tugged at Dex's cock once, growling in his ear.

"You fucking come right now."

Dex didn't hold back, screaming into the music-filled air, cursing up a storm as he came against his chest and Sloane's hand. Sloane milked him of every drop until Dex was a quivering mess, sagging against him, his breath as ragged as Sloane's. Dex lolled his head to one side, and Sloane kissed him, his tongue slipping between Dex's soft lips, drawing out a moan.

"That was kind of intense, huh?" Dex snapped his fingers, and the music turned off.

Sloane chuckled. "I think you have a music kink."

"Hey, nothing wrong with a little mood music."

"Oh, I'm not complaining," Sloane promised. "It's hot as hell."

"I can't move," Dex groaned. "You fucked me numb."

Sloane laughed. "I'll take care of it." He got up and gently laid Dex on the bed before heading into the bathroom to wash his hands and grab a soft cloth, which he ran under warm water. When Sloane got back to the bed, Dex had his eyes closed and his lips slightly parted in a sweet, almost shy smile. His face was still flushed, and he was already asleep. How was it possible to love someone this much? It was pretty scary.

Sloane very carefully cleaned Dex up, smiling when Dex stirred, his voice dreamy as he hummed.

"You're so good to me."

Bending over, Sloane kissed Dex, who sighed against his lips.

"Mm, upside-down Spider-Man kiss."

"You're such a dork," Sloane said with a soft laugh.

"And you love it."

"I do. Now get up, get dressed, and come downstairs. I'll make you some breakfast." Sloane returned the towel to the bathroom, ignoring Dex's grumbling at having to get up, but when Sloane returned, Dex was pulling on a pair of orange boxer briefs, followed by the black V-neck T-shirt Sloane had left on the armchair last night. The shirt used to hang long and loose on Dex. Now, not so much. Sloane let out a groan.

"What?" Dex asked, running a hand through his disheveled hair, his pouty lips quirking up on one side.

"Can you at least put on some pants? I want to be able to cook you breakfast without the possibility of setting myself on fire because I'm distracted by your ass and the way you look in my T-shirt."

With a laugh, Dex walked to the dresser and grabbed a pair of old jeans. They were faded, fit snugger than they used to, and were torn on his knees and under his left ass cheek.

"Better?"

Sloane narrowed his eyes. "Just get that bubble butt downstairs, you troublemaker."

"Hey, I resemble that remark."

Sloane let out a playful growl, and Dex yelped before taking off downstairs, Sloane on his tail. He caught Dex before he reached the kitchen, grabbing him and lifting him off his feet, making him laugh. Sloane lived for that sound. It was full, rich, and genuine. When Dex laughed, it formed little creases at the corners of his beautiful eyes. Sloane put him on his feet and popped a kiss on his lips before heading into the kitchen.

Dex went about making his latte while Sloane got started on breakfast. Thankfully, he managed to do so without incident.

"Everyone got back to me about tonight. They said they'd be there, so I texted Bradley to let him know to expect us around eight," Dex said before taking a sip of his coffee, then releasing a moan that went straight to Sloane's groin every time. He placed the plate holding a breakfast sandwich in front of Dex and earned himself a dreamy sigh. "Sexy *and* a great cook. How did I get so lucky?"

Sloane took a seat beside Dex and turned on his tablet while Dex ate. He held back a smile. "Hm, funny that. I'm pretty sure two days ago you said I had—what was the word you used? That's right, cuckolded. I had cuckolded you and was trying to kill you with my food. Where did that word even come from?"

Dex narrowed his eyes at Sloane. "I'd just finished reading one of Hudson's smut novels. Cuckolded was used several times, and Lady Amelia's husband was totally onto something. Like him, I had been cuckolded by my love! You said you were making breakfast burritos. I expected some yummy burrito goodness in my mouth, and instead I bit into a load of birdseed. There was *birdseed* in my burrito, Sloane. Why was there birdseed in my delicious breakfast burrito instead of bacon and cheese?"

"I already told you, it was quinoa."

"It was birdseed. And I don't care what you say, seaweed belongs in the ocean. Do I look like a mermaid to you? Do mermaids eat seaweed? Never mind. Stop trying to feed me things that have no right being called food."

Sloane hid his smile behind his mug, but there was no way he could keep his shoulders from shaking. Dex bit off a huge chunk of his sandwich, then stilled.

"There's bacon and cheese in this," Dex said around a mouthful of food.

"I know."

Dex gazed at him dreamily and grinned around his sandwich. "I lub you."

Sloane winked at him and playfully nudged his cheek. "I know, sweetheart. I lub you too."

"Come on, people! That the best you got?"

Dex played air guitar across the stage, his fingers moving in time with the sweet riff. He switched to drums as he sang into the microphone, shouting out at the crowd when there was a pause between lyrics.

"Come on, you all know this."

The bar broke off into cheers and sang the chorus of "Juke Box Hero" by Foreigner. Dex hadn't been able to help himself when he'd scrolled through the song list and it popped up. The best part was that every time the chorus sang "stars in his eyes," Dex met Sloane's gaze and Sloane blushed.

Sloane was right. Dex needed this. After their little training session yesterday, he wanted to cut loose and let it all hang out, so to speak. The bar was packed, the regulars all fired up and joining in as he rocked out. Those who weren't singing along were dancing. Dex winked at Sloane, then motioned for him to come up. The crowd cheered, and

Sloane had no choice. He shook his head, his eyes lit up in amusement, and his face flushed as he joined Dex up on stage.

Dex grabbed the microphone and sang loud, the music pumping through his veins, thrumming and reverberating through every inch of his body, deep to his soul. He tapped his foot, his hands grasping the microphone stand. Sloane wrapped an arm around him from behind, and Dex leaned back into him, slipping a hand to the back of Sloane's neck as they moved together. Everyone whooped and cheered. Dex picked a song list guaranteed to keep everyone revved up, passionate, and excited. Tonight they were *all* family. They were invincible, the fire in their spirits never to be extinguished. This right here? He could never lose sight of this. Even Ash was laughing and enjoying himself from the table where Cael sat on his lap as he sang along.

The song ended, and the next one in the queue started up. The crowd went nuts as Dex started singing Kiss's "Rock and Roll All Nite." When the chorus came, he tilted the microphone stand out, prompting everyone to join in, and they did. West was jumping around Dom, fist up in the air as he sang at the top of his lungs. Hudson was laughing as Seb played air drums while Taylor and Angel sang loud, Taylor's arm around Angel's shoulders. Cael was playing kissy-face with Ash, while Calvin and Hobbs did their best *Lady and the Tramp* impression with a mozzarella stick they were sharing, both snickering like a couple of schoolboys. Rosa and Letty were rocking out, and everyone was having a great time.

After a couple more songs, karaoke time was over, and Dex bowed as everyone cheered. He waved at them and took Sloane's hand in his, then gave him a kiss on the cheek before they walked off the stage together. Sloane resumed his seat next to Ash, and Dex sat next to him, thanking Bradley for the frosty bottle of water he brought over to him.

"Killed it again," Bradley said. "This place gets crazy when you do karaoke. They love it."

"You should sell tickets," Hudson teased, winking at Dex.

Ash rolled his eyes with a groan. "Please don't encourage him. His ego's big enough. Next thing you know, he's going to hire a manager and backup dancers." Ash cast Sloane a wicked grin. "Wait, he's got Sloane."

"Fuck off, Keeler," Sloane said with a laugh, everyone joining in. They'd had to put together several tables since their motley crew was growing, with Dom, West, Taylor, and Angel having been officially adopted by Destructive Delta thanks to Seb and Dex. They ordered a truckload of food and drinks for everyone.

A familiar song came over the speakers, and Dex jumped to his feet. "Holy shit." He spun around and thrust a finger at Sloane. "Nobody puts Baby in a corner."

Ash let out a long, loud groan. "Bradley, you're killing me, bro." He shook his head, his frown deep. "How much is he paying you to play this shit?"

"Nothing," Bradley said, his grin wide. "Come on, man. He's getting married. I couldn't say no. Look how happy it made him."

Dex grabbed Sloane's hand and pulled. "You gotta dance with me, babe."

"Really?" Sloane said, his eyes alight with amusement. "Do I *really* gotta?"

Dex nodded. "Yep. We can either dirty dance here or at our reception where it will forever be immortalized by both photographic evidence and video. The choice is yours."

Sloane blinked up at him. "Um, in that case, let's dance. But I get to be Swayze."

"You got it."

Ash shook his head in disgust at Sloane. "You know, the word *no* exists for a reason, pal. You should try it sometime."

"Pot, kettle, Keeler," Sloane called out over his shoulder as Dex led him to the dance floor. They joined several other couples as they got up close and sexy. Sloane put a hand to Dex's lower back and pulled Dex hard against him, making Dex laugh. He slipped his leg between Dex's, and Dex ran his hands up Sloane's chest before wrapping his arms around Sloane's neck. Dex lip-synched to the song as they moved together. As the song neared the end, Dex gave him a wicked grin.

"You know, if I—"

"You are not jumping off a table for me to catch."

Dex threw his head back and laughed. "Damn, I'm getting too predictable. Might have to shake things up."

After a couple more songs, they headed back toward the bar near where their tables were. Dex listened to their friends from several feet away, and it made his heart swell. He could hear Dom's boisterous laugh above everyone else's, and it was hard not to smile. Whatever was going on had everyone in tears. Sloane sat down, and Dex moved his chair in close. He leaned into Sloane as Sloane put his arm around Dex's shoulders.

"What's going on?" Dex asked Cael.

"We're playing that game where you ask who's most likely to be the one to do whatever."

"Oh my God, I love this game. What was the last question?" Seeing as how Hudson was taking several sips of his drink, it was clear he'd been the one pointed at by everyone.

Cael leaned in to reply. "Who's most likely to get a

tattoo while drunk. Then Dom told Seb he should probably keep an eye on Hudson before Hudson ends up with a butterfly tattoo on his ass."

Dex let out a bark of laughter. No wonder poor Hudson lost. If anyone thought getting a tattoo while drunk was a good idea, it would be Hudson. Everything was "brilliant" to Hudson when he had a few too many.

"Okay, my turn," Calvin declared. He cast Dex a wicked grin, and Dex knew he was fucked.

"Who's most likely to get arrested for running naked down Fifth Avenue?"

"Why you gonna do me like that, Cal?"

Everyone pointed at Dex as they burst into laughter.

Dex flipped them all off, two fingers reserved for Calvin especially. "You can all bite me," Dex said as he started lining up shot glasses.

Cael tilted his head to one side, thoughtful. "Didn't you already do that?"

Dex's eyes widened. *Holy shit*. He slid his glance over at Sloane, who was suddenly fascinated by whatever Cael had to say. Dex subtly shook his head, but his little brother promptly ignored him.

"Oh my God! You did," Cael said, loudly. "When you turned thirty, and you took that trip to Europe. You were in Barcelona, and you got drunk." Cael turned to the table. "He streaked naked through a highly populated area filled with tourists and locals, sporting nothing but a souvenir paper fan to cover his boy bits."

The table erupted into full-blown laughter and catcalls. Sloane gaped at Dex, who busied himself taking shot after shot. "You got arrested for streaking in Spain?"

Dex shook his head. "Nope."

Cael let out a snort. "They never caught him. It was in Vegas that he got arrested."

The girls were laughing so hard they were in tears, and Calvin was trying to ask him something but couldn't breathe, much less speak. His friends were asshats.

"What did you do?" Sloane asked, poking Dex in his side. "Tell me. As your soon-to-be husband, I should know these things."

Dex shook his head. Was this shot number seven or eight?

"He went for a swim in the Bellagio's fountain," Cael said with a snicker. "Dad had to go bail him out. But wait, there's more."

Dex narrowed his eyes at his brother. "Or you could stop there."

Letty shook her head, then wiped a tear from her eye. "Oh, no way. We need to hear this."

"Dad was so pissed, but you know what he's like. He doesn't get mad, he gets even. Dad threw Dex a surprise party and invited every ex-boyfriend, every guy Dex had ever flirted with, every guy he never called back after a one-night stand, *and* our aunt Danelle."

That did it. Everyone lost it, and Dex turned to bury his face against Sloane's neck. "Someone shoot me."

Sloane wrapped his arms around Dex and kissed the top of his head. "Remind me never to piss off your dad."

A thought occurred to Dex, and he pulled back. A smile spread across his lips, and Sloane's smile fell away.

"What?"

"Babe, you got drunk, beat him at air hockey twelve times, and called him an old man."

Ash spit out a mouthful of beer that sprayed across the table, causing Calvin, Hobbs, and Dom to dive out of their chairs. Dex couldn't see through the tears in his eyes, he was laughing so hard. If Sloane wasn't pressed against him, Dex would have fallen off his chair.

"Fuck, Keeler." Calvin got up off the floor, then picked up his chair, which had toppled during his swan dive.

Ash grabbed a napkin and wiped his mouth. He gaped at Sloane. "You called Maddock an old man?" Sloane let his head fall back with a groan, and Ash patted his shoulder. "It was nice knowing you, bro."

They all teased Sloane, taking guesses at what Tony's revenge would be. Dex did his best to soothe him, but the fact was, retribution was nigh. His dad did not forget things, and he rarely let them go.

"Excuse us for a second," Ash said, getting up. He took Cael's hand and started leading him away from the table. Well, that was weird. The table went quiet, and Ash gently pushed Cael forward.

"Keep it PG, Keeler," Dex called out. He never knew with this group.

Ash held up a finger in Dex's direction. "Shut your mouth."

Dex opened his mouth to reply, but Sloane leaned in to whisper in Dex's ear, "Don't. He's really nervous."

It took Dex a second to realize Sloane was right. This wasn't just Ash being his usual grumpy asshole self. The guy was genuinely shitting himself over something. What the hell would Ash be nervous about? He walked Cael away from the table to one of the tallboys near the bar.

"What do you think's going on?" Rosa asked. She turned to Letty, then gasped. "You know."

Letty blinked at her innocently. "Know what?"

"You know what's up with Ash."

Letty shook her head, her lips pressed together, though

she was clearly trying hard not to say a word. Dex was about to charm some information out of her, but then he noticed Ash reach into his pocket. Dex almost had a heart attack when he realized it was a key. Ash handed the key to Cael while saying something. Cael's eyes went huge as he stared at the key Ash held out. Dex let out a huge gasp and slapped Sloane's chest.

"Ouch. Babe, what the hell?"

"OhmyGod, he's doing it!"

"Doing what?" Calvin asked, turning to look at Ash and Cael, who'd just nodded and flung himself into Ash's arms. Ash squeezed Cael tight to him before kissing him. Then the two walked over to the table, hand in hand. Cael's smile couldn't get any bigger.

Dex put his elbows on the table and let his chin rest on his hands. "So... what's new?"

Ash rolled his eyes. He resumed his seat, pulling Cael close to him. "I asked Cael to move in with me, and he said yes."

Dex put a hand over his heart as he leaned against Sloane. "Our little lion Therian is growing up so fast."

Ash flipped Dex off as he hugged Cael close.

Sloane sighed. "Seems like only yesterday he was threatening to stab me with knitting needles."

Dex let out a bark of laughter.

Taylor looked over at Angel, mischief in his eyes. "Hey, you know what you should get Cael as a housewarming gift?"

Angel's eyes went wide. "Oh fuck. Don't say it, bro. Please don't—"

"A fern."

The table broke out into peals of laughter, and Ash glared at Angel. "Why? So you can piss on it?"

"Fuck me," Angel groaned. "One fucking time. One time." He narrowed his eyes at Ash. "Okay, Keeler. You want a fern, I'll get you a fucking fern farm."

"Say that five times fast," Calvin teased.

"You think I'm kidding?" Angel nodded. "Just you wait. You're going to have so many fucking ferns, you won't know what to do with them."

Everyone laughed, and Dex sat back to watch his friends tease one another. God, he hoped none of this ever changed. Everyone in their unit knew what was happening with Destructive Delta, but Sparks was scheduled to make the official announcement in a couple of days. Dex didn't even want to think of the media frenzy that would follow. Pushing that thought aside for now, he grabbed the bowl of gummy bears and chucked one over at Calvin, intent on smacking him in the face with gummy goodness when Hobbs pulled a *Matrix* and snatched the little bear out of thin air. He tossed it up and caught it in his mouth.

He winked at Dex, and Dex peered at him. "Okay, hotshot. Think fast." He threw one at Angel, and Hobbs caught it. Damn. *Big guy got some moves*. Dex narrowed his eyes. He whipped out a hand, the gummy zipping toward Rosa. Hobbs dove over three of their friends and caught it.

"Oh my God, my spleen," Angel groaned. He glared at Hobbs. "Dude, have you forgotten you weigh a fuckton?"

Hobbs tossed the gummy bear into his mouth and waggled his eyebrows.

Calvin grinned at Dex. "Ten bucks says he can catch the next one no matter where you throw it from."

Dex jumped to his feet. "You're on, Summers." They both removed ten dollars from their wallets and placed the bills on the table. "Who's in on this?"

Everyone placed their bets, and Dex looked around the bar. "Okay."

Hobbs stood, and Dex crossed the room, garnering the attention of several patrons. More heads turned, curious to see what crazy Dex was up to. He held a thumb up to Hobbs, who didn't move from beside the table. Weird. Hobbs smiled and nodded, his hand going behind him. What was he up to?

Dex took a gummy bear from the bowl and tossed it high into the air. He stared stupefied as Hobbs snapped his wrist and one of Bradley's aluminum plates streaked through the air, hit one pillar, flew across the room, hit another pillar, and then Hobbs dove forward, rolled, and popped up to snatch the plate out of thin air. Dex's jaw hit the floor.

Hobbs winked at him, peeled the little bear off the plate, then popped it into his mouth. The bar went nuts cheering, and Hobbs bowed first in one direction, then another. Dex stopped in front of him.

"Dude, how the—" He gasped, then marched over to Calvin. "Ooh, you took me for a ride."

Calvin counted his winnings, then gave half to Hobbs. "And what a sweet ride it was. You should have seen your face. Oh, wait, you can." Calvin held his cell phone up to Dex, and Dex stared at the video of him and his comically stupefied expression.

"Hustlers, the both of you," Dex grumbled, marching around the table to drop down into his chair beside Sloane, then noticed all the nacho chips were gone. Man, it was every guy for himself with this lot where snacks were concerned. "Gonna get some more chips. Want anything from the bar, babe?"

Sloane shook his head. "I'm good. Thank you."

Dex stood, and Sloane smacked his ass playfully. "Oh, you cad." Dex winked at him before heading for the bar. Dom and West were there, huddled close, talking. One of the barmen came over, and Dex put in his order. West leaned back to smile at Dex.

"Thanks for inviting me, Dex. I always have such a blast with you guys. You're a riot."

"Glad you could make it."

West slipped his fingers into Dom's hair and leaned in close. Dex averted his gaze, not wanting to seem nosy, even though he was totally eavesdropping with his new Therian hearing.

"Just popping to the little Felid's room. Don't go anywhere, handsome."

Dom smiled at him. "Sure. Can I order you another drink?"

"I'm good. Thanks. Back in a minute." West purred, rubbing his chin over Dom's shoulder before hopping off the stool. He ran his fingers across Dom's back as he walked by. When he was gone, Dex turned to Dom.

"So what was that about?"

Dom cast him a sideways glance. "What was what about?"

"Come on, bro. West just totally left his scent all over you."

"Yeah, he does that."

"And?"

"And what?"

"Dude, Therians don't leave their scent on you unless they're your partner or trying to keep other Therians away from you."

Dom took a swig of his beer. "Yeah, I know. I have Therian brothers."

"You do?" Dex blinked at him. "I did not know this." How did he not know that?

"I have three older brothers. Two work for the THIRDS, one in Defense and one in Recon. All of them lion Therians."

"Fuck, I'm sorry."

Dom broke out into laughter, and Dex realized what he'd said. He quickly waved his hands in front of him.

"Shit, I didn't mean it like that, like 'sorry they're lion Therians,' I mean, I don't know them. I'm sure they're really nice guys and all."

Dom let out a snort. "They're assholes, but it's okay, Daley. Relax. I know what you meant. I'm used to it."

Dex couldn't imagine growing up with three lion Therian brothers, much less being the youngest and Human.

"Don't get me wrong, I love my brothers, but I never felt like I fit in with them, you know? I was always the odd one out, and it drove me crazy how they treated me with kid gloves. Like I was this fragile little thing made of glass that could break at any moment. You think you're protective of Cael? Try being Human with three Therian big brothers." He shook his head with a laugh. "It's a fucking miracle I lost my virginity. They scared the ever-loving fuck out of every guy who tried to date me. In high school, I had to ban them from coming to football practice because they'd lose their shit every time I got tackled by a Therian." He sighed and looked down at his fingers. "I know I shouldn't complain because I'm blessed to have a family who loves me and three brothers who would walk through hell and back for me, but that doesn't mean it was easy."

"But look at you now," Dex said, motioning to Dom in all his ginormous Human glory. The guy was a force to be reckoned with. Dex had seen him in action. Being the Human partner of a Therian team leader took fucking balls. Dex should know. It was one of the hardest positions on the team, because when your partner was in Therian form, it was all on you. Then there was the fact that Theta Destructive had more members than Destructive Delta, with five Therian Defense members to Destructive Delta's three. Dom was taller than Dex and had about twenty pounds of muscle on Dex. He was fierce.

Dom chuckled. "Yeah, well, we Palladino men are built like brick shithouses. Take after my old man. He's the lion Therian." Mischief filled Dom's hazel eyes. "Besides, you know how much shit I got away with being the precious baby of the family? Still do." He waggled his eyebrows, and Dex laughed.

"Fuck. Now I feel sorry for your brothers."

Dom's cackle was evil. "I was such a little shit."

"Speaking of handful. West."

Dom narrowed his eyes at Dex. "I heard you like to play matchmaker."

Dex shrugged. "It's a gift."

"No, it's meddling. There's nothing going on between us except some harmless flirting. He flirts with everyone." The frown on Dom's face and his shrug told Dex that maybe that was the problem.

"And you'd rather he just flirts with you."

Dom peered at him, and Dex quickly held up a hand.

"Sorry. I didn't mean to push."

Dom let out a sigh. "It's fine. Sorry, I'm being a dick. I like him. Problem is, so do a lot of other guys, and he likes them right back. Don't get me wrong, he's young, hot, and smart. If he enjoys having lots of casual sex, who am I to judge? It's just not for me. I've never been a one-night-stand kind of guy. I like getting to know someone and spending time with them, the intimacy of it all. With all the shit we see out there, coming home to someone who can make it all go away with just their smile, that's what I want. Someone who'll stick around, be there." Dom shook his head. "West is not a stick-around kind of guy."

"How do you know?"

Dom motioned over Dex's shoulder, and Dex turned to find West wrapped around some random dude, sucking face.

What the fuck, man? That was harsh. Dex turned back to Dom, feeling for the guy. "Shit, I'm sorry."

"It is what it is."

"Have you told him?"

"Told him what? There's nothing to tell. He flirts, I flirt back, and that's it. Besides, it wouldn't be appropriate. I'm going to be his team leader."

Dex arched an eyebrow at him, and Dom laughed.

"Fuck, I forgot."

"You forgot Sloane was my team leader?"

"Yeah. I guess because when I see you two together, I just see the unit, you know. Like two halves of a whole. On his own, I see Team Leader Sloane Brodie, but when you're there, I don't know. I'm not making any sense."

"You're such a romantic underneath all the muscles and curses."

"You're weird."

Dex threw his head back and laughed. "And you're awesome." Dex's chips arrived, and he threw his arm around Dom. "Come on. Let's go see what these trouble-makers are up to." They might be an incestuous little family, but Dex wouldn't trade them for the world.

CHAPTER FIVE

Fall in Central Park was one of Dex's favorite times. The weather was in the high seventies, the sun was shining, and all around them the trees and shrubbery were beginning to change color. Soon the trees would be ablaze in reds, oranges, and yellows. It was a perfect day. Dex zoned in and out, his foot tapping along to the sweet tunes coming through his headphones. Next to his music, the only other sound he heard was the soft chainsaw-like purr coming from his warm furry pillow. Dex turned his head, chuckling at Sloane's contented expression—his eyes were closed, front paws crossed in front of him as he lay tucked against Dex. His tail occasionally twitched where it lay protectively around Dex's left arm.

Reaching up, Dex scratched Sloane underneath his chin, and the purr intensified. This right here was bliss. Lying on a blanket in the grass, the gorgeous scenery—which included Belvedere Castle to their right—a backpack full of snacks, and a PSTC kit for Sloane. Dex plucked an earphone out of his ear and turned to look up at Sloane.

"We should do this more often."

Sloane let out a huff of air, most likely in agreement. He opened his eyes and pushed his nose against Dex's, making Dex chuckle.

"I love you too."

Sloane turned his head, observing the people scattered around them, some having picnics, some napping, others kissing or reading. It was Dex's opinion that jaguar Therians had the best facial expressions. Granted, he was a little biased, but no other Therian in their Therian form could pull off resting bitch face like a black jaguar Therian. Dex was familiar with all of Sloane's quirks. He understood every ear twitch, tail twitch, yawn, or huff, but anyone who didn't know Sloane would look at him in his Therian form and think "that guy gives zero fucks," which in some cases was true.

Unless someone was a threat to him or Dex, Sloane's Felid half was chill. He had no interest in anyone who wasn't Dex or someone close to him. Lion Therians liked to preen. Black jaguar Therians thought you were annoying and needed to go away. The only Therians whose expressions superseded black jaguar Therians on a whole other level were cheetah Therians. Dex didn't have to know the cheetah Therian to understand what they were thinking. It was written all over their furry face. Black jaguar Therians might have the best resting bitch face, but no one did unimpressed like cheetah Therians.

A couple of familiar figures headed their way, and Dex sat up, smiling brightly. "Hey, Cal. Dominic."

"Hey, Justice," Dom replied with a grin.

Dex laughed softly as Sloane arched his neck, his tail thumping against the grass as he watched Seb, Hudson, and Hobbs running and pouncing.

"Go play, fuzzball. I know you want to."

Sloane didn't need to be told twice. He got up and bounded over, hopping through the grass like a giant black bunny. Seb, Hudson, and Hobbs stilled when they saw him, sniffed the air, realized it was Sloane, and lost their furry minds. They were too stinking adorable for words.

"Glad you guys could join us," Dex said. "Ash, Cael, West, and the girls will be here soon."

At the mention of West's name, Dom glanced over at him. "West's coming?"

Dex could tell Dom was trying hard not to look too interested, but his scent had changed slightly, and there was a slight flush to his skin. Calvin had the best poker face ever, but Dex noted the tiny curl of his lip on one side.

"Yeah. He and Cael are like besties now. I swear, when they get together, it's like they're talking another language."

Dom chuckled. "Yeah, I don't understand a third of the shit they talk about. Tech isn't my thing, but it's sweet watching them get all excited about that stuff. It's damn impressive, though. I've seen West do crazy shit with a computer. Makes me glad he's on our side." Dom cleared his throat, and Dex waited. The guy was working his way up to something, but whatever subject he wanted to broach was clearly a difficult one. "So, um, TIN, huh?"

Calvin cleared his throat. "I'm gonna go even the odds. Poor Hudson's out-felined." He got to his feet and jogged over to the guys to play, and Dex turned his attention to Dom.

"Seb told you?"

Dom nodded. "Yeah. He thought he was protecting me by not telling me, but you know how the doc is the voice of reason. He said I'd want to know, and he was right. I'd rather be prepared and know what I'm getting into than be blindsided. Seb's 'promotion' to THIRDS

Recruitment Officer and my promotion to team leader of Theta Destructive goes out while you guys are on your honeymoon. It's going to be one hell of a shock for the team."

Dex cringed. "How do you think they're going to take it?"

"No fucking clue." Dom sighed and ran a hand through his hair. He stared off at Seb bounding across the grass with Hudson, Sloane, Hobbs, and Calvin on his tail. "Not gonna lie. Kinda shitting myself over it. The dynamic was finally perfect. He's one hell of a team leader. Firm but fair. They love him."

"He's a great guy."

Dom nodded, a frown on his face. "Yeah. We worked well together, complemented each other. He bitches and grumbles, and I fuss and mother everyone." He laughed, as if recalling some memory. "Drives the team fucking nuts, but they love it."

Dex put his hand on Dom's shoulder. "You're going to do great, Dom. Do you think he would have left his team to someone he didn't trust?"

Dom blinked at him. "What do you mean? Sparks was the one who approached me."

"Because she asked Seb who he thought would be the best fit to lead your team, and he didn't hesitate. He said it had to be you or he couldn't step away. He refused to leave your team in anyone else's hands."

Dom's eyes got glassy, and he wrinkled his nose. "Asshole. Always looking after everyone." Then he met Dex's gaze, his eyes hard. "You better fucking watch my boy's back out there, Daley."

Dex held his hand out to Dom. "You have my word." It was already agreed that if Dex and Sloane were going to work alongside any other operatives, it would be Seb and Hudson.

"The only one who seems to be taking all of this really well is Nina."

"Hudson told her?"

Dom nodded. "Well, yeah. They're best friends. Also Hudson couldn't keep her in the dark now that Rafe knows."

"Shit. Rafe knows?"

Dom arched an eyebrow at him. "Like you'd keep this shit from your brother."

Dom had a point. And it wasn't like Hobbs didn't know. It made sense for the brothers to all be on the same page. Wait. "Does Rafe know about Hobbs being a TIN Associate?"

Dom nodded. "He wasn't happy about it. You know how protective big brothers are." He winked at Dex, who chuckled.

"I wouldn't know anything about that."

"Yeah, all right. I think I need to sit somewhere else so I don't get hit with the bolt of lightning that's about to fry your ass."

Dex laughed. He really liked Dom and was glad to have him as a part of their ever-growing family. Dom was larger than life, for a Human. He had muscles upon muscles, but he was also smart, sharp, and despite his gruff demeanor and the fact he cursed almost as much as Ash, he was a genuinely good guy. Very sweet and always looking out for those he cared about. Very much a heart-on-his sleeve kind of guy.

"Anyway, Hudson's happy for Nina because she's been at the THIRDS longer than he has, so in his opinion, it's about damn time she got promoted to chief medical examiner. She's worried for Hudson, but she's excited. I think she's also really hopeful that you guys can find a way to help Rafe and Thomas."

Dex nodded. He was determined to find something—*anything*—to help the two Hobbs men. "If there's anything out there that will help, we're going to find it."

"I hope so. Rafe's not going to be able to hide his condition from his parents much longer, and that's just going to shatter Thomas. I think that's really what's driving Seb with this whole TIN thing. He resented the way it happened, but now he's had time to think about it, and whatever he's heard or seen has him on board."

A thought occurred to Dex. "What's Hudson's new title?"

Dom cast him a sideways glance, amusement in his eyes. "The doc *hates* it."

"Why?"

"Because it's typical government posturing bullshit, and long as fuck, so it needs to be abbreviated, but you know no one's going to know what the fuck it means."

"Oh my God, you have to tell me." There was nothing more entertaining than listening to Hudson rant, no matter what he was ranting about, and nothing irked him more than pretentious, unnecessary titles and government posturing courtesy of the bigwigs in Washington. Dex couldn't wait to poke Hudson. "Tell *meeee*," Dex pleaded.

"THIRDS International Chief Forensics Consulting Officer."

Dex fell over laughing.

"You should have seen his face when he read the official letter," Dom said, unable to hold back his laughter.

"Wait," Dex said gasping for breath. "I know *exactly* what you're talking about. His expression goes all blank, which scares the shit out of you because you're like 'fuck, he's broken,' then he narrows his eyes before he goes all deadpan and says in a very calm, collected British voice whatever string of swear words come to mind, and then he loses his shit."

"Yes!" Dom laughed harder. "The doc is fucking hysterical, and he doesn't even realize it. I swear, the shit that comes out of his mouth sometimes..." Dom shook his head and wiped a tear from his eye. "Not even Seb expects half the stuff that comes out of that man's mouth. It's priceless."

"They're adorable," Dex said, sitting up and looking out across the lawn and laughing at the Therian leapfrog going on. Seb, Hobbs, and Sloane were doing their Felid thing, lying in the grass for a lazy cat rest, but because they were a few feet apart, Hudson and Calvin were hopping over them like they were kitty hurdles. They jumped over Sloane, then Hobbs, then Seb, ran circles around them, Hudson's tail wagging before they did it again, jumping over one and then the next. Seb chuffed, and Hudson's ears perked up. He trotted up to Seb and pushed his nose against Seb's before dropping onto the grass in front of Seb. He rolled onto his back, paws up, and Seb threw a paw over him as Hudson licked at Seb's muzzle. When he was done, Seb began to groom him. Man, Dex loved those dorks. Calvin seemed to like the idea, and he dropped onto the grass before playfully annoying his boyfriend by tugging on one ear, then the other, poking until Hobbs pounced on him, making him laugh.

"While you're on your honeymoon, Seb will be getting an operation."

Dex stared at Dom. *What the hell?* "What are you talking about?"

"TIN. They're bringing in some of the best surgeons in

the world. They're going to repair his knee and perform some new unheard-of procedure that'll stop whatever's causing the tissue damage. Hudson explained it to me. Sounds like something out of a science fiction movie."

"You're worried." If Dom was worried, Dex could just imagine how worried Hudson was.

"Yeah, but I tend to do that," Dom replied, laughing softly.

"He'll be okay." Dex turned to the group headed their way. "There's Rosa and Letty." He waved at the girls as they came toward Dex and Dom with Ash, Cael, and West in their Therian forms. Cael dashed over to Dex, chirping happily. He flopped all over Dex, making him laugh. "Yeah, yeah. I'm happy to see you too." He gave Cael a good scratch before looking up at a preening Ash.

Dex gave Ash a nod in greeting. "Mufasa."

Ash sneered at him. Lion Therians were experts at that, and Ash was the king of sneering. West came over, chirping at Dex and bumping his head against Dex's chest.

"Hey, nerd." He ruffled West's fur and scratched him behind the ear. "Hobbs wanted me to tell you guys that if you keep leaving your tech shit all over his BearCat, he's going to recycle it."

The two cheetahs sat up tall, necks stretched, and started chirping their little furry faces off.

"Hey, don't look at me. You got a problem, you take it up with the big guy. Remember when I accidentally dropped that piece of chocolate on the bench and it melted? He put a glitter bomb in my locker. I went out on a call looking like a Human disco ball. Do not mess with the dude's truck."

The two looked at each other, then at Hobbs, who happened to stand up on his hind legs to put his paws on Calvin's shoulders. He was huge. The two bounced over to

Ash, a symphony of chirps thrown at him. Ash flattened his ears back, and Dex felt sorry for the guy.

"Hey, Ash."

Ash perked up, his tail moving subtly.

"Did you hear Sloane calling you? I could've sworn he called you."

Ash bobbed his head before darting off toward Sloane as if someone had set fire to his tail. Cael and West took off after him, but West stopped halfway and turned back. He dashed over to Dom and chirped at him before circling him, rubbing his head all over Dom, then taking off again.

Rosa and Letty went to play Frisbee with the boys, and Dex arched an eyebrow at Dom.

"Don't," Dom muttered.

Dex held up his hands.

The Frisbee came Dom's way, as did West. Dom shot to his feet and snatched the Frisbee out of the air before West could. Dom laughed.

"Oh shit, gotta be quicker than that, rock star."

Dom teased West with the Frisbee, and West jumped up on his hind legs, his front paws on Dom's chest as he chirped at him. Dom laughed as he moved the Frisbee from one hand to the other, keeping it away from West. Changing tactics, West ran circles around Dom before slipping through his legs and tripping him. Dom landed on the grass with a laugh, West rubbing his head under Dom's neck and face.

If Dom wasn't careful, he was going to get his heart broken, and Dex would hate for that to happen.

Dex's phone buzzed a reminder, and he cursed under his breath. He better move his ass, or he was going to be late. One last tux fitting. He might or might not have eaten one too many cake samples. Dex got to his feet and whistled.

Sloane jumped to his paws and craned his neck, tail twitching before he spotted Dex, and then he bounded over. With a big smile, Dex crouched down in front of him.

"I gotta go meet Tony at the tux place. Meet you back here for lunch after, okay?"

Sloane rubbed his head on Dex's face, and Dex hugged him.

"I love you too. I'll text you when I'm done."

Sloane sat on his haunches as Dex stood. He looked up at Dex with big amber eyes.

"Don't look at me with that face. You know you're not allowed to see me in my tux before the wedding."

Sloane huffed, and Dex chuckled. He scratched him behind the ear before calling out to Rosa. She jogged over and gave him a hug.

"I'm gonna leave Sloane's kit with you. I have to run off for a final tux fitting. Shouldn't be too long."

"Ooh!" She clapped her hands excitedly. "I can't wait to see you in your tux. You're going to look so gorgeous."

"Aw, thanks. Keep your eye on this one. He's dying to see the tux, even though he knows he's not supposed to."

"I'm on it," Rosa said. "Say hi to the sarge for us."

"Will do." Dex hugged her and waved goodbye before he called a cab.

~

On the drive over, Dex was actually nervous, which was silly, considering this was the third time he was trying on the made-to-order double-breasted tuxedo. Lou had helped him pick a style that was elegant yet modern.

When he stepped through the door, Martina was there to greet him with open arms. "My darling!" She hugged him close, giving each cheek a kiss. "How are you feeling so close to your big day?"

"Nervous. It comes and goes," Dex said with a smile, following her through the shop, past wooden shelves filled with colorful fabric, displays with shirts, and rows upon rows of ties in all colors and patterns. At the back of the shop were several doors—the middle he knew led to the larger of the private fitting rooms. He stepped inside and closed the door behind him. The Tiffany lamps provided the room with a warm glow, and he liked the light gray wallpaper made to look like connecting sewing patterns of different suit cuts. There was tufted leather seating and a sleek coffee table with fashion magazines, racks of shirts and trousers, and even a silver liquor cart.

Martina walked to the cart and proceeded to mix him a spritz, complete with an orange slice. She brought it to him with a knowing smile.

"I think you need this."

He knew better than to argue. "Thanks." He took the drink and walked over to the large couch.

"Lou says you've eaten too much cake."

"He exaggerates," Dex assured her before taking a sip of his cocktail. *Ooh, tasty.*

Martina hummed and gave him a pointed look. "Lou does not exaggerate," she said, wagging a perfectly manicured fingernail at him. She motioned over to a black garment bag hanging from a hook on the wall.

"Finish your drink, and try on your tuxedo. I'll be outside when you're ready."

Dex smiled brightly at her. "Thank you, Martina. You're the best."

She shook her head in amusement before letting herself out. As he sipped his cocktail and tried to get his pulse to come down a bit, he looked around the room. Sloane had been in this very room trying on his tuxedo. The thought sent the butterflies in his stomach fluttering, and he couldn't help his dopey grin.

Finishing off his cocktail, he got up and returned the empty glass to the liquor cart. He took one of the moist towelettes and cleaned his hands thoroughly, then dried them on the pristine fluffy white hand towel before walking over to the garment bag. Soft instrumental music filled the room, and he stood there, motionless. This was what he would be wearing when he married the love of his life. With a shaky hand, he took hold of the zipper and slowly pulled it down, revealing the flawless black fabric.

Letting out a breath and locating his backbone, he removed the suit from the garment bag and hung it back up. He toed off his sneakers, then started undressing, laying his clothes over the bench to his left. Why the hell was he shaking? Was it because this was his last fitting? Because the next time he wore this it would be his wedding day? He kept waiting to wake up. This had to be a dream, right? He got dressed in a sort of daze, shirt first, then trousers, then tie. He sat down and put on the trendy designer shoes he'd blanked out on the name of, then stood to put on his tux jacket. Once everything was in place, he took a deep breath.

"Sorry I'm late, son. I got held up at work."

"No problem." Dex turned around, and Tony did a double take. He slowly closed the door behind him, his eyes growing glassy. *Don't get emotional. Nope. No.* His dad looked him over, his lips pressed together before he lifted his gaze to Dex's, a big smile spreading across his face.

"You're getting married."

Dex laughed, his eyes brimming with unshed tears. "Yep. That's what the penguin suit's for."

Tony crossed the distance between them and threw his arms around Dex, bringing him in for a fierce hug. Dex shut his eyes tight against his tears, but it was a losing battle. He laid his head on his dad's shoulder, his arms wrapped around his back.

"I'm so proud of you, son," Tony murmured, one hand on Dex's back, the other on his head. "And even though they can't be there with you on your big day, I know they're looking down at you, proud as hell too."

That did it.

The dam broke, and Dex cried on his father's shoulder. He cried for the parents who'd never get to see him walk down the aisle. For the man he loved, and everything Sloane had suffered to get to this moment. He cried because he was so goddamn lucky to have found a family who loved him just as much as his parents had.

"It's okay, kiddo. You get it all out," Tony said quietly, rubbing soothing circles across Dex's back.

By the time Dex was done, his nose was stuffed and his face was hot. He pulled away and thanked Tony for the tissue box, laughing when Tony grabbed a wad for himself.

"God, how am I supposed to make it to the altar without blubbering like a baby?"

Tony shook his head. "If you're a mess, I'm gonna be a mess, and I'm the one marrying you two, remember?"

Dex nodded, a lump in his throat. There had been no question who he wanted to officiate his marriage. He'd be walking down the aisle with Sloane, and his dad would be marrying them, with all their friends and family there to celebrate their love. It would be the first day of the rest of their lives together as husbands.

Once his eyes had stopped leaking and he could breathe through his nose again, he asked his dad to grab Martina.

Her eyes sparkled when she saw him. They always did. Everyone Lou had set him and Sloane up to work with had been amazing, all eager to help and make their big day unforgettable. Dex couldn't have imagined trying to put everything together without someone as fierce and skilled as Lou. The man was a wedding planning guru. Sloane had almost passed out when he saw the calendar spreadsheet Lou had created for them. It came printed on sleek paper, broken down by months, weeks, days, and hours. It contained lists of contacts broken down by type of services, and everything was synched to their online calendars so no appointment was missed, and they received reminders.

"Oh, you look so handsome!" Martina gushed. "Sloane won't know what to do with himself when he sees you."

Dex felt his cheeks flush, and he smiled. "Thank you so much, Martina, for all your help."

She waved a hand in dismissal. "Nonsense. I love what I do. I love to make you happy."

They made idle chitchat for a little while longer before it was time for Dex to take off his suit. Martina kissed both their cheeks and left them so Dex could get undressed. Once he was done, he again thanked Martina and left with his dad. It was such a beautiful day.

"Want to join us for lunch?"

Tony gave him an apologetic smile. "Have to head back to the office, but why don't you boys come on over for dinner? I'll make your favorite, country fried steak and gravy."

Dex wiped at his mouth in case he was drooling. "I would very much like that. Just don't tell Lou."

Tony winked and pointed a finger at him as he walked backward. "Eight o'clock. Love you, kiddo."

"Love you too, Dad. See you at eight." Dex spun on his

heels and strolled down the street in the opposite direction, a dopey smile on his face. There was a great little donut shop on the corner. Surely one donut wouldn't spoil his lunch. One maple donut. With bacon bits. Maybe he'd pick up an order of donutty goodness for the whole crew. He'd definitely need to get a cab back to the park if he did that. No way was he getting on a crowded train with an armful of tasty treats. He'd grab a bear claw for his Broody Bear, though these days Sloane was neither broody nor bearish. The thought of his boo had his smile growing wider.

Sloane was probably going to try and sweet-talk some information out of Dex about his tux. He was adorable. Dex loved that Sloane was just as much of a dork as he was, excited by things like seeing each other in their tuxes and their first dance as husband and husband.

Dex glanced up as a black commercial van with pitch-black tinted windows sped by, nearly hitting a pedestrian. Dex shook his head. He should give the guy a ticket for being an asshat. Tires screeched, and Dex cringed, waiting for the sound of an impact. Instead he heard a strangled cry that turned Dex's blood to ice. His stomach dropped, and the blood drained from his face. He whirled around in time to watch two masked men load Tony up into the van.

"Dad?" Dex's brain misfired, unable to process what he was witnessing. "Dad!" He broke into a run as the tires screeched and the van lurched forward into traffic, uncaring of who or what it ran into. Dex bolted into the street, ignoring the honking horns and shrieking tires. He sped after the van as it swerved through traffic, dodging cars, bikers, and pedestrians. Dex ran as fast as he could, his muscles straining and lungs burning as he attempted to catch up to the van. He couldn't lose it. Whatever happened, he couldn't let them take his father. He couldn't lose that fucking van. There was no license plate, no signage or text, no discernable marks.

Please. No, no, no.

Dex struggled for breath, but he just pushed himself harder, his eyesight sharpening, and his heart pounding in his ears as something inside his gut swirled and expanded, spreading through his chest and exploding out through his body. He had no idea what the hell it was, but as his claws extended and his fangs grew in, he picked up speed. He tried to reach for the handle on the rear door, but the van's careening made him miss, and he only succeeded in scratching the paintjob with his claws. With a feral growl, he launched himself at the van, grabbing the handle and landing on the rubber bumper. He threw a hand up, his claws digging into the aluminum roof. He had no idea his claws were that sharp. Not wasting the opportunity, he grabbed hold of the roof rack with his free hand and climbed on top of the van.

If there was ever a time he wished he'd been on duty, this was it. He had no firepower to aid him, and he couldn't waste a second trying to get backup. He needed to do something to stop this van. Dex retracted his claws, hissed, and unsheathed them again, throwing them forward and sinking them into the roof once more. He used his claws to keep him secured to the van as he crawled forward, his sneakers braced on the rack as he was jerked from side to side. The van ran red lights, and Dex flinched when a truck whizzed across, the van missing the truck's back bumper by a hair.

Rage and desperation exploded through Dex, and he grabbed the roof rack near the front and launched himself over the side of the van on the driver's side, bringing his left fist with him and smashing it through the window, cutting and slicing the hell out of his arm. The van swerved violently, and the driver cursed. Dex grabbed the steering wheel and jerked it to the left. He hung on for his life as the van careened to the side and the driver fought for control. Dex saw the gun from the corner of his eye and hauled himself back onto the roof just as two vehicles came at them, one from each side, T-boning the van.

Dex soared through the air, and then everything went black.

CHAPTER SIX

It was time to eat. After everyone used the privacy stalls at the park to shift back, they received PSTC from their teammates. They grabbed some protein, but they needed a proper meal to regain their strength. Sloane decided to text Dex and have him meet them at the restaurant that way they could all start on some appetizers while Dex made his way over.

"Where do you guys want to go?" Sloane asked, finishing his text, then returning his phone to his pocket. He was starving.

Ash shrugged. "Why don't we just go to the Boathouse? They do Therian-size burgers now. It's like a five-minute walk. Everyone good with that?"

They all cheered for food, and they headed south on one of the many trails. As his friends laughed and talked, Sloane checked his phone to see if Dex had replied, but there was nothing yet. He told himself not to be ridiculous that Dex hadn't texted back right away. Dex probably got caught up in the emotion of it all, especially with Tony there. He was a little more sensitive than usual these days, and Sloane couldn't blame him. There was so much going on in both their personal and professional lives. So many changes.

When they got to the restaurant, Sloane murmured to Calvin, "Where do you guys want to sit?"

Calvin subtly put his hand to Hobbs's lower back, and Hobbs craned his neck to look inside. He shook his head and pointed to the outdoor seating area.

"You got it," Sloane said with a smile. "We should take advantage of this weather while we can, huh?"

Hobbs grinned and nodded.

One of the waiters very kindly put several tables together for them, and once they were seated, menus were brought out. Everyone put in their drink orders, along with appetizers for the table. Once the waiter left, they mulled over what they were going to eat.

Cael leaned into Sloane. "Have you heard from Dex?" he asked quietly, his eyes filled with concern.

"Not yet. I'm sure he's fine. You know all this wedding stuff has him a little restless."

Cael nodded, his attention then seized by Ash, who asked him what he'd like to eat. As Cael rambled excitedly about the menu, Ash looked over his head at Sloane and winked at him. Sloane appreciated Ash distracting Cael. He didn't want to lie to Cael about how worried he was. The waiter returned, and Sloane asked Ash to order for him, then excused himself to go to the bathroom.

He walked into the restaurant and headed for the restroom, then stepped inside. He called Dex, only to get a voicemail. His Felid half was awake now and very unhappy. He had Sloane pacing. Calling Martina yielded the same results, though her voicemail stated she was with a client and would get back to him as soon as possible. The door to the bathroom opened, and Sloane was relieved to see Ash.

"Hey, you okay?"

Sloane shook his head. "Something's wrong, Ash. I can feel it." He paced furiously, his anxiety higher than it had ever been. This wasn't normal for him. He got restless but not anxious, like his body couldn't contain all the frantic energy inside him. He felt nauseous, terrified, and... "Oh God." The pain that hit Sloane brought him to his knees.

"Sloane!" Ash grabbed hold of him and lifted him to his feet. "Talk to me. What's going on?"

"It's hard to breathe," Sloane wheezed. He clutched at his chest. "It feels like my heart's going to explode." His lungs burned, like he couldn't get enough air into them, and his muscles strained, agony shooting through every inch of him. "Something's happening." Fuck, his mate was in trouble. Whatever it was, it was causing Dex an extraordinary amount of physical and emotional pain. Then it stopped. Sloane sucked in a lungful of air and straightened.

"What the hell just happened?"

"It stopped. It just stopped." Sloane ran a shaky hand through his hair. He grabbed onto Ash to steady himself. "It's like he..." Sloane couldn't bring himself to finish his sentence. "I can't feel *anything*."

"Okay, come on. Let's go round up the guys. We can take the stuff to go."

Sloane nodded. Ash was right. If they didn't get some real food in them soon, they wouldn't be any help to anyone. They hurried outside, where thankfully the food had arrived and everyone was digging in. Rosa took one look at Sloane and stilled.

"What's wrong?"

"Something's happened to Dex," Ash said. "Grab your food or shovel that shit, 'cause we gotta go." He grabbed a burger and handed it to Sloane. "Eat."

Years of working at the THIRDS, of not having enough time to fully recover, made them experts in getting food down as quickly as possible so they could get on with saving lives. In three bites, Sloane was done with his burger. The rest of his team was ready to go. They'd still need some time to be back to their full strength, but it was a start.

"Hudson Colbourn?"

Everyone looked over at the huge tiger Therian in jogging attire. He smiled wide at them, and Hudson smiled politely.

"Yes?"

The rustling sound met Sloane's ears seconds before Hudson jerked, a tranq dart sticking out of his chest. Everything happened as if in slow motion. Hudson's eyes drifted shut, and he crumpled to the ground. Sloane made a dive for him, catching him as Seb's roar shook the trees. People screamed and ran as Seb jumped the iron rail and tackled the jogger to the ground. The team scrambled, flipping the hefty ironwork tables and taking cover as gunfire erupted. Sloane said a little prayer of thanks to the restaurant for their choice in sturdy, thick, iron-laden dining furniture. They weighed a fuckton, and the solid wood surface would provide some temporary cover.

They'd come for Hudson.

Ash huddled in beside Sloane, who had Hudson cradled in his arms. "Where the fuck is Seb?"

Sloane peeked around the corner of the table. "He's busy. We need to find one of the shooters and get that gun in Calvin's hands." He scanned the area and saw movement in the trees. "There."

Ash nodded and dashed over to the next couple of tables, where Calvin and Hobbs were. He said something, and the two nodded. Ash lifted the table and walked it over to the rail, covering them. In a swift movement, Calvin and his partner were over the rail. Ash tossed Hobbs the table, and Hobbs caught it, swinging it around to give him and Calvin cover just before Calvin dove into the bushes.

Seconds later, Calvin emerged from the trees, shooting while Hobbs covered him. One bullet was all it took. Calvin aimed with precision and fired. No hesitation, no mistakes. Didn't matter if his target was moving or not. He calculated and pulled the trigger.

Sloane turned his attention to Letty, who was huddled behind another set of tables to his right. "Letty, what's the status on backup?"

"Fifteen minutes," she called out.

"Shit. Okay." These guys had no intention of being here for fifteen minutes. It had to be the Makhai. No one else wanted Hudson as badly as they did.

Ash returned to Sloane's side. "These assholes were waiting for us. How the fuck did they know to strike us now? How the hell did they know we'd be unarmed and vulnerable from post-shift?"

"Probably were watching us."

Ash nodded his agreement. He moved his gaze to Hudson, out cold in Sloane's arms. "They want the doc."

"They can't have him." Fuck, it couldn't be a coincidence. What he'd felt from Dex and now Hudson?

"How the hell are we supposed to stop them, Sloane? There's fucking dozens of them, all in tac gear and armed."

Ash was right. As skilled as Calvin was, there were only

so many bullets in that gun, and from the number of emerging hostiles wearing tactical gear, it looked like they were outmuscled and outgunned. They hadn't recovered enough for another shift.

"We're going to have to retreat." There was no way they could face that many armed Therians in the state they were in.

More gunfire erupted, followed by a small explosion that had Sloane and Ash ducking on instinct. Ash's eyes widened.

"What the fuck?"

Sloane looked around the table. "Holy shit."

Ash joined him, his jaw dropping. "Is that... That's our BearCat."

Hobbs appeared in front of Sloane. He jabbed a finger at Hudson, then in the direction of the truck before making a driving motion.

"Hudson's driving?" Ash asked, confused.

Sloane's eyes went wide. "No. Hudson's brother is driving."

The BearCat came plowing through the parking lot, aiming for every armed mercenary in its path. It soared over the grassy hill, and everyone scrambled out of the way as it skidded and turned, the back of it plowing through the restaurant's fence. A hailstorm of bullets followed.

The back doors opened, and Wolf jumped out. He looked like he'd just stepped out of a damned Armani ad. With a wide grin, he tossed Hobbs the keys.

"There you go. Sorry I'm late. Dreadful traffic in this city."

"Gear up," Sloane ordered, and everyone ran for the back of the BearCat to grab vests and firearms. Wolf crouched beside Sloane, his expression softening when he saw Hudson. He ran a hand over Hudson's head.

"How is he?"

"Okay, just out. You knew, didn't you?" Sloane asked, motioning to the BearCat behind him.

"The Makhai are making their move. Whatever they're up to, it's big. I've been monitoring certain channels of chatter. Unfortunately, the Makhai are very good at what they do, and I was only able to decipher one of their encrypted messages, which stated they planned to take Hudson today."

"So you've been watching Hudson."

Wolf nodded. He brushed Hudson's hair away from his brow. His steel-blue eyes flashed, and Sloane swallowed hard at the transformation.

"Now, if you'll excuse me. I have some Makhai to kill."

Before Sloane could say a word, Wolf was off. He didn't sneak or duck for cover. He stood, unbuttoned his suit jacket, and removed the guns with silencers strapped to the thin black ballistic vest. Sloane had never seen anything like it. Wolf *walked* straight into the zone of fire. One bullet to the head of every Makhai mercenary who made the mistake of showing himself.

Sloane hoisted Hudson onto his shoulder and stood. He ran to the back of the BearCat. His team had their shields out and were positioned around the truck, returning fire.

"Seb," Sloane called out. Where the hell was he?

"In here," Seb said, and Sloane noticed his knuckles were bloodied and there was a splatter of blood across his T-shirt. When Seb saw him looking, he motioned inside the truck. "It's his."

"Help me with him." Sloane turned so Seb could grab Hudson and carry him inside the truck, and then Seb helped Sloane up. Hudson lay on the bench, and on the floor next to him, the "jogger" lay on his stomach, his wrists and ankles zip-tied behind him. His face was a bloody mess, one eye swollen shut. His nose was broken, and there were a couple of teeth on the floor.

"He's not talking," Seb growled, kicking the guy for good measure.

"Sloane."

Sloane turned to Letty, who stood at the back of the truck.

"Yeah?"

"They're gone."

"And Wolf?"

She shook her head. "He's gone too."

Ash appeared beside her. "My guess is he's not going to just let them walk away. Personally, whatever those assholes get, they deserve."

"Everyone okay?" Sloane asked, and received a nod from Ash and Letty. "Good. Backup should be here any minute. They can get this place cleaned up. We need to get this guy to HQ, and—" His phone rang, and Sloane dug in his pocket for it, praying it was Dex.

Unknown Caller flashed on his screen. With his heart in his throat, he answered. "Hello?"

"Sloane."

"Austen?"

"In about a minute, a car is going to pick you up and take you to an undisclosed location."

"Austen, what's going on? Have you heard from Dex?"

"It's about Dex."

The world around him fell silent, and his breathing stopped or at least felt like it did.

"Dex was in a car wreck."

Considering Dex hadn't been driving, all kinds of scenarios entered Sloane's head.

"He was picked up by a TIN medical team and is now at a TIN facility. See you soon." The call ended, and Sloane stared down at his phone.

"Sloane?" Ash put a hand on Sloane's shoulder, startling him.

"Dex... He's been in a car accident. TIN has him. They're going to pick me up."

"I'm going with you," Cael said, stopping in front of Sloane.

Sloane nodded. "Letty, can you...?" He motioned around them, and Letty nodded.

"We'll take care of it, boss. You do what you gotta do, and keep us informed."

"Thank you, Letty."

Letty went off, rounding up the team and relaying information. Sloane was grateful when everyone got to work, and then Calvin stopped by the back of the truck.

"Sloane, there's a black SUV here."

Sloane hopped down from the truck, followed by Ash and Cael. The back doors were opened, and they climbed in. As soon as they were seated, the usual black bags were thrown over their heads. The doors closed and the car drove off. Sloane felt numb. He couldn't even process what Austen had told him. Whatever had happened, Dex had to be okay. Now more than ever, Sloane knew the two incidents were connected. They had to be. Whatever was going on, he was going to get to the bottom of this. If Wolf was right and the Makhai had something up their sleeve, they had to find out what it was and put a stop to it before anyone else got hurt.

The ride was short, and Sloane didn't bother trying to

figure out where they'd gone. He didn't care. All he could think about was Dex. As soon as the SUV doors opened, Sloane jerked the black bag from his head and burst through the facility doors. Austen was waiting for them at the end of the corridor; the look on his face had Sloane breaking into a run to get to him. His heart sounded in his ears, and he was still feeling nauseous from Austen's phone call.

"Where is he?" Sloane demanded.

"I'll take you to him, but first..." Austen turned his attention to Ash and Cael. "I need you two to wait in that room there while I talk to Sloane."

"Screw that," Cael snapped, his face flushed. "Where's my brother, Austen? I want to see him."

"And you will. I promise. I just need to talk to Sloane first. Please, trust me on this."

"I'm his brother," Cael growled, the fear and frustration radiating off him. It was hard to see, but if Austen didn't want Cael going in just yet, there had to be a reason. Sloane put his hand on Cael's shoulder.

"Please, Cael. I promise, the moment I can get you in there, I will. You know I'd never keep him from you."

"I know," Cael sighed, averting his gaze. "I just hate this not knowing. Is this how it's going to be from now on?" Cael looked up at him, his big gray eyes filled with pain. "He's my brother, and no one will tell me anything. I'm just supposed to sit here fearing the worst until someone decides it's time for me to know. How would that make you feel, Sloane?"

It would drive him, and his feral half, out of his mind. What the hell was he supposed to say to Cael? As it was, more people knew about who Dex and Sloane would be working for than was permitted. Most operatives led double lives. They didn't disclose their TIN identities to anyone, not even their spouses. TIN had made an exception for Dex and Sloane because Destructive Delta had become TIN Associates and were being brought in as their assets. They'd made an exception for the others because they were THIRDS—they still hadn't been happy about it, but they'd accepted.

"Just go," Cael said with a heavy sigh, turning to lean into Ash, seeking comfort. Ash wrapped his arms around Cael and brought him in tight against him, laying his cheek against Cael's head as he rubbed his back.

Sloane turned and followed Austen through another set of doors, surprised when Austen stopped halfway down the corridor. "What's going on? Where is he?"

Austen motioned toward the door at the end. Sloane made to go, but then Austen took hold of his arm. "There's something you need to know before you go in there."

"Oh God." Sloane put a hand to his mouth as he tried to get ahold of his emotions. "Please, Austen, just fucking tell me."

"He's going to be okay. Physically, anyway. He's banged up, but thanks to his new Therian DNA, his body has already started to heal. There was a nasty pileup, and he was thrown from the roof of a speeding van. He got lucky and landed on the roof of a car."

Sloane didn't even know where to begin processing everything Austen had just told him. Thrown from the roof of a moving van? "Jesus Christ. What the...? How...? Wait, what do you mean he's going to be okay physically? For Christ's sake, Austen, spit it out."

"The reason he was on the roof of a van was because he was chasing it." Austen ran a hand through his hair before meeting Sloane's gaze. "They took Maddock."

Sloane stared at him. When he spoke, his voice was a whisper. "What?" No. That couldn't be right. He'd heard wrong.

"After the tux fitting, Maddock was going back to THIRDS HQ, and Dex was heading to the park. We don't have all the details, but I managed to get hold of some security footage. Dex was roughly a block away when a man walks past Maddock, turns, and shoots his neck with an injector. Maddock screams, Dex turns, and a black commercial van pulls up to the curb. Two masked men get out. They take Maddock..."

"And Dex goes after them." Sloane felt his knees go weak, and Austen was at his side, an arm wrapped around his waist. That explained everything. What he'd felt back at the restaurant. Oh God. It had been happening while Sloane was in the bathroom trying to call Dex. He blinked back his tears and closed his eyes to get ahold of himself. "Tell me you have something," Sloane said hoarsely, his heart feeling as though it was going to beat out of him. "Austen, tell me TIN has something." He opened his eyes to look at Austen.

Austen shook his head sadly. "These guys were professionals. We've got nothing."

Sloane leaned against the wall and slipped his fingers into his hair. Oh God, this wasn't happening. It had to have been the worst moment of Dex's life, and Sloane hadn't been there. No, he wasn't going to go down that route. Shit.

"They had it all planned out, where and when to strike."

"I'm not following," Austen said.

"They knew I wouldn't be with Dex for the tux fitting. I wasn't supposed to be there. And they knew we'd be vulnerable after our shifts, which is why they waited until just after to try and take Hudson."

"Shit. They tried to take the doc? When was this?"

"Just before you called. In Central Park, in front of the Boathouse. They didn't succeed. Wolf intercepted the message and showed up."

"Okay, I gotta get this intel in. You should go." Austen motioned to the end of the hall, and Sloane flinched. Dex...

Sloane pushed away from the wall and tore off down the corridor, ignoring Austen calling out for him. He ran into the room and came to a halt. Dex sat up on the side of the cot, the only sounds in the room coming from the machines monitoring Dex's vitals. Sloane blinked against the tears welling in his eyes as he took in Dex's bloodied and bruised state. They'd obviously tried cleaning him up, but the white bandages stood out against his stained skin. He was covered in scratches, cuts, and bruises. His eyes were bloodshot and red-rimmed, and he was missing a sneaker. He stared down at the floor, unmoving.

"Dex..." Sloane wanted to go to him, but Dex's stillness gave him pause. He recognized this. It was the calm before the storm.

"I lost him."

Sloane swallowed hard. He remained where he stood. For the first time in his life, he didn't go to Dex, no matter how fiercely his feral half, and his heart, screamed at him to. He couldn't. Sloane could always read Dex, could gauge what his partner needed. Dex had always been good at giving signals—his body language, his vibe, or in this case, nothing but stillness.

"We'll find him," Sloane said softly.

Dex looked down at his hands. "I had him. I could have..."

Sloane took a step forward, and Dex slipped off the cot. Sloane braced himself. He knew what was coming. The hairs on the back of his neck stood on end, and his inner Felid wailed at the agony he could feel radiating from his mate.

The roar that tore from Dex's lips startled the hell out of Sloane, and he instinctively took a step back. It was an inhuman cry; the cry of a wounded animal.

Dex's skin flushed red as he screamed, and Sloane's heart shattered when Dex tore at the tubes and pads attached to his skin. He grabbed the heart monitor and swung it into the concrete-block wall, shattering it into several pieces. The next machine met the same fate, snatched up and smashed against the floor. Dex stomped down on it repeatedly with his sneakered foot, grabbing cables and wires, jerking and tearing. He cursed and yelled as he destroyed the equipment, using a steel tube like a baseball bat to beat the remaining machinery to pieces. Chunks of plastic and wiring sprayed in different directions. Dex punched, pounded, and kicked at anything that wasn't already shattered into dozens of pieces before he tossed the rod and turned to flip over the cot.

The door opened behind Sloane, and Sloane quickly pushed it closed, shaking his head at the operatives through the window on the other side. No way in hell Sloane was letting them in here. It was for their own safety. The room once again plunged into silence, and Sloane turned to find Dex standing in the middle of the room, which now resembled some kind of equipment landfill. Sweat dripped from his face, his chest rose and fell with rapid breaths, the shattered remains of his grief surrounding him on all sides.

Dex collapsed onto the floor, and Sloane ran to him. He dropped down and gathered Dex in his arms, running a hand over his head, and closed his eyes against the tears that fell for his suffering mate, his heart breaking at Dex's sobs. His entire body shivered violently as he clung to Sloane, his fingers digging into Sloane's arms as he screamed and cried himself hoarse. Sloane pressed his head to Dex's, rocking him gently in the hopes of offering some kind of comfort.

Being so close to Tony, unable to help him, was undoubtedly tearing Dex apart. Sloane knew Dex too well. This was happening shortly after the evening when Dex had shut himself in the bathroom because thinking about his parents not being at his wedding had hit him harder than expected. Dex would be thinking about his parents, how he'd been just a little boy, helpless to do anything. And now as an adult, he'd been unable to help Tony. God only knew where Tony was and what they were doing to him.

Sloane held Dex close, rubbing his cheek against Dex's hair. All he could do was be there for Dex and make sure Dex didn't burn down the city trying to get Tony back, because there was no doubt in Sloane's mind that was exactly what Dex would do.

Dex was about to unleash hell on earth to save his father, and Sloane would be there to make sure the man he loved came back to him when it was done. Dex looked exhausted, as expected after what he'd just been through. Everything inside Sloane screamed in agony. His body, his mind, his heart. Yet somehow, he was still numb. Like his brain couldn't quite grasp the truth of what had happened. Like it was a horrible nightmare he had trouble waking up from. Tony always seemed untouchable.

They were supposed to be getting married in a few days. It was meant to be the happiest day of their lives. They'd be surrounded by family and friends. They'd dance, eat cake, and laugh. Tony was supposed to make a toast on their wedding day. Dex had teased him, and Tony surprised them both by admitting he was nervous about it, saying he was just going to talk from his heart because index cards never worked for him and what happened to plain white index cards? Who the hell needed them to be pink, purple, or blue? And what genius created neon index cards? Were they trying to blind him? Sloane shut his eyes tight at the memory. Fucking index cards. It was just another quirk that reminded Sloane of Dex. Tony and Dex shared more quirks than either admitted.

Sloane kissed the side of Dex's head, and Dex opened his eyes.

"Cael?"

"Oh, baby. He doesn't know. I only just found out."

Dex nodded. "Is he here?"

"Yeah, he's with Ash in one of the other rooms."

"Could you...?" Dex didn't finish his sentence, but he didn't have to.

"Of course."

Dex didn't move from where he was; he just leaned away, as if he didn't have the strength to do anything. Sloane made to get up, but Dex's soft voice stopped him. He was staring at the floor, and Sloane wondered if Dex was talking to Sloane or himself.

"Everything's hazy and foggy, a blur of colors and emotions, so jumbled that nothing makes sense. Like I'm drowning. I can feel the fire inside me fading, and I know I need to do something about it, but all I can feel is pain. What if I can't do anything? What if I don't get to Dad in time? What if instead of a wedding, I'm arranging a funeral? I can't lose Tony. What the hell am I supposed to do without him?"

Sloane cupped Dex's face and turned his head so

Sloane could meet his gaze. "We're going to find him, sweetheart, but you need to be strong. Cael's going to need you to be strong."

"Cael." Dex nodded, but the words didn't seem to sink in.

"I'll be right back." He kissed Dex's brow and got up. Thankfully, he didn't have to go far. When he walked out, Austen, Cael, and Ash were standing at the end of the hall. When Cael spotted Sloane, Sloane motioned for him to come over. Cael took off at top speed and was at his side in a heartbeat. Sloane didn't say a word. He walked in after Cael and closed the door behind him. Normally he would have left the brothers alone, but not this time. Not when they might need him.

"Dex?"

All at once, Dex jolted. He sucked in a sharp breath and blinked, as if he were blinking away the haze. He met Cael's tear-filled eyes, and Dex wiped away his own tears, his voice breaking when he spoke.

"I'm so sorry, Chirpy."

Cael kneeled in front of Dex. He looked around the room before turning his attention back to his brother. "It's okay. I'm sure TIN won't care about a little equipment..."

Sloane braced himself. His heart broke for them, and he stood by the door, quiet and still, watching as Dex swallowed hard and met Cael's gaze.

"Not about that," Dex said. "They took him, Cael. They took Dad."

Cael stared at him. "What... what do you mean they took him? Who took him?"

"The Makhai."

Cael opened his mouth, but nothing came out.

"After the tux fitting. They got the drop on him. I heard

him scream, and when I turned around, they were putting him in a van. I chased after them, but I couldn't..."

Cael looked around the room again, really looking this time. Sloane had no idea what was going on in Cael's head, but he could imagine Cael putting it all together, why the room was in pieces. Cael turned back to Dex, a tear rolling down his cheek before he threw his arms around his brother and squeezed him tight. Dex wrapped his arms around Cael, his eyes closed and his lips pressed together, most likely in an attempt not to lose it. Dex would do anything for his little brother, and Sloane could see how desperate Dex was to keep it together. Cael needed him, and Dex would push aside his own grief and despair for Cael. Sloane had watched him do it before.

"We're going to get him back," Cael said, his voice quiet and uncertain.

"We are," Dex promised, running a hand over Cael's head. "And then I'm going to make those sons of bitches pay."

The promise of retribution in Dex's voice sent an icy chill through Sloane. Most people who looked at Dex saw a cheeky, happy-go-lucky guy. The life of the party, the sweet guy who helped old ladies cross the street. They saw the jokester, the sexy guy with the million-watt smile. Few got to see the darkness lurking beneath the surface. It was a side Sloane knew existed because he'd seen glimpses of it over the years. There would be nowhere the kidnappers could hide from Dex.

They'd taken Tony for a reason, and Sloane was certain they'd be hearing from the Makhai soon. Dex stood, pulling Cael along with him. He placed his hands on Cael's shoulders and met his gaze, determination burning through his bright blue eyes. "I swear I am going to do everything in my power to bring him home. You with me?"

Cael nodded, and Dex patted his brother's cheek.

"Good." Dex headed for the door, ignoring the fact he only had on one shoe. Sloane and Cael followed him outside, where a team of TIN medical staff and operatives were gathered. Dex turned to face them. "Tell Sparks I'm going to be at THIRDS HQ. I'll see her there." He turned to go, then paused. "Any of you guys wear size eleven shoes?"

The operatives exchanged glances before one hesitantly held up a finger.

"I need your shoes," Dex said.

The wolf Therian was about Dex's height and weight. He dropped his gaze to Dex's feet, then let out a heavy sigh. With perfect balance, he bent one leg, took off his black shoe, then repeated the action to take off the other. He handed them to Dex in exchange for Dex's beat-up Chuck.

"Thanks. Make sure your boss reimburses you."

Oddly enough, Dex took the shoes but didn't put them on.

"HQ?" Sloane asked as they headed toward Ash, who was talking to Austen. The second they saw him, they hurried over. Dex stopped and looked up at Sloane.

"We're not TIN yet. Get everyone suited up and ready to roll out the moment you give the word. I need you to lead Destructive Delta one more time."

The words filled Sloane with pride. Not just because he'd be leading his team again, but because Dex was doing what he'd promised Sloane long ago. No more lone gunman. They were doing this together. Sloane nodded and removed his phone from his pocket as Dex turned to Austen.

"You too. You're still part of Destructive Delta. I want you to give Cael access to all the camera footage you have of the abduction." He turned to Ash. "That van is going to be smashed to shit. I want it found."

"You got it."

Sloane put in a quick call to HQ and was put through to Calvin.

"Hey, Sloane."

"I need everyone suited up and ready to go by the time we get there."

"Will do," Calvin said, no questions asked, no hesitation.

Sloane thanked him and hung up before turning back to Dex. "Done."

"Good." They headed for the garage where a black SUV waited for them. Dex told the driver where they were going and got in. He put on his newly acquired shoes as Sloane leaned in to talk to him. It was probably time for him to tell Dex about what had happened at the Boathouse.

"The Makhai tried to kidnap Hudson."

"What?" Dex stared at him.

"We went to eat at the Boathouse and were ambushed. They managed to get the drop on us and tranqed Hudson. They sent a whole army of mercenaries for him. They must have been watching us, all of us. They knew we hadn't recovered from post-shift."

"What happened?"

"Wolf showed up, driving the BearCat. *Our* BearCat."

Dex opened his mouth to reply, closed it, and paused before speaking. "I don't even know how to respond to that. I wish I could say I'm surprised, but lately I find that where Wolf is concerned, there's just no telling what you're going to find yourself dealing with. Wait, how did Wolf know?"

"Apparently he's been monitoring the Makhai's chatter—whatever that means—and managed to decipher one of their encrypted messages."

"I'm guessing he didn't take the news well."

Sloane shook his head somberly. "He killed as many of them as he could before they retreated. He disappeared after them."

"Can't say I'm sorry."

"I don't know about you guys, but I'm kinda glad he's on our side. Sort of."

Sloane frowned at Ash. "Wolf's not on anyone's side but his own. The guy will smile at you, tell you how much he likes you, and then put a bullet in your head."

"You're both right," Dex said, causing everyone to turn their focus on him. "Hudson's one of us, and unfortunately, the Makhai have set their sights on him, which means Wolf's going to stick around until he knows his brother's safe from them. We can't afford to turn down his help, no matter how fucked-up that may be. Whether we like it or not, he has connections and skills none of us have. *Yet.*"

Dex had told Sloane his plan of making sure someday soon he could hold his own against Wolf and even surpass him, but he still had a long way to go and a hell of a lot of training to do. As much as Sloane hated to admit it, because of Wolf, the Makhai hadn't gotten their hands on Hudson. The guy might be a psychopath, but it was obvious he cared about his brother and would do whatever it took to protect him. It almost made Sloane not completely hate him. Almost.

A few minutes later, they were being dropped off in HQ's parking garage. Sloane followed Dex straight to the armory. There would be no going home. No shower. No fucking around. Not until they had some answers. The

TIN medical team had cleaned Dex up as best they could while they tended to his wounds without removing his clothes, but according to Austen, Dex had wanted everyone gone from the room as soon as possible, most likely to keep strangers from witnessing his inevitable meltdown.

When they arrived at the Destructive Delta armory, Sloane couldn't help his pride. Their team was there, suited up in full tactical gear sans helmets. They had no idea why they'd been gathered, but it didn't matter. Sloane had made the call, and there they were, ready to move out. Rosa, Letty, Calvin, and Hobbs lined up, waiting, concern etched on their faces as they took in Dex's state. Dex glanced over at Sloane, who nodded and stepped forward. Right now, Dex needed him to deal with anything that had the potential to become too emotional. All his focus and energy were reserved for finding Tony.

"Okay, team. I know you're all wondering what the hell is going on. What's happening is we're preparing for war. Earlier today the Makhai tried to kidnap Hudson. What we didn't know was that at the same time, they were kidnapping Maddock."

Gasps and curses were heard all around. The team stood stunned before they all turned their gazes to Dex, who shook his head at them, his lips pressed together in a thin line. From the state of him, it didn't take much to leap to the conclusion he'd somehow been involved. Sloane was certain Dex appreciated their love and support, but right now he didn't need a shoulder to cry on. He needed someone willing to march into battle with him.

Hobbs squared his shoulders and took a step forward, head held high as he put his right fist to his heart. Calvin nodded in agreement and did the same, followed by Rosa and Letty.

"Whatever you need," Rosa said. "You know we'll be right there with you."

Letty nodded. "We're going to find those assholes, and we're going to bring the sarge home." She walked over to Dex's locker, and he put his thumb to the security pad. It unlocked, and she opened the door. She grabbed his tac vest and handed it to him. "Time to suit up, Daley. One last hurrah."

Dex took the vest from her with a soft laugh. "Yeah."

While everyone turned to discuss tactics, Sloane and Dex quickly changed into their uniforms. As Sloane buttoned up his shirt, it hit home. This was the last time he'd be putting on his uniform, and it would be to save his sergeant. He absently laid a hand over the Destructive Delta patch on his arm. This team had been his from its inception. He'd never led any other team, and no other team leader had led Destructive Delta but him. Together he and Ash had handpicked every member of this team until Dex. They'd all been through so much together and had had so many firsts. When this was done, he'd be hanging up his uniform for the last time.

Pushing back the emotions that threatened to bubble up, he straightened, grabbed his thigh rig, and continued to layer on pieces of his kit. There was no time for him to reflect on the swirling thunderstorm of sentiment coursing through him.

Once every weapon was secured, every piece of equipment strapped, tucked, and clicked into place, he was ready. He grabbed his helmet, now scuffed and dirty, the Destructive Delta sticker faded and distressed. Dex joined him, looking handsome as ever in his full uniform. It had been a while since they'd been sent out on a call, what with all the changes happening around them. He wished they were heading out under different circumstances.

"Ready?"

Sloane nodded. He turned to Dex, who stepped in front of him and straightened the strap of his MP5. They put their heads together, and Sloane placed his gloved hand to Dex's cheek.

"I'm right here with you, okay?"

"Thank you."

Sloane straightened and motioned for the door. "Destructive Delta, move out."

They all waited for Sloane to walk ahead, and Dex fell in behind him. They took formation, following him like they always had to the elevator and then rode it up to Unit Alpha. They headed down the hall and then walked through the doors leading to their unit. When they reached the bullpen, everyone stood. Agents and officers came out from their offices, all to watch them walk through the bullpen, most likely wondering if the apocalypse was upon them since Destructive Delta was ready to head out in full tactical gear. Sloane had no intention of keeping his sergeant's abduction a secret. It would be unfair to the agents who worked with him, respected him, and looked up to him. They had a right to know. They had a right to join in the fight. And he knew Dex would agree with him. Tony was Dex and Cael's father, but he was also a founding member of the THIRDS. He had watched this place grow. He had celebrated and suffered along with every agent in this bullpen. Tony was more than a THIRDS officer. He was family.

Bringing down the Makhai might have been TIN's problem, but that changed when Sloane and Dex discovered they'd had Dex's parents murdered, when they paid to have Dex tortured and killed, and now they had the fucking balls to take Tony away from his family. Sloane didn't care if he had to hunt down every one of those bastards and put them in the ground. He was going to help Dex get Tony back and end this.

CHAPTER SEVEN

"Is this room secure?" Dex stood to one side as Sparks placed her hand on the security panel by the door. After the initial handprint scan, she entered a code, then walked to the front of the room.

Dex pretended not to notice how red her eyes were. She hadn't been at the facility, which was unusual for her. Had she even left her office at HQ until now? How long after his dad was taken had she found out? Despite her reddened eyes, there was no mistaking the promise of unholy retribution in them. She looked very much like how Dex felt.

"The room is secure," Sparks replied, taking a seat at the end of the large conference table. Everyone took a seat except for Dex and Cael, who remained standing near Sparks. "Austen has updated me on everything that's happened today. Hudson is resting in one of the sleeper bays. Seb is looking after him. While the Makhai is out there looking for Hudson, it's best we keep him close. He's being rather stubborn and refuses to allow us to place him in a safe house." Sparks's expression turned grave. "We were wrong about why the Makhai want Hudson."

Dex took a seat in the chair closest to her. "What are you talking about?"

"We thought their doggedness to get their hands on Hudson was due to them actually wanting to get their hands on you." Sparks shook her head. "They want Hudson to get to Wolf."

The silence in the room intensified as Sparks's words sank in.

"They know who Wolf is," Dex said.

"More importantly, they know who Hudson is and what he means to Wolf. When Wolf was recruited, he was given a whole new identity, a new life with no family. Alfie Colbourn is, technically, still dead. He's buried in the family plot in England. That helped ensure Hudson's safety. It's one of the many reasons our operatives lead double lives. Not only to protect the operations but the operatives and their families."

Dex let out a heavy sigh. "They plan on using Hudson to control Wolf or kill him." Wolf had been right about getting Hudson into TIN to keep him safe. With Hudson and Seb training, they'd be better prepared.

"I don't get it."

Dex turned to Cael, who moved closer. "Don't get what? Why Hudson?"

"No, I get that," Cael said, his brows drawn together in concern. "What I don't get is why would they take Dad? They tried to take Hudson because of his connection to Wolf and not you. So if they don't want you, then why take Dad? Who else do they plan to use him against?"

Dex swallowed hard as realization set in. He turned to

Sparks just as the screen on the wall behind them flickered to life. A figure shrouded in darkness appeared.

"Hello, Sonya."

Sparks stood to face the screen. "Who am I speaking to?"

"You can call me the Chairman."

Dex slowly stood. This had to be it. The voice was distorted, and the shadow appeared pitch-black so as to not reveal any distinguishable features. The fact whoever this was managed to breach a room secured by TIN was frightening.

"Where's Agent Maddock?" Sparks demanded. "What do you want with him?"

"You're a clever girl. Why don't you tell me? Why on earth would I take your lover?"

A gasp caught Dex's ear, and he turned, his heart squeezing at Cael's shocked expression. Damn it, this wasn't how he'd wanted his brother to find out. As much as he wanted to go to Cael, they needed to hear what this asshole had to say. Thankfully, his brother seemed to agree because his expression went from stunned to silently fuming.

"Oh dear. It looks like the cougar's out of the bag," the Chairman said with a chuckle. "As much as I would love to hear all the family drama, let's cut to the chase. You have two options here, Sonya. You can do as I ask or have history repeat itself with poor Anthony."

Have history repeat itself? What the hell did that mean? Dex studied Sparks. She didn't so much as blink.

"And what exactly is it you want me to do?" Sparks asked.

"What several operatives in your organization have done. Join the Makhai from the inside. Let's face it, Sonya.

You and I both know there's more than one mole inside TIN. How do you think we've managed to stay out of your grasp for so long? Unfortunately, you and your dear friend Wolf refuse to die, so if you won't die, then I'll have to use your weaknesses against you. It's Spy 101, really. I know you think Dr. Colbourn is safe there with you at THIRDS headquarters, but come now. We're *everywhere*."

"You expect me to betray my organization and become a double agent?"

"I expect you to make the right decision."

Dex swallowed hard, his jaw clenched.

"If not, not only do you lose Anthony, but you lose your new golden boy as well. Oh, but he has so much potential. For a half-breed abomination."

Dex gritted his teeth and clenched his fists at his sides to keep from telling the Chairman what he could do with his backhanded compliments.

"Think about it, Sonya. Do you really think that boy is going to follow you anywhere if you let dear old Dad die a horrible death? Hello, Dexter."

Dex flipped him off, and the Chairman chuckled. "Spitfire, that one. So you see, Sonya. Dad dies, and your precious new weapon becomes an inconsolable mess before he becomes too much of a liability even for TIN. He'll make Wolf look like a Boy Scout. Kiss the rest of the team goodbye, and that includes Dr. Colbourn. No doctor, no rogue assassin. You're alone again, Sonya. You're not very good at this whole family thing, are you?"

Sparks let out a fierce cry and swiped her Glock from her holster before emptying her magazine into the screen right where the Chairman's head was.

Holy shit! Dex took a quick step back, wondering what the hell had triggered Sparks. Nothing ever fazed her. The

Chairman had mentioned something about history repeating itself and then mentioned family. Was it possible Sonya had a family not long ago? Had something happened to them? She never discussed anything personal with any of them. She always kept herself at a distance. *You're alone again.* What the hell had happened? His questions would have to wait. Lucky for them, the Chairman was still there.

"Yes!" The Chairman laughed through the speakers. "That's the fire I want to see. Now you use that, and you get me the information I want from TIN. I'll be in touch."

"Wait," Dex cried out. "How do we know you haven't already killed my father?"

There was a long pause, and for a second, Dex thought the guy had disappeared.

"Boys?"

"Dad." Dex swallowed past the lump in his throat. "Dad, how are you holding up?"

Sloane stepped up beside Dex, his hand coming to rest on his lower back. Dex took comfort in his mate's touch, feeling himself calm.

"I'm okay. When this is over, the three of us are going to Vegas. I love you, boys. Be good, and don't give these sons of bitches—"

There was scuffling before the room went silent.

"Dad?" Cael stepped forward, but there was no reply. He was gone. The quiet didn't last long. Cael headed for Sparks, and Dex caught hold of him.

"You have some fucking nerve," Cael spat out, thrusting a finger at Sparks. "After the hell you've put us through, you hook up with our dad? After what you did to my brother? How could you look him in the eye, knowing what you've done, who you are?"

"Cael. Now is not the time," Dex said gently.

Cael turned his blazing gray eyes on Dex. "Did you know about this?"

For fuck's sake. This wasn't the time. He knew his brother was hurt and angry, but their father's life was on the line. When Dex didn't reply, Cael's expression went from angry to hurt, and Dex flinched.

"You knew." Cael shook his head in disbelief. "You knew, and you kept it from me?"

"It wasn't my place to tell," Dex said softly, hoping Cael would understand.

"Not your place?" Cael pushed Dex away from him. "You're my brother." Cael rounded on Sparks again. "You put my dad's life on the line. He had a right to know what you are."

"He knows."

"What?"

Sparks let out a sigh. "Your father knows I'm TIN."

Dex stared at her. "You actually told him?"

Sparks shook her head. "I was going to, but he beat me to it. Told me I didn't have to say anything, that he's not as oblivious or naïve as we believe him to be."

"We?" Cael folded his arms over his chest. "What the hell do *we* have to do with it?"

"You can be angry at me all you want, but I had my reasons for not telling him who I really work for. What's your excuse?"

"Excuse me?" Cael was indignant.

"While you two went on your secret missions, getting kidnapped, tortured, putting yourselves in all kinds of danger, keeping him in the dark, thinking you were protecting him, he sat there waiting. And before you tell me *I* was the one sending you on those assignments, you better rethink that, because I sure as hell never sent you after

Hogan. In fact, I took your team off that case, but you went behind my back and set off to settle your own score. That wasn't the first time you went off on your own little missions, and it wasn't the last either. Meanwhile, Tony waited for his boys to tell him the truth. When you didn't, he went in search of answers." Sparks stepped in front of them, her voice low and laced with hurt and anger. She pointed to both of them. "Your father has been playing this game longer than you, and he is far better at it than you know. I could have told him what you two were getting yourselves into, but I didn't because that's *your* job. You're his sons."

Dex dropped his gaze, feeling like a shit for not having the balls to tell his dad the truth. They should have confided in Tony from the beginning. They'd convinced themselves they were protecting him, but all they'd managed to do was make him feel like he wasn't good enough, as an agent or a father.

"You're right," Dex said.

Cael frowned at him. "What?"

"We fucked up. *I* fucked up." Dex turned to his brother. "I should have told Dad everything from the beginning. I mean, he's our sergeant, for crying out loud. Instead, I did what I always do, let my insecurities get the better of me." Dex forced himself to meet Sparks's gaze. "You're absolutely right about everything. I got scared, and I thought if he didn't know what was going on, that he'd be safe, and look where that got us?"

Cael's expression softened, and he let out a sigh. "Dex, you can't blame yourself for this. This is on the three of us. We should have told him."

Dex nodded. He needed to learn to turn to his family for help if he needed it, rather than trying to carry the world on his shoulders. What they did was dangerous, and that wasn't about to change, so he needed to change. He'd told himself as much before, but it turned out that changing was harder than expected. It always was when it concerned his family.

"We all have a lot to talk about, but right now, we need to worry about getting Tony back," Dex said. He turned to Sparks. "What are you going to do when the Chairman calls for his answer?"

Sparks placed a finger to her lips and pointed up. Right, the room wasn't secure. "What can I do? I'm going to give him what he wants. Come on. We need to secure Hudson." She headed for the door and motioned for them to follow. They left the conference room and followed her to her office. When the door closed, she took a seat behind her desk. Tapping at the interface, she brought up the security connections to her office and the rest of Unit Alpha. To Dex's astonishment, she shut everything down.

"What are you doing?" Cael asked, eyes wide.

Everything in the office shut down, including security mode. She looked over at their team. "Ash, Hobbs, stand guard outside. I don't want anyone coming within ten feet of this office."

They nodded and walked out, then closed the door behind them.

"The Chairman clearly has access to TIN and the THIRDS, which means until I get someone I trust to reconfigure everything and install a new set of security measures, our technology is useless. We're going to have to go dark and do things the old-fashioned way. We can't trust any intel that comes from TIN, so you and your team are on your own. I'll stall for as long as I can and hope whatever the Chairman has me do isn't irreparable. In the meantime, you need to find Tony before they move him out of the country. After that, there's no finding him."

"How long do you think they'll keep him in the city?" Sloane asked.

"Two or three days at most. They're likely making arrangements to transport him as we speak."

Sloane went thoughtful. "What happened when Moros was investigated? You said TIN arrested anyone who had any connection to him. Were any of them Makhai?"

Sparks nodded. "Three. One killed himself in the interrogation room. Snapped his own neck using the edge of the table. The other two were interrogated by some of TIN's best operatives. The intel collected was verified. I can provide you with access to that product, but it's no longer relevant. All the locations connected to the Makhai were either seized by TIN or abandoned long before TIN arrived. Both places had been cleaned. No trace of anything left behind. They provided us with a short list of names, all belonging to Therians found dead by our operatives. Whoever's running the Makhai, he trusts no one, not even his own organization. The members know as little as possible in case someone is captured, and anyone who does know anything significant kills themselves before the information can be extracted."

"Where are those two Makhai members?"

"In a secure location only I and two other high-ranking operatives know about."

"I need to talk to them," Dex said.

Sparks arched an eyebrow. "You want to interrogate the Makhai members? What exactly do you think you can get from them that we haven't? They've been in our custody too long to have any information on the Makhai's recent activity."

"Wait," Sloane said, turning to Dex. "The guy who shot Hudson with the tranq at the park. We have him in solitary downstairs in the basement."

"You brought in one of the Makhai's men?" Dex turned back to Sparks. "And he's still alive?"

Sparks nodded. She removed a set of keys and tossed them to Dex. "I put him in one of the old cells, sublevel. Call me cynical, but something told me I shouldn't put this guy into one of the regular cells. Unless someone blowtorches those bars, there's no way of getting into that cell, and that's after they get through two sets of steel doors, which they need those keys for."

"I think it's time to ask our friend a few questions."

"You really think he's going to talk to you?" Letty asked worriedly. "The guy didn't even break when Seb was beating the shit out of him."

"Maybe he won't talk to me," Dex said with a wicked grin. "But maybe he'll talk to someone who's much better at interrogation than any of us."

Sparks's eyes went wide. Before she could say anything, Dex turned to Sloane. "We need to go see Hudson."

Sloane nodded. They left the room and headed for the sleeper bays, Ash and Hobbs joining them. Only one of the doors was closed, and Dex knocked on it. He waited for Seb to look through the peep hole. The door opened, and Seb looked Dex over—most likely taking in the fact he was in uniform—and nodded, as if he was on board with whatever it was Destructive Delta was about to do.

"I need to talk to Hudson."

Seb stepped aside, and Dex walked in. When Hudson saw him, he jumped out of bed and pulled Dex into a big hug.

"Thank goodness you're all right. Oh, Dex. I'm so sorry about Maddock."

Dex shut his eyes tight and squeezed Hudson. "Thanks." Clearing his throat, he pulled back and cupped the back of Hudson's neck, keeping him close. They could have lost Hudson too. If it hadn't been for their team, and Wolf, Hudson would have been in the hands of the Makhai, and God only knew what they would have forced Wolf to do to keep Hudson alive. "Are you okay?"

Hudson nodded. "Yes. It was awful, whatever they shot me with, but it's nearly all out of my system now." He looked behind Dex, then turned his concerned gaze back to him. "You're going after them."

Dex nodded. "We've got to find my dad before they try to move him out of the country. I won't lose him again."

"Whatever you need from me, just say the word."

"I'm glad you said that, because I need a favor."

"Of course."

"I need you to call him."

Hudson blinked at him. "I beg your pardon?"

"Call him."

Hudson peered at him. "By *him* are you referring to...?"

"Yes."

"And how exactly am I to do that? It's not as if he's left me a number." Hudson walked over to the bed and dropped down on it with a heavy sigh. He ran a hand through his already disheveled hair. "I wish I could, Dex, but how am I supposed to get in contact with a ghost?"

Dex smiled. "Just use the phone."

Hudson cast him a sideways glance. "I'm afraid I don't follow."

Dex removed his cell phone from his pocket. "He's been

keeping tabs on you. Believe me. He'll get the message. Call me."

Hudson removed his own phone from his pocket, one that was both THIRDS and TIN secure—though there was no telling, considering the Chairman seemed to know exactly what was going on no matter where they were. Hudson found Dex's contact info in his address book and tapped the screen. Dex's phone rang. He answered it but didn't bother putting it to his ear.

Hudson placed his own phone to his ear. "Um, if you can hear me, I need your help. Please. It's very important." He hung up and looked at Dex. "Do you really think that's going to work?"

Seb frowned. "I know we want it to work, but is anyone else as creeped out as I am that he's listening in on us?"

Dex and Hudson both held up a hand.

While Dex agreed, right now he needed Wolf, and he wasn't sure if the guy would have answered had he been the one to make that call. As it was, Wolf tended to pop up whenever he felt like it, but for Hudson...

"You really think he's going to come here?" Seb asked, motioning to the small space around them.

"You're right." Dex motioned for Hudson to follow him. "We need to make it easier for him to get to you."

Outside in the hall, they formed a circle around Hudson.

"Is this really necessary?" Hudson grumbled.

"Yes," Dex replied. "Your brother is a highly skilled assassin, with one vulnerability that's just been exposed."

Hudson stopped walking and grabbed Dex's arm. "What?"

Dex let out a sigh. "They know you're Wolf's little brother. That's why they've been trying to get their hands on you. Not because of me but because of him. If they have you, they can control him or kill him. Depends on how useful they think he'd be to them."

Hudson cursed under his breath and ran a hand through his hair. "Wonderful."

"I know it sucks, but for now, security around you has to be tight, Hudson. That's just how it has to be until we know you're out of danger."

Hudson let out a resigned sigh and nodded.

They headed through Unit Alpha, and Dex was surprised when they were stopped by a group of fellow agents. Taylor and Angel made their way through the center of the group, then stood in front of Dex.

"We heard about Maddock," Taylor said. "I swear we're gonna find him, Dex."

Angel nodded his agreement. "There's nowhere those assholes can hide. Everyone's moving out, including Unit Beta. We're gonna find him."

The rest of their fellow agents joined in, offering words of support. Dex swallowed hard. No matter what happened with TIN, Dex was always going to be a part of the THIRDS. They might not have always gotten along, but they had one another's backs. Dex was proud to be a THIRDS agent, and at heart, he would always be a THIRDS agent. No matter where in the world he was sent, he would always be coming back home to HQ, and that made all the difference.

"Thanks, everyone. I really appreciate it."

The crowd moved so Destructive Delta could walk by. They took the elevator down to Sparta and one of the old school training bays that wasn't in use anymore. There were no high-tech gadgets, no fancy equipment, no speakers.

Nothing but vinyl floors and painted white walls. They stood in the center and waited.

"You think he's just going to walk through the door?" Calvin asked.

No sooner had the question left his mouth than Wolf did just that. He opened the door to the training bay and headed toward them like he was strutting down some fashion runway. The guy never did anything halfway. He never just walked. His posture was perfect, his shoulders were broad, his waist slender, and his legs long. He wasn't even that big. In fact, he was roughly Dex's height and weight. Sloane was taller, larger, and broader than Wolf. Yet Wolf gave off the impression that he was bigger. He always had a twinkle in his eye, like he knew the most amazing secret and *maybe* if you were worthy, he'd share it with you, or he might just kill you.

Whatever hair products Wolf used, Dex had to get some, because the guy never had one hair out of place. His designer suit never wrinkled and his shoes didn't scuff. Dex understood now why they never saw Wolf coming. He was handsome, oozed charm, and for those who didn't know him, they could easily find themselves lulled into a false sense of security. By the time they figured out they were being drawn into his spider's web, it would be too late. The way the guy switched from playful to "stabbing you in the eye with an icepick" was terrifying.

"Is it my birthday?" Wolf asked smoothly. "All of you gathered here for little ole me?"

Dex took a step toward him but made sure to keep out of arm's reach. "I need your help."

Wolf looked from Hudson to Dex and back. He folded his arms over his expansive chest and frowned his disapproval at Hudson. "Explain yourself."

"Please, Al—Wolf. I wouldn't have called if it wasn't terribly important."

Wolf sighed and turned his attention back to Dex, and just like that he was smiling again. "What can I do for you, darling?" He approached Dex and tapped his finger to Dex's nose. "I must admit, I'm rather tickled there's something I can provide you with that your beau can't." Wolf glanced over at Sloane with a smirk. Sloane simply glowered in return. Dex silently thanked Sloane for his incredible patience and understanding. This was too important for anyone to get into any pissing contests.

"Let's get down to it, shall we?" Dex took a step away from Wolf. "I need your help interrogating someone."

Wolf's eyebrows flew up near his hairline. "Say that again? I fear I misheard you."

"You didn't. I need you to get your tools and break someone."

Wolf studied him. "You must be having a laugh."

It was a shitty move, but Dex had to make Wolf understand how serious he was about this. "If they'd succeeded in taking Hudson, how far would you have gone to get him back alive?"

Wolf's steel-blue eyes met his, his expression darkening. "I think you know the answer to that, Dexter."

"Good. Then you know what I'm prepared to do for my father."

"As touching as that is, I'm not in the business of being summoned for charity work."

"You son of a bitch—" Ash caught hold of Sloane before Sloane could launch himself at Wolf.

Shit. This wasn't going well. They had to do something, or they were going to lose him.

Wolf turned and jabbed a finger at Hudson. "Do not,

for one moment, assume I'm about to be at your beck and call. I am not the bloody butler here to clean up your messes. My priority is your safety, and I'm risking a hell of a lot keeping your arse out of trouble. Do you understand me, little brother?" As Wolf turned to go, Seb said the magic words.

"It's the guy who tranqed your brother."

Dex held his breath as Wolf stilled. He turned to Seb, his eyes narrowed, the blue of his eyes nothing but slivers around his blown pupils. "Are you telling me you have in your custody one of the Makhai's mercenaries? Specifically, the one who shot a tranquilizer into my brother's chest?"

Seb nodded. "We figured we could get some information out of him, but he's not talking."

"Oh, he's not going to talk," Wolf said calmly, the ice in his voice sending a shiver through Dex. "He's going to fucking sing." Wolf met Dex's gaze. "Do you realize what you're doing?"

"Inviting the wolf into the henhouse," Dex said with a smirk.

Wolf blinked at him, then let out a bark of laughter. He shook his head in amusement as he reached into his suit jacket pocket and pulled out a pair of black gloves. "You are a treat to work with, Dexter. An absolute treat." He slipped on his gloves and flexed his fingers. "Shall we?"

"Don't you, um, need tools or something?"

"You're absolutely right." Wolf turned to Hobbs. It was kind of amusing to see Wolf have to look up. "My, but they make you Hobbs boys big, don't they? It's like a stepladder of enormity with you three. Anyway, your vehicle was rather impressively stocked. Would you mind bringing me your toolbox?"

Hobbs arched an eyebrow at him, then glanced over at Dex, who nodded.

"We'll meet you downstairs," Dex told Hobbs, and Calvin joined his partner to grab the toolbox from the BearCat. Dex didn't even want to know what Wolf had planned.

"I'll see you boys down there. I'm afraid you draw far too much attention."

Ash stared at him. "*We* draw too much attention? We're actually supposed to be here, unlike you. Like no one's going to notice the guy in the fancy suit and hitman gloves walking through the halls?"

"Actually, you're not supposed to be here. You're supposed to be in your new office, pining for your bestie." He pointed to Rosa, Letty, and Cael. "They're supposed to be in their new office along with the two who just left, pretending to be excited over the new cappuccino machine, and those two," he said, motioning to Dex and Sloane, "are supposed to be on vacation, gazing into each other's eyes and being disgustingly romantic, not in uniform escorting my baby brother around like he's some foreign dignitary. Subtlety is not one of your proficiencies, ladies and gents. It is, however, one of mine." With a salute, he disappeared through the doors.

"Man, I hate that guy," Sloane growled before turning to Hudson. "Sorry."

Hudson shrugged. "What can I say? He is a bit of an arsehole." Hudson's phone rang, and he answered, his eyes narrowing. "Oh piss off, Alfie." He hung up with a huff and returned his phone to his pocket.

"Did Wolf just call you?" Dex asked, starting for the doors.

"Yes, to tell me he heard me call him an arsehole and that it wasn't very nice."

Dex's phone rang, and he answered. "Hello?"

"Darling, would you be so kind as to tell my baby brother he's a little shite?"

"Um, sure."

"Thank you."

Dex hung up and returned his cell phone to his pocket. Next to him, Hudson let out a weary sigh, not at all dissimilar to the kind Dex often heard from Cael when Dex was being a pest. Good to know Alfie and Hudson's relationship was much like any other siblings', except for the whole trained killer part.

"What did he say?" Hudson grumbled.

"He said you were a little shite."

"Lovely." Hudson turned to Cael, his expression deadpan. "Want to trade brothers?"

Cael pretended to think about it. "Hm, deadly assassin or Dex. Deadly assassin or Dex."

Ash opened his mouth, and Dex put a hand to his face. "No one asked for your opinion, Keeler."

Everyone chuckled, and the sense of normalcy it gave Dex was welcome. It helped him remain focused. He had to detach himself from his emotions, or he wouldn't be of any use to his dad. Sloane walked beside him, his presence alone soothing Dex, making him feel like he could get through anything. Whatever happened, he wasn't alone. He was surrounded by people who loved and supported him.

In the sublevel basement beneath the THIRDS garage, away from everyone and everything, the old cellblock was locked behind a huge steel door. Back in the nineties when the THIRDS first opened its doors, it had been one of the most solid holding cells in the state, with thick concrete walls and iron bars. It had been more secure than some prisons, considering most places weren't equipped to hold some of the more dangerous Therians. Soon the prison system caught up, and "Zoos" were opened to contain the most lethal of Therian prisoners. Everything moved to the age of the internet, and new high-tech holding cells were built upstairs, connected to Themis. Unfortunately, Themis wasn't to be trusted, and Sparks had been on the ball putting this guy down here.

Hobbs and Calvin stood to one side of the huge steel door, while Wolf stood to the other, Hobbs's toolbox in one gloved hand. He looked bored. As if he'd been waiting hours for them. Wolf and Hudson glared at each other but remained quiet as Dex unlocked the door to the cellblock. Inside, a small sitting area lay empty along with the guard's station. The lights flickered, and Ash frowned up at them.

"I think I saw this place in a horror movie. Why is everything washed in green?"

Dex followed Ash's gaze up to the ceiling and identified the culprit. The light fixture was growing some funky green stuff. When the hell was the last time anyone was down here besides Sparks?

"I feel like I'm going to contract something just breathing the air down here," Calvin grumbled.

"All right, you bunch of divas, let's get this over with," Wolf said, walking past them to the set of iron bars at the end. He motioned for Dex to approach. "Come on, love. I haven't got all day."

Dex unlocked the door and opened it wide.

"There should be an interrogation room somewhere around here," Sloane said, stepping up to the map on the wall. The place was huge, divided into four sections. "Here." Sloane pointed to the top right section. "Here's solitary confinement, and at the end of the hall, there's a row of interrogation rooms. We'll take him to room 4B." Sloane motioned for Ash, Seb, and Hobbs to follow him. "We'll get him moved, and then Dex and Wolf can go in." Sloane looked over at Dex. "I'll let you know when we're ready."

Dex nodded and handed the keys to Sloane. He stayed where he was while Sloane and the others went off in search of their guy to move him. Cael came to stand by Dex, even though he didn't say anything. Everyone remained quiet, lost in their own thoughts, and Dex leaned against the wall, observing. Calvin gravitated over to the girls, while Hudson went over to one of the chairs. He leaned over to peer at it distrustfully. Meanwhile, Wolf dropped down onto the one next to it and smacked the cushion of the one Hudson was peering at. A cloud of dust puffed up and hit Hudson in the face.

Hudson coughed and gagged while Wolf cackled.

"You wanker," Hudson wheezed. "That was horrid."

Wolf continued to laugh, his eyes bright with amusement. Laughter transformed his whole face and made him look like any other guy.

As Dex watched the brothers being brothers, he was struck by a sense of sadness for Hudson. This couldn't be easy for him. It was bad enough losing Alfie and mourning his death, only to have him back, yet not. Alfie was no longer the beloved brother Hudson had grown up with. There were times, like now, where Dex could see Alfie, and it was hard to believe he was who Wolf had once been.

Realizing Dex was watching him, Alfie was gone in the blink of an eye, and Wolf was back. There was an unspoken challenge in his gaze, as if he were waiting for Dex to try and use the knowledge against him, just like the Makhai had done. Dex couldn't imagine living such a solitary life with no one to trust.

Wolf stood, dusted himself off, and joined Dex. He

looked down at Cael, his voice oddly… kind when he spoke. "Go join your friends. I need a word with your brother."

Cael glanced over at Dex, who nodded. "I'll be fine."

"Okay." Cael went off to join Rosa and the others, and Dex waited for Wolf to say whatever it was he needed to say.

"I can't afford to get close to him."

Dex shrugged. "I didn't say anything."

"You didn't have to," Wolf grumbled. "It's in those big blue eyes of yours. Whatever you may think of me, I'm not trying to hurt him. I just want him to be safe."

"And you think if you stop being an asshole to him, he'll be less safe?"

Wolf's expression hardened. "If I let my guard down, he will be."

"So the Makhai found out who he is to you because you let your guard down?"

"I believe whoever the Chairman has inside TIN unearthed that tidbit of information." Wolf narrowed his eyes at Dex. "You know, you're a bit of a smartarse."

Dex chuckled, and Sloane's voice came through on his earpiece.

"Ready."

"Copy that." Dex turned his attention to his brother and the others. "You guys stay here and keep an eye out. If anyone shows up, make sure you send them on their way, and if they don't want to go, take care of it. We're the only ones with clearance to be down here. Hudson, you come with us. I want you to stick close to Seb."

Hudson nodded and followed them, though he remained lost in thought. Dex and Wolf headed toward the wing where Sloane and the others waited. Wolf was quiet for a moment, his sharp eyes missing nothing.

"Just so you know, you'll be able to do this yourself someday very soon."

The change in conversation threw Dex off. "What are you talking about?"

"Who do you think trained me to do what I did to you?"

TIN had trained Wolf to torture, and they'd soon be training Dex and Sloane. Before his dad had been taken, Dex would have been horrified, most likely believing there was another way, but now... A thought struck him. "Why couldn't TIN break the Makhai guys they have in custody?" It was possible they just didn't have any more information, but Dex couldn't imagine members of the Makhai not being prepared for an interrogation. If they were willing to go as far as to kill themselves, why were the other two still alive? It didn't make sense.

"We are no longer in the good old days of barbaric torture," Wolf said with a heavy sigh. "Even TIN has set parameters they must work within or they'll be getting a good old slap on the wrist from Uncle Sam. After all, even terrorists have rights."

Wolf's snide tone told Dex all he needed to know about how Wolf felt on the subject. That, however, was a debate for another day.

"But you don't operate within those parameters," Dex clarified.

Wolf's smile was evil. "Correct." He headed for the door. "Come along, Dexter. Let's get you some intel and me some satisfaction. If you have the stomach for it."

"Whatever it takes."

They reached Sloane, who turned to Seb. "You and Hobbs stay with Hudson while Ash and I stand guard here." Sloane took hold of Dex's arm and pulled him to one side, speaking quietly.

"Babe, are you sure this is a good idea? We haven't even been sworn in, and you're going to watch someone get tortured by the guy who tortured *you*."

"I know. It's fucked-up. But if this is the only way to get a lead on my dad, I'm going to take it. I lost my parents to these assholes, Sloane. I'm not going to lose Tony. I can't."

Sloane's voice was gentle, his amber eyes filled with love and concern. "I know, sweetheart."

"You don't think I should do this?"

"I think you should do whatever you need to do. Just remember to come home to me, okay? To us."

Dex smiled at him and cupped his cheek. "Thank you." Knowing Sloane would be there when this was done gave Dex the strength he needed. "Do you think I can leave you two out here without you trying to kill each other?" Dex asked, motioning to Wolf.

"I'll behave," Sloane promised.

Dex arched an eyebrow at Wolf, who released a long-suffering sigh.

"Fine. I'll not goad your sensitive boyfriend."

Well, it was something. He'd take it. With that settled, Dex breathed in deep and took hold of the handle to the interrogation room door. It was time to get some answers.

"Dex," Sloane called out, and Dex turned his face, his heart squeezing in his chest at Sloane's nod of encouragement. "Whatever it takes."

He could do this. He *would* do this.

CHAPTER EIGHT

It was now or never.

Dex entered the room and closed the door behind him. The room was twenty-by-twenty, with exposed cinderblock walls, a concrete floor that had seen better days, a steel table bolted to the floor, and a metal chair, presently occupied by a tiger Therian whose face was a testament to what happened when you tranqed a Therian's mate in front of him.

"Are you kidding me? This is who they send?"

Dex stood in front of the table, his hands clasped behind his back to keep him from reaching out and beating the ever-loving fuck out of the guy. "I'm Agent Dexter Daley."

"I know who you are, half-breed."

"Now, that's not very nice," Dex said with a pout. "I'm going to be honest with you... What should I call you?"

"Fuck you."

"I'm going to call you Whiskers. Now, Whiskers, I'm feeling a little fragile at the moment, as you can imagine." Dex walked over to sit on the edge of the table next to the guy. "I mean, your organization tried to kidnap my friend, you and your friends shot at my fiancé, and then you guys kidnapped my father. Did I mention the part where your bosses had my parents killed? Then they contracted a killer to torture me and kill me. I'm not going to lie to you, it's been rough."

"Boo-hoo. Why don't you go home and cry to Daddy? Oh, wait." The guy laughed, and Dex joined in the laughter.

"Oh shit! You're a funny guy, you know that?" Dex wagged a finger at him. "I didn't know you Makhai guys had a sense of humor. Why don't I go home and cry to Daddy? Right. Because you kidnapped my dad, so he's not there for me to cry to." Dex wiped an imaginary tear from his eye. "Funny shit." Dex slammed the guy's head down against the table, blood splattering across the surface before his head bounced back.

"You fuck!" He spat out a mouthful of blood and saliva.

Dex sucked in a sharp breath. "Ooh, that's gotta hurt. Where were we? Right. My daddy issues."

"You're just going to have to kill me because I ain't saying shit."

"Everyone's got a breaking point. Why don't we find yours?"

Whiskers laughed. "You think *you're* gonna make me talk?"

Dex shook his head. "Nope." He walked over to the door and pounded on it. "But I betcha *he* is." The door opened, and Dex took satisfaction in the look of "oh fuck" that crossed the guy's face when Wolf walked in. The guy's eyes were so wide, they looked like they were going to pop out of his head.

"What the fuck is he doing here?"

"You can't just try to kidnap someone's family and not

have to answer to them." Dex turned to Wolf. "Wolf, may I introduce you to Whiskers?"

Wolf arched an eyebrow at him. "Well, that's an unfortunate name for a tiger Therian." Wolf turned a sympathetic gaze on their friend. "I'm so sorry your parents hated you."

"That's not my name, asshole."

"Oh, well, good times, then."

"But since he won't give us his name, Whiskers it is," Dex said cheerfully. He turned back to Whiskers. "Or did you want something more ferocious? Something that'll strike fear in our hearts?"

"Fred," Wolf offered.

Dex cast Wolf a sideways glance. "Fred?"

Wolf nodded. "My auntie had this hideous-looking creature I suspect was some form of cat. It used to attack anything that moved within a five-mile radius of it. I swear it was shat by the devil."

Dex let out a bark of laughter. "Okay, you win. Fred it is."

Fred looked from Dex to Wolf and back to Dex. "You've got to be fucking shitting me. Why is he here?" Before Dex could answer, Fred turned his gaze to Wolf. "How much is he paying you? We'll pay you triple."

Wolf laughed. "Oh, you poor bastard. I'm not being paid to do this. You shot my little brother in the chest." Wolf placed the toolbox in his hand on the table with a *thunk*. He opened it and removed a hammer, which he then pointed at Fred. "Take a moment for that to sink in, Fred. *You* shot *my* sweet, innocent little brother in the chest. Do you know how much that hurts?" Wolf pulled a tranq gun from inside the toolbox and shot Fred in the chest.

"Motherfuck!" Fred cursed and howled in between wheezing breaths.

"Dude, you shot him!" Dex threw up his arms. "Really?"

"They're blanks, Dexter."

"Oh." Dex put his arms down. "Carry on, then."

"You two... are... fucking... crazy," Fred said, gasping for breath.

Wolf grinned broadly at Dex. "You see there? He said we make a good team."

Dex was not impressed. "That is not what he said."

"Are you certain? Because I very clearly heard him say we make a good team."

"Can we get back to Fred?"

"Very well." Wolf returned his attention to Fred. "As you can see, that was very painful. Of course, you were spared the numbing toxin that was spread through my brother's neurological system, paralyzing him and knocking him unconscious, leaving him vulnerable. And then your mates shot at the stuffy agent with the stick up his arse who was holding my baby brother."

"Sloane is not stuffy, nor does he have a stick up his ass."

"Don't interrupt me, Dexter. I'm making a point." Wolf reached into his suit jacket and pulled out a gun with a silencer. He shot Fred in the shoulder, then held the gun up so Fred could see it. Fred was a little busy groaning and writhing in pain. "This one does not have blanks."

Dex hoped they got something out of Fred before the guy bled to death or died of a fucking heart attack.

Wolf sat on the edge of the table in front of Fred, hammer in one hand, gun in the other. "Now, Fred, what can you tell me about Dexter's dear old dad?"

The chains rattled as Fred held on to his wounded shoulder, his teeth gritted as he spat at them. "Fuck you."

"Not the reply I was hoping for." Wolf returned his gun to his jacket before grabbing Fred's hands and bringing the hammer down on one finger.

Dex cringed as Fred's howl filled the room.

"Let's try that again, Fred. I know you have nine more fingers, but time is of the essence. Where is Sergeant Maddock?"

"Fuck you."

Wolf sighed. "Dexter, I'm afraid I'm going to need your assistance."

"Um, sure." Dex walked over, and Wolf motioned to Fred as he pulled a pair of pliers out of the toolbox.

"I need you to hold his head."

Fred tried to get up, but Dex pushed him down. It wasn't like he could go anywhere. The guy's wrists and ankles were shackled and chained to the iron loop bolted to the floor between the chair's front legs. Dex grabbed hold of Fred's head and kept him looking forward.

"Open wide, Fred."

"I'll see you in hell," Fred spat out, and Dex was stunned by how quick Wolf moved. He jabbed Fred in the throat, and the guy let out a horrible gargling, gasping sound. Wolf stuck the pliers in Fred's mouth, and with a quick flick of his wrist, a tooth popped out onto the table.

Wolf picked up the tooth with his gloved hand and held it up to Dex. "L-pill."

"What?"

"Potassium cyanide, Dexter."

"Are you fucking kidding me, Fred? A suicide pill?" Dex smacked Fred on the side of the head. He frowned at Wolf. "Spies still do that shit?"

"It's a little more sophisticated these days. Eyeglasses, pens, tie pins, but yes, still widely used." Wolf turned his attention to Fred. "Of course, the whole point of being a spy, Fred, is to not get caught, but then I suppose you're more hired muscle with a slight payroll increase." Wolf patted Fred's cheek, hard. "Now that we've made certain Fred stays with us a little longer, let's get back to our chat."

Dex walked around the table and folded his arms over his chest. Fred glared at him, then at Wolf.

"Now, Fred," Wolf said pleasantly. "I'm not about to let you die before you give me something useful. Your organization is not coming for you. I can tell you that with certainty."

Fred scoffed. He leaned in to snarl at Wolf. "We can get to anyone."

"Now see, that's where you're wrong. Those fellows out there, as stuffy as they may be, can't be bought. I guarantee you that anyone who tries to get to you will be dealt with. Why? Because they only trust one another."

"They have family," Fred said, his grin smug.

"And you think after this little stunt you've pulled with Sergeant Maddock this lot have left their families out there waiting to be plucked by your friends?" Wolf tsked. "All the families have been moved to secure locations."

Dex frowned. How the hell did Wolf know that? Dex hadn't even known. It made perfect sense. It hadn't occurred to him that his friends' families would be in danger. Why would they be? The Makhai had wanted Hudson and Tony. Why would anyone else be a target? Now he knew. If the Makhai really wanted Fred back, they'd hit Destructive Delta where it hurt most. Why hadn't Sparks or anyone else mentioned it? It was possible Wolf was bluffing. He'd done it before and was an expert at concealing the truth. Either way, Dex would be looking into it as soon as they were done here. Speaking of done...

Dex turned to Wolf. "We need to move this along."

Wolf nodded. "You may want to stand back, darling. Don't want to get blood on that pretty face of yours." He looked up at Dex. "Why don't you step outside? I'll call you when he's ready to talk."

Dex shook his head. "I appreciate it, but I'm not going anywhere."

The Makhai were responsible for so much pain and suffering. They'd shattered his childhood, and Dex had been fortunate to end up in a loving home, raised by a man like Anthony Maddock. Dex wasn't going to let his dad down. Not only was he going to save his father, he was going to have retribution for what the Makhai had done.

"You two think you're going to scare me? I'm prepared to die."

"Who said anything about letting you die?" Wolf's grin betrayed the deadness in his eyes. His pupils were blown, leaving only a thin rim of blue. Dex braced himself. He'd brought Wolf in to do this. Not because he didn't have the balls or the stomach to do it himself, which was quite possible, since he'd never tortured anyone, but he didn't possess the skill. He didn't know how to cause Fred the right amount of pain to break him but not kill him. He knew pressure points. Knew where to hit Fred to incapacitate him, and yes, kill him, but not torture.

Wolf started with Fred's fingers, then he moved on to his teeth. The room filled with screams, sounds of choking, gagging, and gurgling. Wolf didn't so much as blink. He focused on his task and went about bringing Fred as much pain as possible. Dex wiped the sweat from his brow with the back of his gloved hand. His stomach churned on more than one occasion, but he pushed down the nausea each time. He had to get through this. When the room stank of blood, sweat, and piss and they had no information, Wolf spoke up.

"You're going to want to step outside for this, Dexter."

"I said I'm not going anywhere."

Wolf studied him, and Dex was stunned by the look of concern that came into Wolf's eyes. Wait, was it concern or something else? Before Dex could figure it out, Wolf reached inside his suit jacket and removed a familiar leather wrap. He placed it on the table and unrolled it. Dex sucked in a sharp breath, his blood turning to ice at the sight of the long thin needles.

Dex bolted for the door. He yanked it open, ignoring Sloane and everyone else. Dex took off down the hall, Sloane calling after him, but he didn't stop until his stomach decided to empty itself of what little was in there. He used the wall to support himself as he doubled over, his whole body shaking as he threw up to the sound of Fred's screams. *Oh God.* He'd screamed like that once.

A gentle hand came to rest on his back, and Sloane handed him a tissue. Dex wiped his mouth, tears streaming down his cheeks as it all flooded back. The excruciating pain, the terror, the desperation as he'd clung to the hope he'd survive to see Sloane and his family again.

"I'm so fucking stupid," he croaked. "I *asked* for this. I brought him here to do this and convinced myself I had the balls to follow through, but I couldn't... Just seeing those needles again... I couldn't stay in there." A sob tore through him, and Sloane wrapped Dex up in his strong arms. Dex buried his face against Sloane's chest as Sloane pressed his cheek to Dex's hair and tightened his hold on Dex.

"Dex, you're not stupid. There was no telling what

methods Wolf would use. After what you went through, *no one* expects you to be in there, and before you think this reflects on you or your ability to become a TIN operative, you're not Wolf. Sparks knows that. Whatever training Wolf may have received to do what he does, doesn't mean it'll be the same for us." Sloane pulled back and cupped Dex's face. "You're a good man, Dex, with the biggest heart of anyone I know. You're strong. Stronger than you give yourself credit for." He wiped the tears from Dex's cheeks with his thumb. "Feeling the way you do, not being in there, does *not* for one fucking second invalidate your conviction to find your father. Do you hear me?"

Dex nodded. He couldn't help his small smile as he wrapped his hands around Sloane's wrists, his voice quiet when he spoke. "You know me so well."

"So I've been saying," Sloane replied, placing a gentle kiss on Dex's forehead. "I'm right here, Dex, and I'm with you every step of the way."

"Dex?"

Dex wiped at his eyes and stepped out from behind Sloane to see Wolf standing outside the room.

"I believe he's ready to give you some answers."

There was no going back now. Dex understood what Austen had been trying to tell him. What Sparks had warned him of on several occasions. This wasn't a new skill Wolf picked up after he went rogue. This was a skillset TIN had trained him with, one he clearly had experience using to do what needed to be done. How many times had Dex condemned Sparks's actions? Just the other day, she'd asked him how far he was willing to go to protect those he cared about. He'd been quick to stand on his soapbox, criticizing TIN and their methods. He'd been so naïve. Now look at him. Despite what Sloane said, Dex had brought in a killer to do to Fred what had been done to him. What kind of man did that make him? What did it say about him that this was the path he'd chosen? Maybe Sloane was wrong. Maybe he and Wolf weren't all that different.

"Stop."

Sloane's harsh tone snapped Dex out of his thoughts, and he blinked up at Sloane, his chest tight at the heartache in Sloane's warm amber eyes.

"I mean it, Dex. You two are nothing alike, and neither are the situations that led Wolf to you and this guy. That mercenary in there may not have given the order to kill your parents, but he works for the men who did. He chose to cause pain and misery, to kidnap people, and make innocent people suffer. Maybe not all those people were innocent, but some were. Hudson is. Your parents were. They fought for what was right. Maybe they got in over their heads, but they didn't deserve to die for it. They shouldn't have been ripped from your life, from Tony's life. You did nothing to bring on what Wolf did to you, but this guy?" Sloane thrust a finger behind him to the room where Fred was. "If he hadn't been caught, he would have kept on hurting and killing. It's time for him to pay for what he's done."

Dex nodded. Sloane was right. The words may have been difficult to hear, but everything Sloane said was true. Dex thought about his parents, about how the reason they weren't going to be at his wedding was sitting in that room. How if he didn't get some answers, he was going to lose someone else he loved. He couldn't let that happen.

"You're right." Dex headed down the corridor to where Wolf stood. "I'm ready." And this time, he had no intention of backing out.

Wolf hesitated, looking as if he were going to say something, but instead turned and walked into the room. Dex followed, closing the door behind him. He was surprised to find the needles gone. Glancing at Wolf, Dex expected a teasing comment or snide remark, but received neither. Wolf stood quietly with his gloved hands clasped in front of him.

Dex focused his attention on Fred, who was violently shaking. "Give me something, Fred."

"The doctor," Fred replied, his voice hoarse from the screaming. Saliva dripped from his bloodied mouth, his tears mixing with the fluids on his face. "We were going to take the doctor to the theater."

"Keep going," Dex insisted.

"We… were… taking him… to an abandoned theater. In Borough Park. From there we'd keep moving him around the city until it was time to put him on a boat."

"Where were you going to move him after the theater?" Dex asked.

Fred shook his head, his entire body shivering uncontrollably and what was left of his teeth chattering. "I don't know. We'd receive a message the night before the move and would have to get him there by morning. Same thing would happen the next night. The guys are scheduled to change shifts every night, so no one knows where we'd been before that night or where we're going the next night."

"Except for you," Dex said. "You weren't going anywhere. That's why you had that nifty pill in your tooth."

Fred nodded.

"Were the rest of the locations likely to be abandoned?"

"Yeah. We use a lot of abandoned places because of how many there are. Most of them are condemned, full of crackheads or feral Therians. No one goes into those places, especially at night."

"Except you guys."

Wolf stepped up beside him. "You said 'put him on a boat.' Where?"

"I don't know."

"I'm getting tired of that reply, Fred." Wolf grabbed a power drill from the toolbox, then walked around the table. He placed it to Fred's leg.

"I swear! I don't know! Again, we'd get told right before, and then we'd move out. It's usually a shipping yard. We use containers to smuggle them out of the country."

Dex narrowed his eyes. "Them?"

"Anyone the Makhai needs to make disappear."

"Why did you try to kidnap Hudson?" Wolf asked.

Fred sneered at him. "They want their attack dog back."

"Oh, I don't like being called a dog, Fred. It upsets me." Wolf pressed the power drill button, and an agonized cry tore from Fred's throat.

"Fuck's sake, Wolf," Dex growled.

Wolf shrugged. He turned his attention back to Fred. "Explain."

"They wanted someone with your skills under their thumb and figured it was also good revenge for you reneging on your contract to kill Agent Daley. Two birds with one stone."

"And what exactly did they wish to do with my skills?"

"They..." Fred swallowed hard. He looked from Wolf to Dex and back. "After they got what they wanted from Sparks, they planned to use your brother to get you to torture Sergeant Maddock and then kill him."

Dex's blood ran cold. They were going to kill Tony anyway. What the hell was he thinking? Of course they were going to kill Tony. The Makhai wasn't going to just let him loose, especially after they got what they wanted. No, they'd string Sparks along until the damage to TIN was done and the Makhai was well and truly in control, and then they'd kill Tony.

"I swear, that's all I know. Please."

Wolf nodded. "I believe you, Fred." He placed the power drill in the toolbox, then pulled out his gun and shot Fred in the head.

Dex stared at him. "What the fuck did you just do?"

Wolf returned his gun to the holster inside his jacket. "Removed a loose end, Dexter. What were you planning on doing? Arresting him? You certainly couldn't hand him over to TIN, not with the Makhai on the inside. He had no more information. You arrest him and the Makhai would simply find him and do what I just did, only they'd make it look like he'd done it to himself. I saved the city time and money. Lucky for you, you happen to have the chief medical examiner just outside."

Wolf opened the door, and Dex ran after him.

Damn it, he should have known Wolf wasn't going to just walk away from Fred. He'd probably made the decision to kill the guy from the moment he'd agreed to interrogate him. Hell, maybe that was *why* he'd agreed to this whole thing, knowing that at the end he could end the guy's life. How much killing had Wolf done to feel no remorse for his actions? He didn't think twice about pulling the trigger and planting a bullet in Fred. Was that what TIN expected from Dex? From Sloane? Dex quickly shook those thoughts from his head. Right now, the only thing that mattered was finding his father. Everything else would have to wait.

"What happened?" Sloane asked the moment Wolf and Dex emerged from the interrogation room. The look on

Dex's face said it wasn't good. *Damn it.* Sloane had hoped that son of a bitch would give them something. One lead. They just needed a place to start.

"We got a lead," Dex said somberly, "but it's not much. I doubt they've taken Tony to where they were going to take Hudson, but we need to check it out anyway. They tried to kidnap Hudson so Wolf would do what they wanted."

"Which was what?" Hudson asked.

"After they got what they wanted from Sparks, they were going to get him to torture my dad and then kill him."

Sloane balled his hands into fists at his sides and told himself to breathe.

"And we're just going to let him walk out of here?" Ash asked, pointing to Wolf. "What if, God forbid, they manage to get their hands on Hudson? You really think Wolf isn't going to do exactly what they want him to do?"

Hudson looked horrified. He turned to his brother. "You will do nothing of the sort."

Wolf arched an eyebrow at him. His expression turned dark. "You expect me to do what? Stand by and allow them to kill you?"

"You honestly believe they won't kill me anyway? That they'll hold up their side of the deal? Like they plan to do with Sergeant Maddock? *I* will not be the source of someone else's grief, Alfie! Do you understand me?"

"And who bloody said I'd leave the decision to you?" Wolf growled at Hudson, crowding him menacingly.

Hudson held his head high. "You won't have a choice." There was no mistaking the conviction in Hudson's voice.

Wolf stared at him. "What are you saying?"

"I will not allow myself to be used to hurt someone I care about. Perhaps you forget who I am. Death is not your specialty alone, brother."

"You wouldn't dare."

"Try me."

Wolf turned to Seb. "Talk some sense into your bloody husband, will you?"

Seb swallowed hard, pain in his eyes. "I wish I could."

"What?"

"Come on, Wolf. You really think he's going to listen? If it was me, and I knew someone was going to use me to hurt Hudson or my brothers… I'd do the same."

Wolf looked around at everyone and their determined expressions. "I'm surrounded by fucking martyrs. Unbelievable."

"Are you saying you wouldn't do the same?" Dex asked. He stepped up to Wolf and put two fingers to the sides of his temple. It took everything Sloane had not to grab him and move him away from that asshole. "Someone puts a gun to your head and says to Hudson, 'kill your friends, or your brother dies,' what do you do? Do you let him do it, knowing what it will do to him? Knowing there's a chance he's going to turn into *you*?"

Wolf stilled. He closed his eyes and let out a sigh. When he opened them, he took hold of Dex's fingers, tucked them under his hand, and brought Dex's hand to his lips for a kiss. Dex arched an eyebrow at him. What the hell was this guy's deal? He was always flirting with Dex or finding an excuse to touch him. It drove Sloane, and his Felid half, insane.

"You're a very dangerous man, Dexter. I imagine you would be very bad for my reputation." He released Dex and headed for the exit. "You have your answers. I would move quickly."

"What are you going to do?" Dex called out after him.

"Seeing as how my little brother has some very stupid

ideas knocking around that annoying brain of his, I'm going to do what I do best. Find those who do not wish to be found. I'll be in touch. Keep the little wanker safe, will you?" He turned and winked at his brother. "Have fun cleaning up my mess for once."

"What's he on about?" Hudson turned to Dex.

"Wolf shot Fred. In the head."

Sloane groaned, and Hudson let out a slew of curses, but by the time he turned to look for Wolf, he was gone.

Dex put a hand on Hudson's shoulder. "We gotta go. You okay to handle this?"

"Yes. I'll get Nina to help."

"Okay." Sloane turned to Seb. "You stay with him. The only people we trust are family. Everyone else is considered a possible threat. You need backup."

"I'll get Dom and Rafe," Seb replied without hesitation.

Sloane nodded. He agreed with Seb's choices. Dom could be trusted, and Rafe was a given. Also, Rafe was just as fierce as Seb, if not more. He'd be one hell of an obstacle to get through if Seb went down. "We'll keep you posted. Destructive Delta, we're moving out." Sloane led his team down the corridor toward the exit, while Dex filled him in on the information they obtained before Wolf put a bullet in Fred's head. They joined up with Rosa, Letty, and Calvin, and together they made for the elevator and headed up to the garage where the BearCat was parked. Sloane opened the back doors, and everyone took their positions except for Dex, who grabbed a bottled water from the mini fridge, rinsed his mouth out, and spit it out into the small trash bin inside one of the compartments. Taking the bottle with him, he took a seat on the bench. Hobbs got behind the wheel, with Calvin buckling up in the passenger seat. Cael took a seat behind the security console, and everyone else took the bench. They buckled up, and Hobbs got them moving.

"Where are we heading?" Cael asked.

"Queens," Sloane replied. Dex shifted beside him, and Sloane quickly removed his phone from his pocket. He held it up so everyone could see it, then turned it off. He tapped his earpiece, the light turning from blue to red. Everyone pulled out their phones and did the same. Hobbs handed his phone to Calvin. Cael turned and powered down the security console. Once everyone's earpiece was off, Sloane spoke up. "No tech," Sloane reminded them. "We gotta go dark until we get some tech the Makhai can't use against us. No cell phones, no security console, no earpieces, no GPS, nothing. Hobbs, we're heading for Brooklyn. Off Eleventh Avenue and Forty-Sixth Street."

"Wow," Ash said with a whistle. "That's really specific, bro. How do you know where it is?"

Sloane shrugged and looked down at his gloved hands. "I know the area really well. I spent a lot of nights driving aimlessly through the streets. It's near Green-Wood Cemetery." Sloane gave Dex a small smile. "That's where Gabe is buried."

"You okay?" Dex put his arm around Sloane, and Sloane kissed his cheek.

"I am, sweetheart. I promise." It was the truth. Dex had played a major role in helping Sloane heal, and although he still missed Gabe, he was now able to draw fond memories rather than painful tragic ones.

They were making good time, despite traffic, and needed to get in there before the sun set. Not that he could recall the place having any windows. The old theater had been bustling with activity back in the twenties and had held some pretty epic concerts up until the seventies when the neighborhood got tired of the noise. Sadly, the place was falling apart. It had been owned by a furniture company once and used for storage. It was then sold to another furniture company, which also used it for storage. Considering the Makhai had planned to use it, even if it was for one evening, it most likely had been abandoned for some time.

Hobbs drove up Eleventh Avenue and made a left on Forty-Sixth Street. The old brick building looked pretty much like it had the last time Sloane had seen it, with the addition of some more scaffolding along the front and side. Back when he'd aimlessly roamed these streets, he'd felt a tinge of sadness whenever he'd gone by the old theater. Its façade showed remnants of elegant molding, and Sloane couldn't help but wonder what she must have looked like in her heyday. Now the building looked much like the hundreds of other abandoned places around the city, with its heavily boarded-up entrances and mismatched brickwork where windows had once been.

The BearCat came to a stop beside the theater, and Sloane unbuckled his belt. "Let's try to get in there as quietly as possible. We don't know what we're walking into. Our priority is the sarge. Once we're inside, turn your coms on and stay safe. Ready?"

Everyone nodded. They secured their helmets, then grabbed their rifles and shields. Sloane opened the back doors and jumped out. He waited for the rest of his team and then closed the doors. They fell into formation and quickly ran under the scaffolding. There were plenty of vans and commercial vehicles parked in the area, thanks to the lumberyard across the street and the surrounding businesses.

"It looks like it's scheduled to be demolished. I saw a banner back there," Cael said.

"That would explain why the Makhai picked it. They only needed it for one night." Sloane went straight for the back. It was very unlikely the Makhai were going to camp out on the other side of the building, which had been converted into a storefront some time ago, complete with large glass windows. No, if the Makhai were here, they would be on the other side of the wall, where the rest of the theater remained untouched. They reached a set of heavy metal doors. "Ash, help me out here." Ash joined him, and Sloane took hold of one door while Ash took the other. "Lift and pull." They did, and the doors opened. They exchanged glances.

"Well, that's a good sign," Ash murmured before returning to formation. Sloane motioned for them to follow, and he raised his rifle, keeping an eye out for any movement as they entered the makeshift alley. More scaffolding and an aluminum roof had been placed between the buildings, with heavy mesh and a string of lightbulbs. Sloane would hazard a guess that this was the entrance the demolition crew intended to use before they brought the whole thing down. To his left there was another set of double doors. This one wasn't locked either. The hairs on the back of Sloane's neck stood on end as he reached for the handle.

"What's wrong?" Dex asked from behind him.

"I don't know," he said. "Something doesn't feel right." It wasn't just the convenience of finding no locks on either set of doors. His gut was telling him something was off. He checked around the doors, the hinges, the frame, looking for any trip wires or any evidence of something suspicious, but he found nothing.

"Do you want to find another way in?" Dex asked.

Sloane shook his head. "Everyone, stand back." Gripping the handle tight, he carefully inched the door open.

Nothing. He opened it and motioned for Hobbs to come forward and check it out.

Hobbs stepped in, rifle at the ready. He quickly checked the area, his sharp eyes not missing anything. Hobbs knew exactly what to look for. He inspected the walls, the ceiling, the floor, checked the dust, the splintered boards, everywhere. He sniffed the air and then turned to Sloane, shaking his head.

"Okay." Sloane nodded, and Hobbs rejoined the formation. "Area's clear," Sloane said, motioning for his team to follow. They headed through the dilapidated corridor, the walls plastered with old fliers and posters, the floor still littered with old ticket stubs and candy wrappers. Sloane held his rifle at the ready, his Therian vision helping him see into the shadows. He listened for any sounds that shouldn't be there. So far there was no movement. They reached the door that led out into the orchestra level of the theater, and Sloane turned. He signaled for Ash, Letty, Hobbs, and Calvin to take the stairs up to the balcony level. If there was any trouble down below, he wanted his sniper up there with a full view of everything and everyone. Ash, Letty, and Hobbs would provide cover for Calvin, should he need it. The rest of the team would go in with Sloane.

The old blue doors had seen better days. They were rotting, the paint crackled and chipped. Pieces of the decorative molding had broken off over the years. Sloane took hold of one handle and motioned for Dex to take the other. He mouthed the words "on three," and Dex nodded.

Sloane counted down on his fingers, and on three, they opened the doors with a loud creak. Sloane cringed, but there was no way around it. This place had been built in the twenties and abandoned decades ago. What was left of it was crumbling around them. Sloane quickly took the lead once more, and the rest of the team entered behind him and spread out into the orchestra pit filled with broken furniture, debris, and empty boxes. They each checked a section, making sure there was no one hiding behind the mountains of rubble and garbage. Each one of his teammates came back with the same reply. The area was clear.

"Sloane."

Dex's tone had Sloane running over, and he gently put his hand on Dex's shoulder when he saw the weathered black leather bomber jacket hanging from the back of a bloodstained chair.

"That's Tony's," Dex said, reaching out to take the jacket, then hesitating. There was a note sticking out of the front breast pocket. Dex pulled it out and opened it for them to read.

Predictable. Nice try. We'll say hi to dad for you.

Dex crushed the paper in his hand. Before he could reply, Ash shouted from the balcony.

"Everybody out!"

Sloane grabbed the jacket and Dex. They turned to run as a *boom* shook the theater. Sloane's eyes widened as the balcony popped up and for a moment, Ash, Calvin, Hobbs, and Letty were floating before everything came down.

"Ash!" Sloane took off, a cloud of dust smacking into him when the balcony hit the floor. Pieces of rubble flew out in different directions, chunks of plaster and wall. Sloane coughed and covered his nose and mouth with his arm as he walked through the fog. Somewhere behind him, he heard Cael shouting for Ash and the rest of the team calling to the others.

"Up here!" Ash coughed, and Sloane took a step back, looking up. As the dust began to settle, he could make out several hanging dark shadows. Dex, Cael, and Rosa stood beside Sloane. A tiny section of balcony remained, the chunk of concrete holding a row of chairs hung precariously from several steel rods that had bent downward but not broken. Ash was clutching one of the chairs, Letty wrapped around his waist and legs, and Calvin hanging by one arm from the strap of Ash's rifle, which was thankfully strapped to Ash's vest.

"Ethan!" Calvin called as he tried to get purchase.

"Fuck." Sloane looked around. He'd seen a mattress somewhere around here. "There! Guys, grab that mattress and bring it over." It was a mighty small target to hit if Calvin fell, but it was better than the jagged slabs of concrete. If anyone could make it, it would be Calvin. As the rest of the team went for the mattress, Sloane kept his attention on Ash and the others.

Hobbs was in the doorway on solid ground, kneeling and quickly pulling out the grappling rope from his backpack. He secured it to himself, then around an exposed beam in the wall. He jerked on it, and seeming satisfied it would hold his weight, he turned, and as quickly as possible, rappelled down the wall to the hanging piece of balcony.

Dex, Cael, and Rosa returned with the mattress. They placed it where they thought Calvin would land. It wasn't an exceptionally long way to fall, but with all the dangerous debris on the floor, it could cause some serious injury.

Hobbs placed a boot on the edge of the broken structure, and it shook. Ash cursed, and Calvin cried out, the pain from hanging from one arm jolting him. Hobbs pressed his lips together and shook his head. It wasn't going to work. Ash looked up at Hobbs, and Hobbs motioned downward and made a swinging motion.

"Shit." Sloane took a deep breath.

"What's going on? What's he going to do?" Dex asked.

"He's going to come down fast and swing toward Ash. Ash is going to have to grab him on the first attempt and make sure he gets a good grip or they're all coming down. The section they're on won't hold Hobbs's weight, and there's no time for me to get up there and get them down." Dust was raining down from the chunk of balcony, and the crumbling sounds told him all he needed to know. Sloane held his breath, and Hobbs counted down on his fingers.

On three, Hobbs sped down the rope and swung right, making sure he was lower so when Ash fell, he wouldn't miss Hobbs. Gasps were heard all around as Ash and everyone hanging on to him fell. Ash latched on to Hobbs's vest with both gloved hands. Everyone bounced and shouted, but they held on tight.

"Everyone okay?" Sloane called out.

"Peachy," Ash replied with a growl. "Get us the fuck out of here, Hobbs."

Hobbs planted his feet against the balcony, and Sloane ushered everyone to the doors they'd come in from. The balcony was about to come down. They ran for the stairs leading up to the balcony, and Sloane placed Tony's jacket on the floor to one side so he could grab the rope.

"Everyone pull," Sloane ordered. Dex, Cael, and Rosa all grabbed the rope with him and heaved. Sloane gritted his teeth, his muscles straining. They each took one step back at a time, one foot first, then the other. If Dex hadn't been part Therian, there was no way they would have been able to pull up Hobbs, Ash, and their two Human teammates. As strong as Cael was, Sloane would have been doing most of the heavy lifting, and Hobbs would have been challenge enough.

As soon as Hobbs's shoulders were up, they grabbed him and carefully pulled him in through the doorway until he could rest his arms on the floor before Sloane. They all clipped their rappelling ropes to his vest and secured them around the exposed beams to each side of him. They held on to the ropes just in case. Sweat dripped down Sloane's face. When Hobbs was secure, Sloane leaned over.

"Cal, you need to climb up!"

Calvin cursed under his breath and let out a pained growl as he swung himself and grabbed onto Ash's vest with his other hand. He let his head rest against Ash for a second before he started to climb up Ash, then Ethan. When he was close enough to reach, Sloane grabbed him by the vest and hauled him inside.

"You're next, Letty," Sloane called down.

Letty climbed up Ash, then Hobbs, and when she was close, Sloane pulled her in as well.

"Ash, buddy, come on." Sloane prepared himself as Ash climbed up Hobbs. He crouched down, feet firmly planted on the ground as he grabbed hold of Ash's vest and pulled hard, Ash landing on Sloane as he hit the floor.

"Fuck," Ash said, breathless. He patted Sloane's cheek and rolled off him before pushing himself to his feet. It was a group effort getting Hobbs up. "Jesus, pal," Ash grumbled. "How much do you fucking weigh now? Because it's definitely more than before."

"It's all the training," Calvin said as he tried to catch his breath. "He's over three hundred now." Hobbs flicked Calvin's ear. "Ouch, what? It's true. Besides, it's all muscle, Ethan." He rubbed his arm, and Hobbs fussed over him, checking him over and touching his arm. Calvin grumbled, but it betrayed the gentleness in his eyes. "I'm fine. Just sore." Hobbs wrapped an arm around Calvin's shoulders and brought him up against his much larger frame.

"Let's get the hell out of here," Sloane said, grabbing

Tony's jacket and handing it to Dex, his voice soft when he spoke. "They're gone."

"Is that...?" Letty didn't finish her sentence, her eyes on Tony's jacket.

"Yeah," Dex replied gruffly. He turned and walked off. Sloane let him go on ahead, knowing Dex needed some time on his own. He followed several steps behind, with the rest of the team close by.

Ash walked beside Sloane, talking quietly. "They knew we were coming."

"Yeah, they left a note." Sloane told Ash what the note said, agreeing with Ash's curses. "I doubt they were here long. The bloodstains on the seat looked pretty fresh. I didn't have time to really look."

"Fuck. Now what?"

That was a good question. They had no leads, no van, no Makhai to interrogate, and they were running out of time.

CHAPTER NINE

DEX STARED down at the jacket in his hands. His father's jacket. Had the bloodstains on the chair come from Tony? They'd looked relatively fresh. Had Tony been there, or were the Makhai just playing games? They'd known Dex would be there. That's why they'd left the note. Taunting him. Dex pulled off his helmet and threw it against the wall.

"That son of a bitch is toying with us!"

"Dex."

Dex kicked at the scaffolding's metal bars. "Motherfucker! Son of a fucking bitch!"

"Agent Daley!"

Dex jerked to a halt. He blinked at Sloane, then looked around him at the gathering crowd of pedestrians. Shit. Clearing his throat, he held up a hand. "Sorry. I'm sorry."

"Hobbs, check the truck. I'm not taking any chances. As soon as it's clear, we head back to HQ." Sloane handed Dex his helmet and pulled Dex to one side, turning him toward the building so his bigger frame blocked the onlookers' view of him. Despite his closeness and his hand on Dex's arm, it just looked like he was having a quiet word with a team member rather than a lover. "I need you to keep it together, sweetheart. I know it's shitty of me to ask you that, but we need to keep our heads if we're going to find Tony. Yes, this is a setback, but we've been in tight spots before. We'll find something."

Dex nodded. He was pissed. No, he was beyond pissed. It was bad enough his father was in the hands of murderers; now they were taunting him, throwing his failures in his face. Dex swallowed hard, and he met Sloane's gaze, allowing the love and support he saw there to wash over him, to bring some calm to his turmoil.

"We got nothing, Sloane."

"So we go back to HQ, follow up with Sparks, and see what's happening on her end. I'm guessing the Chairman's been in touch. Then we check in with Austen and see where he and his CIs are on locating that van. We can start with that and go from there, okay?" Sloane pulled their heads together, and Dex closed his eyes. He took a few deep breaths. When he was ready, he opened his eyes.

"Okay."

"Dex?"

Dex turned to find his brother standing there, his gaze on the jacket in his hand. "Hey, Chirpy," Dex said softly, walking to Cael.

"That's Dad's, isn't it?"

"Yeah," Dex replied quietly. As much as he didn't want to add to his brother's worry, he was done hiding the truth from Cael. "We found it on a chair inside. There were bloodstains. They looked fresh. I don't know if the blood was Dad's or if the Makhai are just fucking with us, but..." Dex swallowed hard, and Cael sucked in a sharp breath, followed by another. Dex quickly pulled him into a hug, murmuring in his ear, "We're going to find him, okay? He's stronger than those assholes realize. This is Dad we're talking about. He survived our teenage years, so he can survive anything."

Cael sniffed and let out a quiet laugh. "You mean *your* teenage years. I never stole his car to go on a date with a junior when I was fourteen."

Dex pulled back. He shrugged and held back a grin. "I didn't steal it. I was borrowing it. Besides, you never would have reached the pedals at fourteen." Dex winked at him and laughed when Cael shoved him, grumbling under his breath that he was a jerkface.

Cael returned to Ash's side, his anxiety visibly easing as Ash once again occupied his attention. Dex's smile fell away, exhausted by the pretense.

After Hobbs cleared the truck, having scanned it for any devices that didn't belong there or any signals out of the ordinary, they all climbed in and headed back to HQ. Everyone was quiet, and Dex held a tight grip on his father's jacket. Sloane was right. He had to keep his shit together.

~

Back at HQ, they dropped their gear off in the armory before heading upstairs to the locker rooms for a quick wash while they waited for their meeting with Sparks. After the announcement went out in the media about the changes to Destructive Delta, she'd been inundated with phone calls. The timing was shit-tacular. Dex stood in front of his open locker, staring at his father's jacket hanging neatly on the wooden hanger.

"Dex?" Sloane came to stand beside Dex and put a hand on his shoulder.

Dex smiled sadly as he motioned to the jacket. "It was John's, you know."

"The jacket belonged to your dad?"

"Yeah. The right pocket has a hole. Tony says he was always bitching at Dad to get it fixed because of course that was the pocket that my father kept shoving all his change into. The coins would fall into the lining, and whenever they had to chase someone down, Dad would jingle and give their position away. It drove Tony batshit crazy." Dex slipped his hand into the pocket, his lashes growing wet as he laughed softly. "The hole's still there."

"And Tony never gave it to you?" Sloane asked gently.

Dex shook his head. "He tried to, a long time ago, but I could see how much it meant to him. Besides, my dad had given it to him after my mom bought him a new one for Christmas." Dex's jaw muscles tightened. "That was the one he'd been wearing when he was killed. Tony couldn't bear to see it. John's blood had soaked into the leather." Dex slammed the locker shut. "Let's go talk to Sparks."

The team was waiting for them outside, and together they headed for Sparks's office. The door was open, and she motioned for them to enter. As soon as they were in, she put the room into privacy mode.

"Is that going to work?" Cael asked.

Sparks nodded. "I have a small team of operatives who I trust with my life. I had them install a new system. It'll take the Makhai weeks to break through it, so we have some time." She reached behind her desk and pulled out a metal case. After placing it on the desk, she opened it. There were eight earpieces and eight cell phones. "Everyone take an earpiece and a phone. Seb, Hudson, Rafe, and Dom have already received theirs." She tapped the one she was wearing. "These are secure and use a private tower, which will keep the Makhai guessing. The same software has been installed in your BearCat's security console. Unfortunately, Themis is still compromised."

"What about everyone's families?" Dex asked, not mentioning it was Wolf who'd brought up the information. "What if the Makhai decide to go after them to get to one of us?"

"Several hours ago, I had everyone moved to a secure location under the guise of official THIRDS protocol concerning a possible threat to their safety due to a sensitive case your team is working. I assured them you were all well and would see them as soon as you were able. They're safe."

"And what about the Chairman? Has he been in touch?" Dex asked.

"Yes. So far he's instructed me to upload whatever is on this drive. It arrived by courier an hour ago." She placed a small black USB fob on the desk. "I've managed to deter him for a few hours since the fob needs to be plugged into one of TIN's servers. One only I have access to. Fortunately for us, I can't get to any of our facilities due to the current media frenzy over today's announcement."

A thought struck Dex. "Wait, you made sure the announcement went out. You were buying us time."

Sparks nodded. "Under the current circumstances, the announcement would have been canceled. I made certain it wasn't, making it look like a clerical error. Based on the intel we have on the Makhai, I knew whatever they had in mind was a long time coming, and they're not about to risk everything by having me go out there with all this media attention. They've waited years. I'm sure they'll wait a few hours until things die down. The PR department is handling everything, but several news stations want to hear from me. I've bought us several hours, twelve at most."

That was a few more hours that Tony would be safe. They needed to make the most of that time. Dex looked up at Sparks. "Have you learned anything about this Chairman asshole?"

"From the small amount of intel I've managed to gather, I believe he's the one in charge, which would mean everything orchestrated by the US branch of the Makhai has happened because of this Chairman. If we find him, we can cause the Makhai some serious damage."

"Any luck figuring out who he is?" Sloane asked.

Sparks shook her head. "Nothing. It's very possible the Chairman is one of the founding members of the Makhai. No one knows who he is or what he does outside his role as 'the Chairman.' What I do know is we're getting close. That's why they're hitting us hard. As calm as the Chairman seems, I'm thinking he's starting to get desperate. With Moros gone, along with several of their associates, and Wolf not only working with us but against the Makhai, I think the Chairman is getting worried."

"Good. He better be fucking worried." Dex studied Sparks. She looked like she wanted to say something but wasn't sure. "What? You want to say something."

Sparks let out a heavy sigh and took a seat behind her desk. "This is bigger than we imagined and possibly connected to the events of 2005."

Dex's brows drew together. "What happened in 2005?"

"My team and I were on our way to seize a Therian we believed played a major role in the Makhai. Someone in our organization warned them we were coming. They were waiting for us. I was almost killed. One of our top operatives wasn't so lucky. It was also the day Fang became Wolf."

"You're talking about when Wolf's partner, Tucker, was killed?"

"Yes. We need to find the Chairman and get him to divulge who his contacts at TIN are. Until then, I'm afraid we have to be careful with our intel."

"Any word from Austen?" Ash asked.

Sparks looked at her watch. "He should be calling in three, two..."

Sloane's new cell phone rang, and he picked up. "Hello? Hold on, I'm going to put you on speaker. Yes, area's secure." Sloane tapped the phone, and Austen's voice came over the line.

"I found the van."

"What? Where?" Dex asked, ready to head out.

"Sorry, Dex. Place has been wiped clean. I swept the place myself from top to bottom. They cleaned it good."

"Fuck," Dex spat out. He was getting sick and tired of this.

"Hold your horses, Daley. I said we were down, not out. The place was cleaned professionally not too long ago. The smell was strong and really familiar. I remember another location we checked out having the same smell. It was one of the locations given to us by Moros's associates. While I was combing the place, I found a small droplet of cleaning solution someone had left behind. A reliable contact of mine is analyzing it as we speak. He'll be able to get us the formula and a breakdown of all the ingredients because my guess is this compound can't be bought at your local supermarket."

"Which means we should be able to trace and cross-reference it," Dex said, trying not to get too excited. "Nice job, Austen. How long until we have that information?"

"It's going to take two to three hours at least. I'll be sure to call you."

Damn it. "Thanks, Austen. I appreciate it." Austen

hung up, and Dex turned to Sloane. "We need to look into abandoned places around the city. Anything that's seen unusual activity."

Before Sloane could reply, Sparks spoke up. "All available units were sent out and are questioning anyone who might have seen anything unusual, but there are dozens upon dozens of abandoned locations in this city, not to mention a vast amount of camera footage to analyze. It's going to take time. I've also put out a call to THIRDS HQ in Princeton, New Jersey and in Philadelphia. They've sent out several units as well. It's very possible they've moved Maddock out of the city but are still keeping him close. For now, I need you all to get some food in you and discuss the next course of action."

Dex was ready to protest, but Sparks put up her hand to stop him.

"It's getting late. None of you ate properly after your shifts at the park. I'm surprised you're still standing. Dex, you haven't eaten at all. None of you will be any good to Maddock if you're not at your best. Shower, eat, and when you're done, you're each scheduled for a brief session with Dr. Winters."

The room filled with groans.

"Are you kidding me?" Dex shook his head in disbelief. "We don't have time for that."

"What do we need to see the doc for?" Ash grumbled.

Sparks's brows shot up. "Do you want me to make you a list?"

Ash glowered at her, and Sparks's expression softened.

"I'm sorry, that was insensitive and uncalled for. It's been... a challenge for all of us. Maddock's abduction is officially a THIRDS case. As you all know, anyone connected to Sergeant Maddock can volunteer to see Dr. Winters.

However, in the case of Destructive Delta, it's protocol and not an option. He's your sergeant, and in Dex and Cael's case, a parent. Dr. Winters has to sign each of you off after your sessions or the team will be pulled from the case. As it was, I had to fight to keep you lead on this. If it weren't for the respect everyone has for Sergeant Maddock and their desire to see him found alive, they would never have allowed Destructive Delta to work this case. It's not my call."

"And if I don't get cleared," Dex said, leaning his hands on her desk to meet her gaze. "You think I'm going to just step aside and let someone take lead on this?"

Sparks let out a heavy sigh. "We all know better than that, Dex. Please, just see Dr. Winters. It's not as if he isn't familiar with you or the rest of the team, and he knows how important this time is for you, which is why he's made an exception and is keeping the sessions short. Give him a chance. Emotions are running high right now. Maybe he can help with that."

Damn it. He didn't have time for this. Instead of being out there in the streets, he had to be sitting on a couch, sharing his feelings with a shrink. As soon as he thought that, he felt like shit. It wasn't Dr. Winters's fault. The guy was just doing his job. Dex liked the doc, he really did. The guy was always there with a smile and word of encouragement. Dex probably spent as much time in Dr. Winters's office as he had in the principal's office when he was a kid. Hmm... interesting.

"Fine." Dex took the room off privacy mode and stormed out, the others following behind. They headed for the locker room, everyone lost in their own thoughts. They agreed to meet in the canteen after a quick shower. He stood under the showerhead, hoping the hot water would ease some of the tension in his muscles, but that didn't help. When he was done, he brushed his teeth to get rid of the nasty taste in his mouth, changed into a clean uniform, and walked with Sloane to the elevator. Forty-eight hours until their rehearsal dinner. The wedding was in less than ninety-six.

"I'm not hungry," Dex grumbled, tapping his fingers against his thighs. He was jittery as hell, like he was going to crawl out of his skin if he didn't do something, but there was nothing he could do. The elevator was empty, so Sloane stepped in front of him.

"Hey, look at me."

Dex did. He looked up into Sloane's amber eyes filled with pain and sorrow. Dex didn't want to see pain there. They'd been so happy just a few short days ago. He wanted that back. He wanted his father and his fucking life back.

"Talk to me."

Dex shook his head. "I have all this anger and energy inside me that's just building and building, and I don't know what the hell to do with it, Sloane. And now I have to sit around for hours, talking instead of doing, and I feel like I'm going to go out of my fucking head." The elevator doors opened, and Dex swept past Sloane. He knew Sloane wanted to help, but talking wasn't going to help him, and now he had to sit and talk for who knew how fucking long. He couldn't lose his shit with Winters. He had to prove he was in control, that he could do this, that it wasn't all crashing down on top of him.

"You sit," Sloane said softly. "I'll get you something to eat."

"Thanks," Dex replied, summoning a smile. He took a seat at the table, and he could tell everyone was trying not to look at him. They were his friends, his family. They knew him well by now. They all talked quietly among themselves. Cael was quiet across from him, and even Ash looked worried. Sloane put a tray in front of Dex. There was a Therian-sized burger, a chocolate milkshake, and a blue frosted cupcake. Dex frowned at the cupcake. "Maybe I should call Lou and call the whole thing off."

The piercing blow to Sloane's heart was unexpected, as the words that had come out of Dex's mouth had been. Sloane swallowed hard. He turned to Dex and took hold of his hand.

"You know that I'll support you on whatever you decide, but if you make this decision, it can't be because you're giving up. That I won't allow."

Dex's jaw muscles worked, but he didn't tear his gaze away from the damn cupcake. Sloane had hoped to cheer him up a little, but instead he'd made things worse.

"Dex?" Sloane took hold of his chin and turned his head to meet his gaze. The grief and heartache in his big blue eyes was like a punch to the gut, but he wasn't going to let Dex give up. Wasn't even going to let Dex so much as *think* about giving up. "Now you listen here. We have been to hell and back together. We've faced all kinds of ugly out there and come back with scars, some of which can't be seen, but we have *always* had one another's back, and that sure as hell is not going to change now. Your dad is one of the strongest men I know, and so are you. We're going to find him, and he's going to make that damned speech in four days and be nervous and grumpy and curse and rant about fucking index cards." Dex laughed, and Sloane kissed his cheek. "I know it seems like none of us can catch a break, but this will end soon, baby, I promise. We'll get through this."

Dex nodded, a wobbly smile on his face. He turned and peeled the film off his cupcake before tearing it in two and giving Sloane half.

"Thank you." Sloane took it with a smile.

They ate, and Sloane was grateful for the team distracting Dex and Cael by bringing up all the hilarious shit Tony loved to rant about. Nobody did ranting like Tony. It was epic. Especially since Tony didn't consider himself funny. The man had no idea how hilarious he was. He genuinely hated colored index cards, though not as much as zucchini noodles. Good grief, the man could go on for hours about vegetable noodles.

Once they were done eating, they headed for the elevator. "The second we hear from Austen, we move out. In the meantime, Ash, I want you to get a list from Sparks of all the teams that are out scouting locations. Rosa, Letty, Cael, I want you to contact each of their team leaders and find out where they've been and who they've talked to. Have them send the info to your phones rather than Themis."

Calvin pulled his phone out of his pocket and sighed. "Just got a text from Dr. Winters. Looks like I'm up first."

Sloane nodded as he held the elevator doors open for his team. "Soon as you finish, you take over for whoever's up next. Same goes for everyone else. By the time we get intel from Austen, I want to have a list of places that have been cleared, a list of where everyone's heading next, and a list of places no one's been to yet. We're covering a lot of ground here."

On the ride up to Unit Alpha, Dex had become restless again. He was tapping his fingers against his legs, worrying his bottom lip with his teeth, and couldn't seem to spend longer than a few seconds in one spot. This wasn't good for any of them. As they headed into Unit Alpha, Sloane took hold of Dex's arm.

"We'll catch up with you guys. Call me if you find something."

Everyone headed off, and Sloane walked Dex through the bullpen, past the conference rooms, and around the corner toward the corridor leading to the sleeper bays.

"Sloane? What are you doing? I hope you're not about to suggest I take a nap."

"And lose my spots?" Sloane shook his head. "No sleeping." He opened the door to one of the empty bays and nudged Dex inside. He closed the door behind them and locked it.

"Sloane, I know you're worried, but this isn't—"

Sloane brought Dex up against the door, his knee shoved between Dex's legs and his mouth all over Dex.

"I want you to fuck me," Sloane growled, sucking Dex's earlobe into his mouth. "I think we could both use the release."

A shiver went through Dex, and he nodded, his lips on Sloane's. The heat coming off his sexy partner was driving Sloane crazy, along with his heady scent, the taste of his lips, and the feel of his breath against Sloane's skin. Sloane allowed Dex to take the lead and walked backward toward the bed until the back of his legs hit the mattress, and then he sat. He reached down and took hold of Dex's boot, lifting it up so he could undo the laces, his eyes never leaving Dex's.

Molten amber spread into the blue, and Sloane hurried, pulling off Dex's boots, then his own. Dex quickly undressed, while Sloane did the same. There was no time to waste. They were frantic to get their hands on each other, and when Dex was naked in front of him, Sloane pulled him close so he could keep his hands on all that delicious skin. He gazed up reverently at Dex, astounded by the wonder that was this amazing man.

"I love you so much," Dex said softly, caressing Sloane's jaw.

"I love you too." Sloane waited for Dex to say whatever was clearly on his mind. Dex motioned between them.

"This here, us, is home. Wherever we are, no matter what's going on, we do our best to leave the world out there, and in here it's just you, me, and our love for each other. I know it won't always be possible, but you're my sanctuary, Sloane, and I need that. I need to have my home to come back to after whatever it is we face out there, and I need to know I'll be the same for you."

Sloane took hold of Dex's hand and brought it to his lips for a kiss before placing it over his heart. "I promise."

Dex's smile was glorious, and Sloane pulled Dex onto his lap, needing to kiss him, to feel their bodies pressed together. This time, their kiss was slow and sweet, filled with promises and trust. There was no one he had more faith in than the man right here in his arms. For the rest of his life, Dex would be who he turned to first, who he confided in, and who he asked for help when he needed it. Dex would shelter him, protect his heart, and love him.

Sloane pulled away, and Dex got up so Sloane could move back on the bed. Dex crawled over him, their lips once again locked in a passionate kiss, their tongues tangling and savoring. It was slow, like they had all the time in the world even though they only had a few minutes. Dex laced his fingers with Sloane's and moved his arms above his head. He spread Sloane's legs, and Sloane brought his knees up. Dex left him long enough to grab the packet of lube from his tac pants before returning to him and kissing him.

Even with this being about them needing release, it didn't diminish their love for each other. Sometimes they made love. It was sweet and sexy and amazing. Sometimes they were both horny and needed to get their hands on their mate, and sometimes they just needed a good hard fuck. Dex trailed scorching kisses down Sloane's chin to his neck and down his chest. He scraped his nails across Sloane's skin, running his fingers down every curve of muscle and every dip. Sloane wanted to close his eyes, to lose himself in the sensations Dex was bringing him, but instead he watched Dex, memorizing the way his blond hair fell over his brow, the flush on Dex's skin, the plumpness of his sweet lips, and the heat Dex left behind with every kiss he placed against Sloane's skin. Dex wasn't just going to fuck him, he was worshipping him, pouring his heart and soul into every kiss.

The tear of the lube packet was followed by cool liquid against Sloane's hole as Dex pushed one finger in. Sloane hissed at the intrusion, wriggling underneath Dex as Dex continued to drive him wild with his mouth. Sloane's cock was hard, jutted up against his stomach, and he groaned when Dex licked at the pearl of precome at Sloane's rosy tip. He sucked the head of Sloane's cock into his mouth, and Sloane bucked underneath him. A second finger joined the first, and Sloane couldn't help but release a low moan. He slipped his fingers back into Dex's hair, stroking softly as Dex's hot mouth moved on Sloane, swallowing Sloane down to the root before moving back up.

"Dex," Sloane pleaded, tugging at Dex's hair. Dex took the hint, moving up to kiss Sloane, his fingers still working Sloane's entrance, stretching him. Sloane grabbed a pillow from beside his head and lifted his hips to slip it underneath him. He wrapped his legs around Dex's waist, and Dex replaced his fingers with his cock. Sloane groaned into Dex's mouth as the initial burn gave way, and pleasure rippled through Sloane's body as Dex began to move inside him. Sloane wrapped his arms around Dex to keep him from moving away. Sloane loved having Dex's weight on him, loved feeling the strength of the man in his arms. He ran his hands down the delicious curve of Dex's spine to cup Dex's ass, digging his fingers into his plump cheeks.

Not long ago, he would have held himself back, not just physically but emotionally. Now he left himself completely exposed. His heart was right there between them, vulnerable, open for Dex to do with as he pleased. He'd bared his soul to Dex, put what little faith he'd had at the time in Dex. It was terrifying how easily Dex could shatter him.

"I'm yours, always," Sloane whispered, nuzzling Dex's temple before placing a kiss behind Dex's ear. He inhaled deep, allowing Dex's scent to envelop him. There was nothing like the scent of his mate. Dex's muscles pulled and strained as he moved.

Dex moved back enough to look down at Sloane, an almost shy smile on his face. His cheeks were flushed, his kiss-swollen lips slightly parted. Sloane ran a thumb over one of Dex's thick eyebrows.

"You're so beautiful."

Dex kissed him, his movements growing quicker, their panting breaths the only sounds in the room. Sloane held on tight to Dex, his head thrown back as Dex snapped his hips. Dex nipped at his exposed neck, then followed up with a kiss. He drove himself deep into Sloane, their bodies moving together, their skin flushed and beaded with sweat. At that moment, nothing existed outside the two of them.

"Sloane," Dex breathed, his face a study in pure ecstasy.

"Do it," Sloane growled, urging Dex to take what he

needed. Dex pulled out and flipped Sloane over onto his stomach. He looked at Dex over his shoulder, moaning at the sight of Dex stroking himself, his bottom lip between his teeth, before he parted Sloane's ass cheeks.

"Fuck, your ass is a thing of beauty."

"Fuck my ass is what I'm waiting on."

Dex leaned in to pull Sloane's earlobe between his teeth before murmuring, "Who's in charge here?"

"You are," Sloane said with a groan. "Please."

Dex hummed and ran a hand over Sloane's flank before slapping his ass cheek, leaving him tingling. Sloane sucked in a sharp breath and arched his back in response.

"Fuck me, Dex. Please."

Dex pressed himself to Sloane's back, rubbing his cock against Sloane's crease. "Tell me what you want."

"I *need* you to fuck me."

"How bad?"

"I need your cock inside me so fucking bad. I want to feel you for hours."

"Baby, you're going to be feeling me for days." Dex drove himself inside Sloane, and Sloane cried out. He grabbed fistfuls of the bedsheets, and Dex plastered himself to Sloane's back, one arm around Sloane's neck, his free hand grabbing a handful of Sloane's hair as he pounded Sloane into the mattress, his thrusts deep and hard.

"Oh, fuck. *Fuck*," Sloane growled, his fingers digging into Dex's forearm. The sound of skin slapping against skin filled the room, and Sloane was grateful for the soundproofing. Not to mention the Therian-size bed that rocked beneath them. Dex's hips lost their rhythm, his panting breath in Sloane's ear as he lost himself in fucking Sloane. He snapped his hips once more, and Dex turned Sloane's head, bringing their mouths together as Dex came inside him, his body trembling with his release. After one final hard thrust, he turned Sloane onto his back and swallowed Sloane's cock. When Dex slipped his finger between Sloane's cheeks and along the trail of come, Sloane's release exploded through him. He cried out, his muscles tightening and his toes curling. He came inside Dex's mouth, and Dex took all of him. When he was done, he licked his lips and moved up Sloane's body, letting his head rest against Sloane's.

"When I'm with you, it's like the world slows down and I can just... be. You ground me, Sloane. I'd be lost without you."

Dex's body trembled, and Sloane smiled lazily as Dex moved down to lay his head on Sloane's chest. Sloane wrapped an arm around Dex's back and absently stroked Dex's shoulder.

"We should clean up and get dressed," Sloane said, chuckling at Dex's groan.

"But I'm so comfy."

"What if I make it worth your while?"

"I'm listening."

"How about if you get up, I do all the work, and when this is all over, I'll bring you breakfast in bed."

There was a pause.

"Death Star pancakes?"

Sloane held back a smile, relieved to have his Dex back. "You got it."

"You sure make it tough for a guy to be lazy," Dex grumbled, pushing up onto his elbows. He gave Sloane's lips a quick kiss. "But I like you anyway."

"I'm glad to hear it."

Dex climbed off the bed, and Sloane rolled onto his side,

propping himself on his elbow as he admired Dex's lean muscular frame while he stretched.

"And you make me pancakes."

"There is that," Sloane replied, amused. He got up and smacked Dex's ass before darting over to the small sink and the towel rack.

"You really think I'm going to let you get away with that?" Dex grabbed the washcloth away from Sloane, then wrapped his arms around Sloane's waist before Sloane could turn the water on. Dex backed Sloane up against the door, pinning Sloane's wrists against it.

"I sure hope not," Sloane teased, nipping at Dex's chin. As they kissed, Sloane made a promise to himself. He'd never allow Dex to lose what made him so special—his heart. Sloane would protect it with everything he had. Always.

"Hello, Dex. Please, make yourself comfortable," Dr. Winters said as he closed his office door.

"Thank you, Doctor." Dex took a seat on the comfortable floral-print couch, pulling one of the soft blue pillows onto his lap. There was a plush blanket in the same color beside it, and he absently ran his hand over it. The office was designed to create a sense of calm with its soothing tones and soft lighting. A lovely smell floated up from the aromatherapy diffuser. The space was elegantly decorated but cozy, with potted plants around the room and a window that let in the sun during the day. From what Dex could gather, everyone except him, Cael, and Sloane had been in to see Dr. Winters. The rest of the team had been signed off and cleared.

Winters took a seat in the wingback chair across from Dex and crossed one leg over the other. He tapped the screen of the tablet on the coffee table beside him. "I'm going to start our session." He turned to Dex with a sympathetic smile, his amber eyes filled with concern. "I know this is the last place you want to be right now, but you understand how important your well-being is to the THIRDS and to me."

"I know. You're just doing your job."

Winters frowned at him. "I hope you don't believe you or any of the agents I see are just a file to me, Dex."

"I'm sorry. No, I know that." Dr. Winters had helped Dex work through a lot of emotional upheaval during his time at the THIRDS. From his acclimating to the team when he first joined, all the way through his supposed "ambush." Everything Dex and Winters talked about was confidential, but Dex never disclosed any information regarding TIN. The last thing he wanted to do was place the good doctor in danger for just listening to him. "You've done a lot for me, for Sloane, and the rest of the team, and I appreciate it, I really do. It's just frustrating. This isn't where I should be spending my time. We're working against the clock. Every minute I'm not out there looking for my father, chasing down leads, is a minute closer I get to never seeing him again."

Winters nodded. He was roughly Tony's age. A tall wolf Therian with a kind face and gentle eyes. He was soft-spoken, always calm and ready with a smile. A lot of agents hated seeing him, mostly because they didn't like having their emotions prodded. Dex didn't mind. He understood Winters's role, and he genuinely believed the guy wanted to help. This was just bad timing.

"Dex, you're an incredibly resilient man," Winters said,

leaning forward. "I know I shouldn't get personal, but I have never met anyone with a heart as strong as yours. Everything you've been through, everything you've suffered, and you always find a way to pick yourself back up and keep fighting. You might be a little worse for wear, but you dust yourself off and jump back into the fray. I admire that about you."

"Thank you."

"How are you holding up under all the pressure? You've had a lot on your plate recently with months of wedding preparations. Thank you for the invite, by the way."

Dex smiled. "I meant what I said. I appreciate everything you've done for me and Sloane. You were there to help me work through some things when Sloane got hurt in the car explosion, when my brother was taken and Tony was shot." He shook his head as he thought of all the other times he'd been in here. "Do I get like a special badge or something for most office visits?"

Winters chuckled. "You know you're always welcome to come talk to me. No flying bullets or apocalyptic events needed."

Dex nodded, grateful for the support. He squeezed the pillow to his chest and let out a heavy sigh. "It feels like I'm getting slammed from every angle, and I'm trying to focus on one thing at a time, but it's hard. I mean, I'm supposed to be getting married in a few days, and I keep thinking maybe I should call Lou and have him cancel the whole thing, and I said as much to Sloane, and man, he's just so amazing. He always knows exactly what to say or do to pull me back from that ledge. But even then, I can't stop thinking about how what if instead of me enjoying the happiest day of my life, I'm arranging a funeral? I don't know if I can come back from that. How am I supposed to come back from losing another father?"

Dex ran a hand over his face in frustration. "And then I get pissed, because *really*? One time wasn't enough? Am I so fucking cursed that the universe keeps trying to take people I love away from me? I lost my parents, I almost lost Sloane, my brother was kidnapped by Hogan, Tony was shot, and God knows how that could have turned out, and now he's out there somewhere in the hands of killers who are just biding their time." Dex swallowed hard and blinked back his tears. "I don't know if I can do this."

"You can," Winters assured him. He sounded so confident. Like if Dex just agreed with him, it would be so. "You're strong, Dex. What's more, you have a brother who looks up to you and depends on you. What would happen to Cael without you? What if the worst comes to pass, and he no longer has his father? What will he do if he doesn't have you to turn to?"

"No. I know. You're right. I'm just... tired. To be honest with you, Doc, right now, I'm exhausted. My head is a mess, but my heart is, like, 'don't you fucking dare.'"

"Then it's clear you need to listen to your heart."

Dex nodded his agreement, and Winters sat back in his chair. "You're not as restless as you once were. It's good to see Sloane's influence helping you through such a difficult period."

Dex couldn't help his smile at the thought of Sloane. "There's something about him that makes me... breathe. Just having him close by makes me feel calm, and if I start not to be calm, he touches me, and it's like everything's going to be fine. He grounds me."

"You're both perfectly suited for each other, and I'm so happy for you both. You've come such a long way."

Winters's words touched Dex. "Thank you."

"Now, are you prepared to do what needs to be done? Are you confident you can perform your duties to the best of your abilities? That your teammates can rely on you?"

Dex nodded, putting as much conviction behind his words as possible. "Yes, I'm confident in my abilities, and I'm here for my team. We're going to find Tony and bring him home."

CHAPTER TEN

THIS WAS REALLY HAPPENING.

Sloane stood in the middle of the empty training bay. It was one of the biggest in Sparta. The most high-tech with the newest equipment. This was where he'd be training agents and team leaders. At the end of the bay was a large locker room split into two for male and female agents, and to the right of the bay was his new office.

He headed into the sleek office twice the size of the one he shared with Dex. As he looked around, he wondered why a training officer would have such a big office with so much hardware and gadgetry, and the answer became clear. When he wasn't out in the field as a TIN operative or at home with Dex, he'd be here. He'd need everything at his disposal because this wasn't who he was first; he was a TIN operative moonlighting as a training officer. It was all so very surreal.

"Where the hell is he?"

Sloane checked his watch for the third time. It wasn't like Ash to be late. His best friend was always punctual, and he expected everyone else to be. If he got delayed, he always sent a quick text. Sloane decided to go see what was holding Ash up. He walked out into Sparta, greeting his fellow agents along the way as he headed up to Unit Alpha, stopping by his old office. It was tough, seeing only one desk in there now. Ash's desk. Sloane imagined Ash wouldn't be spending much time in there. While Dex and Sloane had been off, they'd moved Rosa, Letty, Cael, Calvin, and Hobbs to a much bigger space they now shared, each with their own desk. As soon as Dex and Sloane were sworn in, Destructive Delta would start in their new role as training team, so it made sense that they'd need to share the same space to collaborate and plan.

Sloane walked through the bullpen toward the conference rooms, and he found what he was looking for, well, the second thing; Ash was still nowhere to be found. The shiny new digital screen beside the door read Destructive Delta—THIRDS International Training Team.

Sloane opened the door, and five sets of eyes greeted him.

"Sloane!" Cael jumped from his chair. He rushed over to Sloane, surprising him when he threw his arms around Sloane and hugged him.

Sloane laughed. "What's all that about?" It had only been a couple of hours.

"He's feeling a little nostalgic," Rosa said, motioning around them.

The room was impressive, but then it had been one of Unit Alpha's largest conference rooms. It was state-of-the-art, with sleek new desk interfaces and a wall-to-wall digital board. Another wall had a huge flat screen built into it, while the third wall was lined with comfortable seating. At the far end were three doors, the left the bathroom, locker room, and shower for the female agents. The middle door led to the kitchen, where Sloane could see vending machines and all kinds of appliances, and the right door led to another bathroom, locker room, and shower for the male agents. It was a pretty sweet setup.

"It's a nice office," Calvin said.

Cael nodded. "We got our own kitchen."

"But it's still weird," Rosa added.

Sloane understood. They were still together, but separate. "Hey, when this is all over, the sarge will be just down the hall, Ash will be just around the corner, I'll be downstairs in Sparta."

"When you're not away," Cael said, frowning.

Anyone who heard Cael's words would think Cael meant when Sloane wasn't off training abroad or in another state, but what Cael actually meant was when Sloane was off on an op with Dex for TIN.

"Dex and I still represent Destructive Delta. We haven't left, and when we're not... on assignment, we'll be right here. We're family. That's not changing. I'm proud of you guys. This is a huge deal for the THIRDS. You're the first International Training Team. Sparks wouldn't have given this to you if she didn't think you could make a difference in these agents' lives. They need to see what a real family's like, and no one can do that better than Destructive Delta."

Rosa came over to Sloane and hugged him with a sniff. "Jerk. You're not supposed to be the one reassuring us."

"We're supposed to reassure you," Letty offered, hugging Sloane from his other side. He wrapped his arms around them and tried not to give in to his emotions, but when Hobbs stood, Sloane couldn't help it.

"Oh fuck me," he said with a laugh as everyone crowded him for a hug.

"Don't tell Dex," Calvin muttered.

"We'll never hear the end of it," Rosa said.

"Don't forget, you guys are going to have to be ready for when Dex and I need you. You're our backup, same as it's always been." Destructive Delta might be the new training team, but they were also Dex and Sloane's assets. It was going to be a challenge for all of them, balancing their old lives with the new.

"Hell yeah!" Letty wiped at her eyes before turning to head back to her desk. "Your boy's in the new team training bay, feeling sorry for himself. He's been in there since he got back from seeing Winters. I think they talked about him being team leader."

"Really?"

Cael nodded sadly. "When I asked him what was wrong, he said he just needed a few minutes on his own, how Winters had talked to him about his new role on the team and how he was going to do a great job."

Shit. "Okay, thanks, guys."

Sloane left Unit Alpha and took the elevator down to Sparta. He needed Ash to be at his best. Strangely enough, Sloane found himself feeling nervous all of a sudden, which was ridiculous. This was Ash. No one knew Sloane better than Ash. Dex might know Sloane intimately, but Ash and Sloane had been together for almost thirty years. Fuck, he was getting old. He couldn't help his smile, knowing Ash would curse him out for thinking that since they were the same age.

Just next door to his personal training bay was the Destructive Delta's new team training bay, the one Ash had asked Sparks for when she offered Destructive Delta the position. It was just as high-tech as Sloane's, but much bigger. It was divided into different training sections, and he found Ash on a bench, hunched over, near the boxing ring, his hands covering his face. Knowing Ash would hate being caught in an emotional state, Sloane called out as he approached.

"There you are, Keeler."

Ash jolted upright. He wiped at his face before clearing his throat, his voice rough when he spoke. "Fuck. Sorry, I didn't even realize what time it was."

"That's okay. I stopped by the office. Saw everyone's new digs. Cael seems happy about the kitchen."

Ash chuckled. "Yeah. Him and Hobbs. Couple of dorks. They already stocked the fridge."

Sloane took a seat on the bench and patted the space next to him. "Talk to me."

"Oh no. Fuck that. I ain't having no come-to-Jesus moment with you. I'm fine. This is all so... fucked-up. I can't stop thinking about the sarge out there, and now all this shit. Anyway, I'm fine."

Sloane called bullshit. Ash had just been sitting in an empty training bay, hands covering his face, and from his reddened eyes, it was more than obvious this was all hitting him harder than he expected.

Sloane nodded. He glanced over at the ring and grinned. "Okay. How about a few rounds?"

Ash eyed him. "If I bruise you, your annoying fiancé is going to bitch at me."

Sloane shrugged before he started to remove his boots. "Guess I'll have to make sure you don't bruise me."

Ash laughed. "Oh shit. So now that you're TIN, you think you can kick my ass?"

"I still have a few days before it's official. What's the matter? Afraid your CQC isn't up to snuff? What have you been doing during all those TIN training sessions?"

"Fuck you. I can kick your ass no matter what title you got."

"Come on, then."

"When your man comes whining, just remember you asked for it." Ash grabbed a pair of gloves and began slipping them on.

"Gloves? What happened to 'you asked for it'?"

"Are you kidding? Sarge will kick my ass if I bruise that pretty face of yours just before your wedding." He wrinkled his nose, and Sloane got it. None of them wanted to think otherwise. Tony had to be okay. They *had* to get him back.

Ash hit his gloves together and winked at Sloane. "I'll make sure they're small bruises that'll heal quickly."

Sloane pulled on his own gloves. "Or you could just not hit me in the face."

"Where's the fun in that?"

"Right. Okay, then." Sloane climbed into the ring as Ash did the same. He hit his gloves together, hopping on his toes and squaring his shoulders as Ash prepped himself. When Ash was ready, he hit his gloves together.

"Okay, hotshot. Show me what you got."

Sloane shook his head, amused. Ash had no idea.

"No? Okay. Me first, then." Ash approached, and Sloane readied himself. He waited patiently as he'd been taught to do.

Over the course of the last few months he'd been trained in all kinds of different martial arts and combat techniques along with Dex, until they each found a fighting style that worked best for them. For Dex it had been easier. He was fast, adaptable, and far more flexible than Sloane. Sloane was bulkier, heavier, and although he could be quick, his movements were better suited to techniques that required less fancy moves and more focus on precision and force. Moves that aimed to get the job done as quickly as possible and fewer of them. So when Ash threw a fierce left hook, Sloane dodged it, slapping his arm away and retaliating with a right hook to the ribs.

Ash cursed under his breath, quickly pulling back.

"Come on, Ash. You left yourself wide-open," Sloane teased.

Ash came at him again, keeping close to Sloane, who worked to anticipate Ash's moves. He'd watched Ash train and fight for years. He was familiar with Ash's strengths and weaknesses. Ash liked to mix things up, and although his left was almost as strong as his right, he tended to favor his right. Out in the field, they didn't come across a lot of perps trained in CQC, at least not until lately. For someone as big as Ash, he moved fast, but most importantly, he hit hard. Sloane was quick to block Ash's fists, making sure to stay away from Ash's elbows and knees. They moved around the ring, and Sloane could see Ash getting frustrated with Sloane not only constantly blocking him but not hitting back.

Ash struck with a fierce combination of left and right hooks, the last of which Sloane ducked under, rolled, then popped up behind Ash and kicked at the back of his knee, sending Ash down onto one knee. With a growl, Ash got to his feet and turned.

Sloane held his arms out to his sides and shrugged, his grin smug.

Ash laughed. "Okay. So that's how it is. I was gonna go easy on you, but now"—he hit his gloves together—"it's on."

Sloane grinned. "I hear a lot of trash talk, and yet I'm still looking pretty."

Ash threw his head back and laughed, and it was a good sound to hear. With a nod, he pulled off his gloves and tossed them out of the ring. Sloane smirked and followed his lead. This was the Ash he knew and loved. Confident, cocky, and ready to take on the world.

Ash charged, relentless in his attack, and Sloane put his training to the test, blocking Ash's punches, anticipating the blows by what he knew of Ash and his fighting technique. Sweat dripped down Sloane's face as he protected himself from an elbow to the head, uppercuts, punches to his ribs and kidneys. The more Sloane blocked, the fiercer Ash became. Lion Therians had incredible stamina. They would fight until their dying breath, and Ash was no exception. He was fueled by his inability to land a hit. Sloane knew if he kept this up, he'd eventually tire Ash out, but what would be the fun in that?

Sloane brought his hands down on Ash's fists, smacking them away from his body before kicking out, sending Ash reeling. Sloane moved in close, striking Ash in the chest, hearing his sharp intake of breath. He threw his arms around Ash's waist, lifted him off his feet, turned, and brought them both hard against the canvas with Sloane landing on top of him. He tried to roll off, but Ash was quick.

"Fuck!" Ash threw his arm around Sloane's neck and wrapped his leg around Sloane's waist.

"Are you... seriously... trying to fucking knock me out?" Sloane asked, feeling his airway constrict. He grabbed Ash's wrist and pulled down with all his strength, bringing his chin toward his chest as far as he could go, giving himself more breathing room.

"That's right, fucker. You're not the only one who's learned a few new tricks."

Sloane laughed. He managed to roll onto his side, bringing Ash with him, and got to his knees.

"What the fuck are you doing?" Ash growled.

"This." Sloane lifted them both just enough to make it hurt when he dropped down.

"Fucker!" Ash ground out, but he didn't let go of his death grip on Sloane.

Sloane punched Ash in the ribs, receiving a smack to the head. "Ouch! What the fuck?"

"That's what you get for leaving me, asshole."

"I'm not... leaving," Sloane grunted, punching Ash again on his side.

"Fuck! Stop doing that."

"Then let go."

"Fuck you!"

Sloane rolled over, pushed up again, and dropped them, landing on Ash again.

"Motherfucker," Ash laughed.

"Remember when we were kids, and we'd push our beds together so we could pretend we were wrestlers?" Sloane pushed at Ash's arm, but Ash was having none of it.

"I recall kicking your ass," Ash replied, panting. His grip loosened, and Sloane smiled.

"Only because you were bigger."

"And stronger," Ash added.

"But you always made the same mistake."

"Oh yeah? And what's that?"

"Thinking you'd won before the fight was over." Sloane grabbed Ash's right foot, pulled it toward him, and jammed his elbow into the side of Ash's knee.

"Son of a bitch!" Ash let go of Sloane's neck, and Sloane rolled off him, landing next to Ash. They both lay on their backs, panting.

"I know you're not *leaving*, but you're not going to be with us. We've done everything together since we were kids.

We've been on the same team since we joined the THIRDS, before you were a team leader."

"Yeah, and you remember how weird that was at first? Me giving orders, and you following them?"

It had been a big transition for them. Ash had always been the one to look after Sloane, to advise him and lay some hard truths on him. Sloane had happily followed Ash in everything when they were kids, and suddenly, Sloane was the one leading, and Ash was the one following.

"I remember," Ash muttered.

"But no matter what, you always had my back."

"I still do." Ash sat up, and Sloane followed suit. "Don't get me wrong. I know why you're doing what you're doing, and I support that." He averted his gaze, his lips pulled into a frown. "I'm proud of you. Not a lot of people would have the balls to do what you're about to do. I just hate that everything has to change." He motioned around them. "Look at this place. There's going to be teams of agents in here looking to *me* for help. These guys are already at their lowest point, and Sparks thinks I can bring them back from that? I mean, Jesus, Sloane. Most people are offended just by my presence alone."

Sloane stood with a chuckle. He held a hand out to Ash and helped him up. They climbed out of the ring and grabbed a couple of towels from the shelf. Sloane looked around at the new equipment, unused and pristine. Everything was stocked. Soon it would be full of life. It would also be full of pain, loss, and desperation. Taking a seat on the bench, Sloane looked up at Ash.

"Do you think Sparks made you team leader just because you said so? She made you team leader because she knows you're ready, Ash. You've been ready for some time. You're also not alone in this. You have Cael, me, Dex, the rest of our family to back you up. I know Dex and I won't always be here, but that's okay. I'm marrying your boyfriend's brother, for crying out loud. There are still going to be date nights and movie nights and dinners at Tony's. Plus, you'll be plenty busy now that Cael's moving in."

Ash nodded and shoved his hands into his pockets before deciding to take a seat next to Sloane. The mix of concern, uncertainty, and fear in his best friend's amber eyes squeezed at Sloane's heart. Something was really bothering Ash, and it wasn't just Sloane working for TIN.

"What is it?"

"I received my new security clearance last week, giving me access to the list of teams who are being considered for our training program. I started looking through them, and it scared the shit out of me." Ash shook his head, and he let out a heavy sigh. "You have no idea, Sloane. Some of the fucked-up shit that's happened to these guys... No wonder their teams are broken. I'm not just talking about a loss within their team, a difficult case, or any of the messed-up stuff that we encounter out there. There are things that have happened to some of these agents that no one should have to go through." Ash ran a hand over his face. "How am I supposed to get through to a team leader who watched his entire team get blown up right in front of him?" Tears welled in Ash's eyes. "How do I help the agent whose partner was kidnapped, raped, and shot in the head, right in front of her?" Ash shook his head as he tried to keep it together. "We've dealt with a lot of shit, but nothing compared to what some of these agents have been through. Why would Sparks think I'm the right guy for this job? And what if we lose the sarge? Jesus, Sloane, we're going to end up on the same list, just as broken as the rest of these teams."

Sloane stood and took hold of Ash's face, forcing him to meet his gaze. "First of all, we're *not* going to lose the sarge. Second, we sure as hell are not going to end up broken. We're a family, Ash. Whatever happens, we're going to be there for one another and get through it together. As for the other agents, no one says you have to hold anyone's hand. Sparks knows you, knows how you handle things. Maybe your in-your-face, no-nonsense approach is what some of these agents need. If a softer touch is needed, you have Cael. If you need a gentle hand, you have Hobbs. Or if an ass-kicking is what someone needs, you have Letty. Rosa can patch them up afterwards and feed them."

"If I want someone sniped, I have Cal," Ash said, blinking back his tears. His wobbly smile and the mischief in his eyes made Sloane laugh.

"Exactly." Sloane released him. "My point is, you're not alone. You're going to do great. I'm proud of you too. This is your chance to do for these agents what you did for me. You taught me that no matter how bad things get, that if I kept fighting, if I trusted in you, that we would make it through, and things would get better. You never lied or gave me false hope. You taught me there are no easy answers in life, no shortcuts. Because of you, I learned the real meaning of strength, loyalty, and family."

Ash wrinkled his nose, tears welling in his eyes again. "Asshole."

With a dopey grin, Sloane brought Ash into a hug, and Ash returned his embrace. Sloane was going to miss having Ash at his side like nothing else. As if reading his thoughts, Ash spoke up, his voice rough with emotion.

"Remember your promise. If you need backup, you fucking call me."

Sloane squeezed Ash tight. "I promise."

A round of applause startled them, and Sloane turned to find their family.

"Yeah, yeah," Ash growled, wiping a tear from his eye. "Nothing to see here. Drop and give me twenty burpees."

Calvin laughed, and when Ash joined in the laughter, the rest of the crew weren't far behind. Sloane knew better. Ash's humor vanished, and his expression turned hard.

"I'm not fucking kidding."

"What?" Letty groaned.

They all dropped and got started, with only Cael standing there.

"You too, sweetheart. No favoritism."

Cael narrowed his eyes. "Are you saying Sloane never showed Dex favoritism?"

Sloane shook his head. "Not where training was concerned. In fact, you know better than anyone that I was harder on him than the rest of you."

Cael huffed. "Fine." He joined everyone else, grumbling as they followed orders.

"When you're done here, I'll see you guys in the conference room," Sloane said, waving at them as Ash walked with him out of the training bay. Ash grinned wide and threw an arm around Sloane's shoulders.

"You know, I think I'm gonna enjoy this whole team leader thing."

Heaven help them.

Sloane's phone went off. It was a text from Sparks. Dr. Winters was ready for him. "I gotta go see the doc."

"Good luck." Ash gave his shoulder a pat. "I'll let you know if we hear anything from Austen."

"Thanks."

~

Sloane left Ash and headed back upstairs to Dr. Winters's office. As soon as he'd walked into the waiting room, the door to Dr. Winters's office opened, and Dex walked out. Butterflies fluttered in Sloane's stomach at the sight of Dex's beautiful smile. He loved that Dex still caused that reaction in him. Sloane returned Dex's smile and waited as Dex made his way over. He laid a hand on Sloane's upper arm, squeezing subtly.

"Try not to give away too many of my secrets," Dex teased, winking at Sloane before he walked off. Sloane shook his head in amusement. He joined Dr. Winters, greeting him as he walked through the door.

Winters closed the door with a smile. "Sloane. Thank you for seeing me. As I told Dex, I know this is a most inopportune time, but circumstances dictate we make sure you and your team have the support you need."

"Thank you, Doctor." Sloane took a seat on the couch, picking up Dex's scent on the throw pillow beside him. He took it and placed it on his lap.

Winters smiled warmly at him. "I'm happy to see he brings you comfort."

Sloane tilted his head in question, and Winters motioned to the pillow. "His scent is on that pillow. I imagine it's why you picked it up."

"Oh, um, yeah," Sloane replied with a sheepish grin.

"You've both brought a sense of calm to each other. Well, I would say you bring *him* calmness, and he lifts your spirits. There's a lightheartedness to your soul you didn't have when he first joined."

Sloane nodded his agreement. "I wasn't in a good place, but you know that."

Winters's gaze was sympathetic. "I do. It was a very difficult road for you, but you've come such a long way, opening yourself up to the healing process. You stopped believing you were incapable of finding happiness again. I'm very proud of the progress you've made, Sloane."

"Thank you." Sloane swallowed hard. It *had* been a difficult road, and there had been times when he'd stumbled. When everything looked bleak, and he was surrounded by pain. Dex had been his guiding light, helping him steer through the darkness to safe shores.

"How are you handling the current situation? Sergeant Maddock has been a father figure to you since you joined the THIRDS, and he's your fiancé's father."

Sloane let out a heavy sigh. "It's difficult, but I'm doing the best I can for my team and for Dex." Just like Ash was doing his best for Cael. Between Dex and Ash, they didn't allow Cael to get swept up in his anxiety, and Ash had managed to prevent Cael from having a bad panic attack like he'd had when Tony had been shot. "It's been stressful for all of us, with all the changes, the wedding, and trying to bring Tony back home safe."

"And how are you juggling your roles as team leader, future training officer, and soon-to-be husband?"

"Right now, my focus is on doing everything I can to support my team and find our sergeant. Dex and I have had some time to get used to our dual roles over the years. Sure, this time it's more of a challenge because I want to be there for him emotionally, but we both have a job to do, and we acknowledge that."

"I'm glad to hear it. You seem to be handling the situation well."

Sloane shrugged. "I have to. That's my job as team leader. To be the touchstone for everyone on my team."

"Lead by example," Winters said, nodding.

"Yes. My team looks to me to keep it together. To keep them going no matter what. I have to be confident in what I say and what I do."

"And if the worst comes to pass?" Winters asked gently. "If you're wrong. What do you think will happen to your team? To Dex? You've assured them they can bring Sergeant Maddock home. Should you be making those kinds of promises? What if you can't deliver?"

Sloane thought about that. It would tear them apart, but... Sloane wouldn't let them fall. He'd been in this position before. He knew grief intimately. Suffering was an old friend. One Sloane had turned his back on some time ago. He knew the path to darkness like the back of his hand. There was no way in hell he would let Dex or the rest of his family end up there. Sloane met Winters's eyes.

"They're strong. Whatever happens, we'll get through it. Together."

Winters opened his mouth to reply, but Sloane's phone went off. "I'm so sorry, Doctor. I need to take this."

"Of course. Good news I hope."

"Fingers crossed," Sloane said, getting up. "I need to go. Thank you for everything."

"I'll see you soon," Winters said.

Sloane left the office and hurried out into the hall, his phone to his ear. "Talk to me, Austen."

"I have the list of ingredients from the formula. As I

suspected, it's a homemade concoction created by a professional cleaner. I've got good news and bad news."

"What's the bad news?"

"The bad news is that they're all common elements that when bought individually wouldn't raise any red flags. I did a cross-reference across the three states, and as suspected, there's no one place where all these ingredients were purchased."

"And the good news?"

"The sale of these particular ingredients is higher in Jersey than in New York City. So if you're going to start somewhere, start there. It's very possible the cleaner is either located in Jersey, or he's making the stuff there and bringing it over."

"Thanks, Austen."

"I'll call you if I find out anything else."

"Okay, well, we got somewhere to start."

Sloane quickly sent Ash a text, and they met in the one conference room Sparks had set up for them. The only one that was secure at the moment. His team was in there waiting for him.

"Jersey," Sloane said, before relaying the information he'd gotten from Austen. "You got the information I asked for?"

"You know how many abandoned places there are in New Jersey?" Ash asked, shaking his head and handing over the lists his team had compiled. It was lengthy. "They got almost as many as we do."

Sloane took a look at the printouts. Shit. Even with all their units and those in other states helping, there were way more on the list than they could get to in time.

"Maybe Sparks can get THIRDS HQ in Princeton to

accept some of our units over there to help," Letty suggested. "Put a task force together."

Ash let out a snort. "Come on, Letty. You know how fucking long that shit takes, and then it turns into a pissing contest, and we don't got time for that shit."

As his team discussed possible ways to expedite the search across multiple locations in the short amount of time they had, Sloane joined Dex and Cael in reviewing the recording of the Chairman's conversation. He watched Dex pace as Tony's voice filled the room. After the recording ended, Dex replayed the part with Tony as he and Cael both frowned. Finally, Cael spoke up.

"I keep thinking about what Dad said about Vegas."

"What about it," Dex said, folding his arms over his chest as he started to pace again.

Cael faced his brother. "Dad hates Vegas. Like *hates* it with a fiery passion. He would never volunteer to go there, not even to celebrate."

Sloane went pensive. "Wasn't Vegas where Tony had to go bail you out of jail?" he asked Dex.

"There's that too," Cael said. "Dex was arrested in Vegas. He's banned from, like, half the casinos there. Why would Dad suggest going there?"

Dex's eyes widened. "Holy shit."

"What?" Sloane asked, straightening.

"Fuck me, I'm such an asshole. He was trying to tell us something." Dex walked over to Sloane and grabbed the printout with all the abandoned places. He held it up. "He was trying to give us a clue without the Makhai figuring out that's what he was doing. If they look up my record, or arrest records in Vegas, they'd find nothing because thanks to Dad pulling in a favor, my arrest was never made official.

They'd have no idea why he said that except that maybe he wanted to celebrate with his sons. *We* know I was in jail."

"Jail. Abandoned locations." Sloane cursed under his breath. He grabbed the sheet from Dex and scanned for what he was looking for as Dex confirmed his thoughts.

"He's in a fucking prison."

"Here," Sloane said, pointing to one particular location on the list. "There's an old abandoned jail in Newark."

Cael leaned in, then tapped away at his phone. "This place has been closed since the seventies and is notorious for feral Therians, dealers, and illegal activity. The city plans to demolish it. It's decayed, rusty, and falling apart, but there're any number of places where you could hide someone."

Sloane removed his cell phone from his pocket and put in a call to Austen, who answered on the first ring.

"Hey, Sloane. You got something for me?"

"Yeah, I need someone to check out the Old Essex County Jail over in Newark. I'll be waiting to hear back from you. I'm thinking this is it, and if it is, we need to mobilize right away."

"I'm not far from there. I'll call you as soon as I have something."

"Be careful."

"Will do."

Austen hung up, and Sloane headed for the door of the conference room, everyone following close behind. "While Austen confirms visuals, we need to inform Sparks and put together a plan of attack."

"Hope everyone's had their tetanus shot," Ash said. "Might I also suggest we go in with full armor. This place is going to be one giant landfill of rusted metal and used drug paraphernalia. Oh, and mercenaries shooting at us."

Sparks's door was open, but Sloane knocked anyway, just in case. She looked up from her desk and motioned for them to come in. She placed the room in privacy mode and laced her fingers on her desk's surface.

"I was about to call you. Tell me you have something because I've run out of time. I had my last interview of the day, and the Chairman just made contact. He wants me over at the closest TIN facility getting this USB plugged in."

"We think the sergeant's in Jersey. I'm just waiting on confirmation. If we're right, we're going to need backup. A lot of it."

Sparks nodded. "Take Theta Destructive and Beta Ambush to back up your team. From there, get whoever else you need. Call in every team we have out there in the city. I'll deal with Princeton HQ and anyone else who wants to waste our time with paperwork bullshit. If there's an agent on this floor, I want them out there bringing Maddock back." Her eyes were filled with a fury Sloane had never seen before. "They want a war, we'll give them one. Consider the Makhai's men armed and dangerous. Take them down."

"What are you going to do about the USB?" Dex asked. "Whatever's on there can't be good."

Sparks stood and smoothed out her pantsuit jacket. "Whatever the Makhai want, I have no intention of giving it to them, but they won't know until it's too late. I have someone who's going to make sure whatever is supposed to happen, doesn't happen. You know what that means."

Sloane nodded. He turned to face his team, his eyes falling on Dex. "If we don't get Tony back by the time the Makhai figure out Sparks has screwed them..."

"Then Tony's dead," Dex said, balling his hands into fists at his sides.

Sloane's phone rang, and his heart leapt into his throat. "Austen?"

"Get your ass moving, Brodie. They're in there, and from the looks of it, they won't be for long. I can't confirm visuals on Daddy Maddock, but there's a fuckton of firepower around, and it ain't because of the scenery."

"Shit. Thanks, Austen."

Dex looked at him expectantly.

"Austen confirmed the Makhai's men are at the prison. We're looking at a lot of firepower. Everyone in full tactical gear and armor. We're going in hot." Sloane turned back to Sparks. "We'll send you a text the second we have Tony secured."

Sparks nodded, and Sloane hurried out into the bullpen to put together an army of his own.

CHAPTER ELEVEN

He had no words.

Dex couldn't bring himself to open his mouth, much less attempt to speak. When Sloane put out the call to arms in Unit Alpha, the speed at which their fellow agents volunteered and got geared up left Dex speechless. Their unit had ten squads. A total of five had been available to mobilize, and of those five, not one had remained seated when Sloane asked that anyone willing to help them march into battle to retrieve Sergeant Maddock stand. Dex had never seen anything like it. Not that he'd expected any less from his fellow agents, but it still struck something deep inside him. At the HPF, he'd thought he'd been a part of a brotherhood, one that would have his back and fight along with him for what was right. But in the end, they'd turned on him and cast him out for doing what he'd sworn to do when he'd picked up his badge. They hadn't even given him a chance. By contrast, everyone in his unit was there because they believed in what they were doing. They believed in fighting for a better world.

Sixty THIRDS Defense agents filled the armory,

preparing for nothing short of a military strike, twenty in their Therian forms, including Hobbs and Ash. Taylor was attaching pieces of armor to his uniform as he gave his team a pep talk. Seb was checking on each member of Theta Destructive, and Rafe was talking to his team, Alpha Ambush. Alpha Pride and Beta Pride, two fierce teams with twelve total Therian Defense agents who were solely lion Therians, were all in their Therian forms and ready to tear shit up. All together they had fourteen lion Therians in Therian form, and six tiger Therians in Therian form.

Dex's gear weighed a fuckton with the armored plates, pads, and additional weapons, the special material of his uniform making it more difficult to be fatally wounded if the Makhai's men were using armor-piercing rounds. Of course, no armor or uniform was completely impenetrable. There were only so many hits it would be able to take before it fractured and something made it through. If they hit him, he had to hit back harder.

Sloane turned to everyone now gathered in Destructive Delta's armory. Seb let out a loud whistle that got everyone's attention. They all turned to Sloane.

"I wish there was time for me to tell you all what this means to us, but for now, I hope a thank-you will be enough. Every team leader has their entry point. Destructive Delta will focus on finding and retrieving Sergeant Maddock. He's our priority. We have direct orders from Sparks to retrieve the sarge at all costs. We're going in hot. Stay safe, and we'll see you on the other side." Sloane swallowed hard and smiled, his eyes glassy. "Being a part of this unit has been an honor."

Everyone cheered, whooped, or roared before rushing out toward the garage and the awaiting BearCats. Each team's set of Recon agents were on standby and ready to move out should their teams need the backup.

Dex climbed into the BearCat and strapped himself in next to Sloane on the bench. With Hobbs and Ash in their Therian forms, Rosa did the driving. The engine of the massive vehicle roared to life, rumbling and growling as they headed out for the turnpike. If luck was on their side, at this time of night, they could make it in half an hour. Sloane and Ash had come up with entry points for all the team leaders, and while they were busy distracting the Makhai, Destructive Delta would come up alongside the light rail line. Sparks had already put in calls to delay the train at Norfolk Street Station and Warren Street Station. Between their Therian sight and night-vision gear, they'd be able to see what they were walking into, though they had to be extra vigilant as they ventured into the pitch black of the crumbling structure. The darkness could either work for them or against them, especially since the Makhai's mercenaries were all Therians.

Time went by in a blur, and before Dex even blinked, the BearCat came to a stop. Sloane gripped Dex's gloved hand, giving it a squeeze, and Dex squeezed back. Everyone stood, and while his team picked up their shields, Dex turned to Cael and grabbed him by the vest, pulling him close. They put their helmets together, and Dex patted his brother's chest.

"Be safe, Chirpy. I want Dad back as much as you do, but we go home together, okay?"

Cael nodded. "I know."

Letty opened the back doors. As their team jumped down, Dex turned to Sloane. Feeling kinda out of sorts, he was overcome by a sense of yearning to be close to Sloane, which was funny, considering Dex carried Sloane's DNA inside him. How much closer could they get? He kissed his fingers and placed them to Sloane's visor. With a soft smile, Sloane mouthed the words "I love you." They jumped down from the back of the truck Rosa had backed up between two large rental trucks in a parking lot off Central Avenue.

Dex's earpiece crackled to life, and they heard Seb's quiet voice.

"Theta Destructive in position. We've got movement all around the property. From my location, thermal shows at least twenty outside and an undisclosed number inside the three structures."

Seb was followed by Rafe, Taylor, and the other team leaders confirming their positions. Everyone was ready.

"Standby, we're moving into position," Sloane replied. He motioned for everyone to follow, and they fell into formation, hurrying after him as they took the long way around the station to the Norfolk Street entrance in case there were spotters close by. The station had been cleared as Sparks had instructed, with a guard blocking each set of stairs, four in total. The huge tiger Therian stepped aside as Destructive Delta headed his way. They swiftly made their way down the steps to the platform and jumped down onto the lines.

"Watch your step," Sloane ordered as they hurried down the tracks and through the tunnel beneath Newark Street to the other side. They stayed close to the building. Thanks to the dilapidation of the place, it was surrounded by a dense forest of overgrown trees and shrubs. The roofs were one bad storm away from blowing off, which meant no one would be up there.

Their earpieces came to life again, this time it was Austen. "Okay, teams. We're looking at twenty armed hostiles guarding the perimeter off Newark, Central, Lock, and New. Rutgers's parking lot is a no-go. We got a couple of snipers on the roof of the health institute across the street, and one on the roof of the truck rental place across from the prison. He's facing Central at the moment."

"Copy that," Sloane said quietly.

Shit. That was right next to where they were. Sloane signaled for Calvin to keep an eye on the roof to their left. Sloane motioned to the ledge on his right, then signaled Hobbs and Ash over. The two leapt up onto the grassy ledge with ease. Sloane placed his shield on the ground before turning to Dex and lacing his fingers together. Letty took Dex's shield from him so Dex could grab hold of Sloane's vest and hoist himself up onto the grassy ledge. He took his shield from Letty and silently leaned it against the brick wall surrounding the prison. The rest of the team followed suit, each helping the others get up and move equipment. Then it was just Sloane, and everyone put their backs into it, pulling up a two-hundred-fifty-pound Therian wearing almost sixty pounds of gear.

Once Sloane was up, they fell back into formation. The brick wall became lower as they got nearer the student parking lot. One by one, just as they had before, they got up over the wall and landed on the other side in a thicket of trees. The area was pitch black, but Dex had no need for night-vision goggles. He had his own built in. His eyes picked up what little light there was, helping him make out shapes and movement in the shadows. The closer he was, the clearer the image, but where he once would have seen nothing but black blobs, now he could see objects.

"Destructive Delta in position. Begin extraction," Sloane said into their earpieces. "Cael, you're up."

Cael walked ahead of them. He removed his backpack

and pulled out his thermal imaging binoculars. Once he'd secured his backpack, the team covered him as they moved silently forward, Cael scanning the structures. There were three buildings on the property, each one as derelict as the other. Mountains of illegally dumped trash littered the ground, along with whole sections of brick wall that had fallen off the buildings, windows that had collapsed outward, shattered glass panes, hills of drug paraphernalia, and a sea of empty food and water containers. The smell of rusted metal, mold, rot, piss, and shit burned Dex's nose, and for the first time he regretted his Therian sense of smell. Holy fuck.

Any feral Therians or poor souls unfortunate enough to end up here had either been run off by the Makhai or were hiding. Dex would guess hiding. He could hear subtle rustling in the trees around them and had spotted several glowing eyes low to the ground, but nothing advanced toward them.

"Shit." At Cael's curse, Dex stilled, along with everyone else on the team. "I think I found him."

"That's good, isn't it?" Rosa asked.

"He's in that center building there on the third floor. It's a cellblock with four floors. There's dozens of armed Therians on each floor, just inside the entrance and around the building." Cael handed Dex the binoculars, and Dex looked at the building. He swallowed past the lump in his throat. There on the third floor, in the center inside what looked like a cell, was Tony, sitting in a chair, his head hung low. Six armed Therians were inside the cell with him. Suddenly there was a flurry of activity.

"Shit, I think we've been made," Dex said, handing the binoculars to Sloane, who took a quick look before his voice came in over their earpieces. How the hell did they know?

"Alpha teams, go, go, go!"

A symphony of machine gun fire and bursts of light filled the night as all six teams moved in. Fierce roars shook the leaves in the trees as THIRDS agents and Makhai operatives charged one another. Destructive Delta rushed the cellblock, and Dex fired at everyone who moved who wasn't one of their own. The bullets came hard and fast against his shield as he moved. The Makhai's mercs came out of the woodwork like roaches. One rushed Dex from his right, and Dex spun, slamming into the guy with his shield and sending him flying back. Anger and adrenaline roared through Dex. There was no way these fuckers were keeping him from that cell.

Mercs turned in his direction from every angle, like sharks sensing fresh blood. They advanced and Dex's senses went into overdrive. He released his MP5, letting it swing from its strap attached to his vest and drew out his claws. His fangs pierced his skin, and he let out a fierce roar as they rushed him. They had no idea who they were fucking with.

Dex ducked under one fist and used his shield to slam into another Therian, spinning and bringing his claws with him, slashing across another Therian's throat. Blood splattered across his shield and the corner of his visor. A hard body slammed into him, knocking him off his feet, and when he hit the ground, he realized it had been two hard bodies. His shield was kicked away, and one of the Therians made to lunge, but then he was tackled by a huge ass lion Therian in his Therian form. It was Ash, and he tore the guy's throat out with one move.

Scrambling to his feet, Dex faced the six Therians moving slowly toward him. In the distance, he could see Sloane fighting off another half dozen or so Makhai with a ferocity Dex had never seen before. Sloane was pissed, and he was letting it all out on these assholes. Dex turned his focus back on the Therians in front of him.

"You waiting for an invitation?" Dex growled. "Come and get some."

Dex didn't bother with his shield. When the Therians advanced, he put his training to use. There was no holding back. It was him or them. They all rushed him at once, and Dex grabbed the guy closest to him, propelling him into the others to give him the advantage he needed. He ducked and dodged the fists coming at him, used his claws to slash at anyone stupid enough to get close to him. Snagging hold of one Therian's tactical vest, he jumped and kicked out with both feet, getting another in the chest and knocking the guy onto his ass. Dex used a combination of swift moves to bring down the Therians, using his claws and swiping his Glock from his thigh rig and shooting. Any Makhai mercenary who went down would not be getting back up.

Four down, two to go. He didn't have time for this. With a roar, Dex ran and scissor kicked around one huge guy's neck, bringing him down. As he fell with the guy, he used his legs to snap the guy's neck while firing at the Therian lunging for him. The guy's visor splintered, red splashing from the inside, and he fell facedown onto the ground.

Dex jumped to his feet, returned his Glock to his holster, snatched up his shield, and ran into the cellblock. He took a sharp right turn and headed for the stairs. Three Makhai goons blocked his path, but before Dex could do anything, they crumpled, one of them rolling down the stairs. Dex's head shot up in the direction the bullets had come from, and he grinned.

Calvin was up on the top floor, looking through his scope. He gave a thumbs-up, and Dex gave him a salute. Calvin was clearing a path for him, and as Dex hurried up the rusted and crumbling stairs, hopping over the bodies of fallen Makhai, he spotted Sloane and the rest of the team down in the middle in a tight circle, shields up as they fired on the Makhai and anyone who tried to get to Calvin or Dex.

Several Therians in their feral forms scrambled into the cellblock building, but they were too busy fighting one another to pay attention to Destructive Delta. The battle was fierce, claws shredding, teeth tearing at flesh and fur. The roars of Felids filled the air. Dex made it to the third floor and slowed down. There were several cells, all open. There was no telling who or what would be lurking inside. Quickly but cautiously, he checked every cell before walking past it. Just as he neared the cell Tony was supposed to be in, a jaguar Therian plowed into him, sending him crashing through the oxidized bars. The putrid bars gave way, and Dex landed on the walkway on the other side. He moved to get up when a loud crack had him going still. He looked down and realized the walkway was made of glass sections, each pane held up by rusted bars. The glass was so filthy, he'd mistaken it for concrete.

The jaguar who'd launched himself at Dex roared from the safety of the other walkway. Dex hissed back. He released his rifle and motioned at the jaguar to advance.

"Come on, asshole. Come get me."

The jaguar roared again and leapt. Dex rolled out of the way, grabbing the steel frame as the glass shattered under the jaguar's weight. Dex hung from one arm, and the jaguar's claws latched onto his tactical vest. It released a pained roar as bullets pierced its bulky frame, and Dex unhooked the claws with his free hand, watching as it fell onto the walkway below, the glass shattering, and sending the jaguar falling to the first floor with a *thud*.

This time it was Sloane who'd fired. While from above Calvin took care of anyone trying to get to Dex, Sloane covered Dex from below. Grabbing hold of the ledge to his right where he'd crashed through the bars, Dex climbed onto the more secure walkway. He pushed himself to his feet and ran up to the edge of the doorway one down from where his dad was supposed to be.

"Cal, any visuals?"

"Five armed hostiles. Three on the left, two on the right. Sarge is sitting in a chair in the middle."

"Copy that." Okay. Dex inhaled deeply and closed his eyes briefly as he released the breath through his mouth. He put his shield on the floor behind him, pulled his Glock from his thigh rig, and the backup tucked into the holster at his hip. There was no room for hesitation. No room for error. He crouched low and ran to the wall beside the open cell door. The second he stepped foot in front of that door, they were going to shoot him. Or he could shoot first.

"Dad?" Dex called out. It wasn't like the Makhai didn't know he was out there.

"Dex? Don't come in here!"

There was shuffling and noises, Tony grunted as someone hit him. Son of a bitch was going to pay for that. Dex readied himself and reached for the flashbang clipped to his vest. "Remember the first time I watched the ending of *Alien*?"

"I remember." Tony's reply told Dex he was as ready as he was going to be.

Dex pulled the pin and tossed the flashbang into the room. He slipped into the smoke-filled room of stunned Therians, using his sharpened senses, pleasantly startled when he realized he could make out the Therians in the smoke with enough detail to take them down. The Therians fired wildly toward the door. They might have had experience with flashbangs, but so did Tony. He had been dealing with them since he was Cael's age, and thanks to Dex's warning, Tony had shut his eyes tight, covered his ears, and looked away just as Dex had the first time he'd watched the ending to *Alien* when he'd been eight years old.

In rapid succession, Dex fired both guns, one shot for each Therian. They crumpled to the filthy floor around Tony. They hadn't even restrained his dad, knowing there was no way he could get out of there with the number of armed Therians. Tony was skilled, but as a Human, he was at a disadvantage, especially unarmed and in the dark.

Tony stood, wavering from his disorientation, but managed to throw his arms around Dex, hugging him tight. Dex allowed himself a couple of seconds to hug him back. He swallowed down his emotions and returned his guns to their holsters before he grabbed his dad's arm and headed toward the door.

"I've got the sarge," Dex declared. "I'm going to need cover to get him out of here. Walking out the front door." It was their only option. It also meant anyone who was left was going to come gunning for them. Outside on the walkway, Dex grabbed his shield and headed for the stairs, but his path was blocked. He turned and found the other end blocked as well.

"Fuck. Guys, I need an exit." Dex ducked back inside with his dad. "Guys?"

"We got company. I think they called for backup," Sloane replied. "We're taking heavy fire. You need to get out of there, Dex. Calvin's got his hands full."

Shit. "Copy that. Cael?"

"I've got this. Get Dad out," Cael replied, Ash's roar echoing in the background.

Dex worried his bottom lip. They had to move. If they stayed in here, they were sitting ducks. An idea struck him, and he handed his Glock to his dad. "Be right back." He didn't wait for a reply. He ran out, using his shield to cover himself as he kicked at the rusted bar in front of him. It snapped off and rolled to the glass walkway. The top bar met the same fate. As the Makhai slowly approached from both sides, Dex ran in and handed his shield to his dad before turning around.

"Climb on."

"What?"

"Climb on, Dad. We don't have time."

"Boy, are you out of your ever-loving mind?"

"Just do it!"

Tony jumped onto Dex's back, one arm wrapped around Dex's shoulders and grabbing onto his vest, his legs around Dex's waist, and his free hand gripping the shield tight. This was going to hurt like a motherfucker. There was no way he was letting his father fall onto all that shit down there. Exposing himself to the sea of oxidized steel, shards of glass, bloody needles, and fuck knew what else could be just as much of a death sentence.

Fuck. *Fuck.* If he didn't go now, they were both dead. There was only so much his armor could take.

"What are you doing?"

There was no time to rappel down. Dex squared his shoulders and reached down deep to that swirling mass of *something* he kept feeling in there. *Come on. Whatever the fuck is in you, now's the time for it to make itself useful.*

Dex moved back into the cell and took a calming breath to center himself. He grabbed the doorframe and propelled himself forward. He screamed for his dad to hold on and jumped onto the glass walkway. His instinct would be to roll when he hit the ground floor, but he couldn't do that. As he expected, his weight combined with Tony's brought the glass pane down, and Tony protected his head as they fell through the glass. Dex landed in a crouched position, the force of the impact making its way up his body. He didn't stop to think about what the hell he'd just done. When his dad jumped down, they took off like a bat out of hell.

A storm of bullets rained down on them, and Tony held the large shield close. One, two, three bullets struck Dex's armor in the back, the pain reverberating through his body with the shock of each hit, but he kept going. A tiger Therian in feral form leapt out from behind a mound of debris, and Dex intercepted, putting himself between the Therian and his dad. He slammed his head forward, cracking his helmet against the tiger's skull. His visor splintered, and the Therian dropped to the ground, out cold. They turned to go and found themselves surrounded by roaring and snarling Felids.

Dex stepped in front of his dad, his rifle ready. There was no way he could take down this many before he and Tony were swarmed. A lion Therian took a step forward and roared, and something inside Dex shattered. His throat closed up, he heard a painful snap, and he let loose the scream that traveled up from somewhere deep in his gut. Except it wasn't a scream. It was a roar. A jaguar Therian roar.

The Felids around them freaked, ears flat as their gazes darted to one another. Before Dex could take a step forward, whatever the fuck he'd just done did the job, and every THIRDS agent in feral form appeared, fangs bared and claws unsheathed, and started tearing the shit out of the Makhai.

Dex grabbed Tony, who was staring at him, stunned.

"We gotta move."

"Did you just roar?"

"Not the time, Dad." Dex had no idea what he'd done. It sounded like a roar, but—holy fuck, did he just roar? He shook himself out of it, and they ran for the exit. Dex kicked at the fence, it opened, and he hurried Tony out onto the sidewalk.

"Sloane, I got the sarge!"

"They're retreating," Sloane replied, breathless. "See you at the rendezvous."

"Copy that." Dex ran down New Street and took a left on Lock. They jumped over the campus community fence and ducked into the shadows against one of the buildings. They collapsed onto the grass to catch their breaths. Dex pulled off his helmet and let it drop onto the grass. He tapped his earpiece. "Sloane, what's your status?"

"The Makhai have called off the attack. They're bailing. Anyone left who's got a pulse is being hauled off to hospitals, and from there to a much prettier prison than this place. Sent word to Sparks the moment you got the sarge out. She's on her way back to HQ. The Chairman got dick."

"He's not gonna be happy about that," Dex said, letting his head fall back against the wall. He reached out to put his hand on Tony's shoulder, needing to reassure himself his dad was safe.

"Like I give a fuck," Sloane growled, then shouted at someone. "Grab that fucker, will you? I don't know where the hell he thinks he's going. You okay?" Sloane asked Dex, his tone softening.

"Yeah. Ready to head home." Dex swallowed hard. "Everyone else?"

"A little worse for wear. Some bullet wounds and minor

injuries, but everyone's present and accounted for. We're heading to the BearCat now. See you in a minute."

"See you."

Dex turned to face Tony, who was smiling warmly at him.

"What?"

"I knew my boys would find me."

Dex opened his mouth to reply but instead grabbed his dad in a crushing hug. He shut his eyes tight, the last of his adrenaline leaving his body. As hard as he tried to keep the tears at bay, he couldn't. The relief that flooded through him was overwhelming.

"I love you too, kiddo." Tony kissed the top of his head, and Dex pulled himself together.

"You scared the shit out of me."

"I know," Tony replied. "The whole time I was there, all I could think about was my boys." His jaw muscles worked as he shook his head. They heard the rumble of the BearCat as it got near, and Dex pushed himself to his feet. As they headed for the street, Tony cast him a sideways glance. "So, we gonna talk about the fact you roared like a jaguar Therian?"

Dex shook his head. "Nope. You got bigger things to worry about."

Tony arched an eyebrow as the BearCat pulled up to the curb, and Cael was the first to jump out of the back.

"He knows about you and Sparks."

Tony stilled. "Fuck. I wanted him to find out from me."

"Yeah, well, he found out when the Chairman called to threaten your girlfriend. I say you got until tomorrow before he brings it up."

"She's not my girlfriend," Tony said quietly. "We're taking things slow. It's not easy for either of us."

Before Dex could ask, Tony climbed over the fence, and Dex did the same. Actually, in Dex's case, it was more like crawled. He was suddenly feeling exhausted, which was odd. Yeah, he'd pushed himself, but he wasn't injured or anything. His muscles strained, and his body felt sluggish. He was also starving. Like he hadn't eaten in days. What the hell was wrong with him? Sloane ran over and helped him down. He didn't say a word, just wrapped Dex up in his strong arms and rubbed his cheek against Dex's temple.

"You're okay," Sloane murmured.

Dex nodded, clutching onto Sloane's arms. Cael hugged the life out of their dad, the rest of the team soon joining in. Dex closed his eyes and laid his head under Sloane's chin, a rumbled sigh coming up through his chest. Dex and Sloane pulled back at the exact same moment, their wide eyes meeting. Dex's jaw dropped.

"Did you just...?"

Dex shook his head fervently. "Ixnay on the purring-bay," Dex ground out through his teeth.

"You did," Sloane said, stunned. "Holy fucking shit, babe. You just purred like a Felid." Everyone's head whipped around to stare at Dex. Sloane cringed. "I said that kind of loud, didn't I?"

Dex gaped at him. *Oh my God.* He was going to strangle that sexy beautiful neck. Sloane had not just outed him. With a glower, he poked Sloane in the vest, announcing loudly, "Well, now that makes two of us."

Ash let out a bark of laughter, and Sloane groaned. "Why would you do me like that?"

"Because if I'm going to suffer, so are you, darling, precious, love of my life. You and your sexy mouth let the jaguar Therian out of the bag."

"Wait," Ash said, walking over, motioning between Dex and Sloane. "You two can purr in Human form?"

"Human form is my only form," Dex replied with a sniff, crossing his arms over his chest.

"Which purrs like a jaguar Therian?" Ash turned to Sloane. "You purr in Human form?"

Sloane let out a long-suffering sigh. "Just get it out of your system, Keeler."

Ash did not get it out of his system. He laughed his ass off on the way back to the BearCat. He laughed all the way to the drive-thru where Dex ordered Therian-sized everything and polished it off in minutes. He immediately felt better afterward. Like his energy had been restored by the meaty-carby goodness. Ash was still laughing.

"Jesus, Ash, you making up for the whole of your freakin' life?" Dex asked, shaking his head in disbelief. Every time he thought Ash was going to shut it, he started laughing again. His face was red, he was crying. He was actually shedding fucking tears. Dex let his head fall into his hands with a groan. He was *never* going to hear the end of it. *Never*.

Back at HQ, they tried to get Tony to go to the hospital or at least have Hudson look him over, but Tony was stubborn as hell. While they'd all put their weapons and armor back in their respective armories, Tony had showered quickly and changed into a clean pair of jeans and a black long-sleeved henley. Then in Unit Alpha, he personally thanked every agent who had gone out there to bring him home. Those who were injured, he called. Tony had spent hours in the hands of murderers who'd planned to kill him, and instead of going home, he was here at HQ. This was where he wanted to be. Though Dex noticed that Tony made sure to stay close to Dex and Cael. Every so often, he would reach out and squeeze their shoulders, put an arm around them to pull them in for a brief hug, or just stand with his arm against theirs, as if seeking their comfort.

When Tony was done speaking to the other agents, he headed for Sparks's office, and Destructive Delta followed. He stepped foot through the door, and Sparks stood, her gaze darting to Dex before moving back to Tony. She waited, and Dex could tell it was killing her. Usually Sparks was unreadable, her expression guarded. It was a skill she'd mastered to perfection. But as Tony rounded the desk, a crack appeared in her armor.

Tony stopped in front of her. "I'm sorry."

The crack fractured and splintered. His soft words struck something inside Sparks, and she launched herself into his arms. Although they were the same height because of her heels, she looked small in his beefy arms. He turned his face into her red waves and murmured something Dex couldn't hear despite his Therian hearing. Tony kissed her temple, and Sparks nodded. She cleared her throat and pulled away, straightening her formfitting suit jacket. With a smile, she turned to address Destructive Delta.

"It's probably no surprise that expressing emotion is not something that comes easy to me. In my position and experience, becoming emotionally involved with anyone, forming any kind of attachment, means putting myself and those I may come to care about at risk. Over the years, it's been difficult to keep myself distanced from all of you, and although I still believe that there's a great risk involved in letting people in, I will say that I've learned a great deal from Destructive Delta." She swallowed hard and took a seat behind her desk. "I learned the true meaning of family. I also learned that your emotions don't make you weaker but stronger. Thank you for all you've done." She smiled warmly at them. "I am exceptionally proud of you. All of you." She faltered, her eyes getting glassy before she quickly looked away, and the emotion was gone. "You should all get some rest before the celebrating begins." She smiled at Dex. "You have a wedding rehearsal to prepare for."

"What about the Chairman?" Sloane asked. "Someone obviously put in the order for the Makhai to fall back."

"Intel informs me that the Chairman is in the wind. It's possible he's going to try and leave the country to regroup. We're monitoring all aircrafts. I'll let you know as soon as I know more. In the meantime, remain alert."

Everyone turned to go, but Tony spoke up. "Dex, Cael, could you stay?"

Sloane put his arm to Dex's elbow and leaned in. "I'm going to hit the showers. I'll wait for you in the locker room."

Dex nodded. The door closed, and it was just the four of them. Cael crossed his arms over his chest, the stubborn set of his jaw telling Dex this was not going to be fun.

"I'm not talking about this," Cael said, eyes narrowed.

"Cael," Tony said with a soft sigh. "I'm sorry things came to light the way they did. That's not how I wanted you to find out."

"That's the problem, Dad. You kept this from me." He frowned at Dex. "You *both* did." He turned back to Tony. "Were you even going to tell me?"

"Of course I was." Tony took a seat on the edge of Sparks's desk. "I was trying to find the right moment."

"There is no right moment," Cael replied heatedly. "I

mean, really, Dad? *Her*? Out of everyone you could have picked to get into bed with, you pick *her*?"

Tony's expression hardened. "Mind your manners, son. I taught you better than that."

Cael pressed his lips together in a thin line, his fists at his sides before he replied. "Yes, sir."

"My relationship is my business, just like your relationship with Ash is yours, and Dex's relationship with Sloane is his. We're all adults who know how to handle ourselves."

"Really? Because when you found out about Ash and Sloane, you showed up at Dekatria with Old Betsy."

Sparks's eyes went comically wide, and Dex had to put a fist to his mouth to keep from laughing. Shit. Cael totally called their dad out on that one.

Tony blinked at Cael before rubbing his chin. "I did, didn't I?"

"Yes," Cael replied, crossing his arms over his chest again. "Because you thought they were messing with your boys." Cael shot a look at Sparks. "So, tell me, Dad. How is this situation different?"

"The difference is, no matter how worried I was, I love those boys. I watched them grow from uncertain youths to fierce grown men. I may not have trusted them with your hearts, but I trusted them with your lives. Whereas you two never failed to let me know how much you disliked and distrusted Sonya. Yes, I should have told you both sooner, and this is on me, but you didn't exactly make it easy for me. I love you boys. The last thing I ever wanted to do was let you down, and I felt like somehow by developing feelings for Sonya, I had."

Dex glanced over at Sparks, who was looking off to the side at nothing, lost in her own thoughts. It was obvious she knew, and for the first time, Dex felt bad for her. She knew

Tony felt like he was letting his sons down by being with her, and she still stuck by his side? Dex frowned at his dad. "That last part was, uh, kinda harsh, Dad."

Tony arched an eyebrow at him. "I know, but I was honest from the beginning."

Dex turned to Sparks. "And you just accepted that?"

Sparks lifted her gaze, her expression unreadable again. She was hiding from him. "Why wouldn't I? I never gave either of you a reason to feel any differently toward me. You and Cael are your father's whole world. Of course he would feel that way. Whatever you may believe, I never intended for this to happen. We both fought it for a long time."

Dex turned his attention back to his dad. "You've never let us down."

"I must have at some point. I mean, why else would you two not confide in me? When did I start needing to be coddled and protected?"

It struck Dex then just how bad they'd shaken their dad's confidence. "You're right. We should have confided in you from the beginning. We told Sparks as much when she called us out on our bullshit."

Tony's brows shot up. "She did?" He turned to her. "You did?"

She nodded but remained quiet.

"She was right. How long have we been going behind your back, getting caught up in all kinds of shit, and keeping it from you? We thought we were protecting you, but this whole thing has proven that no matter what we do, we live in a world with no guarantees. We're family. Of course we're going to worry, but we need to trust in one another, and that means trusting in the decisions we all make."

Dex turned to Cael, who was scowling at him. "So, does that mean we're telling the truth about everything?" Cael narrowed his eyes, and Dex knew exactly what his brother was talking about. Tony might know about Sparks being TIN, but there was no way he knew about Dex being tortured by Wolf, or they'd be having a completely different type of conversation. From the corner of his eye, Dex saw Sparks tense, a barely audible gasp escaping her. There was something there. Something Dex couldn't quite put his finger on. Dex met his brother's gaze. Cael's big gray eyes waited expectantly.

"It means we need to trust one another. It also means we need to trust that the decisions we're making are the right ones for the right reasons." With that, he walked over to his dad and hugged him. When he pulled back, he swallowed past the lump in his throat. "I'm glad you're okay. You need anything?"

Tony smiled warmly. "Got everything I need right here. You boys go on. Get some rest. The next few days are gonna be kind of intense."

Dex stared at Tony and let out a bark of laughter. Only his dad would call a wedding intense after what he'd just been through. Dex headed for the door, waiting for Cael, who'd stopped to give their dad a big hug. After some murmured words between them, Cael joined Dex. The door to the office closed behind them, and Cael frowned at Dex.

"What happened to telling the truth? Let me guess, it's not your place to tell."

When had his little brother become such a smartass? "There's a reason she hasn't told him," Dex said, making his way to the locker room. He was looking forward to a nice hot shower and then going home and crawling into bed with his man.

"Yeah, she's saving her own ass. She knows if she tells him, he's done."

"No, there's something else. I'm sure of it." Dex paused outside the locker room. "You think Dad's really okay after everything that happened?"

Cael sighed. "You know Dad. He doesn't sit and think about things. They happen, it's over, and he moves on. Either way, after he gets debriefed, he has to see Dr. Winters. Hopefully the doctor can get through to him."

Dex hoped so. Their dad wasn't big on sharing his worries or insecurities. He wasn't a big talker, especially when it came to his own well-being.

Inside the locker room, Sloane sat on a bench talking to Ash, and Dex took a moment to admire his beautiful mate's profile. Sloane was down to his black undershirt and charcoal gray boxer briefs. He had one ankle up on his opposite knee, his big hand and long fingers resting on his ankle. The V-neck T-shirt was snug, stretching across his broad shoulders and over his biceps, since he was slightly turned to face Ash. His stubble had grown in thick. Dex stalked over and straddled the bench beside Sloane, who was engrossed in whatever he and Ash were talking about. Dex slid his arm around Sloane's waist and rested his chin on Sloane's shoulder. They were pressed together from head to toe.

"Mm, comfy," Dex said. He inhaled deep and groaned. "You smell so good."

"And on that note," Ash said, tugging at one of Cael's belt loops playfully. "Hey, sweetheart. Want me to get you anything from the canteen while you shower?"

Cael smiled brightly as he leaned in and kissed Ash. "A hot chocolate?"

"You got it." Ash stood and kissed Cael in return before Cael headed off to the showers.

“I guess I should shower,” Dex mumbled, not wanting to move from where he was pressed up against Sloane. Sloane turned his head and patted Dex’s thigh.

“Make it a quick one. I just want to get you home.”

Somehow Dex found the energy to spring up and off the bench. He cupped Sloane’s face and kissed him long and deep until he heard Ash grumble beside him.

“Do you mind? No one needs to see you two sucking face.”

Sloane laughed against Dex’s lips, and Dex reluctantly pulled back. He smiled knowingly at Ash. “You’re just jealous because that’s what you wish you were doing right now with Cael.”

Ash’s face flushed, and he muttered something under his breath before walking off. With a laugh, Dex stripped down to his boxers. He grabbed his toiletry bag from his locker as Sloane stepped up behind him, nuzzling his hair, his voice low and husky when he spoke.

“You really need to hurry up.” Sloane trailed a finger down Dex’s spine, making his body shiver. “I want to get you in bed and see what it takes to make you purr.”

Dex shut his locker and turned to Sloane, his toiletry bag covering the erection he now sported. Sloane licked his bottom lip, and Dex followed his sinful tongue. He lifted his gaze, a moan escaping him at Sloane’s blown pupils.

“I, uh, guess I better go shower.”

“Quick.”

“Quick,” Dex agreed before walking around Sloane and jogging toward the showers, a wide grin spreading across his face. So, Sloane wanted to see what it would take to make Dex purr? Challenge accepted.

CHAPTER TWELVE

"Dex, this place is stunning."

Dex chuckled at his aunt's huge eyes as they walked through the estate gardens where the wedding ceremony would take place. Months ago, Lou had presented him with a slideshow of possible venues, but when the photographs of this place came up, Dex knew immediately this was it. The historic French chateau-style castle and estate on Long Island was exactly what he'd wanted. They were surrounded by miles and miles of greenery, or rather a host of fall colors. The lush trees that stretched as far as the eye could see were beginning to burst with yellows, oranges, and reds. It was blissfully peaceful. No traffic and no city noise. They were in their own little bubble of serenity.

The estate was dazzling with its elegance, and for the next three nights, its thirty-two guestrooms would be occupied by Dex and Sloane's family, friends, and their friends' loved ones. Those attending the rehearsal dinner had arrived and were all currently touring the impressive and prestigious estate. Tony and Danelle had been the first ones to arrive, followed by the entire Hobbs clan, along with

Darla and her beau, Armel. Julia and Darla wasted no time in bringing Vivian Keeler into their circle of awesome momness. Then Lucia Huerta arrived with her husband, Thiago, and the parental monarchy was complete.

Having them all under the same roof was terrifying. Dex had never witnessed Ash so well-behaved. It had scared the ever-living crap out of Dex, and Sloane couldn't stop from snickering every time Vivian was near Ash. If she wasn't fixing the collar of his shirt, she was brushing something off his shoulder or picking a stray hair off his sleeve. She'd gushed over him, about how proud she was, and what a good boy he was. Dex and Sloane were all but ready to grab some popcorn and just follow the two around, it was so entertaining. Taylor, and especially Angel, thought it was the most hilarious thing ever.

"I wish you could visit more often," Dex said, saddened that he didn't get to see his aunt as often as he used to when he and Cael were kids, but she had moved to Philly several years ago to take care of her and Tony's mom, who needed looking after. Dex had met his adoptive grandmother once, but it had been brief. Tony had tried to include her in their lives, but the woman could hold a grudge something fierce. She'd never forgiven Tony for joining the THIRDS or for adopting a Therian son. Not after her husband had been killed on the job by a Therian.

"I know, baby. I miss my boys." She let her head rest against his arm as they walked in companionable silence. His aunt had been a constant in his life when he'd been little. She would babysit him and Cael, and she took care of them when they were sick and Tony had to work. She'd fed them, bathed them, read them stories, and taught them how to be kind and compassionate yet stand their ground. At fifty-two years old, Danelle Maddock was a tall, slender, stunning woman with flawless dark skin and striking hazel eyes. She was the sweetest, gentlest woman Dex had ever known, but if someone made the mistake of messing with her boys, well, hell hath no fury like a pissed-off Danelle.

After walking through the gardens with his aunt, it was time for dinner inside the beautifully decorated formal dining room with its soft yellow walls and ornate white crown molding. Music played softly in the background while they ate and chatted.

"Okay, everyone, settle down," Ash said as he stood, tapping the side of his glass. "When I was asked to make a best man speech, I knew exactly what I was going to say. And then I remembered my mom was going to be in the room."

Everyone laughed, and Vivian waved cheerfully.

"So I had to rethink things, especially when it came to my initial thoughts on Dex after his grand entrance his first day on the job."

Dex pointed to himself and blinked innocently. Ash shook his head at him.

"Yeah, nice try. No one here is fooled by that face." Ash turned back to address the room. "Let's just say that when I first met Dex, I wasn't a fan. At the time, the team wasn't in a good place. I was angry and mean."

Dex put up a finger and opened his mouth, only to have Sloane clamp a hand over it.

"Thanks." Ash smiled brightly and winked at Sloane. "See, that's what I'm talking about. Sloane has always had my back. He's like a brother to me. Before I got my mom back, he was the only family I had. No one knew me like Sloane. Back when Dex joined our team, we had this missing piece, one we not only couldn't find a fit for, but didn't want to. Dex didn't leave us a choice. He did what he does best, and he got under everyone's skin. Whether you liked him, loved him, or wanted to push him off the Brooklyn Bridge, he was there with that dopey smile of his, ready to go to war for you. We might not have always gotten along, but I learned pretty quickly that if you needed someone in your corner, Dex was your guy. He's fearless, relentless, and I've never seen anyone with a greater sense of justice than the guy with the same middle name."

Ash swallowed hard and turned to meet Sloane's gaze. "Sloane, I didn't understand what you saw in Dex, but as I watched your relationship with him grow, I started to see it. He was everything you needed and everything you deserved. He didn't just bring you back to us, he helped you heal and proved to you that you weren't broken but instead, worthy of every bit of love he offered. Seeing you two gave me hope." He reached down and Cael took his hand. "Because of you both, I found the courage to give my heart away, and I couldn't be more grateful. Thank you."

Sloane rose and stepped up to Ash. They hugged tight, and Dex blinked back his tears. Everyone stood and clapped. Dex joined them, and when Sloane stepped away from Ash, Dex held his arms out.

"Bring it here, big guy."

Ash shook his head at him, but his amber eyes were filled with amusement. As he hugged Ash, Dex murmured quietly, "Thank you for taking such good care of him. I promise I won't let you down."

Ash squeezed him before releasing him and sitting. As everyone enjoyed their meal, Dex and Sloane visited each table, spending time with their friends and family, knowing the next couple of days would be a whirlwind of activity. With two hundred guests attending the wedding, they wouldn't be able to spend as much time at each table as they would like, which was why this evening was for family and close friends before the other guests arrived.

After dinner, Lou grabbed Dex, Sloane, Tony, and the rest of their wedding party to begin the rehearsal, showing them what rooms they'd be waiting in. They ran through the music and Dex's cue for joining Sloane in the sitting room. From there everyone would exit out to the gardens, where the ceremony would take place. Lou lined everyone up in the order they'd be walking down the aisle, made sure everyone remembered how much space to leave, and how they should walk at a normal pace.

Dex stood in the doorway next to Sloane, staring out at the garden, which on Saturday would be decorated, filled with two hundred guests, and at the end have an altar where they'd be married.

"Oh my God," Dex said. He turned to Sloane, eyes wide. "We're getting married the day after tomorrow."

Sloane smiled warmly, his eyes filled with love. He cupped Dex's cheek and brushed his lips over Dex's. "And I couldn't be happier."

Dex leaned into Sloane and hummed. "I think getting married must be an aphrodisiac because all I can think about is jumping your bones."

Sloane opened his mouth to reply, but whatever he'd wanted to say had to wait because Lou showed up. They ran through the whole thing a couple of times to give Lou peace of mind. By the time they were done, they were all desperate to get to the dining room for a few drinks.

On the way back, Sloane took Dex's hand, and when no one was looking, kept walking instead of going into the dining room.

"Where are we going?" Dex asked, hurrying along as Sloane led him down the hall and through the door that led to the grand staircase. They went down the stairs, and the butterflies in Dex's stomach went wild. He felt kind of giddy, and he loved Sloane's sudden bout of spontaneity. It was dark outside, but the estate was aglow with warm light. They crossed the courtyard to an alcove at the far end that was shrouded in shadows.

Sloane pulled Dex inside, and before Dex had a chance to speak, Sloane had him up against the wall, kissing him and stealing the breath from him. Dex moaned against Sloane's lips, his fingers curling around the sleeves of Sloane's black dress shirt. Dex had all but melted when Sloane had finished dressing earlier in the day. He'd decided on a black button-down long-sleeved shirt and black dress pants. He looked sexy as hell, huge, and imposing, the most gorgeous man to walk these halls, and he was Dex's. His hair was neatly combed to one side in a retro style, and he had a jaw full of rough stubble. Dex could come just from looking at him.

A shiver ran through Dex, and he groaned when Sloane cupped him through his trousers. "Sloane," he breathed. They couldn't be out here for very long before someone would come looking for them. After all, they were sneaking away from their own rehearsal dinner. As if reading Dex's thoughts, Sloane quickly got to work unbuckling Dex's belt and shoving Dex's trousers, along with his boxer briefs, down to his thighs. He turned Dex to face the wall, and Dex spread his legs as far as he could, his hands braced on the smooth stone. He heard the tear of a lube packet and then felt the cold of Sloane's lubed finger penetrating him.

Dex groaned, and Sloane pressed his chest to Dex's back. He nipped at Dex's jaw while his fingers stretched Dex, first one, then two. Dex writhed beneath Sloane, and he pushed his ass back against Sloane's fingers, fucking himself on Sloane's long, slicked-up digits.

"Fuck, you're so goddamn hot," Sloane growled. He smacked Dex's ass cheeks, and Dex almost came right then.

"I need you inside me."

Sloane turned Dex's face so they could kiss—it was sloppy, wet, and filled with painful need. Sloane removed his fingers from inside Dex and replaced them with his cock. Afraid of making too much noise, Dex bit down on his bottom lip, his forehead pressed to the wall as Sloane slowly sank into him, the burn so delicious Dex couldn't help moving his hips. There was so much emotion swirling inside him that he feared his body wouldn't be able to contain it. He needed something to distract him, to leave him unable to think.

"I want it hard, Sloane."

Sloane kissed Dex's cheek. "Are you sure?"

Dex nodded. He needed to channel all the emotions inside him threatening to explode into Sloane taking him, into carnal desire from his soon-to-be husband. Out here with the sounds of nature, in the middle of a fairy-tale castle, just hours before their wedding, after the hell of the last few days, he wanted to feel Sloane down to his core. Sloane thrust the rest of the way in, and Dex gasped. He arched his back, and Sloane closed his hand around a fistful of Dex's hair, tugging his head back and claiming his mouth, a feral growl rising from his chest as he pumped himself inside Dex. They kissed like they'd been starved for each other's touch, tongues dueling, lips sucking, teeth nipping.

Dex thrust his hips, impaling himself on Sloane, and Sloane plunged into him over and over. Dex threw a hand back, his fingers digging into Sloane's thigh, the claws of his right hand growing out and scratching at the wall. Sloane palmed Dex's erection, his fist pumping in time with his deep thrusts. Sloane changed his angle and hit Dex's prostate, covering his mouth with his free hand to muffle Dex's cries.

"That's it, baby," Sloane said, breathless. "You're so beautiful like this, your face flushed, your gorgeous lips open as you make the sweetest noises. Do you feel that?" Sloane asked, snapping his hips, and Dex thought his eyes were going to roll into the back of his head. "Do you?" Sloane snapped his hips again, and Dex nodded. "When you walk back in there, you're going to still be feeling my dick inside you."

Dex moved Sloane's hand from his mouth and looked at him over his shoulder. "I love you, Sloane. I love you so fucking much."

Sloane's expression softened, and he kissed Dex, his thrusts remaining sharp and deep inside Dex. He stroked Dex, jerking him off as he murmured against Dex's mouth, "I can't wait to get you on that beach, to make love to you on the sand, in the ocean, my hands all over you." Sloane's free hand roamed Dex's body, caressing his skin, slipping under Dex's shirt and tweaking one of his nipples. Dex sucked in a sharp breath.

"Sloane," Dex warned. He was so close. Sloane nipped at his jaw, his hand moving quicker as his hips lost all rhythm.

"Come for me, baby. Spill yourself all over my hand so I can suck your come off my fingers."

"Oh God." Dex's orgasm plowed through him, his body trembling with the force of his release as Sloane pumped himself once, twice, then muffled his hoarse cry in Dex's hair as he came inside Dex. They stood together unmoving, Sloane's arm around Dex, his cheek against the back of

Dex's head. With a hiss, Sloane carefully pulled out of Dex, and Dex turned, groaning when Sloane met his gaze and did as promised, licking his hand clean before he kissed Dex so Dex could taste himself. They helped each other set their clothes to rights, and then Sloane leaned into Dex and lifted his chin, their eyes meeting.

"I should be nervous about Saturday, but I'm not."

"You're not?" Dex asked quietly.

Sloane ran his thumb over Dex's bottom lip. "I've never been surer of anything in my life. I love you, Dex, and nothing will make me happier than being your husband."

Dex wrapped his arms around Sloane's neck, his heart squeezing in his chest. As he kissed Sloane and thought about their upcoming exchange of vows, excitement bubbled up inside him. In just a few days, he would be married to this amazing man. He couldn't wait.

Sloane had never been happier. They kissed until they couldn't stay out here any longer and snuck back inside. As they approached the dining room, it was oddly quiet. They exchanged glances before Sloane opened the door, and they walked into a pitch-dark dining room. The lights suddenly came on, and they were taken aback by the collective shout.

"Surprise!"

Sloane gaped at their colleagues, all coming to stand together in the center of the room, now decorated in tangerine and turquoise balloons, streamers, and paper lanterns. A huge banner read: Congratulations!

"Oh my God, you guys." Dex gave a sniff, his eyes glassy. "I can't believe you did this."

"Believe it," Taylor said, grinning wide as he

approached. He held out his hand to Sloane, who took it, returning Taylor's smile. "Whatever our differences in the past, Sloane, you are one hell of a team leader. I knew my team was in good hands when Destructive Delta was out there with us. Thank you for everything."

"Thank you for always backing us up," Sloane said, his throat thick from Taylor's words. They didn't always see eye to eye, and yeah, there had been some rough moments between them, but Taylor was a great team leader who took pride in his job and did his damned best to keep everyone safe. Sloane had never questioned the man's skill or leadership ability.

Taylor nodded, his eyes bright with unshed tears. He turned to Dex, his expression softening. "PR, huh?"

Dex chuckled. "Yeah, somebody's gotta look pretty for the camera." He winked at Taylor, making him laugh. Taylor averted his gaze, his voice quiet when he spoke, and Sloane could tell he was trying to keep hold of his emotions.

"Not gonna lie, Daley. I'm going to miss having you out there."

Dex surprised Taylor by bringing him in for a hug. "I'll be around anytime you need me."

Taylor nodded. "Thanks. We'd arranged to do this in Unit Alpha, but you know..." His expression softened. "With everything going on with the sarge, we canceled it. When the sarge found out about it, he talked to Lou, and they arranged for us to surprise you here."

Tony came to stand next to Dex, who turned and hugged him tight. "Thanks, Dad."

"You're welcome, kiddo. Your unit wanted to give you a proper send-off, so here they are."

Dex wrinkled his nose and gave a sniff before turning to announce boisterously, "Let's get this party started!"

Everyone cheered, and Sloane laughed when eighties music started playing. He kissed Dex's cheek, smiling at the light in Dex's bright blue eyes. His partner was clearly touched by all the love they were being shown. Their colleagues took turns approaching them and congratulating them on their upcoming wedding and their promotions, teasing Dex about all the different PR stunts he was likely to be involved in. Most everyone seemed to agree that although it would be a shame Sloane would no longer be out in the field, the knowledge and experience he'd accumulated over the years would be of great value to team leaders in training. Better trained team leaders would mean stronger teams, all of whom would help move THIRDS HQ toward a better future. With the resources they had, they could make a big difference, not only in the lives of agents from all over the world, but also in the lives of the people they helped.

Their team came over once everyone had finished, and Ash gave Sloane's shoulder a squeeze. He didn't say anything, but he didn't have to. He knew Ash was touched, same as Sloane was. They really had one hell of a unit here. Sloane grinned at Ash. "So which one of you made sure no one came looking for us?"

Ash coughed into his hand, and Dex laughed.

"Aw, Ash. You big softie."

Ash rolled his eyes. "Whatever." He so wasn't fooling anyone.

As Sloane and Dex chatted with their friends and colleagues, they heard cheering. They looked up, and Sloane laughed at the giant, six-tiered donut wedding cake several fellow agents wheeled in. Dex gasped, and Herrera winked at him.

"We know you guys have your own fancy cake, but

seeing as how Dex has been going on about a donut wedding cake for months, we figured this would be the perfect time to get him one."

Dex wiped a tear from his eye. "It's so beautiful and looks so delicious." He pointed to the top of it. "I especially like the cake topper." It was two gummy bears, an orange one and a blue one, and between them they held a red gummy heart. Dex clasped his hands together. "Okay, everyone, dig in!"

Plates were handed out, and everyone laughed when Dex didn't bother with a plate. He just took the top two tiers filled with donuts off the cake. He blinked up at Sloane, innocently.

"What? It's technically two pieces."

"Yeah, I don't think so." There were enough donuts on those two tiers to feed their team. Or at least Hobbs. The last thing they needed was Dex on a sugar high, bouncing off the walls while Lou was trying to maintain some semblance of order. The poor guy had enough on his plate with the wedding and reception. Sloane had no idea how Lou managed it all.

Hudson and Seb joined them, with Nina and Rafe not far behind. Dex offered them donuts. "Take some. Mr. Scrooge McDonut over here won't let me stuff my face."

Nina laughed as she plucked a pink frosted donut with shredded coconut from the top tier. "Well, you do have a tux to fit into. Lou will murder you if you need to get it adjusted. Again."

"That wasn't my fault," Dex complained. "It's all the training I've been doing."

"And all the cake you've been eating," Letty teased, taking a blue frosted donut with white swirls.

"You said cake, but what I think you meant to say was

bench pressing." Dex narrowed his eyes at Hobbs, who took six donuts, three around each index finger. Dex turned to Sloane, his bottom lip jutting out. "How come Hobbs gets to stuff his face?"

"Because Hobbs isn't the one getting married on Saturday," Sloane said, kissing Dex's temple. "After the ceremony, you can stuff your face with all the wedding cake you want."

Dex waved a finger at everyone. "You all heard him. None of you are getting wedding cake. It's all mine."

Everyone laughed and continued to pilfer Dex's donuts until there was only one left, the one with the gummy bear grooms. Dex peered at Sloane, who had yet to take a donut.

"Don't even think about it, Brodie."

Sloane leaned in to kiss Dex, and while he had his partner distracted, swiped the donut. Dex's scandalized expression made Sloane laugh.

"You're adorable." He took Dex's hand in his and placed the donut on his palm. "And I love you."

Everyone *awwwed*, and Dex plucked the gummy heart from atop the donut. He handed it to Sloane. "I love you too, holder of my precious squishy heart."

Sloane opened his mouth, and Dex popped it in.

"You two are making my teeth hurt," Ash declared. "I need something to drink. Preferably with vodka or something." Ash walked off, and Cael cheerfully followed.

Sloane was touched by the effort everyone made to put together the surprise party. Zach came over with a big smile.

"Thank you for inviting me and my siblings to the rehearsal dinner and the wedding," Zach said. "They're very excited." He pointed over to his three bear Therian sisters and six giant bear Therian brothers, all chatting and laughing with members of Unit Alpha.

Dex patted Zach's bulging bicep. "Of course. How could we not? You're part of the gang, and you sort of played an important role in mine and Sloane's relationship."

Zach arched an eyebrow at him. "Oh? How so?"

"You made sure my first impression was a memorable one," Dex said, winking at him.

Zach chuckled. "I'm glad I could help."

They spent the next couple of hours talking to their colleagues and answering questions about their new promotions and the wedding. Everyone wanted to know when they'd be hearing the pitter-patter of little Sloanes or Dexes. The thought didn't terrify Sloane like it once had. It was still too soon, but it was no longer out of the question.

While everyone enjoyed the party, Dex and Sloane stood to one side, leaning against the wall and observing their friends and family. Several members of Unit Alpha hovered around Tony, and Sloane caught more than one of his colleagues scanning the room for the sarge, as if making sure he was there and safe. Sloane had a feeling Tony had just earned himself a protective detail whether he liked it or not.

"Hello, fellas." Hudson smiled brightly as he approached, Seb at his side. "A donut cake? You'd think you were at the office."

Dex let out a snort. "Where else am I going to get my sugar high?" As if realizing what he'd said, Dex blinked up at Sloane and ran his tongue over his bottom lip. "What I meant to say was, where else am I going to get all my healthy snacks? Yum, so many delicious veggie sticks and... nutritious rice cakey things."

Sloane shook his head, amused. "I love how you think I don't know about your afternoon donut run or that every fifth trip to the bathroom is actually a trip to the canteen."

Dex gasped, a hand flying dramatically to his chest. "Why, I have no idea what you're speaking about, sir."

"Right," Sloane said, "just like Hudson has no idea how all those boxes of cookies got into his locker."

Seb turned to Hudson and arched an eyebrow at him. "I thought you said you were going to cut down?"

Hudson shoved his hands into his pockets and suddenly found his shoes of great interest. "And I will."

Seb folded his arms over his chest. "You said that three weeks ago, remember?"

Sloane held back a smile as Hudson lifted his chin high with a sniff.

"I can quit anytime. I simply don't want to."

Dex and Sloane laughed. Poor Seb, as if he could ever deny his husband anything. He was worse than Sloane. At least Sloane had managed to get Dex to eat vegetables. Hudson never had that problem, but his cookie addiction was as bad as Dex's sugar one.

Dr. Winters approached, smiling warmly at them. "I just wanted to thank you both again for inviting me. It means so much. I don't normally accept invitations for events outside of work, but I feel I had to make an exception for you two." He extended his hand to Dex, who shook it, smiling wide, then he held his hand out for Sloane. "Congratulations."

"Thank you," Sloane said, shaking the doctor's hand. "Saturday."

"I'm so very happy for you both."

Dex looked at Winters's empty hands. "You don't have a drink. Let me get you one."

"Thank you," Winters replied, and Dex headed to the bar.

No one liked having to go see Dr. Winters because

usually that meant something was seriously wrong. It wasn't because he wasn't a nice enough guy or compassionate or understanding, but he was the guy they saw when they were in pain. Sloane had spent months in Dr. Winters's office talking to him about Gabe, and it had been agony, having to constantly pick at the scab of his wounds before they were even properly healed. It was the process. Talking to Winters was supposed to help him, but he hadn't been ready to talk to anyone, much less a THIRDS-appointed doctor. Everyone on his team had spent time with Winters, some more than others, but in the end, the man had helped them in many ways.

After Ash had infiltrated the Coalition and then been shot, he'd seen Winters. Calvin had seen the doctor on several occasions due to his position as sniper on Destructive Delta. Cael had several sessions after being kidnapped by Hogan, after his encounter with Fuller, when Dex had been taken by Pearce, and then Dex's "ambush." Dex had been in to see Winters almost as much as Sloane. The list was long.

As if sensing his thoughts, Winters placed a hand on Sloane's shoulder. "You two have been through so much, you deserve to be happy."

"Thank you, and thank you for everything you've done for me, and for Dex."

Winters chuckled. "He's a strong one, that one."

Hudson nodded his agreement. "Resilient little bugger."

Sloane stiffened. Those were words he never wanted to hear from Hudson, not after he'd heard them come from Hudson's brother the day Dex had died.

. . .

"Here you go." Dex returned with a drink for Winters, who thanked him with a wink and laughed softly at something Hudson said.

"That he is, Dr. Colbourn. You know, you remind me of an old colleague I worked with a long time ago."

"Oh?" Hudson asked.

"Yes. I should probably get in touch with him soon. It's been far too long."

Dex had no idea who they were talking about, but before he could ask, Tony called Winters over, and the doctor excused himself.

The lights dimmed before blue-and-purple club-style lighting turned on as the music kicked into high gear. The tables were moved to one side, exposing the dance floor, and it was open bar. Lou had arranged for cars to pick up their colleagues after the party and take them wherever they needed to go, so Dex had a feeling they were all going to be celebrating late into the night. The parental folk all said their goodnights as it got later in the evening, and everyone kicked up their heels, shots in hand.

Dex had been in the middle of impressing his husband-to-be with his Running Man skills when Seb rushed over. He stopped in front of Dex. "I think you might want to see this." The look on his face sent a chill through Dex, and he took off after Seb. *Now what?* If someone else tried to mess with his wedding, he was gonna cut a bitch.

Outside in the foyer, Seb came to a halt. "Everyone be quiet for a second." The foyer fell silent. "You hear that noise?"

"What?" Sloane asked.

"Listen?"

The rumbling, whirring sound got louder. Ash ran to

the window and looked around. "Seb's right. There's something in the sky... What the hell is that?"

Letty joined him, her eyes going wide. "That's a helicopter."

"Shit, someone order a chopper?"

"Ash, Seb, come with us," Dex said. "Everyone else stay here. We'll be right back."

Dex dashed off with Sloane right beside him. They hurried down the grand staircase that led out to the entrance courtyard, where a black helicopter landed, its bright white and red lights a sharp contrast to the warm atmospheric lighting of the courtyard.

Dex couldn't believe it. "It can't be."

"Tell me I'm not seeing what I think I'm seeing," Sloane said.

Dex wished he could, but they were all seeing the same thing.

"You've got to be fucking kidding me," Ash growled, his hands balling into fists at his sides.

The chopper's propellers slowed as the beast of a bird powered down. The door opened and out hopped Wolf in a pristine, expensive, designer three-piece suit. He removed the pilot's helmet and tossed it onto the pilot's seat before buttoning his suit jacket and sauntering over to them. He stopped in front of Dex, flashing a wide grin filled with perfect white teeth that Dex wanted to punch him in.

"Hello, Dexter."

"You've got some fucking nerve showing up here," Sloane growled, and Dex readied himself in case he had to keep Sloane and Wolf apart. One of these days Sloane was going to decide enough was enough, and Dex was not looking forward to that day. It didn't help that Wolf gave no fucks what Sloane thought and continued to pop up in places where Dex was, flirting like he always did.

"What are you doing here?" Dex asked.

"I've brought you a wedding present." Wolf leaned in with a wink. "Though it's not too late to change your mind. You can still ditch that stick-in-the-mud and travel the world with me. Oh, the mischief we could cause together."

"I'm going to fucking kill you," Sloane growled, and Wolf held up a hand to stop him.

"Easy there, mate. You have some uninvited guests heading your way."

Dex groaned. "Are you kidding me? What now?"

"There's an army heading this way."

Dex froze. "What?"

"The Makhai," Wolf said, motioning around them. "It would seem the Chairman is making one last go of it rather than retreating. I imagine he's grown quite tired of losing. His army will be surrounding the estate at any moment. Which is why I brought you a little present."

Wolf tipped his head toward the helicopter, and Dex followed him, Sloane not leaving his side. Ash and Seb weren't far behind, and Dex was grateful for their support. Wolf was still too unpredictable. There was no telling what he had in store for them or why he was here. Not that Dex didn't appreciate the warnings. Wolf was far more connected than the rest of them, but that didn't mean his intel was reliable or that he was even telling the truth.

Wolf motioned to a huge black crate inside the chopper before looking at Ash and Seb. "Hop to it, fellas. You're going to need all those muscles to get that out of there."

Ash let out a low growl but joined Seb and Sloane in grabbing the crate and pulling it out.

"I can't believe we're taking orders from this asshole," Ash grumbled.

"Said arsehole can hear you, Agent Keeler. I've killed men for far less."

Dex frowned at Wolf. "You killed someone for calling you an asshole?"

"Sounds awful, doesn't it?" Wolf shook his head in amusement. "Of course not. Don't worry that pretty little head of yours. Merely entertaining myself with your delightful friends."

Dex rolled his eyes, and Wolf chuckled.

The guys grunted as they lowered the crate, and as soon as it was on the ground, Sloane punched Wolf across the face.

Holy shit.

Wolf stumbled back, and Sloane glared at him as he shook his hand out. "You've had that coming for months," Sloane snarled.

A low growl escaped Wolf, and he narrowed his eyes as he took a step toward Sloane. Dex quickly moved in front of Sloane, putting himself between the two. With his hands up in front of him, Dex met Wolf's gaze and quirked a smile.

"You can't say you didn't deserve that."

Wolf arched an eyebrow at Dex before letting out a chuckle. "Fair enough." His eyes turned hard as he moved them to Sloanc. "You get one shot. Try that again, and not even your sweetheart will be able to save you from me."

Ash and Seb moved behind Sloane, and Dex quickly spoke up. "Okay, everyone. Let's just chill before the testosterone chokes us all to death." He motioned to the crate. "You want to tell us what's in that thing?"

Wolf pressed his hand to the digital display. The locks

clicked, and he opened the lid. They all stood around the crate, staring at it.

"Oh my God." Dex looked up at Wolf. "You brought an entire arsenal." He gasped and threw up an arm. "I call dibs on the rocket launcher!"

Wolf laughed. "A man after my own heart. That should even the odds a bit, don't you think?"

"Why are you helping us?" Sloane asked, peering at Wolf.

"For one, I'm not helping *you*. I'm helping your delectable fiancé. Two, the Makhai tried to kill me, then tried to kidnap my little brother in order to use me to kill for them. Consider me offended."

"The enemy of my enemy is my friend," Dex said.

"Something like that," Wolf replied, grinning wide. "Though I have tried to convince you to venture beyond acquaintance, but you're frustratingly loyal."

"So you're just giving this to us?" Dex asked eyeing him.

"I will take a thank-you kiss." Wolf tapped his lips.

Dex narrowed his eyes. "Yeah, that's not going to happen."

"It was worth a try." Wolf winked at him, then gave him a one-fingered salute before turning on his heels and heading for the pilot's seat.

Dex turned to Seb. "I need you to round up anyone who isn't a civilian." With Seb running off to do as asked, Dex quickly turned back to Wolf. "Wait, you're just going to leave?"

Wolf's smile was sinful. "Why? Do you *need* me, Dexter?"

"If we don't stop these guys, they're going to keep coming after us."

"Yes, they will, but they won't catch *me*." He made to climb in, but Dex's words stopped him in his tracks.

"And what about Hudson?"

Wolf slowly turned to meet his gaze. "Careful, Dexter." His voice was clipped and almost as terrifying as the coldness in his eyes.

"I'm not trying to manipulate you. It's the truth, and you know it. While the Chairman is out there, knowing who Hudson is to you, he won't stop."

The fear that flashed through Wolf's gaze was so quick Dex questioned whether it had been there at all. As if on cue, Hudson came running. Seb and the rest of their THIRDS friends and colleagues weren't far behind. Hudson's smile broke Dex's heart.

"Alfie," Hudson greeted cheerfully, as if his brother had just dropped by for a chat.

Wolf pressed his lips together. He faced Sloane and the others. "Arm yourselves, secure your civilians, and do what you do best. There's no room for hesitation or a conscience. It's you, and everyone you hold dear, or them." Wolf grabbed an MP5 submachine gun and a tactical vest.

"Are you ignoring me?" Hudson asked, scowling at his brother.

Wolf turned to Hudson. "Go inside."

"With the civilians," Hudson said before looking around at everyone putting on tactical vests and arming themselves with all manner of firearms. He moved his gaze back to Wolf, and Dex stifled a groan. He knew that look. "No."

Wolf peered at him. "What do you mean *no*?"

"I'm not going to hide. I'm going to fight alongside you and Seb." He took the machine gun from Wolf, who snatched it back with a snarl.

"Don't be so bloody pigheaded! Go inside!"

"No." Hudson squared his shoulders. "I'm a THIRDS agent, and... you know."

"You're a medical examiner."

Hudson narrowed his eyes. "I have training, Alfie."

"Stop calling me that," Wolf ground out through his teeth. "Go inside, or I swear on our grandmother's grave, I will pick you up and carry your arse in."

Hudson folded his arms over his chest. "I'd like to see you try."

Wolf opened his mouth to reply, then seemed to think better of it. "How about this. If you agree to go inside and stay there, I'll allow you to ask me *one* question."

Hudson worried his bottom lip, and Dex knew his friend was warring with himself. It was clear Hudson wanted to fight alongside them, with his husband, and although Hudson was right that he was a trained THIRDS agent, Wolf was equally right. Hudson's training wasn't the same as everyone else's. As far as TIN training, he'd only just started recently and had even further to go than Dex and Sloane. Were Dex in Wolf's shoes, he would have done what he could to keep his brother safe. Hudson glanced at Dex, and Dex nodded. Thankfully, Hudson gave in.

"Very well. How did you become... this?" Hudson asked, motioning to Wolf in general.

"That's a very complicated question that would require far longer than the few minutes we have, so I'll give you the abridged version. I was never dead. Only made to look as if I were." Wolf thrust his machine gun and tactical vest at Dex so he could remove his suit jacket, which he draped over Hudson's shoulders. Then he took the vest from Dex and strapped himself into it.

"TIN arranged it. They had been watching the both of

us for some time, but decided to approach me first, knowing if I joined, you were sure to follow. My falling to certain doom was the perfect opportunity. Fate decided I wasn't going to die at the bottom of those cliffs that day. It had a far more sinister design in mind."

"TIN forced your hand?" Hudson asked, his eyes filling with anger.

Wolf frowned at him. "Don't be ridiculous. They made me an offer. I could return home, back to living under my father's thumb, fall into line like our siblings and be miserable, watch you be miserable, or I could change our lives, starting with me as a TIN operative. I could be whoever I wanted to be, do what I wanted to do. The sky was the limit. I'd have a freedom I never knew was possible. I wasn't as brave as you. I never would have left for the States, not if it meant leaving you behind, but you weren't ready. You needed a push, and my death gave you that push. I accepted the offer on one condition—that Sparks would look after you and get you away from that bastard father of ours. She made sure when you applied to the THIRDS, a position at THIRDS HQ in Manhattan was open for you."

Hudson's brows drew together. "You're the reason I was hired to the THIRDS?"

"No. *You're* the reason you were hired. I just made sure you were close to where she was."

"Why?"

"So she could keep you safe. It was part of the deal."

"What deal?" Hudson asked.

"Why don't you tell him, Sonya?"

Everyone turned to stare at Sparks, who stood several feet away, Tony and Cael behind her. Dex was stunned by the tears in her eyes. When she spoke, her voice was almost a whisper.

"I would keep Hudson safe, away from anyone who might try to use him against Wolf, and Wolf would keep my daughter safe."

Wait, what? Dex walked around Wolf to stand in front of Sparks. "You have a daughter?"

Sparks nodded.

"That's why she's been trying so hard to track me down." Wolf turned to Dex, and Dex was taken aback by the sympathy in his blue eyes. "It's why she allowed me to take you, knowing you would be tortured. She was desperate to get her hands on me."

"Why?"

"While TIN was working to close in on the Makhai," Sparks explained, "the Makhai was getting to us. I needed to make sure my daughter was safe. Wolf was the only one who knew where she was, and if he was working for the Makhai..."

"Then you had no way of knowing he wouldn't betray you and give them your daughter."

Sparks turned to Wolf. "I never believed you would betray me. I was afraid they'd leave you no choice."

"Because they'd discovered who Hudson was." Wolf cursed under his breath. His jaw muscles clenched, and he met Sparks's gaze. "You were right to have worried."

Hudson drew closer to Wolf, his expression pained. "You would have turned over a young girl to those heartless monsters?"

"And what would you have me do?"

"Not sacrifice a child to save me," Hudson replied, indignant. "You should know better!"

This was insane. Dex didn't even know where to begin with all these truth bombs that were being let loose. My

God, did he know *anyone* who led a normal, uneventful life?

"Wolf," Sparks pleaded. "Just tell me..."

"She's a perfectly healthy, well-adjusted teenager, leading a very happy life," Wolf said softly. "She was accepted into the college she'd set her heart on, with a full scholarship, all of her own accord with no help from me. Her boyfriend is a lovely young Human who worships the ground she walks on." Wolf walked up to Sparks and put a hand to her cheek. "She's happy, Sonya, and safe." He smiled warmly, and for a moment, Dex saw Alfie, the man he'd been before betrayal had twisted his heart and turned him into a killer. "She has your eyes and that fiery red hair of yours. A force to be reckoned with, that one."

Sparks covered her mouth with her hand, a tear rolling down her cheek. "Thank you." It was then that Dex glanced over at his dad and saw the crushed expression on his face. Dex cursed under his breath. Tony had heard. As if coming to the same realization, Sparks whirled to face Tony.

"You let that psychopath kidnap and torture Dex?"

Sparks opened her mouth to reply, but Tony held up a hand to stop her.

"Did you see him?" Tony asked, pointing at Dex as he took a step closer to Sparks, the quiet fury burning in his brown eyes. "Did you see what he looked like? And I'm not talking about the blood or bruises. I'm talking about underneath." He shook his head in disbelief. "I understand going to the lengths you did for your child, but you did it knowing that was *my child* you were doing it to. Jesus Christ, Sonya, he put needles underneath my boy's fingernails!" As if remembering Wolf, Tony turned to face him.

"You coldhearted son of a bitch," Tony growled before lunging at Wolf. Dex moved quickly, and it took Sloane,

Dex, and Ash to hold Tony back. He spat in Wolf's direction. "You listen to me, asshole. This isn't over. I don't care how long it takes me, I'm going to make sure you end up locked up in a hole somewhere, do you hear me? You're going to pay for what you did to him."

"Dad, please."

Tony shook his head. "How can you even be talking to this guy, Dex?" Tony looked hurt and confused. Dex pulled him to one side, talking quietly.

"I know. Sometimes I don't believe it myself, but it's complicated, and no way am I excusing what he did, but if it wasn't for him, Seb and Hudson might not be alive now. He, um, he's Hudson's brother."

Tony stared at him. "What now?"

"It's a long story. Basically, Wolf is Alfie, who supposedly died several years ago, but as you can see, he's alive. He was hired by the Makhai to torture me and then kill me after finding Mom's file, but when I got away, he voided the contract and pissed them off. We've kind of got a weird arrangement of sorts. He has a habit of popping up and helping me out. He helped us find you, and, uh"—Dex cleared his throat—"he kind of has a thing for me, I think."

Tony's eyebrows shot up near his hairline. "I'm sorry, but are you saying the psychopath who tortured you and was going to kill you, shows up to help you out because he likes you?"

"Yeah, and to protect Hudson."

Tony narrowed his eyes. "Son, you hang out with some fucked-up individuals."

Despite the current circumstances, Dex couldn't help his bark of laughter. "Yeah, my world is pretty interesting. Would you mind if we talked some more about this later?

There's an army of trained mercenaries on their way to kill everyone, so I could really use your help."

Tony's eyes widened, but he quickly pulled himself together. "What do you need?"

"We need to put this place on lockdown and get everyone to the most secure areas of the estate. Thomas is going to need help."

"I'm on it." Tony brought Dex into a hug. "Be safe." With that, he turned and headed inside without so much as glancing in Sparks's direction.

"Excuse me, I just need to..." She turned to run after Tony.

Wolf turned his attention back to Dex. "I know this means little coming from me, Dexter, but if there is one person you can trust at TIN, it's Sonya. Never forget that everyone answers to someone, and that includes Sonya Sparks. The path you have chosen is a minefield of secrets and uncertainties. You'll need allies. Strong ones. We could all hope to be as strong as she is."

"The Chairman said if Sparks didn't do what he asked, that history would repeat itself. What did he mean? Does it have to do with her daughter?"

Something in Wolf's eyes said it did, but before Dex could ask, Wolf shook his head. "It's not my story to tell."

Hudson and Cael had gone back in to check on everyone. They'd split into two groups, one to guard the estate and everyone in it, and one to take down the Makhai army. Dex strapped himself into a tactical vest.

"So you're the only one who knows where her daughter is?"

"Correct," Wolf said.

"Are you really looking after her or using her as collateral."

"I gave my word, Dexter."

"Right."

"You really are so wonderfully sweet and naïve." Wolf crooked his finger. "Come here, darling. Allow me to give you another wedding gift."

Dex glanced over at Sloane, who looked uncertain. "What the hell."

When Dex walked over, Wolf wrapped an arm around his waist and pulled him in close to whisper in his ear, "Do you honestly believe that with all of TIN's resources at her disposal, and years of knowing me, Sonya Sparks couldn't catch me if she wanted to?"

Dex's eyes widened. They'd been right. Sparks had been keeping TIN away from Wolf. It was only when the shit started hitting the fan that she decided she needed to bring him in. This whole time, she'd been protecting him.

Gunfire erupted, and everyone scrambled.

"Take cover," Sloane ordered, running over to Dex.

"They're coming in through the gardens," Ash shouted from the doorway where he'd plastered himself.

"Motherfuckers!" Dex released the safety on the MP5 submachine gun. "These assholes are not going to ruin our wedding, Sloane."

Sloane grabbed his shirt and hauled him close for a quick but passionate kiss that had Dex's toes curling. "Be safe."

Dex nodded.

"You boys are adorable," Wolf said. "And such fun! I may have to visit with you more often."

"Please don't," Sloane said, making Wolf laugh.

Their wedding was only a day away, and Dex was going to be at that altar with Sloane if it killed him.

"Move in!" Sloane ran out first and Dex was right on his

heels. Everyone else charged, making sure to take cover when the bullets started flying. These weren't just brainless thugs; they were trained mercenaries. Even so, anyone who'd armed themselves was either a trained THIRDS Defense agent or a TIN operative. Dex was once again thankful for his new Therian DNA, making it possible for him to see into the darkness without needing special gear like his fellow Human friends, something that slick bastard Wolf had considered when he'd packed his wedding gift to Dex.

As Dex and Sloane dove into the fray, their friends were right beside them, from Sparks, who'd once again joined them, to Dom and his fierce lion Therian brothers. Zach and his six huge-as-fuck bear Therian brothers were tearing the shit out of the Makhai. A booming sound shattered the night sky, and Dex glanced up at the balcony. Oh yeah. And their resident badass sniper was having fun with Dex's rocket launcher.

The Chairman made a huge mistake sending what was left of his army here, and it had nothing to do with the wedding. They'd chosen to attack Dex while his family and his friends' families were under the same roof, and for that reason, not one of these hired killers was going to make it out of here alive. The Makhai started this war, and now Dex was going to finish it. Maybe not during this battle, but he wouldn't rest until those bastards were where they belonged, either behind bars or dead. These weren't innocent casualties. They were Therians who had accepted killing innocent civilians. It would be a cold day in hell before Dex let any of these assholes lay a hand on Danelle, Thomas, Julia, Darla, or anyone else in that house.

Dex let out a fierce growl as he twisted out from under a mercenary's grip. He brought his fist up with him, catching the bastard under the chin. The guy staggered back, and Dex fired before turning to shoot at any Makhai merc who crossed his path. He dodged one guy's charge, turned, and kicked out, all his weight behind the move, shattering the guy's kneecap. The man howled in pain and reached for the knife in his belt. Dex swiped it, spun, and plunged it into the side of the tiger Therian's neck. He jerked it out, then straightened in time to see a lion Therian charging toward Sloane, who was engaged in hand-to-hand combat with another jaguar Therian.

Dex placed his thumb on the spine of the knife, squared his shoulders, brought his right leg back, raised the knife, and threw it. It plunged into the Therian's thigh and brought him crashing down, distracting Sloane's opponent just enough for Sloane to get the upper hand. He slammed the guy's face into his uplifted knee, and the guy was out.

"Yes, sir."

Dex's hearing picked up chatter, and when he turned, he found one mercenary talking to himself, or rather to whoever was on the other end of his earpiece. Someone was giving these guys orders, and Dex was willing to bet that someone was the Chairman. Dex took the opportunity to strike and slammed into the guy from behind. They both tumbled to the ground, and Dex fired before the guy could get off a shot. He stole the guy's earpiece and listened in time to hear a man growl on the other end.

"I want both of them alive. Kill everyone else and burn the place down. You know what to do."

Dex's blood ran cold. It couldn't be. He knew that voice. They'd spent hours talking, even laughing together. Sloane shouted from somewhere behind him.

"Dex, look out!"

All he had was seconds. He spun and shouted, "Wolf!"

Wolf took off toward him, but Dex knew he'd never reach him in time. That wasn't why Dex's last words were to a man who'd tortured him. He wasn't looking for Wolf to save him. He was looking for the killer in Wolf, the man once referred to as Reaper. The last thing Dex saw before his world went black was the promise of retribution in Wolf's gaze after Dex unearthed the traitor among them. The Therian who'd pretended to be their friend, all the while stabbing them in the back and tearing TIN apart from the inside out. The man who was here on this very property to celebrate his and Sloane's wedding.

"It's Winters!"

CHAPTER THIRTEEN

Fuck. My. Life.

Pain flared through every inch of Dex's body as he stirred into consciousness. His brain was foggy, his head was killing him, and his body was on fire. Especially his shoulders and arms. Like someone was trying to rip his arms out of their sockets. He pulled his arms on instinct, only to be met with resistance and the clinking of metal. What the hell? His eyes flew open, and he jerked his arms again. His wrists were bound by thick leather cuffs attached to a thick chain hung over a giant metal hook dangling from the ceiling. His feet didn't touch the ground, and he was missing another shoe. Who the fuck kept taking his shoes? A groan met his ear, and his head shot back up. He stamped down the panic that threatened to rise inside of him.

Just a few feet ahead and to the right, Sloane sat in a metal chair, thick leather straps across his chest and around his wrists and ankles. He was out of it, eyes closed and head hanging forward. Dex took in the area around them. It was long but narrow, shrouded in darkness, with a couple of utility lamps hanging from hooks on what appeared to be aluminum walls. The place was grimy, dirty, with questionable stains on the floor in several places. Several armored crates were stacked toward the far wall, and to the left of that, a steel table contained a laptop and several pieces of tech. A small silver-colored rolling cart was parked beside Sloane, another beside Dex.

"Sloane," Dex hissed quietly. "Sloane, wake up."

Sloane groaned, his head lolling to one side as he started to regain consciousness.

"Come on, baby. Wake up for me."

Where the hell were they? How...? Everything came flooding back in a tsunami of pain and heartache. Oh God. This couldn't be happening, and yet it all made sense. Everything finally fell into place. As if he'd had this huge jigsaw puzzle with all these pieces, but he couldn't fit them together because there was one giant fucking asshole of a piece missing, and it had been under his nose the entire fucking time, right from the beginning, messing with them, waiting for the right moment to strike. *Fuck. Fuck. Fuck. All the fucking fucks!*

"Hello, Dexter."

Dex's blood ran cold, and he swallowed down the bile rising in his throat. He grabbed hold of the chains attached to the cuffs around his wrists and pulled, bouncing and swinging. Nothing budged. "Fuck. *Fuck.*"

"Such language."

Dex stopped struggling long enough to glare daggers at the man who'd shattered his reality. *Really*? Since when did swearing become more obscene than torture, murder, and *betrayal*?

"I'm sorry, did I offend your oh-so-delicate sensibilities? Good. Fuck you, you fucking traitor! You underhanded, arrogant, sociopathic son of a bitch!" Dex was so livid he was practically vibrating with fury. For years they'd bared their souls to this man, willingly and naïvely turning over every little detail of their lives, their loved ones, sharing their deepest, darkest secrets. There was no one Dex knew whose life hadn't been touched by this man. Cael's, Sloane's... Tony's. "We trusted you. We *all* trusted you. How could you look us in the eye, after everything you've done? How could you look my father in the eye?" Then he remembered his last words before everything had gone dark. Suddenly he found himself grinning.

Winters came to stand before him, his hands shoved into the pockets of his gray slacks as he tilted his face up to study Dex. "You seem to be rather pleased about something. Would you care to share?"

"I'm *pleased* because whatever happens to me, your days are numbered." Dex's grin widened as he met Winters's eyes. "He knows."

Realization dawned on Winters, the smugness falling from his face and making Dex laugh.

"That's right. He knows who you are and what you did. There's *nowhere* for you to hide. He's going to find you, and when he does, he'll make sure you get what you deserve. That's if I don't get my hands on you first," Dex hissed. He flinched as his claws pierced his skin. A swipe of his claws was all it would take, and Dex wouldn't hesitate.

Winters tsked. "My dear Dex. What kind of unsavory individuals have you been associating yourself with? Have you forgotten he tortured you? Tried to kill you?"

"Believe me, I haven't forgotten. Just like I won't forget *you're* the one who sent him after me. *You* paid him to torture me, to kill me. *You're* the puppet master who's been pulling everyone's strings for decades. Shultzon, Moros,

Wolf, Sparks... TIN. You're so fucked, not even hell is going to want you."

Winters smiled, his eyes cold and empty, like the man's soul. "Let's see if we can knock that cockiness down a peg or two."

Good luck with that. Right now, his cockiness and anger were all Dex had. That, and the hatred he felt down to his core. Criminals he understood. Thugs like Hogan, Collins, and the Coalition he got. Hell, Dex even understood where a guy like Isaac Pearce was coming from. He might have been unhinged, but Dex could see how the guy had gotten to where he ended up, could pinpoint the exact moment the final thread of sanity snapped. Winters? *The Chairman*? This was why Dex had signed up for TIN, to stop monsters like him.

Dex opened his mouth for another smartass remark when a huge Therian in a black tactical uniform appeared from somewhere behind Dex, walked past him, and wheeled over a strange-looking machine with dozens of thin long wires attached to small pads.

"What are you doing?" Dex demanded, watching in horror as the guy moved the machine to Sloane. "Get the fuck away from him!"

The lion Therian leaned over and tore Sloane's dress shirt open, the buttons popping and pinging as they hit the floor and the aluminum walls. He tore at Sloane's white undershirt and rolled up Sloane's sleeves before he began taking the pads one by one, removing the backing, and sticking them all over Sloane, at his temples, his arms, and his chest. Dex fought fiercely against the chains holding him, screaming as the Therian flicked switches, then pressed a red button.

Electricity crackled, and the lights flickered. A guttural

cry shook Dex to his core just as a jolt of pain sparked through him. He gasped, his back arching and tears filling his eyes. *No. Please God. No, no, no.* Another jolt was accompanied by a scream that had Dex crying out. The lights flickered once again, and another surge of high voltage shocked his system. His body trembled involuntarily as Winters held up a hand.

Sloane's chest heaved with panting breaths, his eyes wide as he struggled to figure out what the hell was going on. He turned his head, the heartbreak on his face tearing at Dex's insides. "Dex..."

"You son of a bitch!" Angry tears welled in Dex's eyes, and he wanted nothing more than to tear Winters apart. The man had listened to Dex pour his heart out. He'd given Dex advice on dealing with the heartache he'd faced over the years, and now he stood there as if none of it had happened? It had all been a lie. The sympathy, the gentleness, the kindness had all been bullshit. A façade to hide the disturbing truth.

Sweat dripped down Sloane's face, and Dex could tell his soon-to-be-husband—because screw these assholes, they were getting out of here and getting married—was trying hard to keep it together. The lion Therian reached for the red button again.

"No! Back the fuck off!" Dex jerked at the chain to no avail. Sharp pain shot through his arms and wrists. "Don't you fucking touch him!"

The guy pressed the button, and Dex's scream joined Sloane's as the current surged through Sloane. Dex's body convulsed, and Winters hovered near Dex.

"Fascinating. Make a note that the hybrid feels his mate's pain."

The hybrid.

Another jolt, and Dex gritted his teeth against the nauseating agony. His insides felt like they were on fire, the smell of burning flesh stung his nostrils, and he almost gagged. He struggled to draw in air, his muscles straining as if being torn from his bones. Whatever suffering Dex was experiencing, it was far worse for Sloane, who was receiving the shocks directly. As bonded mates, they felt each other's pain if it was significant enough, and holy fuck was this significant. Dex had never, *ever* felt anything like this. Not even when he'd been tortured by Wolf. He turned his head to look at Sloane, a lump forming in his throat at the tears that escaped Sloane's beautiful amber eyes. His chest rose and fell in rapid pants, and his body shook so badly the chair rattled.

"Baby," Dex pleaded. "Stay with me."

Sloane nodded. "I... love... you."

"Disgusting," Winters said with a sneer. "Do you know how painful it was to watch you two? Every time I thought one of you was going to do the right thing and walk away, you didn't. Then I had to listen to you both babbling on about each other and your unholy affections." Winters nodded at his companion. "Hit him again."

"No!" Dex jerked at his restraints over and over, putting all his strength into the movements, but nothing budged. "I'm going to tear you motherfuckers apart!"

"You won't." Winters pointed up to the chain securing Dex to the ceiling. "No zip ties this time. You won't be getting out of that."

"Why?"

Winters put a hand up to pause the next shock, and Dex didn't dare show his relief.

"Why?" Winters leaned in, repulsion and hatred burning in his eyes. "Because you're an abomination. It wasn't enough to copulate with one of our kind, but to be marked, bonded, and then have the audacity to steal DNA from him? How *dare* you try to be like us." He punched Dex in the gut, and Dex gasped. He coughed and wheezed as the breath left his lungs. His body swung, and Dex gritted his teeth against the jolt to his shoulders.

Winters smoothed a hand over his hair, calm as can be. He nodded, and another bolt of lightning crackled through Dex's body. He shut his eyes tight to Sloane's scream, his heart beating in his ears. Sweat dripped down Dex's face, blood trickled from his nose, and he shivered violently. The lights in the room flickered, or it could have been his vision. They had to find a way out of this. Sloane wouldn't be able to hold out much longer.

"We can't allow Sloane to live and infect another Human. Once he's dead and you're left a bereaved, weak mess of a thing, we're going to take you apart piece by piece. Then we'll use what we've learned from your tainted carcass to destroy every other abomination out there."

Sparks had been right. There were more like him. The shock must have shown on his face because Winters laughed.

"Did you think you were the only one of your kind? My, but we have quite the ego. There are more out there, hiding, foolishly believing we won't find them. We found those that came before you. We'll find the rest of the mistakes."

Mistakes.

As if reading his thoughts, Winters shrugged. "That's what you are. Nothing more than a mistake. A freak of nature."

"Kind of hypocritical, don't you think? Calling me an abomination, a freak of nature, a mistake. Everything you've been called since the virus made you."

"Only the Pre-First Gens were made. The time will come for them to be exterminated as well, leaving only the pure to inherit the earth." Winters strolled over to Sloane and petted his head. He let out a heavy sigh. "It's a shame we have to destroy him. I always admired him. Never understood his attraction to Humans, but that could have easily been remedied. He'd have made a fine soldier. If it weren't for the anomalies in his blood, we could have used him. We need strong Therian specimens like Sloane to help us create a better world, a world run by Therians. Those Humans who don't fall in line will know what it's like to live in zoos. To live in fear, hiding in crumbling hovels like Greenpoint, fighting for scraps of food like savage beasts." Winters ran his finger absently over the classification tattoo on Sloane's neck. "We'll see how Humans like being branded."

"Why would you kill Therians? *You're* a Pre-First Gen." The guy was older than Sloane. That made him a Pre-First Gen. Dex understood Winters's hatred for Humans, and he'd never agreed with the marking. Hell, he'd lost his shit the day they'd marked Cael. The Human race, and the world's governments, had a lot to answer for where Therians were concerned, but what the Makhai wanted to do was insane, and it sure as hell didn't explain the genocide they had planned for their own race.

"Pre-First Gens aren't pure Therians. They're diseased, sickly remnants of our Therian origins. As for me and my associates, someone needs to oversee the new world."

"Of course." Typical. Genocide was always so much easier when you didn't include yourself among the diseased.

Winters turned to him, a smile Dex had seen dozens of times making him feel sick to his stomach. He approached Dex and spoke softly.

"When the cleansing begins, I'm going to start with the THIRDS and all your diseased friends. That little problem you seem to think I have? He'll be under my thumb once he sees I have his precious little brother, and *then* I'm going to start with *your* brother, until everyone you know and love becomes the casualty of a war long overdue." He stepped back and clapped his hands together excitedly. "But first, we're going to have a little fun."

"If you're going to kill us, just do it," Sloane grumbled, spitting out a mouthful of blood and saliva. "Don't bore us with your bullshit."

Dex shook his head, his lip curled up in a sneer. "He's probably got a couple of monologues planned. What if we do a quick-fire round instead? Liven things up a bit."

Sloane laughed, though his smile didn't reach his eyes. "We could play charades. Two words, eight syllables."

"Egotistical maniac?"

Sloane beamed at him. "Baby, you're so smart."

"Thank you, boo."

"Mind you," Winters said, rubbing his bottom lip with his finger, "and this is just my professional opinion, but it's possible you may both suffer from several underlying psychological disorders."

Dex let out a bark of laughter. "Oh shit. I hope you're not planning on charging us for that one, because let me tell you, that ain't news. I mean, isn't that why we came to see you?"

Sloane let out a snort. "Of course, that's a little bit hypocritical, Dr. Winters. I mean, you've got two of your former patients shackled in your"—he looked around—"whatever the fuck this is. Box. And you're telling *us* that *we're* screwed-up? It's okay to admit it. Nothing to be ashamed of. We do just fine."

"And seriously? The *Chairman*?" Dex scoffed. "*That's* what you chose to name yourself? Out of everything you could have chosen, you give yourself the title of corporate douchebag? How is that scary?"

Sloane gasped. "What if he takes away our 401(k)?"

Dex shook his head in mock horror. "What's next? Dental?"

"You know what that means," Sloane told Dex somberly. "No more gummy bears."

"Nooooo!" Dex's bottom lip quivered as he turned his attention to Winters. "Talk about kicking a man when he's down." He perked up. "Maybe he named himself after that movie." He cringed. "That was a terrible movie. I'd go with the corporate douchebag."

Winters rolled his eyes at Dex. "I get the feeling neither of you is taking this situation with the amount of gravitas it merits."

"Yeah, I went to college too, Doc. You and your gravitas can sit on it and rotate."

Silent fury filled Winters's eyes, and he nodded at his companion. Dex cried out against the pain jolting through his body, the chains noisily clinking above his head as his body shook, the sound of Sloane's screams reverberating around them. After the third time, everything went black.

Dex groaned and slowly opened his eyes. His ears were ringing, and his vision was sharpening. He flexed his fingers to fight the numbness creeping in.

"Welcome back."

Shit. What happened?

"You and your fiancé passed out there for a second." Winters smiled up at him. "I gave you both a little something to perk you up. Can't have you missing out on all the fun."

Sloane...

Dex looked over at Sloane and almost choked on a sob. "Sloane..." His voice was hoarse, and his body ached all over. Sloane let out a groan, and Dex almost cried with relief.

"Aw, look how happy you are. Don't worry, he's simply resting. Astounding specimen, but then, I expected no less from him. He's a survivor. A true Therian warrior." Winters shook his head with a tsk. "You've brought this on him, Dex. Sentenced him to death. You should have let him be."

"Fuck you," Dex spat out, hissing at the pain of slowly unsheathing the claw from his left index finger. He discreetly tucked it close. They had to find a way out of this, and they didn't have long. Winters intended on killing Sloane and dissecting Dex. This wasn't a simulation. It wasn't a training exercise. If they didn't do something, they were dead. If they could just get themselves out of this, they could contact someone on their team. He wasn't about to underestimate Winters and how many goons he probably had around here. There was no doubt in Dex's mind that their family was out there searching for them. Tony was probably losing his damn mind.

Dex's entire body was in agony, but whatever Winters had given him provided a nice little boost of energy. Could it have been the same thing Wolf injected him with when he'd tried to keep Dex awake? That seemed to really do the trick. Whatever the case might be, Dex needed some time, and with a guy as egomaniacal as Winters, he knew just how to get that. Winters didn't seem to be in any particular hurry, which meant he was feeling confident Dex and Sloane were going to meet their demise at his hands.

"Dr. Winters, please."

Winters chuckled. "Oh, it's Dr. Winters now, is it?"

"How did you do it?"

"Do what?" Winters asked as he went about arranging surgical tools on the silver medical tray he must have placed on the cart beside Dex when he'd passed out. There were four guards with tranq rifles now posted around the room and four medical staff members. Seeing as how Dex couldn't see behind him, there was no telling how far back the room stretched or who else was there. Since he couldn't see any kind of door, he had to assume it was behind him.

"How did you spend day after day, month after month, year after year acting like you gave a shit? Consoling us, offering advice, spending hours talking, laughing, being our friend."

"I'm very good at what I do. It wasn't so much pretending as playing a role, one I used to my advantage to gather intel. Other than Themis, who else at the THIRDS could gather as much sensitive information as I could? No covert ops needed, no sneaking about or trickery. All that was required on my part was patience, and the information would come to me. Fortunately, patience is something I possess in spades."

"You really think you're going to walk away from this? TIN will find the mole."

Winters's laugh sent an icy chill through Dex. "Oh, sweet, naïve Dexter." His grin curdled Dex's blood, but not as much as the words he whispered when he leaned in. "I *am* the mole."

Dex's heart almost stopped, and he stared down at Winters. "You... you're TIN?"

Winters returned to add more tools to the tray, including a bone saw. Dex swallowed hard, pretending he hadn't seen it.

The smile dropped from Winters's face. "When I was

infected by the virus, I thought I was going to die, and after I was given the vaccine, when I shifted, I believed I had been cursed. I was treated like a rabid animal and shunned by my family, friends, and peers. It was a dark, painful time in my life. Then I was approached by the THIRDS, and the thought of working with others like me, in a healing capacity, was enough to give me purpose. That's where I met General Moros. We became very good friends, and I realized I wasn't alone. He taught me I shouldn't be ashamed of what I was, that I wasn't cursed but blessed. That we had evolved past Humans, were better in every way, and why should we allow ourselves to be branded and spit on by a species weaker than us?"

Winters turned his back, and Dex cast Sloane a glance, thankful to find Sloane had his head turned in his direction, watching him. Discreetly, Dex lifted his gaze to his hand and stretched out his clawed finger. He moved his index finger before tucking it back against the restraint. When he lowered his gaze back to Sloane, Sloane's eyes were closed, and he winced in a way that was all too familiar to Dex.

That's it, baby. You can do it. Stay with me.

Dex turned his attention back to Winters just as the man returned to the tray. What the hell did Winters plan on doing? Actually, he didn't want to know. "So, if you're TIN, why didn't Sparks know?"

Winters moved the tray closer to Dex and lined up several syringes filled with foggy liquids. One of his cronies wheeled over a gurney with numerous straps hanging off the sides. "What happened to the boring monologue and charades?"

Dex glared at Winters, and Winters laughed.

"Now who's being a spoilsport? Sparks doesn't know I'm TIN because my clearance level is higher than hers."

Fuck. "How much higher?"

Winters met Dex's gaze. "There are five high-ranking officials with national security clearance higher than even that of the POTUS. They run TIN. I'm one of them."

No wonder Sparks didn't know.

"No one knows my identity as Dr. Winters other than my four colleagues, and none of them know I'm the Chairman. After Moros and I formed the Makhai, I was made an offer by TIN. I accepted immediately. Moros and I needed to know what we were up against, and it was worse than we thought. TIN didn't want to put Therians in power. They wanted to ensure equality between Humans and Therians. They wanted to make certain Therians didn't abuse their power. The absolute gall.

"We couldn't have that, so I spent years moving up the ranks, keeping the Makhai informed and one step ahead of TIN. My hope was that one day the Makhai would be strong enough to overpower TIN, and TIN operatives could be convinced to join our fight." Winters shook his head. "But soon it became apparent the disease within TIN had spread far and wide, taking hold of exceptionally talented Therians. Certain operatives had to be taught a lesson. When Sonya and her team got too close, we made an example out of them."

"You were behind the ambush that killed Tucker?"

Winters smiled. "Yes. Wolf—Fang at the time—was too much of a threat, too good an operative. I needed to act quickly. Operatives can't afford to form attachments, or someone will try to exploit it. I knew what Tucker meant to him. Wolf made it so simple. I had hoped Sonya would meet her demise along with Tucker, but unfortunately, Wolf intervened. A minor setback. Sonya made the same mistake as Wolf. She truly believed we would never find out about her little secret family. I put an end to that quite quickly. She arrived in time to watch her home explode with her husband and child inside. It was a shame about the child. I do dislike extinguishing Therian life, but the Human mate had to go."

Oh God. A husband. That's what Winters had meant when he said history repeating itself. Dex thought he was going to be sick. The only thing keeping his dinner in his stomach was the fact that Sparks's daughter was safe, thanks to Wolf. As long as the Makhai believed she'd died in that explosion, she'd be safe. How could Winters justify what he'd done? How many had he killed to pave the way for the Makhai?

"You can only hide the truth from them for so long," Dex said, feeling the leather cuff tear. If his claws could pierce aluminum, they could sure as shit cut through leather.

Winters tapped at the syringe before turning to Dex with a grin. "By the time my colleagues discover the truth, it'll be too late. Are you done trying to buy yourself more time? I'm a little disappointed in you, Dexter. Surely you don't think I'm that much of an amateur. We have all the time in the world to chat. By the time your friends discover where you are, they'll arrive to find nothing but an empty lot. I never spend longer than I have to in one place, so my men are making arrangements to move us as we speak. Now this will hurt quite a bit. It's a little concoction that will paralyze you but keep you awake while I slice into you." He called for a couple of his men and motioned to Sloane. "It's time."

The lion Therian who'd been shocking Sloane turned the setting up on the machine. What did it take to be that coldhearted? Did the Makhai pay *that* well?

Dex glared at the lion Therian. "You're an asshole."

The guy arched an eyebrow at him before turning his attention to Sloane, who started murmuring something.

"What's he saying?" Winters asked, frowning.

The guy leaned in, and Sloane slammed his head so hard against the Therian's face, Dex heard bone cracking. The guy let out a howl and went stumbling against the equipment, everything going down with him as he hit the floor, tearing the wires attached to Sloane right off his body. Using the distraction, Dex jerked at the cuffs he'd been cutting away at, and they tore the rest of the way. He dropped to his feet and rolled as Winters lunged to stab Dex with a needle. Popping up, Dex swiped a sharp surgical knife from the tray before he could achieve his goal and swung it at Winters, who jumped out of the way, the knife slicing through his suit jacket like butter.

Winters shouted for backup, and next to Dex, Sloane had managed to slice through one of his straps, his left arm now free.

"You're not getting out of here alive," Winters snarled, grabbing one of the knives, the syringe still in his other hand. He lunged at Dex just as Dex snatched the tray, sending everything on it flying before the tray collided with the side of Winters's head, momentarily stunning him and throwing him off-balance.

Dex bolted toward Sloane and managed to slice through the strap restraining Sloane's right wrist. He handed Sloane the knife, then darted off to draw the guards away from Sloane. He swiped the tray as Winters shouted at his men.

"What are you waiting for? *Get him*!"

Dex hurled the tray at one of the guards, striking him in the neck. He choked and gurgled, grabbing onto his neck and dropping his rifle. Dex made a dive for it, snatched it up, and rolled onto his back. He shot at the guards charging toward him. While Winters wanted Dex alive to perform his little experiment, they had a fighting chance. Three guards went down and the others scattered, including Winters, who ducked behind a refrigerator that looked like it belonged in some fallout bunker. Dex scrambled to his feet as one of Winters's men charged Sloane, who was busy cutting at the strap around his chest. Dex blocked the guard's path, claws unsheathed and fangs extended. His blood boiled, his pulse quickened, and his muscles pulled tight. His vision grew sharp, and his senses were heightened as he hissed at anyone stupid enough to come between him and Sloane.

"Restrain him!"

"I got this," Sloane told Dex as he stood, his knees buckling. Dex caught him and shook his head.

"We need to get you to a hospital."

Sloane breathed in deep, squared his shoulders, and straightened, his amber eyes ablaze. He stepped away from Dex, the calm fury coming off him in waves. Dex sniffed the air and grinned. His partner's feral half was mighty pissed, and anyone who knew anything about Felid Therians knew you didn't want to incur the wrath of a jaguar Therian.

The room wasn't a room but what looked like... *Shit.* Dex stepped closer to Sloane. "I think we're in a shipment container." That would explain the lack of windows and just the one exit.

Sloane nodded. "That means there's only one way out."

The way out was currently open on one side as several armed Therians hurried inside. There was no telling where they were or how many more of the Makhai's goons were out there.

The men charged, and Dex turned to his training and

the fighting techniques he'd learned, along with some good old Human-Therian hybrid slashing the shit out of anyone who got close enough.

"The hell with this," Winters snarled. "Just kill them!"

Shit. They needed to think fast. Turning the gurney Winters had planned to dissect Dex on onto its side, they lifted it and tossed it at an approaching group of guards, knocking them off their feet. A rifle skidded past Sloane, and he dove for it and picked it up as he rolled to his feet.

"The crates!" Dex motioned behind them, and they fired at the group of guards as they made a break for the stack of armored crates. The shipping container filled with the sound of bullets hitting the crates and aluminum walls. Dex peered out around the side of the crates and fired, while Sloane did the same on his side, shooting any and everything that moved. Several of the guards rushed back out, using the doors of the container to shield themselves since there was nowhere else for them to take cover inside. Well, there was one place, and it was currently occupied by Dex and Sloane. Dex set his sights on Winters, who was walking briskly toward the end of the container toward the doors. He was talking into his cell phone.

Shit. They couldn't let that son of a bitch get away.

"Sloane, Winters."

"Go! I got this!" Sloane provided cover while Dex made a break for it. Sloane could handle himself, and Dex trusted his partner to get the job done and survive. Judging by the way Sloane came at Winters's men, his money was on Sloane.

Dex fired at the guards behind the left door as he slammed into the right door with all his strength, sending the guards on the other side flying. Between him and Sloane, they took out the guards, leaving the ones in the container and anymore that might show up. Dex took off after Winters, who turned, saw him, and bolted into a run, dropping his cell phone in the process. Dex swiped it up, dialed a code sequence, and put it to his ear as he sped after Winters. He'd been right. They were in a shipping yard. Outside it was bright, which meant they'd been in there for hours. The line rang once, and a somber voice picked up.

"Identify yourself."

"Sparks, it's me!"

"Dex? Where are you?"

"With the Makhai, chasing after Winters in a shipping yard. We need backup. Can you trace the phone?"

"We're on our way."

"Sloane's inside one of the containers with these assholes. I'm going to get Winters." He left the phone on and shoved it into his pocket. Fucker was fast, but Dex was part Felid now, so he was faster. He pushed himself and started closing in until Winters made a sharp left, then a right, tearing down the dock where several boats were anchored, including a speedboat. The bastard had been prepared.

Dex lunged at Winters and tackled him to the ground. Winters rolled onto his back, kicked at Dex, and landed a blow to Dex's chest that sent him rolling, his back hitting one of the pier's iron bollards. Pain rippled through Dex's back, but he quickly pushed to his feet. Winters came at him fast and hard. The guy might have been playing doctor, but he was clearly trained. Dex had to push himself to keep up with Winters's moves.

In the distance, Dex could hear a speedboat. They were coming for Winters. There was no fucking way Dex was letting him walk away.

"Don't fight this, Dex," Winters growled, producing a

knife from inside his sleeve and catching Dex off guard. He sliced at Dex's thigh, and Dex momentarily faltered. It had been a split second, but it was enough for Winters to get the upper hand. "Just think of it like this. You'll be joining your dear mom and dad."

Winters kicked at Dex, and Dex's back hit another bollard, knocking the wind out of him. Winters sliced at him again, but Dex managed to grab his wrist and knock the knife out of his hand. It bounced on the rickety dock and plunged into the water. Winters was relentless. He threw an arm around Dex's neck and put him in a choke hold, his knee pressing into Dex's groin. Throwing a hand back, Dex grabbed the thick rope hanging from the bollard, quickly loosened it, and tossed it around Winters's neck. With a fierce roar, Dex jerked the rope, and Winters choked, his fingers clutching the rope around his neck as Dex spun him, and kicked at the back of Winters's legs, forcing him to his knees.

Gunfire erupted around the docks, and Dex pushed Winters down onto his stomach, kneeling on his back and pulling on the thick rope, tightening it around his neck. The speedboat that had been heading toward the dock made a sharp turn and headed in the opposite direction. Dex turned toward the lot of shipping containers he'd come from, and his heart swelled when he saw Destructive Delta sweeping through, rifles in hand as they moved in on Winters's men.

Dex leaned in, snarling in Winters's ear, "I should snap your neck."

"Then do it," Winters growled. "That way I won't have to listen to any more of your mommy and daddy issues."

Dex gritted his teeth and pulled on the rope, Winters gagging and gasping for breath under him. All he had to do was twist the rope, and it would be done. The man beneath him had caused so much pain. So much suffering. He'd had Dex's parents killed. He'd tried to take Tony from him and had sent a killer to torture him.

"You don't deserve mercy," Dex ground out through his teeth. He wanted to do it. God, he wanted to do it so bad.

"Dex."

Dex looked up, surprised to find Sparks standing there. He hadn't even seen her approach.

"Give me a good reason I shouldn't end him right now."

Sparks's blue eyes moved from Dex to Winters, the black spreading until only a sliver of blue remained.

"Because death is too good for him."

Dex considered her words. "Meaning?"

"Meaning I'm going to put him in the deepest, darkest, filthiest pit of hell, where he's going to be made to suffer every hour of every day, but first he's going to give up his operatives inside TIN before any more lives are lost."

Winters let out a harsh laugh. "You stupid, deluded little girl. My people will find me."

Sparks put her heel to Winters's temple and leaned in. He hissed at the pain. "Your people are already bailing on you. How long do you think before they all jump ship to save their own hides? Especially since I let my superiors know we've detained you? Also, I may have alluded to your cooperation."

Winters glared at her as he spat, "No one will believe that."

"Thanks to your people, who are now turning traitor on *you*, TIN is moving in on your organization. Intel says the US branch of the Makhai is done."

Winters went still. Guess they had their answer. Dex hauled Winters to his feet, and Sparks clamped black cuffs around his wrists and another around Winters's neck. A row of red lights turned on, glowing on each device, accompanied by a brief high-pitched beep.

"I control these cuffs. One command, and enough electricity will go through your system to fry your insides."

Dex smirked as he dropped the rope to the ground. "Talk about irony." He turned to Sparks. "What about Wolf? How are you going to keep him from killing Winters?"

"I don't need to."

"I don't understand."

The coldness in Sparks's eyes sent a chill through Dex.

"I've already made a deal with Wolf. I get Winters first, and when I'm done with him, he's all Wolf's."

Dex patted Winters's shoulder. "I wish I could say it was nice knowing you, but I hope you rot in hell."

TIN operatives flooded the scene, and they escorted Winters toward an unmarked armored car. Dex hoped Winters sucked in as much of the sun as he could because the asshole wasn't going to be seeing the light of day any time soon. Whatever Sparks had in store for him, there was Wolf waiting at the other end.

Sloane hurried toward him, looking a little worse for wear. His arm was bloodied, and he held on to his side, but he gave Dex a reassuring grin. Destructive Delta jogged behind him, helmets on, full tactical gear and rifles in hand, all ready to kick some more ass. Dex stood there a moment, just taking in the sight, unable to keep from puffing up his chest a little bit. This was his team. His family. Even with Dex and Sloane heading for new adventures, their family was always going to be there to back them up.

When Sloane reached him, he threw his arms around

Dex. "Thank God you're okay." Sloane held him close, his hand cradling Dex's head.

"I'm okay." He pulled back and looked Sloane over. "What about you? Are you hurt?"

"You mean besides feeling like I've been struck by lightning? I'm good. Just a few grazes."

"I'm a little confused," Ash said, coming to stand beside them. "Winters is alive. How is he alive after all the shit he put us through?"

Dex nodded. "Winters killed Sparks's husband, he's the reason she can't see her daughter, and he's responsible for Tucker's death. If there's anything left of the guy when Sparks is done with him, she's promised him to Wolf after."

"Fuck." Ash shook his head. "Yeah, he's going to wish you'd killed him."

"I can't believe he was lying to us this whole time," Calvin said, shaking his head, his eyes glassy. "He fucking sat there in front of me, acting like he cared, when really he hated me and what I was."

Dex opened his mouth, but then Hobbs pushed past them, heading down the pier. Calvin was going to follow, but Dex stopped him. "Let me have a word with him. Please."

Calvin nodded.

Dex left his team and headed down the pier. Hobbs had stopped to one side, his back turned to Dex as he gazed out at the water.

"Hey, big guy."

The tears that Hobbs wiped from his cheeks broke Dex's heart. Out of all of them, Dex understood how Winters's betrayal had crushed Hobbs the most. Although Hobbs never talked to Winters using words, he still communicated with him often because he'd trusted Winters.

Hobbs shook his head, his fists balled at his sides and his green eyes filled with anger.

"Talk to me, Hobbs."

Hobbs shook his head fervently, his lips pressed together. He swiped a hand over his mouth and jerked his hand out, like he was tossing his voice into the ocean. Dex's heart stopped, and he grabbed Hobbs by the arms.

"No. Don't you fucking dare. That asshole does not get to undo all the progress you've made. Hobbs, look at me."

Hobbs shook his head, tears streaming down his cheeks. Desperation and panic rose inside Dex.

"Ethan, look at me," Dex demanded.

Hobbs looked down at him, his bottom lip trembling and his face crumbling. Dex stepped close and took hold of his face.

"Ethan, you can't let what that asshole did stop you from being you. Yes, he betrayed us, and I promise you he is going to hell for that, but all the progress you made over the years was *you*. What he did doesn't change the fact that you're fucking amazing, and brave, and the best at what you do. It doesn't change how much Calvin adores you or how proud your family is of you." Dex smiled through his tears. "It doesn't change how much I love you. Winters has taken so much from us. Please don't let him take you too."

Hobbs lost the fight against his tears, and the dam broke. He hugged Dex tight to his chest and lowered his head, whispering in his ear, "I love you too. I'm sorry. I was mad."

"I know. And there's nothing to be sorry for, big guy." Dex closed his eyes, relief running through him as he ran a hand over Hobbs's back. When he opened his eyes, Calvin was there, heartache and concern all over his boyish face. Dex tapped Hobbs's shoulder, and Hobbs pulled back. He turned and drew Calvin into his arms, his face buried in

Calvin's hair. Dex wiped at his cheeks as he made his way over to Sloane. This wasn't something they would get over easily, and the THIRDS would no doubt expect them to see another appointed psychologist. Dex felt for the poor soul who'd be taking Winters's place.

"He okay?" Sloane asked, worried.

"He's taking it hard, but I think he'll heal. It'll take some time." He cleared his throat before he got emotional again. "So where are we at?"

"TIN's rounded up everyone here," Letty said, motioning behind them. "We've hit the Makhai hard, and with Winters off the board, the rest of them don't stand a chance."

Dex let out a shaky breath. He stared up at Sloane. "It's done."

Sloane pulled him close and kissed the top of his head. "Yeah, baby. It's finally over."

As they walked back toward the yard where the container had been, Ash spoke up. "I hate to be the one to bring everyone down, but you all heard Sparks. This is just one branch of an organization whose reach stretches who knows how far."

"And we'll get to them too," Sloane promised, slipping his hand into Dex's and lacing their fingers together. "Right now, we have something equally important to get to."

Dex beamed up at Sloane, but then he remembered Tony. "Where's Dad?" he asked his brother.

"Back at the estate," Cael replied. "He was determined to come out here, but thankfully Sparks convinced him someone needed to stay and keep everyone safe in case Winters had anything else up his sleeve. With your aunt, Thomas, and the other parents there, he gave in. We had plenty of agents on-site, but I think she was just afraid of something happening to him so soon after we just got him back."

Dex was relieved. His father was stubborn, but when it came to the safety of those he cared about, he put his pride aside. "How are things between him and Sparks?"

Cael's expression turned sympathetic. "Dad said they're taking some time apart. I don't think he'll ever be able to forgive her for what she allowed to happen to you."

"She did it for her daughter," Dex said gently.

"Yeah, and I get that. I guess that's why I'm conflicted. Either way, how can they have trust between them after that?"

"You're right," Dex said with a sigh. Whatever happened, he just hoped his dad would be happy.

Dex was quiet as he walked hand in hand with Sloane, surrounded by his team. Men, women, Therians, all of whom he loved and considered his family. It struck him then how none of them were related to him by blood, not even his dad and brother, and yet the bond they all shared could never be broken. They'd been through it all together. They'd laughed, cried, bled, mourned, and loved. Whatever the future held, they were the one constant in his life. His home.

CHAPTER FOURTEEN

DEEP BREATH.

Fifteen minutes.

Fifteen minutes and the wedding processional music would start, and the wedding party would begin their march toward the altar until it was Dex and Sloane's turn. Dex let out a shaky breath.

"Okay, it's happening. This is happening." He paced in front of the door he'd walk out of before he'd head for the sitting room where Sloane would be waiting to walk him down the aisle, the start of their new journey. Dex swallowed hard when something big blocked his path. He looked up, and Hobbs grabbed his shoulders.

With a big dopey smile and watery eyes, Hobbs leaned in and whispered in Dex's ear, "You got this."

Dex's eyes welled up, and he quickly blinked away his tears. He nodded, afraid if he said anything he'd lose it.

"You look amazing," Letty said, kissing his cheek.

"You look beautiful." Dex beamed at her, loving how she looked in the strapless black gown, the long tangerine-colored sash tied around her waist and the bouquet of tangerine roses giving it a perfect pop of color. He turned to the rest of his wedding party. "Look at you guys."

Cael, Hobbs, and Hudson were all dashing in their black suits with tangerine ties and little tangerine rosebuds pinned to their lapels, matching the one pinned to Dex's tuxedo lapel. Sloane's wedding party would have Ash, Calvin, and Seb in black suits with turquoise ties and a turquoise rosebud pinned to their lapels, which would match the one Sloane would have pinned to his. Rosa, much like Letty, would be in a strapless black gown with a turquoise sash, and holding a bouquet of turquoise roses. Everyone was stunning.

Hobbs waggled his eyebrows and lifted the legs of his black trousers, revealing tangerine and turquoise socks. Hudson and Cael followed his lead, revealing their matching socks, and Dex laughed. He tugged at his trouser legs, showing off his all tangerine socks. Sloane's would be all turquoise. It had been Sloane's idea. The reason behind the suggestion being the need to have "a little bit of that Daley charm."

Hudson stepped up to Dex and smiled brightly. Tears welled up in his eyes, and Dex wiped at his own eyes.

"Stop it. You're going to fog up your glasses."

Hudson laughed and hugged him tight. Bracing himself, Dex wiped his sweaty hands on his pants as Cael stepped up to him. His bottom lip trembled, and Dex shook his head.

"Come on, Chirpy. Don't make me smear my makeup."

Cael laughed and grabbed him, pulling him into a tight hug. "I love you so much, Dex."

Closing his eyes, Dex hugged his little brother fiercely, his voice cracking when he replied, "I love you too, Chirpy." With a sniff, he pulled away. "You got the ring?"

Cael nodded and patted his front breast pocket. A knock on the door was followed by Lou poking his head in. He opened his mouth to speak, looked Dex over, and flew into the room to throw his arms around Dex. He pulled back and kissed Dex's cheeks, his eyes glassy.

"Sloane's a very lucky man," Lou said softly. "Make sure he never forgets that." Wiping under his eyes, he motioned to the door. "It's time for me to take Cael and the others to the sitting room. I'll be back for you. All the guests are in their seats, Tony's in position, and the photographers are in place."

"And Sloane?"

Lou smiled brightly. "Looking handsome as ever. He's in the sitting room with Ash and the others."

"Is he okay?" Dex asked. It was almost time. In less than an hour, he'd be married. Was Sloane as nervous as he was? Was he freaking out? Now that they were here, was he having second thoughts? Cold feet?

"Dex." Lou put a hand to his cheek. "It's your wedding day. Stop worrying and enjoy this moment."

Lou was right. These were memories that would stay with him for the rest of his life.

"Come on everyone." Lou opened the door, and Dex waved at his brother and friends as they all walked out. Just before the door closed, his aunt Danelle walked in, her coral dress looking stunning against her dark skin.

"Hey, you're not supposed to outshine the groom," Dex teased.

She laughed and cupped his face. "Oh, baby, no one can outshine you. Never have, never will. Now, whatever you're worrying about, don't. That man of yours adores you. I know he's going to do right by you."

"You do?"

The twinkle of mischief in her big hazel eyes made Dex chuckle.

"Honey, if he doesn't, he's got me and Tony to answer to. Your man is brave, but he ain't that brave."

Dex let his head fall back with a laugh. He wrapped her in his arms and hugged her tight. "Thank you, Aunt Danelle. I love you so much."

"I love you too." She pulled away with a dainty sniff, turned him around, and smacked his butt. "Go knock his socks off."

Dex winked at her before she headed for the door. "That comes later."

"I should check on him. Someone needs to check on him."

Sloane paced from one end of the sitting room to the other. It probably didn't help that he could see out ahead into the formal garden and the rows of white chairs filled with two hundred wedding guests and Tony standing at the gorgeous altar at the end of the stunningly decorated aisle. Lou had really outdone himself. The tangerine and turquoise were softened by the white, resulting in pops of color rather than overpowering the décor. The sky was blue, the weather perfect, and at any moment, he'd be faced with his future.

It was fine. Dex was fine. Why wouldn't he be? Dex loved him. Loved him more than Sloane could have ever dreamed. Dex was the most amazing man he'd ever met. Beautiful, funny, brave, kind, generous, with a heart so big there was no question why he was so loved. It was like before Dex, Sloane had been living an incomplete life. He hadn't known he was capable of the kind of love he felt, that he could be as happy as he was. Before Dex, he was afraid to hope. He'd been broken, the pieces all put back together precariously with glue that never seemed to dry or fill the cracks properly. Then Dex came into his life, and one tiny piece at a time he took Sloane apart and pieced him together, healing the cracks and setting fire to his soul, waking up something inside Sloane.

Sloane closed his eyes, thinking of everything they'd been through together. They'd faced and survived bullets, explosions, kidnapping, torture, and ghosts from their pasts. They might have stumbled along the way, but they always picked each other up and their relationship was all the stronger for it—and that was before they were bonded.

"Sloane."

Sloane blinked up at Seb. "Hey."

Seb put a hand on his shoulder. "Stop worrying. Dex is crazy about you. There's nothing he wouldn't do, or hasn't done, for you."

Sloane smiled and nodded. Seb was right. He hugged Seb. "Thank you." He pulled back and found Rosa smiling, tears in her eyes. She smoothed down his tuxedo jacket and fixed the turquoise rosebud in his lapel. "Rosita Bonita, you look beautiful."

"You don't look so bad yourself," she replied with a sniff.

Sloane chuckled. "Thanks." He winked at Calvin, who stepped up to him, all glassy eyes and bashful. "Come 'ere." Sloane pulled him into a hug. "Thank you for being such a good friend."

Calvin pulled back and wiped a tear from the corner of his eye.

"All right, enough crying." Ash stepped in front of Sloane, frowning at him. "This is Daley we're talking about. The guy's not just nuts, but he's nuts about you. Has been since the beginning. There's no one out there more committed to you and your happiness than he is."

Sloane swallowed past the lump in his throat. He pressed his lips together, and Ash gave him a pointed look.

"No. Nope. You suck that tear back in."

Sloane laughed, his eyes welling. Ash's bottom lip trembled, and he shook his head, refusing to give in. At least until Sloane found his voice.

"My mom might not be here, but having you with me makes it okay."

"Oh, for fuck's sake." Ash crumpled and brought Sloane in for a fierce bear hug. "I fucking love you. Don't ever, *ever* forget that. I might not have Arlo, but I have you. You're my brother."

Sloane closed his eyes against the falling tears and squeezed Ash tight. "Brothers," Sloane agreed. No matter what, Ash would always be his family, and having him here meant the world to Sloane.

The music started, and Sloane pulled away, thanking Rosa for the tissues. Ash took a couple with a grumble. Since Ash was his best man, he had Dex's wedding ring in his pocket. Sloane and Dex had picked out their rings together. A matching set that represented him and Dex. Two black ceramic Tiffany bands, each with a yellow gold inlay set with twenty-one black diamonds. The gleaming black band was Sloane, and the sparkling gold center inlay was his heart, Dex. But the part he loved most was the engraving inside each band.

Forever yours. Faithfully.

"It's time," Ash announced, stepping up to the doorway, with Calvin standing behind him, then Seb and Rosa. The door to the sitting room opened, and in walked Cael, Hobbs, Hudson, and Letty. They took turns hugging Sloane, telling him how good he looked and how happy they were for him. Ash kissed Cael's cheek, his smile wide.

"You look beautiful, sweetheart."

Cael's smile was dazzling as he took the arm Ash held out to him. "Thank you. You look amazing."

Ash winked at him, and they faced forward. Everyone paired up and got in line. Sloane squared his shoulders and stood behind Rosa. He tugged on his shirt cuffs and blew out a breath to steady himself. It was finally happening. *Fuck.* He'd never been more terrified. Not because he was getting married but because soon he would be a husband. He was committing himself to being everything Dex deserved.

The door to the sitting room opened, and he turned, his breath catching at the sight of Dex in his double-breasted tuxedo, looking more beautiful than ever. There was a sparkle in his stunning blue eyes, an adoration reserved only for him. Sloane swallowed past the lump in his throat as Dex stepped up to him.

"Hi," Dex said quietly.

"Hi," Sloane replied, his voice rough with emotion. "How is it you always manage to steal my breath away?"

"It's only fair since you stole my heart." A tear rolled down Dex's cheek, and Sloane wiped it away with his thumb. He held his hand out to Dex, and Dex placed his hand in Sloane's. They laced their fingers together, and the double doors were opened for them. The music changed, and they walked out into the garden, down the white carpet that stretched to the altar, where their family and friends stood to each side of Tony.

As they walked hand in hand past their friends, everyone snapping pictures, in tears, or smiling brightly, Sloane tightened his grip on Dex's hand. Their friends and family were here for them, to see them off on this new adventure. They reached the altar, where Tony stood dressed sharply in a black suit and black tie, a microphone pinned to his lapel. He smiled wide at them, his eyes watery. Clearing his throat, he squared his shoulders.

As Tony began the ceremony, Sloane and Dex faced each other, Dex's hands in his. Dex's flushed cheeks and beautiful smile had Sloane grinning like an idiot. God, he was so in love with this man. Tony thanked their guests for being here with them to witness their union on this beautiful day. He talked of celebration and love and how everyone here played an integral part in their lives.

"Love is truly a gift. As the inspirational Maya Angelou once said, 'Love recognizes no barriers. It jumps hurdles, leaps fences, penetrates walls to arrive at its destination full of hope.' In the time that Dexter and Sloane have spent together, they've built the sturdy foundation for a lifelong relationship." Tony continued, speaking of love forever binding them together and how they'll spend each day nurturing their love.

"The love you share must be guarded and cherished. It is your most valuable treasure. Dexter and Sloane, I invite you to declare your vows. Dexter, you may begin."

Dex took a deep breath and nodded. Sloane had never seen Dex this nervous before. It spoke volumes about what this meant to him. Very little rattled his sweet, fearless man. Dex met Sloane's gaze, and Sloane winked at him. With a soft laugh, Dex nodded again, as if finding his courage. He lifted his chin and spoke confidently.

"I, Dexter, take you, Sloane, for my lawfully wedded husband, to have and to hold, from this day forward, for better or worse, for richer or poorer. I promise to be true to you in good times and in bad, in sickness and in health. I will love you and honor you all the days of my life, until death do us part. This is my solemn vow."

Tony looked to Sloane. "Sloane, you may now make your promise."

Sloane smiled at Dex and brought Dex's hands to his lips for a kiss before he started. "I, Sloane, take you, Dexter, for my lawfully wedded husband, to have and to hold, from this day forward, for better or worse, for richer or poorer. I promise to be true to you in good times and in bad, in sickness and in health. I will love you and honor you all the days of my life, until death do us part. This is my solemn vow."

"Dexter, do you take Sloane to be your lawfully wedded husband? Do you promise him love, faith, and tenderness? Do you promise to cherish him, put your trust in him, and comfort him in difficulty, so long as you both shall live?"

"I do."

"Sloane, do you take Dexter to be your lawfully wedded husband? Do you promise him love, faith, and tenderness? Do you promise to cherish him, put your trust in him, and comfort him in difficulty, so long as you both shall live?"

"I do."

"You may now exchange rings. Let these rings remind you always of that love, and of the promises you have made here on this day."

Dex turned and gently took Sloane's ring from Cael, and then Sloane turned to take Dex's ring from Ash, winking at his red-eyed friend. Ash shook his head at him as he stepped back behind Sloane.

"Will each of you please repeat after me as you place the ring on your loved one's hand? I, Dexter, give you, Sloane, this ring as a symbol of my love and commitment. With this ring, I thee wed."

Dex lifted Sloane's left hand and slid the black band

down Sloane's ring finger. "I, Dexter, give you, Sloane, this ring as a symbol of my love and commitment. With this ring, I thee wed." A tear rolled down Dex's cheek, but his smile was breathtaking. All Sloane wanted to do was grab him and kiss him senseless.

"Repeat after me," Tony instructed, making sure Sloane didn't get ahead of himself. "I, Sloane, give you, Dexter, this ring as a symbol of my love and commitment. With this ring, I thee wed."

Sloane lifted Dex's left hand and slipped the black band onto his finger. "I, Sloane, give you, Dexter, this ring as a symbol of my love and commitment. With this ring, I thee wed."

"By the power vested in me by the state of New York, I pronounce you married. You may now kiss."

Everyone erupted into cheers as Sloane moved in to kiss Dex, laughing when Dex grabbed him, turned, and dipped him. Dex waggled his eyebrows before kissing Sloane. He brought Sloane back up with him, and Sloane couldn't help it. Before Dex could turn away, Sloane cupped his face and brought their lips together. Dex melted against him, the crowd cheering and catcalling as Dex grasped the lapels of Sloane's tuxedo. They wrapped their arms around each other, lost in the kiss, the world disappearing, leaving only the two of them. When they were breathless, they came up for air, and they rested their heads together as Tony declared loudly.

"Ladies and gentlemen, it's my pleasure to present to you Dexter and Sloane Daley!"

They faced the crowd, their fingers laced together as they headed back down the aisle, waving at their friends and family, and everyone threw handfuls of rose petals. As they walked through the shower of colorful petals, Dex beamed up at him, his eyes glowing amber.

They kissed again, cameras going off, smartphones snapping away, and Dex let out a dreamy sigh that made Sloane chuckle. They posed for more pictures before heading inside with their wedding party and family for photos on the grand staircase. They took countless pictures with just the two of them posing, being sweet and being silly. They took photos with their friends and with family. They kissed, made funny faces, and laughed. Everyone flashed their tangerine and turquoise socks. Soon it was time for them to go to the terrace room for the reception, including Sloane and his husband. Husband. No matter what job they did, what name or title they'd end up going by, *husband* was the most important one, and it would never change.

Dex sat beside Sloane at the long, elegant table set up for them and their wedding party. Cael sat to Dex's right, with Ash next to him, then Rosa and Letty. Seb sat to Sloane's left side with Hudson, then Calvin and Hobbs. They faced the huge terrace room filled with guests, the twinkling lights around the room and the dazzling sparkle from the crystal chandeliers giving everything a magical, fairy-tale glow, and that was almost what it felt like, as if he were in a fairy tale. A round table to their left had the exquisite wedding cake. It wasn't six tiers; it was better. It was white with tangerine and turquoise accents. It was also nine cakes.

Six individual cakes made the base, each with a turquoise edible ribbon along the bottom and an edible tangerine rose in the center. They held a large tier stylishly decorated in white and turquoise stripes, the next tier white with a tufted design and tiny turquoise pearls, and the top tier white with swirls, the first letters of their names lovingly scripted on the side. The topper was an arrangement of edible tangerine roses. Each cake was a different flavor because there was no way Dex could pick just one, so he'd asked each member of Destructive Delta to pick their favorite flavor.

As the salads and appetizers came, Tony stood and tapped a spoon to his glass to get everyone's attention. There were whistles and catcalls. He shook his head at them as if they were too much, but his eyes shone with amusement.

"Yeah, all right. Enough of that now. I want to welcome you all to tonight's celebration."

Everyone clapped and cheered. Tony put his hand up, and the room immediately fell silent. Dex winked at Sloane, whose brows shot up. No one could command a room like Anthony Maddock.

"Although they're not with us today, I know John and Gina Daley are here in spirit." He lifted a glass toward the small round table near the door that contained beautifully framed photographs of Daley-Maddock family members who couldn't be with them but who Dex had wanted to honor. There were framed photos of Dex's parents, of Tony's father, and two cheetah figurines exquisitely carved from wood painted in gold and black, since no photos of Cael's parents had ever been found. Sloane had placed a vase of pink peonies, his mother's favorite, and together they lit several white candles. It had been an emotional moment for the two of them, but it had also been cathartic in a way.

"John and Gina were my family, and when I lost them, my world shattered. I found myself lost and terrified, not just because I'd lost two of the most important people in my life, but because they'd left me their most precious gift." Tony turned to smile at Dex, tears in his eyes. "Their little boy."

Dex wiped at his cheek and let out a shaky breath. He'd resigned himself to the fact he was going to be bawling his eyes out for most of today. Sloane wrapped his arm around Dex and brought him in close, kissing the side of his head, soothing.

"I was young, scared, and up to that point had never given much thought to being a father, and suddenly, I had this tiny person looking up to me and relying on me. My actions from that point forward wouldn't just reflect the kind of man I was but the kind of man Dex would become. I prayed every night that I would do right by John and Gina and their little boy. Now when I look at the man Dex has become, I see parts of John and parts of Gina." Tony held his glass up again. "Most importantly, I see a man they would have been proud of, and as our son heads off on this new adventure with the man he loves, I can be at peace knowing I did all right."

Everyone clapped, and Dex stood. He ran around the table to where Tony was and threw his arms around him, hugging him close, both of them sniffing and laughing.

"I love you so much, Dad."

Tony cradled Dex's head against his shoulder. "I love you too, kiddo."

With a wobbly smile, Dex headed back to the table. He resumed his seat next to Sloane and buried his head against Sloane's neck to a collective *aww*. Dex waved his hand at them, his voice muffled but loud as he did his best Linda Richman impression.

"Talk amongst yourselves."

Everyone laughed, and Sloane rubbed his back. "Okay, sweetheart?"

Dex wiped at his eyes, then blew out a shaky breath. "I'm good." He turned back, and everyone cheered.

"Yeah, yeah. Eat your salads." That got him more laughs, and soon the staff was serving dinner. As they ate and chatted, instrumental music played in the background. Dex couldn't wait to get his jacket off. The photographer was going around snapping photos of all the guests at their tables and recording messages from everyone to Dex and Sloane. He couldn't wait to watch them later. After the reception, a car would be waiting to take them to a snazzy hotel closer to the airport, their packed bags in the trunk and everything ready for their flight out tomorrow afternoon.

Cael stood, facing the crowded room, and Dex braced himself. At least he'd managed to eat something so he wasn't weeping on an empty stomach. The room went quiet, all eyes on Cael, who looked nervous, but then that was just Cael. Ash placed his hand to Cael's lower back, and the transformation was instant. Cael relaxed and smiled brightly. He turned his attention to Dex.

"Dex, I don't know that I can find the right words to describe you."

Ash opened his mouth, and Cael put a finger to his lips without even having to look at him, making everyone laugh.

"Not those words."

Dex laughed along with everyone else and winked at Ash. Did Ash know just how full his hands would be now that Cael was moving in? Dex couldn't wait to see what that looked like.

"But then, that's always been you. Larger than life, standing out from the crowd. Like a supernova whose star never dies but whose light is explosive, lighting up everyone's life."

Dex sniffed and wiped away his tears as Cael tried to fight his back. His bottom lip shook, and Dex stood to bring his baby brother into his arms.

"I love you, Dex."

"I love you too, Chirpy."

Cael pulled back and let out a slow breath. "When I first found out about you and Sloane, I admit, I was worried. The two of you were so different, and both of you were working through some pretty tough changes. It was bumpy at first, but I don't need to tell you that."

Dex sat and Cael looked over at Sloane, his expression softening.

"Sloane, the more I saw you with Dex, the more I saw that you two were meant to be. No one made my brother light up the way you did. He has this smile that's just for you, and no one can mistake the look in his eyes. It's there for everyone to see. He adores you. The reason I knew you were meant for him was because no one, and I mean *no one*, has ever gotten Dex to just be. My brother never stopped moving. He was always the constant blur of activity, a whirlwind of restless energy that needed to be unleashed. Then he fell in love with you, and with one touch, Dex slowed to a stop. I had never seen anyone have that effect on him. Which is why I believe that long before you were mates, you were already bonded. Welcome to the family, Sloane. I'm proud and honored to be your brother."

Sloane stood, and Cael walked over to hug him. Everyone clapped and cheered, and Dex had never felt prouder. He was so blessed to have all these amazing people in his life. It was important he never take that for granted or lose sight of what really mattered.

After Cael's toast, they went back to eating their dinner, talking, and laughing. Then Sloane turned to Dex and held his hand out. Dex's heart swelled in his chest as he took Sloane's hand, and everyone clapped. The lights dimmed, and Sloane led Dex to the dance floor as Journey's "Faithfully" started playing.

Sloane drew Dex in close, one hand to Dex's lower back, the other holding Dex's hand. With a soft sigh, Dex let his head rest against Sloane's shoulder as they danced, his arm around Sloane's waist.

"I remember the first time you sang this to me," Sloane said, resting his cheek against Dex's head. "I tried so hard to tell myself it didn't mean anything, that the song didn't strike something deep inside me. And then you looked at me while you sang, looking so damn beautiful up there. I thought you were the sexiest thing I'd ever seen. I was mesmerized."

Dex pulled back enough to gaze up at him, his heart in his throat. "I picked that song because it's what I wanted so badly. I wanted to be yours always."

Sloane cupped his cheek and leaned in for a kiss. It was sweet, gentle, and had Dex melting against Sloane. Everyone clapped, and the song ended. Another slow song started, and Dex called out across the room.

"Okay, I want all the parents up here to join us. Julia, Thomas, move your sweet little keisters. Ash, bring your mom up here. Darla, Armel, Dad, come on." The parents all made their way to the dance floor, and Dex walked to Sparks and took her hand. She looked striking in a royal blue figure-hugging dress. Like a movie star from the forties.

"Dex, what are you doing?" Sparks asked through her teeth, her smile never leaving her face.

"Tony needs a dance partner." Dex brought her to his dad and smiled brightly.

Tony narrowed his eyes at Dex.

"Sorry, Dad. My wedding, my rules." He patted Tony's shoulder, then rejoined Sloane on the dance floor.

"You really think that's a good idea?" Sloane asked. "They look kind of uncomfortable."

"I'm not the only one in my family who's stubborn," Dex said. "They need to talk, and can you think of two people less likely to share their feelings than those two?"

Sloane nodded his agreement. "I think your dad's even worse than Ash. I didn't think it was possible, but yeah."

As the parents danced, Dex snuck a peek at his dad and cringed. Jesus, it was painful. "Babe, I'll need you to run interference for me. Wait for my signal."

"Um, okay," Sloane said with a chuckle, his eyes filled with amusement. Dex kissed him, then walked over to Sparks and Tony.

"May I cut in?"

"Sure," Tony said, taking a step back. He turned to go, and Dex took his father's hand and pulled him into a dance. Tony rolled his eyes at him.

"Sweet baby Jesus."

"What? You're my parent, so tradition states I get to dance with you. Suck it up, buttercup."

Dex pointed behind him, and Sloane headed toward Sparks to dance with her. Tony glared at him, and Dex's grin widened.

"You're not allowed to be mad at me. It's my wedding."

"I have not forgotten," Tony muttered.

"Good, so when are you and Sonya going to talk?"

"What is there to talk about?"

"Dad, I'm not about to tell you what you should do, but

I need you to know that I'm okay with her. Yes, what she did was wrong, but none of us can say we wouldn't have done the same in her situation. She watched her husband get blown up and lost her daughter. Should she have told you? Yes."

"Dex," Tony warned.

"All I'm saying is I'm willing to forgive her. I'm alive, Dad, and I'm going to be okay." Dex hugged his father tight before leaving him and finding Sloane, who had taken his seat behind the table as the music picked up and the parents got down and jiggy with it. Dex and Sloane had agreed the parents should have the dance floor before all the crazy started. Dex took a seat next to Sloane as the floor erupted into cheers as everyone on the dance floor formed a circle around Julia and Thomas.

"Look at them," Sloane said, lacing his fingers with Dex's as Julia danced around Thomas, who was pulling some serious moves from his wheelchair, arms in the air like he just didn't care. "After everything they've been through, they look at each other like they're falling in love for the first time."

Dex hummed as he leaned into Sloane. "You think we'll look at each other like that when we reach their age?"

Sloane kissed Dex's temple. "I have absolutely no doubts."

Dex looked out across the room at all their guests, so many of whom he'd met when he first joined the THIRDS. How was it possible these people had only come into his life a few short years ago? It felt as if he'd known them his entire life. Had it really only been a few years since he'd been salivating over Darla's cooking? Or plotting with Thomas on how best to smuggle Hudson's Cornish pasties out of the kitchen without Julia noticing?

Hadn't he always been conspiring with Hobbs on all the different ways they could annoy Ash? Rosa had taught Dex how to make empanadas so he could bribe Sloane, and Letty texted him pictures of dumb things she knew would make him laugh.

"Hey, you okay?"

Dex nodded, swallowing past the lump in his throat. "Just thinking about how incredibly blessed we are."

"Yeah, we are," Sloane said quietly, bringing Dex's hand to his lips for a kiss. The song ended, and everyone cheered. "Ready?"

"You bet." Dex jumped to his feet, and they walked out onto the dance floor. They turned to their guests, and Dex undid the first button of his suit. There were catcalls and whoops as Dex started to move his hips as the Bee Gees's "You Should Be Dancing" started playing. Sloane came to stand next to him, moving along with him, both of them unbuttoning their jackets.

"Take it off!" someone shouted, and Sloane laughed.

At the same time, they pulled open their jackets, revealing the tangerine waistcoat Dex had been hiding, and Sloane's turquoise waistcoat. The crowd went nuts, and the rest of their wedding party joined them, the guys removing their jackets, and the girls unsnapping the bottom half of their long gowns to reveal a flowy knee-length skirt. They lined up in two rows behind Dex and Sloane, and together they all danced in unison, even Ash. They performed John Travolta's routine from *Saturday Night Fever* as an ensemble. The first time they'd pulled it off in rehearsal, they'd played back the recording, and Dex had been impressed, especially with Ash. He'd grumbled about it at first, but when it came down to it, the guy had come through. The moves were energetic and intense. By the end, they were all sweating and panting, but everyone jumped to their feet cheering and shouting.

Dex laughed, breathless as Sloane lifted him off his feet and spun him.

"Let's party!" Dex shouted, and the dance floor flooded with their friends and family. The music was a fantastic mix of oldies, eighties, and modern dance tunes, all carefully selected to keep everyone buzzed and out there dancing. Dex and Sloane danced with all their guests, and soon even Dex was ready for a break. The music faded, and he held up a hand.

"I think it's time for some cake. What do you guys think?"

They were met with loud cheers, so Dex joined Sloane over by the table, and the photographers snapped away as Dex put his hand over Sloane's and together they cut the first slice of cake. Sloane scooped some frosting off and touched it to Dex's nose, making him laugh. They fed each other before Dex grabbed a handful. He turned and smooshed it into Ash's face at the exact moment Ash hit him with a face full of frosting. Apparently, they were both extremely predictable. They laughed along with everyone as the staff began dishing out cake and champagne.

Sloane pulled Dex close and licked his cheek as Dex laughed, a flash going off to capture the moment.

"Mm, strawberry." Sloane waggled his eyebrows. "I always thought you were a little fruity."

Dex laughed and shoved a piece of cake at Sloane's face. He poked his tongue out and licked the corner of his mouth.

"Ooh, salted caramel. This was my pick," Sloane announced.

They cleaned each other off, giggling and laughing like a

couple of schoolboys, then Dex stuffed himself full of cake like Sloane had told him he could. He made sure to have a piece of each flavor. By the time dessert was over, Dex was bouncing. He grabbed Sloane's hand, and they headed back to the dance floor as the music kicked off again. Everyone crowded together, doing everything from the Twist to the Electric Slide. When "Time of My Life" came on, everyone cleared the floor.

Sloane took Dex's hand, and he winked at the crowd. "Come on, you all knew this was coming."

Dex nodded. "Because he loves me."

"Because I'm a sap," Sloane added before turning to Dex. "Plus, I get to be Swayze."

Dex threw his head back and laughed as he played his part, dancing the routine with Sloane, their eyes on each other as they dirty danced. Then Sloane kissed his hand, and Dex backed up, watching Sloane go all sinfully sexy Swayze on him, and the crowd lost their minds. Sloane spun around, and the wedding party danced behind him, following his moves. He stopped and nodded to Dex, who couldn't believe he was actually going to do this without a mat.

Dex ran, and when he neared Sloane, he hopped, and Sloane lifted him, his arms spread out for balance just like the choreographer had taught him. Sloane's strong hands held him at his waist, and when he lowered Dex to his feet, everyone joined them again on the dance floor.

"Have I told you how amazing you are for agreeing to this?" Dex asked, beaming up at Sloane. Who else would have gone along with his shenanigans? Whenever Dex suggested something crazy, Sloane never thought he was being ridiculous or stupid. He was always receptive, incredibly sweet, and open to being crazy right along with Dex.

There was no one who was better suited for Dex than his wonderful husband.

"Are you kidding? And miss the look you're giving me right now? Never."

"And what look is that?" Dex asked, feeling as though his heart was going to beat out of him with how happy he was.

"Like you're the luckiest guy in the world because you have me."

Dex brought his arms around Sloane's neck and drew him in for a kiss. "Babe, I *am* the luckiest guy in the world because I have you. I won't ever forget that."

The rest of the night went by in a blur of music, dancing, and laughter. The wedding couldn't have gone better, and Dex would remember this day for the rest of his life. When the time came for them to leave, everyone blew bubbles as Dex and Sloane walked by their loved ones toward the sleek vintage Rolls Royce waiting for them.

They stopped at the end of the aisle, where the photographer stood to take more pictures. Sloane turned to Dex, wiped the tear from his cheek, and leaned in, murmuring against his lips, "I love you, Mr. Daley."

Dex returned the sweet kiss. "I love you too, Mr. Daley. For as long as I live, my heart is yours."

The driver opened the door, and Dex climbed in first, followed by Sloane. The evening was cool but lovely, so the top was down. The driver closed the door and climbed behind the wheel. As they drove away, they waved to everyone. Dex blew a kiss to his dad, his eyes misty. He turned in his seat, his hands in Sloane's, and smiled at his husband.

"Kind of feels a little bit like the end, doesn't it?"

Sloane brought Dex's fingers to his lips for a kiss, mischief in his stunning amber eyes that were also filled with passion and adoration. "Sweetheart, this is just the beginning."

Dex let out a loud whoop before pouncing on Sloane. Whatever future they faced, they would be doing so together. Sloane was right, this was just the beginning, and Dex couldn't wait to get started.

Looking for more stories from the Destructive Delta crew? Ever wonder about those moments between Dex and Sloane that we don't see in the books? How about when Ethan and Calvin became best friends? Or when Sloane and Ash first met?

Join us as we celebrate the THIRDS universe with two collections of flash fiction stories written to prompts submitted by fans. Sometimes we want to know more about our favorite characters. Where they came from, how they became who they are, their families, friendships, and past heartaches. These snippets of moments in time offer an inside look at the lives of our favorite THIRDS characters. Whether it's first shifts, the forging of unbreakable bonds, or a night full of shenanigans, these stories are sure to enrich your THIRDS reading experience.

THIRDS Beyond the Books Volume 1 and *Volume 2* Available now on Amazon and KindleUnlimited.

Looking for Austen and Zach's book? *Love and Payne*, A THIRDS Universe Novel, is also available on Amazon and KindleUnlimited.

A NOTE FROM THE AUTHOR

Thank you so much for reading *Tried & True*. I hope you enjoyed the THIRDS series. If you did, please consider leaving a review on Amazon. Reviews can have a significant impact on a book's visibility, so any support you show these fellas would be amazing. Want more of the THIRDS crew? Check out the THIRDS Beyond the Books Volume 1 and 2, available in March from Amazon and KindleUnlimited. Want to read Austen and Zach's story? *Love and Payne*, A THIRDS Universe Novel is also available on Amazon and KindleUnlimited.

Want to stay up-to-date on my releases and receive exclusive content? Sign up for my newsletter.

Follow me on Amazon to be notified of a new releases, and connect with me on social media, including my fun Facebook group, Donuts, Dog Tags, and Day Dreams, where we chat books, post pictures, have giveaways, and more!

Looking for inspirational photos of my books? Visit my book boards on Pinterest.

Thank you again for joining the THIRDS crew on their adventures. We hope to see you soon!

CAST MEMBERS

You'll find these cast members throughout the whole THIRDS series. This list will continue to grow.

DESTRUCTIVE DELTA

Sloane Brodie—Defense agent. Team leader. Jaguar Therian.

Dexter J. Daley "Dex"—Defense agent. Former homicide detective for the Human Police Force. Older brother of Cael Maddock. Adopted by Anthony Maddock. Human-Therian Hybrid.

Ash Keeler—Defense agent. Entry tactics and close-quarter combat expert. Lion Therian.

Julietta "Letty" Guerrera—Defense agent. Weapons expert. Human.

Calvin Summers—Defense agent. Sniper. Human.

Ethan Hobbs—Defense agent. Demolitions expert and public safety bomb technician. Has two older brothers: Rafe and Sebastian Hobbs. Tabby tiger Therian.

Cael Maddock—Recon agent. Tech expert. Dex's younger brother. Adopted by Anthony Maddock. Cheetah Therian.

Rosa Santiago—Recon agent. Crisis negotiator and medic. Human.

COMMANDING OFFICERS

Lieutenant Sonya Sparks—Lieutenant for Unit Alpha. Cougar Therian. Undercover operative for TIN (Therian Intelligence Network).

Sergeant Anthony "Tony" Maddock—Sergeant for Destructive Delta. Dex and Cael's adoptive father. Human.

MEDICAL EXAMINERS

Dr. Hudson Colbourn—Chief medical examiner for Destructive Delta. Wolf Therian.

Dr. Nina Bishop—Medical examiner for destructive Delta. Human.

AGENTS FROM OTHER SQUADS

Ellis Taylor—Team leader for Beta Ambush. Leopard Therian.

Rafe Hobbs—Team leader for Alpha Ambush. The oldest Hobbs brother. Tiger Therian.

Sebastian Hobbs—Team leader for Theta Destructive. Was once on Destructive Delta but was transferred after his relationship with Hudson ended in a breach of protocol and civilian loss. Middle Hobbs brother. Tiger Therian.

Dominic Palladino—Defense agent. Close-quarter combat expert for Theta Destructive. Human.

Angel Herrera—Defense agent. Pilot and BearCat driver for Theta Destructive. Human.

Osmond "Zach" Zachary—Defense agent for Alpha Sleuth in Unit Beta. Has six brothers working for the THIRDS. Brown bear Therian.

West Delray—Recon agent for Theta Destructive. King cheetah Therian.

OTHER IMPORTANT CAST MEMBERS

Gabe Pearce—Sloane's ex-partner and ex-lover on Destructive Delta. Killed on duty by his brother Isaac. Human.

Isaac Pearce—Gabe's older brother. Was a detective for the Human Police Force who became leader of the Order of Adrasteia. Was killed by Destructive Delta during a hostage situation. Human.

Louis "Lou" Huerta—Dex's ex-boyfriend. Human.

Bradley Darcy—Bartender and owner of Bar Dekatria. Jaguar Therian.

Austen Payne—Squadron Specialist agent (SSA) for Destructive Delta. Freelance operative for TIN. Cheetah Therian.

Dr. Abraham Shultzon—Head doctor during the First Gen Recruitment Program who was personally responsible for the well-being of THIRDS First Gen recruits. Was also responsible for the tests that were run on the Therian children at the First Gen Research Facility. Recently apprehended by TIN for creating an unsanctioned Therian mind-control drug and for kidnapping THIRDS Therian agents for an unauthorized project.

Wolf—AKA Fang, Reaper. Former TIN operative turned rogue. Wolf became a freelance agent for hire after feeling he was betrayed by TIN, the organization that caused the death of his partner. Wolf Therian.

John Daley—Dexter J. Daley's biological father. Anthony Maddock's best friend and partner at the Human Police Force. Killed during a shootout in a movie theater during the riots. Human.

Gina Daley—Dexter J. Daley's biological mother. Worked for the CDC in NYC. First to volunteer to work with Therians. Killed along with her husband during a shootout in a movie theater during the riots. Human.

Darla Summers—Calvin Summer's mother. Human.

Thomas Hobbs—Ethan, Sebastian, and Rafe Hobbs's father. Suffers from Therian Acheron Syndrome. Tiger Therian.

Julia Hobbs—Thomas Hobbs's wife and mother to Ethan, Sebastian, and Rafe Hobbs. Human.

Benedict Winters—THIRDS-appointed psychologist. Wolf Therian.

Admiral Abbott Moros—Chief of Therian Defense. Tiger Therian.

Arlo Keeler—Ash's twin brother, killed during the riots in the 1980s.

Beck Hogan—Leader of the Ikelos Coalition. Killed during confrontation with THIRDS agents. Tiger Therian.

Drew Collins—Beck Hogan's second in command. Cougar Therian.

Felipe Bautista—Drew Collins's boyfriend. Wolf Therian.

Milena Stanek—Works in antiques acquisitions. Rosa's girlfriend. Leopard Therian.

James Kirk—Firefighter. Letty's boyfriend. White tiger Therian.

GLOSSARY

Melanoe Virus—A virus released during the Vietnam War through the use of biological warfare, infecting millions worldwide and killing hundreds of thousands.

Eppione.8—A vaccine created using strains from animals immune to the Melanoe virus. It awakened a dormant mutation within the virus, resulting in the alteration of Human DNA and the birth of Therians.

Therians—Shifters brought about through the mutation of Human DNA as a result of the Eppione.8 vaccine.

Post-shift Trauma Care (PSTC)—The effects of Therian post-shift trauma are similar to the aftereffects of an epileptic seizure, only on a smaller scale, including muscle soreness, bruising, brief disorientation, and hunger. Eating after a shift is extremely important, as not eating could lead to the Therian collapsing and a host of other health issues. PSTC is the care given to Therians after they shift back to Human form.

THIRDS (Therian-Human Intelligence

Recon Defense Squadron)—An elite, military-funded agency comprised of an equal number of Human and Therian agents and intended to uphold the law for all citizens without prejudice.

Themis—A powerful, multimillion-dollar government interface used by the THIRDS. It's linked to numerous intelligence agencies across the globe and runs a series of highly advanced algorithms to scan surveillance submitted by agents.

First Gen—First Generation of purebred Therians born with a perfected version of the mutation. Any Therian born in 1976 is considered a First Generation Therian. Any Therian born after 1976 is simply considered Therian.

Pre-First Gen—Any Therian born before First Gen Therians. Known to have unstable versions of the mutation resulting in any number of health issues. Most possess the ability to shift, some don't. No medical research was available on Therians before 1976 as Humans were not classified as Therians until then.

BearCat—THIRDS tactical vehicle.

Human Police Force (HPF)—A branch of law enforcement consisting of Human officials dealing only with crimes committed by Humans.

Sparta—Nickname for the THIRDS agent training facility at the Manhattan THIRDS headquarters.

TIN—Therian Intelligence Network. Therian equivalent to the Human CIA.

Tin Man—TIN operative. Nicknamed after the Tin Man in *The Wizard of Oz*, as TIN operatives are rumored to have no heart.

Anti-Therianism—Prejudice, discrimination, or antagonism directed against Therians.

Therian Classification—Tattoo marking on a Therian's neck displaying the Therian's classification, including family, genus, and species.

ALSO BY CHARLIE COCHET

FOUR KINGS SECURITY

Love in Spades

Be Still My Heart

Join the Club

Diamond in the Rough

FOUR KINGS SECURITY UNIVERSE

Beware of Geeks Bearing Gifts

THE KINGS: WILD CARDS

Stacking the Deck

LOCKE AND KEYES AGENCY

Kept in the Dark

PARANORMAL PRINCES

The Prince and His Bedeviled Bodyguard

The Prince and His Captivating Carpenter

The King and His Vigilant Valet

THIRDS

Hell & High Water

Blood & Thunder

Rack & Ruin

Rise & Fall

Against the Grain

Catch a Tiger by the Tail

Smoke & Mirrors

Thick & Thin

Darkest Hour Before Dawn

Gummy Bears & Grenades

Tried & True

THIRDS BEYOND THE BOOKS

THIRDS Beyond the Books Volume 1

THIRDS Beyond the Books Volume 2

THIRDS UNIVERSE

Love and Payne

COMPROMISED

Center of Gravity

NORTH POLE CITY TALES

Mending Noel

The Heart of Frost

The Valor of Vixen

Loving Blitz

Disarming Donner

Courage and the King

North Pole City Tales Complete Series Paperback

SOLDATI HEARTS

The Soldati Prince

The Foxling Soldati

STANDALONE

Forgive and Forget

Love in Retrograde

AUDIOBOOKS

Check out the audio versions on Audible.

ABOUT THE AUTHOR

Charlie Cochet is the international bestselling author of the THIRDS series. Born in Cuba and raised in the US, Charlie enjoys the best of both worlds, from her daily Cuban latte to her passion for classic rock.

Currently residing in Central Florida, Charlie is at the beck and call of a rascally Doxiepoo bent on world domination. When she isn't writing, she can usually be found devouring a book, releasing her creativity through art, or binge watching a new TV series. She runs on coffee, thrives on music, and loves to hear from readers.

www.charliecochet.com

Sign up for Charlie's newsletter:
https://newsletter.charliecochet.com

facebook.com/charliecochet
twitter.com/charliecochet
instagram.com/charliecochet
bookbub.com/authors/charliecochet
goodreads.com/CharlieCochet
pinterest.com/charliecochet

Made in the USA
Middletown, DE
05 August 2022

70673242R00203